RUTHLESS ALCHEMY

RUTHLESS ALCHEMY

JEN BAIR

Copyright © 2024 by Misplaced Adventures

Cursed Dragon Ship Publishing, LLC

6046 FM 2920 Rd, #231, Spring, TX 77379

captwyvern@curseddragonship.com

Cover © 2024 by We Got You Covered Book Design

Developmental Edit by Tracy Leonard-Nakatani

Proofread by Kelly Lynn Colby

ISBN 978-1-951445-80-5

ISBN 978-1-951445-81-2 (ebook)

All rights reserved

No part of this book may be reproduced in any form or by any electronic or mechanical means, including information storage and retrieval systems, without written permission from the publisher, except for the use of brief quotations in a book review.

This book is a work of fiction fresh from the author's imagination. Any resemblance to actual persons or places is mere coincidence.

<u>Anthology</u>

Last Night at the Jolly Chicken

<u>Misplaced Mercenaries</u> by Kevin Pettway

A Good Running Away

Blow Out the Candle When You Leave

Big Damn Magic

Illusions of Decency

Heroes Kill Everyone

<u>Hettie Stormheart series</u> by Jen Bair

One Good Eye

Ruthless Alchemy

<u>Huntress and Harvester series</u> by Jessica Raney

A Seed Once Sown

<u>Wrong Way series</u> by Kevin Pettway

Wrong Way to Heaven

Wrong Way Home

<u>Invasion of the Chromium</u> by William LJ Galaini

Chromium Rise

<u>Pick's Pocket</u> by C.M. McGuire

Beer For My Corpses

<u>The Kin</u> by Ethan A. Cooper

All Hail the Kin

All Hail the Kin

Gullhome
Oldam's Temple
Norrik
Raiders Sea
Icebite
Spiny Oyster River
Summervatn
Vikkan
Krysuvik
The
Disn
Badiron
Majloe
Tyrra
Knarrax
Summer Trades
Mirrik
Gradesh
Pippi
Bramland River
Green
Sheaf
Low
Rousca
Wood
Watchpost
Rousland
The Arlean
Dalut
Arlea
Sleed
Sejent
N
W E
S
Sedrios
Wlege
Soulduu
The Paradisals
Bangut
Runfish
Port Placid
Polf

Full-color map at KevinPettway.com

For Suzy Olear (a.k.a. Northern Lights). Twin powers activate! Fantasticorns like you make writing worthwhile. This Zeloxahad is for you.

CONTENTS

CHAPTER 1

SWORDS AT A MAGIC FIGHT

Hettie

Hettie stumbled down the dark streets of Garpoint listening to the scuff of her boots echoing off the buildings. Four men tailed her from a distance. It didn't take a flickerwit to figure out what they had planned, but it irritated her they were doing such a poor job of it.

Fish-brained marshtrotters. At least have a little pride in your work. She led the men along, careful to hide her frustration behind her drunken swagger. It wouldn't do to scare them off.

The men weren't local to Poll's Wander. They'd come from the far reaches of Sedrios to join the Widows' Will, seeking glory in the coming battle against Lord Vincent. The sojourn to Stonehaven, Vincent's estate, should have required minimal planning, but they'd had to adjust for the influx of soldiers flooding in from all over Sedrios and beyond. Over two months later, they were finally ready to head for the mountains of the Little Gods.

Some of the newcomers preferred the army depart without Hettie.

A balmy breeze drifted through the streets, ruffling her long dark hair. The truth was, Poll's Wander was beginning to feel like home. At least it was before the excess soldiers had swarmed in. She couldn't complain. The larger their army, the better their chances.

Deryl chuckled. *"If they weren't drunker than a Pirate at a Blood Bay Festival, they'd probably be stealthier."* Once a man, Deryl had been cursed for eternity as a sentient eyeball and now hung in a sleek black pouch around Hettie's neck. She had magically bonded to him, allowing them access to each other's thoughts and he talked to her incessantly because nobody else knew he existed.

"Smarter too," she replied, listening as the four men closed on her. A few cups of guapi yeti made her head buzz pleasantly, though she was far from drunk.

She turned down a side alley in hopes the secluded setting might embolden the men. Hettie didn't look like much, an average-sized Pavinn girl just into adulthood. An easy target, though she knew it wasn't her appearance that drew them.

The men narrowed the gap to a few dozen paces.

A low warning *grawp* told her Ouri was watching from his perch overhead. Hettie made a hand gesture, indicating she had the situation under control. Her amber hawk, one of the largest birds in all Andos, would scare the pants off her pursuers if he flapped down into the shadowed alley where the enclosed space would act as an echo chamber for his piercing shrieks of outrage.

The men finally stopped talking when they entered the alley a dozen paces behind her. Their scuffling feet mingled with their inebriated attempts to shush each other.

"Servio has to know he's painting a target on his back every time he runs his mouth," Deryl said.

General Servio was one of the many newcomers. He'd been throwing barbs at Hettie since he'd arrived. Over the past week, he'd done everything he could to convince Liselle to leave "the witch" behind. He was lucky he hadn't been thrown out on his ear.

"I'm positive that's what he's counting on," Hettie said grimly. *"If he can get me to act out, or even kill someone, he'll have plenty of ammunition for his argument."*

"Liselle would never agree to keep you out of the battle. They have no idea what they'll face at Vincent's fortress. They need us. Besides, we were here first."

"I don't think calling dibs works on the battlefield."

"Sure," Deryl said, *"but we're not on the battlefield. We're still in the city, where logic and civilization rule."*

"Hey, witch!" came a call from behind Hettie.

Her smile was humorless. *"What was that about logic and civilization?"*

"We got a bone to pick with you," one of the men said.

The four men picked up their pace, approaching fast until one of them tripped. Hettie winced at the sound of bone meeting stone.

"If you're waiting for them to chase you down, that may take longer than you want to spend. We set sail tomorrow. I assume you want sleep at some point." Deryl said that last bit with a sour note. He didn't sleep. He usually spent his nights talking to Ga'Kinlon, a large cloth that doubled as a magic portal. He went by Gak for short.

Hettie listened to the men's curses and knew he was right. She turned to face the men, three of whom were helping the clumsy one to his feet several strides away.

The men were Pavinn, as were all but a handful of the newcomers.

"It's late," Hettie said. "Say your piece."

The clumsy one wobbled woozily. A cut from his forehead leaked blood into his eye. Hettie could have healed it easily if she'd had the inclination.

Two men helped the injured friend lean against a wall.

"You're not going with us tomorrow," the remaining man said. He was the tallest of the four and had a lithe build. His hand rested on the hilt of his sword.

As if his sword would do him any good against magic even if there wasn't a ten-foot gap between them.

"You're the interloper here," Hettie reminded him. "We defeated Vincent's army the first time while you were sipping on ale in a brothel somewhere. We don't need some half-wit drunkard along for the counterattack. If you don't want to fight alongside a witch, then find another army to join."

The influx of people had brought bar fights, muggings, and a general rise in stupidity. Getting physical with tavern maids had practically become a sport over the last couple weeks. One man had tried to set fire to the house of a woman who'd slapped him for grabbing her rear.

Garpoint's locals were eager for a big send off so they could get back to being a cozy port city. They didn't care much for the rougher soldiers.

Hettie felt right at home with ruffians, but she wasn't used to them singling her out. The magic-haters seemed to be the dumbest of the troublemakers.

The man in front of her slowly pulled his sword almost like he was trying to prove her point.

"Was that supposed to be ominous?" Deryl asked. *"He can't possibly think you're intimidated by a sword."*

"You underestimate his stupidity," she assured him.

The two men left their injured friend to stand by the swordsman. They pulled swords of their own, one of them accidentally whacking the leg of the other with the flat of his blade when he attempted to flourish it. The offended friend glared but didn't say anything.

"Agree to stay behind," the lead man said.

"Or what?" Hettie fought back a yawn. Deryl was right. She needed sleep.

"Or we'll poke you good with these sharp sticks," the flourishing idiot replied.

Hettie tipped her head to one side. "Think you can reach me without beheading your companions over there, slick?"

His lip lifted in a sneer. "Don't think that would stop me from stabbing you through the neck."

His companions turned to look at him. "What? It's not like I'm *planning* to stab you, but accidents happen. Just saying it wouldn't stop me is all."

Hettie held up a hand and started ticking off fingers. "You brought swords to a magic fight. First mistake," she said. "Your swords are wielded by idiots. Second mistake. And you let your idiots get drunk before the confrontation. Third mistake. I'm telling you now, you should sleep this night off."

"I wouldn't have thought to apply these words to this situation, but you're in danger," Deryl said, clearly confused. Part of his curse was to warn of imminent danger.

Hettie immediately flared her senses, searching for the source and the results made her blood run cold. *"My magic doesn't seem to be working at the moment."* She managed to keep the words calm in her head despite the panic clawing its way up her throat.

After the falling out with her family—a fight that had left Elkin, the love of her life, dead—she'd had no home, no family, and no future.

Her magic was all she had left. The idea that it could be taken from her was terrifying. Without it, she was just a girl in a world full of dangerous people. Black spots danced before her eyes, and she realized she'd forgotten to breathe.

"Calm down," Deryl soothed.

"What part of this situation warrants calm?" she snapped.

"Right, poor choice of words."

Their mind speak was quicker than thought, so only a brief moment had passed since Deryl's warning. The lead swordsman lunged forward. Hettie would normally have stopped him with a muttered phrase and a twist of her hand. Instead, she was forced to defend herself the old-fashioned way.

She dodged and the sword stabbed the air between neck and shoulder. Lightning quick reflexes honed by sparring matches with pirates and cutthroats had her leaning forward to let the blade slide along the shoulder of her red leather vest. She grabbed the hilt of the sword, locking it against her, and planted a boot between the man's legs.

A hollow thud told her she wasn't the only one using leather protection.

With a grin, the cocky man spun, launching Hettie into his two friends. Instinctively, Hettie tried to flare her magic to sense their positions, but she couldn't feel her magic.

"What in the nine hells?"

"You didn't have that much to drink," Deryl reasoned.

"I've been half-conscious with more magic than this."

She swept her arm around as she plowed into the men, knocking aside their blades. She spun, hauling at the man on her left so he was between her and the flourishing idiot. The man stumbled, and she snaked one hand around the hilt of his sword and gave two quick jabs at his throat.

He released his sword, and she snatched it from the air. One good shove had the way clear to the flourishing idiot. A single smack on his sword hand had him disarmed.

Hettie shook her head in disgust. *"Who gave this man a sword?"* He was lucky he hadn't cut himself with it.

Eyes wide, he backed away from her until he cowered against the wall where his bloody-headed companion slouched. The man she'd throat punched was huddled on the ground, writhing weakly.

Hettie squared off against the leader, who rushed her almost before she'd planted her feet. They traded blows, rapid and precise.

"Aren't you going to make my eyes dribble out of my head?" the man taunted.

"Crap," Hettie and Deryl said at the same time. The shock of it made her miss a step, which earned her a slice along her chin. She scrambled to fend off a flurry of blows. A moment later, the man retreated a step, waiting for her reaction.

Whatever was wrong with her magic, he clearly knew about it. She'd assumed the men were idiots for chasing down a witch in the dark with only swords to protect them. The realization that she'd underestimated them filled her with a cold dread.

Deryl said, *"I don't think it's possible to completely strip someone of their magic."*

Her reply was immediate. *"Yes, it is."* She'd done it to her sisters. After Nuala's jealousy led her to use a book of magic to suck up an island's worth of raw magic, including Deryl's life force, Hettie had been forced to absorb the raw magic herself in order to save him. She'd stripped her sisters of magic in the process and permanently blocked off the source of it for good measure.

The magic she'd siphoned from them had been building pressure inside Hettie all these months. She'd saved it for the big battle, but it had become more of a struggle every day to control her power, especially for complex spells.

She should have noticed the absence of that roiling pit of power within her. The guapi yeti had dulled her senses more than she'd thought.

"You can't block magic without having magic," Deryl insisted. *"Whatever this guy did is temporary."*

"Unless someone with magic is here with him," Hettie reasoned, thinking of her most troublesome sister. Nuala didn't have magic anymore, but the younger siblings of the Daughters' Coven did. Nuala was manipulative. She could have convinced one of them to block Hettie's magic.

"From what I can tell, you guys didn't learn that spell growing up," Deryl reasoned. *"And you took the book of magic from her."*

He was right. Nuala had stolen a book of magic from Liselle, who insisted Hettie keep it when she'd tried to return it. Months of studying the book taught Hettie she wasn't great at formal learning. *"What makes you think that book is the only thing Nuala stole?"*

"I think it's more likely the Temple of the Sky sent these guys."

The Temple was a religious organization determined to eliminate sorcery. She didn't like the idea that she'd already drawn the Temple's attention.

The swordsman suddenly came at her with a flurry of blows that kept her on her heels. She'd relied too much on her magic, and it showed.

He backed her up against the wall with his blade pressing in on her throat. Her own sword held it at bay, but he had brute strength on his side.

Magic typically gave her a boost in both strength and speed, but without it, she struggled against the weight of him. Her arms shook. She tried to slip along the wall to divert the pressure.

He shifted with her, keeping her cornered.

Sensing victory, a grin spread across his face. "Your head will earn me a hefty sum."

She grimaced, turning her head from the smell of liquor on his breath. "Too bad your head won't earn me anything of worth."

She gave a low whistle.

CHAPTER 2
THE MAN IN BLACK

Hettie

The whistle wasn't loud, but it carried far enough for Hettie's purposes.

A heartbeat later, Ouri arrived in a flurry of wings and an ear-splitting screech, clawing at the man's head. Hettie used the moment of surprise to wrench his sword from his grip.

With a startled yell, the man leaped back, swatting at the bird briefly before taking off for the end of the alley.

The fight was abruptly over. Hettie stood panting as she took stock of her circumstances. The other three men were still down, with the flourishing idiot the only one conscious. Despite only having received a slap to the wrist, it may have been broken, judging by how he clutched it to his chest.

She could have healed that wrist with magic. They were too worried about magic's potential for harm to consider the benefits.

Deryl snorted. *"As if magic is needed to hurt someone."*

Hettie turned to the flourishing idiot. He was dressed in threadbare clothing with a short, scrubby beard, and close-set eyes. "How did you block my magic?" she demanded.

The man blubbered to himself. Then, quick as a rat, he turned to face the wall and bashed his head into it.

Alarmed, Hettie lunged for him. He'd only managed two blows by the time she stopped him, but his head bobbled comically.

"What in Arlea's blessed name did you do that for?" she asked.

His eyes rolled up in his head, and he slumped.

Hettie crouched over him, aghast. *"What is going on with these guys?"*

She scanned the alley, silent but for the groaning man with the head wound. The man she'd throat punched hadn't twitched. The leader was her only option if she wanted answers.

Without a second thought, she took off in pursuit.

"Are you sure chasing this guy is a good idea with your magic out of commission?"

"You think letting him go is a better idea? I need to know what he did to me." At the mouth of the alley, she paused to scan the street in both directions. The lanterns did a passable job of lighting the area. A flicker of light from up the street marked Ouri as he flew past.

Two men stood facing off, one with a short blade no more than a couple feet in length, the other tall and lithe with his hands in the air. Hettie stalked toward them.

"Who's this guy?" Deryl asked.

The newcomer's blade was unique. Despite the shadows cast by the flickering lantern, the black metal seemed to glow with swirling lines of gold, lending it a hypnotic beauty.

Both men turned at the sound of Hettie's boots. The taller man bared his teeth and hissed at her.

Smooth as butter, the new guy flicked his blade, slapping the tall man in the mouth with the flat of it. New guy muttered what sounded like, "Be nice."

The tall man hissed again, but in pain this time. He covered his mouth with one hand.

Hettie came to a stop near the men. Her blade at her side, but ready.

Dressed head to toe in black leather, the man had a slender face and wore an expression somewhere between amusement and disinterest.

Ouri let out a greeting call and the new guy's gaze flicked up to the bird before returning to his captive. He gestured with his odd black blade. "What did you want with this guy?" It was clear he knew how to handle himself in a fight by the position of his feet, his grip on his blade, and his relaxed, confident posture.

"Sensing any danger from him?" she asked Deryl.

"No, but it would be just your luck to run into someone else *wanting to kill you."*

The last thing she wanted to do was pit her skills against the man in black. Her head was beginning to pound, and her vision blurred around the edges—a side effect of whatever the men had drugged her with, she suspected.

The man in black had asked her a question, and she focused her sludgy thoughts on answering. "I'm going to question him, assuming *you're* not going to give me any trouble."

He grinned and it lit up his face in a way that reminded her of Elkin so much she had to avert her gaze. "I've tempted fate many times," he said, the words honest and without even a hint of arrogance. "I've learned it's best to avoid crossing sorcerers whenever possible."

Hettie nodded, though it made the world wobble unpleasantly. She was glad at least something was going right.

"Ask him where he got that blade," Deryl said. *"Maybe we could get a sword like that."*

"This isn't a shopping trip."

The man she'd chased spat at Hettie's feet. "I'm not telling you nothing. I'll go to my grave before I tell you what you want to know."

Hettie's eyes narrowed, though he faded in and out of focus. "We'll see about that."

Before she could raise her sword to poke him in the forehead, a trio of men came in from a side street. It took a moment, but Hettie recognized them as local soldiers. She waved them over.

"Arrest this man. I'll want to question him in the morning," she said. "There are three more in the alleyway back there." She pointed with her sword and stumbled when her vertigo increased.

Judging by the rosiness in their cheeks, the soldiers had been drinking as well, but they were quick to respond. Two of them headed for the alleyway. The third reached for the unarmed captive.

"What about him?" he said, nodding a chin at the man in black.

"Leave him be," she said.

"Your words are starting to slur," Deryl said. *"Maybe you should get back to your room."*

The world tilted slowly. Hettie gave her head a brief shake, trying to dispel the vertigo.

"It's the drugs." Even the words in her head were slurred.

"Obviously. You didn't have that much to drink," Deryl said. *"Shameful for a pirate."*

The man in black was studying her. She ignored him. *"Unlike you, I don't have a deep, burning passion to consume entire taverns. I'm glad you don't have a stomach. You're irritating when you're sober. You'd be an unbearable drunk."* Gods. Now she was rambling.

She gave the man in black a curt nod before making her way down the street. Which way was her room again?

"I was a fantastic drunk," Deryl said. *"Charming and hilarious. The ladies couldn't keep their hands off me."*

"Are you sure they were laughing with you and not at you?" Exhaustion hit her. It was all she could do not to stop and lean against a building.

"I'd be offended if I thought you had a sense of humor. You wouldn't know funny if it jumped up and bit you on the chin."

"I know funny just fine. You're not it." A wave of dizziness convinced her she wasn't going to make it to the inn. She kept walking until she was ready to fall over.

A quick glance behind her showed an empty street. At least she thought it was empty. It was hard to tell with the buildings swaying. Ahead she spotted a darkened section of wall, which marked a narrow passageway. She entered to find it so slim she could easily reach out and touch both walls.

"This should be a safe place to sleep this off, right?"

"It's safer than sleeping in the middle of the street."

The drugs didn't give her a chance to object. The world was spinning. She wouldn't last much longer.

She shuffled down the narrow alley. The pungent reek of decaying fish was overwhelming. She knew that smell. It belonged to a fish cutter's shop.

Sure enough, a dozen feet down the path, a cart of fish scales and guts blocked the way forward. By the smell, it was overdue for emptying, but with the chaos of launch preparations, they were likely holding off.

In case they decided to empty it first thing in the morning, Hettie decided to sleep by the back end of the cart. She climbed over it and slid beneath the edge to lay in the dirt, waiting for the dizziness to consume her.

Ouri landed overhead with a gentle flap of wings and a chirrup. She was comforted knowing he would be watching over her.

She was plunged into a dream of Elkin. His blue-black hair fluttered in the wind. He smiled his dimpled smile at her while rainbow-colored mist slid around them, hissing as it went. A strike like thunder rattled the heavens and Elkin's expression twisted to one of shock.

In slow motion, he collapsed.

His look of shock turned to accusation.

Hettie's life with him assaulted her in flashes: the first time she saw him, the first time they kissed, his stories of adventure, their farewell on the docks of Garpoint, and fighting the fish-men together.

Each memory was interrupted by the scene of him falling, his eyes so accusing.

He had died trying to keep her safe. He'd tried to tell her about her family so many times. She'd refused to listen.

Slago take her heart, he'd had so many more adventures left to enjoy. Adventures with her.

The emotions tied to the flickering memories—joy, longing, love, wholeness—were plunged into panic, replaced by a need to do something—to save him. With each flashing image of his death she tried to run to him, to heal him, but he continued to fall, and her dream-self moved so damned slow.

He hit the ground and the life went out of his eyes.

A scream echoed in her mind. One without breath. One without end.

For all her efforts, she was as far from him as she'd ever been.

She'd never stood a chance.

Hettie woke with a start.

Yelling from inside the fish cutter's shop disoriented her at first. "Bring in the next load! It'll be a busy day with the harbor emptying!"

A pounding thrummed just behind her eyes. She squinted in the morning light, trying to slow her racing heart. *Just breathe.*

Ouri sat on the edge of the wagon. He nuzzled her hair when she finally sat up. She buried her fingers in the plumage at his neck, grateful for his presence.

"Good morning, Smelly."

It took Hettie a moment to remember why she was in an alley full of fish scales. She reached out to feel for her magic.

Overwhelming relief flooded her when she managed to touch that well of power within her. Her magical sense was still groggy, like that part of her was numb, but it was there. That was a good sign.

"You should be good as new by the end of the day," Deryl said.

"Let's hope. I'm not comfortable using it with this weird numbness. It's been hard enough to control these past few weeks."

Deryl grunted in agreement.

Hettie gave Ouri one final scritch before climbing back over the wagon of fish scales. The vertigo from the night before had passed and only a mild headache remained. She needed to visit the jail and get answers on what they'd done to her.

"You need to get to your meeting. You're already late," Deryl reminded her.

She glanced up. The narrow strip of sky overhead told her she'd already missed the start of it. She cursed, hurrying out of the passage only to stop short when she reached the main street. The man in black leaned against the wall a foot from her.

"What are you doing here?" she blurted.

He raised an eyebrow. "Ensuring your rest went uninterrupted." He reached out to languidly flick a chunk of fish skin from her shoulder.

His proximity unsettled her, and she was all too aware that she smelled.

She flushed in embarrassment but refused to look away. "The men from last night have been detained, I assume?" Before he could answer, she moved past him to put some distance between them.

He followed her. "Somewhat."

She paused, turning back to him. "Somewhat?"

"The soldiers rounded them up. I went to check on you. I heard a commotion and went back. Somehow, one of the men got hold of a sword and killed the other three."

"Slago take him, he what?" she breathed. Hettie felt like she'd been stabbed herself. She needed answers from those men, and you couldn't question the dead.

It didn't take much work to guess which man had killed the rest. "Where's the last one? That conniving wither-brained goat-skimmer is going to get a piece of my—"

The man in black winced. "I may have killed him."

Hettie exhaled in exasperation. "May have?"

"Did," he corrected. "I did kill him."

"Bloody nails!" She swore with more volume than was strictly necessary. So much for getting answers.

He gave her time to collect the shattered remains of her patience, then said, "For what it's worth, he would have killed your soldiers if I hadn't stepped in."

That didn't surprise her much. The swordsman had stripped her of magic and taken her by surprise in that alleyway. It had been dangerously easy to underestimate him. She'd sent drunken soldiers after him. She was lucky they hadn't been killed too.

"At least this way you won't have to worry about him coming after you again."

"I still want to know what they dosed me with."

"You and me both. There's no help for it, though. You can still make your meeting."

Deryl found it entertaining to watch people argue. With Servio around, there was always arguing.

Hettie glanced at the sky. It was early enough that the meeting might not have concluded yet.

She turned to the man in black. "What's your name?"

"Some call me the Sly Hand. You can call me Tallori." Again, his words were unpretentious.

She didn't have time to get the story behind the name. "You're here to join the army?"

He shook his head. "I was hired to guard a merchant bringing a shipment of swords from up north. They were loaded on the ships yesterday. I head out today once I've gathered supplies."

Hettie had a couple potions she'd made before leaving Storm Flower. One was uniquely deadly and Tallori looked like the kind of guy who would put it to good use. "Before you leave, stop by the Flickerfish Inn. I'll have something for you."

Before he could respond, she took off for the merchant hall, hoping she hadn't missed the entire meeting.

CHAPTER 3
NO

Hettie

Hettie ran until she hit the docks.

Soldiers loaded ships while merchants hawked their wares, knowing business would die once the city emptied later that day.

"Slow down," Deryl said as they approached the meeting hall. *"You're going to burst in there smelling of fish guts and panting like you just birthed Bukker's pups."*

The imagery curled her lip, but she understood his point. Servio would have a field day with her state of dishevelment. He needed no ammunition where Hettie was concerned. General Poll Servio was a retired big shot with an even bigger mouth.

Hettie wanted nothing more than to sew his lips shut.

She slowed her steps, taking in Garpoint's brightly colored buildings. They varied in height, mainly because they were slowly sinking into the marshlands. Her destination, the merchant hall, stood in contrast as a large, squat building on stilts painted the bland color of sand.

Hettie climbed the steps and took a final deep breath to steady her nerves. The smell of fish didn't bother her. She'd grown up on an island.

She entered to find the hall half filled with various leaders of the segmented army, as well as those in charge of the supply train, engineers, and the like. The front of the room held a low stage with five chairs.

Servio was old, fat, and balding, but his eyesight didn't suffer. He spotted Hettie the moment she stepped in. "Nice of you to join us, Witch," he greeted in a dry tone. The very words seemed to frown in disapproval.

Hettie ignored him.

Sitting in order atop the stage was Servio, Vammi, Jonathan, and Liselle, followed by a glaringly empty seat reserved for Hettie.

Liselle had taken responsibility for returning Poll's Wander to stability in the wake of Vincent's first attack. She was level-headed and likable, so nobody balked at her temporary leadership. Her dark hair framed an oval face with pale gray eyes that were stunningly unique.

Jonathan was Liselle's trusted advisor and the leader of the Widows' Will. With his dark hair trimmed and neatly combed, he sat straight-backed and dignified in a blue shirt, gold vest, and black pants. His lean, lanky form made him appear taller than his average height.

Vammi looked sharp, as always, with his angled jawline, curly black hair, and smoldering eyes. As captain of Lady Tuigasi's Steppers, he wore his standard uniform, black with vibrant green highlights.

The Steppers were the only force within the Widows' Will that had not been scattered in Vincent's initial attacks and folded into the greater army. While still part of the Widows' Will, they were a special subunit.

Hettie was there to assist in any way she could. Turning Servio into a lizard was high on her list of priorities.

"Servio," Liselle said sweetly. She was a master of honeyed words, but she'd grown increasingly waspish with him. "Hettie has so graciously shown you where the door is. Please remember you can use it at any time."

Liselle had yet to insist he leave, but she'd come close. As brash and annoying as he was, he did have a reputation for knowing war strategies. Hettie and the rest had decided to tolerate him for the time being. He tested that tolerance every time he opened his mouth.

In hindsight, Hettie wasn't sure suffering the man was a good idea. While he was at least moderately respectful to everyone else in leadership, he undermined her at every turn. Still, if it would save lives, she would swallow her pride and do her best not to strangle him mid-sentence.

"Come join us." Liselle's warm smile turned to a grimace when Hettie climbed onto the stage. "Oh my. What happened to you?" Liselle wasn't the only one with a wrinkled nose.

"She can't hold her drink, I'd wager," Servio muttered.

He grunted as Vammi elbowed him in the ribs. Despite the force of the gesture, Vammi wore a smile. Very little ruffled Vammi.

Even with the jab, Hettie found it hard not to smack Servio in the back of the head as she walked past him to her seat. "I was ambushed by a bunch of surly twit bits," she quietly told Liselle. "I'll tell you more after the meeting. In private."

"Good call. You definitely don't want it getting out that there's a way to block your powers."

Liselle's eyebrows rose. She ran a searching gaze over Hettie. "You're sure you're okay?"

Hettie gave a curt nod and motioned for the meeting to resume.

"You haven't missed much," Liselle said, raising her voice to include the others on stage. "We've confirmed the plans we made yesterday and established that you, Servio, Vammi, and Jonathan will each be on a different ship."

Servio muttered something, but he was too far away for Hettie to make out. He'd wanted all the leaders on the same boat, no doubt so he could try to persuade Jonathan and Vammi to toss Hettie overboard. Of course, that would never happen.

At least she didn't think so. She had trouble making statements like that after her sisters' betrayal. Did you ever really know a person?

"The weather seems to be holding for now and the journey to Stonehaven won't take long," Liselle continued, drowning out Servio's comments. "So all that remains is overseeing the last-minute changes."

"Speaking of last-minute changes," Servio spoke up, "I'd like to—"

Liselle, Jonathan, and Vammi all turned to Servio as one. "No," they said in unison.

"Every day is the same with this guy," Deryl commented.

"Let me be perfectly clear." Liselle's tone took on a sharp edge. "If you ask one more time for Hettie to remain behind, you will be forbidden from accompanying my army."

Servio traded glares with Hettie, but he wisely kept his mouth shut.

When the meeting was over, Liselle motioned for Hettie to exit through the side door. A buttressed strip of walkway encircled the merchant hall, leading around to the stairs. The path conveniently allowed them to bypass the majority of the building's occupants.

Liselle wove through the bustle of people along the docks, her gray-green dress flaring out behind her in the breeze. Hettie followed on her heels. When they reached a less crowded side street, Liselle spun and gave Hettie a hug.

"You're going to smell like fish," Hettie warned. Despite her words, she felt a warm glow in her chest. If she could have traded her sister Nuala for Liselle, her life would have been so much better.

"I can take a bath later," Liselle said. She pulled back. "Tell me what happened."

Hettie relayed the night's events, watching Liselle's eyes grow wide with alarm.

"They took your magic?"

She waggled a hand in the air. "They didn't take it so much as block it. I can feel it again. Whatever they put in my drink seems to be wearing off."

"The downside of guapi yeti's flavor, I suppose." Liselle didn't have to ask what Hettie was drinking. The fermented guapi juice, tart and purple with little white seeds floating in it, had quickly become her drink of choice.

"Anyway they're dead now, which means I won't have to worry about them. But I need to know what they used on me."

Liselle's brow furrowed. "I haven't heard of anything like that, but then, you're the only person I know with magic. I'll make inquiries while you're gone."

"I'd appreciate that." She didn't have to ask Liselle to be discreet.

Hettie was leaving Garpoint, but so were all the foreigners. The newcomers were all part of the army, which meant she'd have to be on her guard. Her confidence in taking care of herself had been shaken. She wasn't nearly so formidable without her magic.

You left your sisters without theirs. The reminder made her stomach churn with guilt.

"I'm glad you made it to the meeting," Liselle said, interrupting Hettie's thoughts. "Listening to Servio's commentary was driving me crazy. Are you sure you want him along?"

"No. But we might need him." They'd had this conversation before.

What Hettie hadn't told her closest friends was that she felt like an imposter.

It didn't help that Servio kept trying to get rid of her. Hettie stood her ground in part because there was nowhere else for her to go. She liked being with her friends. They were the closest thing to a home she had.

Confidence had been easy to come by as the First Daughter, leader of the Daughters' Coven. Everyone looked to her, and she almost always knew what to do. When she didn't, her mother had the answer.

Her sisters had shown her how fallible she was. Powerful or not, Hettie wasn't the leader everyone thought she was. She was just faking it. She had been all along. She just hadn't realized it.

She had no experience leading an army on a cross-country expedition to fight a battle against unknown enemies. Neither did Jonathan or Vammi, though they both wore the mask of leadership the same as she did. She was willing to wager they both felt incompetent in their positions.

Despite being an overbearing pig's anus, Servio was the only one with the skills for the job. Hopefully, they'd need him like a hole in a boat instead of a cork.

"I worry he'll cause trouble for you."

Liselle's words triggered a memory. She had said something similar before in reference to Nuala. Her words had proved prophetic.

"I can handle him," Hettie said with more confidence than she felt.

Liselle put a hand on her arm. "You can take care of yourself, I know." She hesitated before reaching into a pocket of her dress and pulling out a curved white trinket. "I want you to have this," she said.

It was a bracelet, white like bone with dark, stained carvings on it.

Hettie took it, studying the markings. She recognized some, others she didn't, though a few looked similar to markings she'd seen in her book of magic.

"It's an artifact," Liselle said with a sparkle in her eye that told Hettie a history lesson was coming. Liselle collected historical arti-facts. It was her passion.

"According to an ancient text, a man named Horquil was visited in a dream by Al Dagos, who told him to gather stories from all over the world. The only problem was that Horquil was a farmer and could only speak the language of his land. Al Dagos took a bit of bone from men all across the land and combined it with magic to create this bracelet. It's called the Bangle of Discernment. Supposedly, it lets you understand any language."

Hettie looked closer at the markings. The stain used to darken them was reddish-brown, almost like blood. If the bangle was made of bone, the stain might well be blood. Hettie wasn't sure bones and blood were the look she was going for, but that wasn't the only reason she was nervous about wearing it. The last time she'd activated an artifact, she'd ended up with a long dead man stuck in her head.

"I'm not that bad."

"Eh," she said, noncommittal. He clearly wasn't thinking of the

many times she'd threatened to throw him in the ocean. *"Some things are better left alone."*

"Where's your sense of adventure?"

Liselle said, "I don't know what you'll find in the mountains, but it may come in handy. It can't hurt, in any case."

"See?" Deryl said. *"It can't hurt."*

"Says the woman who's never had to deal with you." Regardless of her misgivings, Hettie slipped the bracelet on. The bone was stark and pale against her brown skin.

"I wish I was going with you," Liselle said with a sigh. "I never took myself for an adventurer. That was always Griff's hobby. Now that he's gone, it's like I can't stay busy long enough to keep my mind from dwelling on him." While her expression was carefully neutral, Hettie could see the sadness beneath.

When she and Liselle first met, Lord Holden's death wasn't a topic of conversation. That changed after Elkin died. It had connected them in a way nothing else could.

Hettie was keenly aware losing a boyfriend of a couple years wasn't nearly as bad as losing a husband of decades. Her situation paled in comparison to Liselle's. While she understood the feeling of having the future erased, she couldn't comprehend a feeling of loss magnified so far beyond her own.

Their connection was one of several aspects that made Poll's Wander feel like a second home. Hettie tried not to think like that though. She was all too familiar with how quickly circumstances could change when a body got too comfortable with their place in life. She had no home. It was best she remember that.

"I wish you could come too," Hettie said. "If for no other reason than to exact vengeance."

Liselle smiled. "Vengeance was something I never thought much of either. It always seemed so petty before."

Before Lord Vincent had invited the Lords of Poll's Wander to his castle, then butchered every last one of them. Before he sent a letter to the five widows telling them he planned to take over their land.

It had been a brutal ploy for power. One that had ultimately failed.

A distant call came from the boardwalk. Vammi had spotted them and jogged their way. He flashed them a boyish grin as he approached. "You two left too quickly for Servio to get in any last jibes."

"I'm sure he'll survive," Hettie said wryly.

Vammi had a way of lightening any mood. He was roguishly handsome and deviously charming with a reputation for pushing the bounds of propriety.

"Besides," Liselle said, "I doubt he wants to talk to Hettie before she bathes."

"Masterful plan for repelling him." Vammi's eyes smoldered. "If you need someone to help you remove the smell, consider me an avid volunteer."

Vammi was 80 percent flirtation and 20 percent bravado.

Hettie hadn't been sure what to think of him when they'd first met. His flamboyant comments were enough to make her blush, despite being raised on an island of pirates with little sense and no sensibilities to speak of. But she'd gotten used to him quickly.

Of their group, only Jonathan was perpetually disturbed by his comments. Jonathan had more propriety than a Darrish priest.

"I can bathe myself just fine, but I'll keep you in mind if there's anywhere I can't reach."

Liselle rolled her eyes. "I want to tell you two to watch out for each other while you're gone, but I'm afraid you'll take it the wrong way."

Vammi chided her with a look and held his hands out to the side. "Don't be jealous. I have two hands. I can wash you both."

Liselle swatted at him. "Behave yourself." She turned back to Hettie. "I'll be planning a great feast for when you get back. We'll sit beneath my beautiful new tapestry."

Hettie had used magic to embed the image of a fighting peacock, the Holden family emblem, on Gak. He was hanging in the feasting hall at Penelope.

"Gak says thanks for the remodel, by the way," Deryl said.

Hettie smiled. It was one of the few spells she'd been able to make sense of from the new spell book. *"That spell isn't as useful as the night vision spell, but he does look rather dashing in blue and gold."*

CHAPTER 4

CHEATERS AND LOSERS

Hettie

Two days later, Hettie stood aboard *The Lucky Lass*, one of the biggest cogs Garpoint had to offer for the trip around the southern edge of the Little Gods. Over a dozen ships sat in the tiny bay off the southern coast of Sedrios where the mountain range sloped down to the golden sands of the Yellow Sea. Tucked into the base of the mountain sat the path to Stonehaven.

Being on the water again had felt strange to Hettie, like she was closer to her mother and farther than ever from Elkin. Strangely enough, she missed Liselle more than anyone and was homesick for Penelope.

At the railing, she closed her eyes and lost herself to the gentle rocking of the ship beneath her feet as she considered the problem of how to get on shore.

The rhythmic creaking of the rigging overhead was interrupted by Deryl. *"I'm beginning to think we don't give old Vinnie enough credit."*

Hettie snorted. *"Said nobody ever."* From her perch atop the aft castle, she studied the blackened remains of a dock protruding from the rocky shore, if one could call it a shore at all. It was more an encrustation of boulders.

Lord Vincent's estate was nestled into the Little Gods, which divided the Sedrian marshlands from blistering desert. Poll's Wander had never considered him a threat. It was a mistake they wouldn't make twice. With luck, taking down Lord Vincent would protect them from future threats.

Word had spread in the weeks after the Battle for Poll's Wander and the Widows' Will had swelled to four times its original size. Men and women from Deep Knotting and beyond had flocked to join them. Some sought purpose; others wanted adventure. A small minority wanted trouble.

Now over a thousand strong, the soldiers expected an easy victory.

Hettie wasn't so sure.

The victory in Poll's Wander had relied on Hettie's sisters working together, as well as a pirate navy. They currently had neither, thanks to the colossal falling out between Hettie and her family, plus the death of Elkin, the leader of said pirate navy.

They'd only just begun their journey, and the burning of the docks indicated Vincent would prove to be as unpredictable as ever.

"Too bad you didn't bring more rowboats," Deryl said.

Rowboats hadn't seemed necessary when they needed that space for supplies. They hadn't even left sight of shore. Rowboats had been low on the priority list with only a handful sprinkled in among the entire procession.

"Even rowboats won't help without a dock," she countered. The morning sunshine reached beyond the looming mountain tops, illuminating the glistening shoreline. *"The rocks are mossy and it's a six-foot vertical climb up to the path."* She sucked on her teeth. *"We should have planned for something like this."*

"You spent too long planning already. If you'd planned down to the tiniest detail, you'd have never left. This adds a bit of spontaneity. It adds to the adventure."

"This isn't an adventure," she reminded him for the thousandth time. *"It's war."*

"War can be an adventure."

"Only if you're immortal."

Shouts rang out from beneath the sail of *The Lucky Lass*. Surrounded by cheering soldiers, two men raced to strip off their clothing.

Hettie sighed. *"What are these idiots up to now?"*

Deryl let out a little squeal of glee. *"I don't know, but it looks fun. Let's see if you can strip faster than they can."*

Hettie ignored him and watched the scene unfold.

Stripped down to skivvies and boots, one man sprinted for the railing and bounded overboard with practiced ease.

Hettie couldn't figure out how he'd gotten his pants off over his boots.

"Go fool!" Deryl cackled, caught up in the excitement. *"Whatever they're doing, I hope that guy wins."*

"What in Handoon's gullet?" Hettie wondered, peering down at the spot where the man had disappeared beneath the waves. The dim morning light made it difficult to see below the surface. *"Is he swimming for shore?"*

Close to the desert as they were, the water temperature was comfortable, but a man couldn't go to war naked, so swimming for shore alone and unclothed was a stupid plan.

"Stop whining and start cheering," Deryl said.

The second man finally untangled his feet from his britches and stalked over to the railing, still wearing his shirt and skivvies. "You left your boots on, Fish-for-Brains!" he hollered when his competitor's head breached the surface not far from the boat.

Hettie descended to the main deck and pushed her way through the gathered men. She found Captain Pulley near the railing, his bushy white eyebrows drawn together as he frowned at the man in the water.

"Are the men getting bored, Captain?" she asked.

He stiffened but avoided looking at her. He was more terrified of her magic than most Sedrians she'd met. "Blessed be your mother," he said in greeting. "The men are young and eager to help." He shook his head and muttered to himself, "Perhaps too eager."

Hettie had her doubts on how swimming naked was supposed to help, and she said so.

The captain tipped his head in a way that indicated he, too, had no idea how the men planned to help.

On most ships, the captain's word was law. Captain Pulley had been terrified enough of Hettie to avoid asserting himself during their short voyage and the lack of discipline showed.

"What are you up to, Zacha?" the captain called to the man in the water.

Zacha did a lazy backstroke, pulling away from *The Lucky Lass* while keeping an eye on his competitor overhead.

The half-naked man spoke up before Zacha could answer, voice pitched to carry so his friend in the water could hear. "We *were* gonna race to shore. We can get up those rocks no problem."

"We?" Zacha called. "You lost this race before you started."

"Because you're a dirty cheatin' fin stuffer!" hollered the other.

"It ain't cheatin' if I'm quicker!" Zacha took a breath and ducked his head, thrashing around as he tried to get his boots off while staying afloat.

The crowd watched in amusement until Zacha suddenly jerked. His head shot up, his expression terrified.

"What is it?" Hettie asked.

Flailing, he spun in a circle, peering down into the water.

Hettie reached for her magic, ready to scan the area. Before she got that far, a slimy, purple head emerged directly behind Zacha.

Hettie froze at the sight of a fish-man. She'd fought them before at Elkin's side. The memory was like a punch to the gut, a blatant reminder that he would never fight at her side again.

CHAPTER 5

FISH-MEN AND GLASS SHARKS

Hettie

A gasp from the ship's passengers echoed across the water. In a flash, the gelatinous fish-man disappeared beneath the surface with Zacha in tow.

"He's quicker all right," Deryl said. *"Quicker at dying."*

The half-naked man still aboard began muttering a prayer.

Hettie's magic had returned after her confrontation in Garpoint, and she was grateful for the familiar pressure of it now that she needed it. She flared her senses, finding Zacha in moments only to find his heartbeat stuttering. The fish-man was firmly clamped to his neck. Hettie hadn't managed to get a bubble of air around him before he went under. A heartbeat later, he was dead.

Hettie slammed her hands on the railing in frustration.

She turned her attention to the surrounding water, searching for more of the creatures. One hovered near the surface, a silent sentinel watching for others foolish enough to enter the water. Another was

29

down near the silty ocean floor. Three more fish-men circled the dead man before lunging. They tore poor Zacha to shreds in moments.

Hettie was a healer, but she couldn't heal death.

"Swimming is out," she said through clenched teeth. "We're going to need another way across." She regretted sending Ouri off to find food. He would have been a good lookout.

Without warning, the fish-men retreated beyond the range of her magic.

It didn't take long for her to figure out why. Bubbles rose from the murky depths as if the sea were boiling. Muttered curses from soldiers and sailors alike filled the air.

"Hettie," Deryl said. *"That sea turtle is staring at you."*

She sensed the turtle directly below the railing before she spotted it. Huge and reddish brown, it watched her from beside the boat.

Another wave of homesickness struck her. "Hello, Mother. It's been a while."

Captain Pulley let out a sound of distress from beside her. She wasn't sure if it was because of her words or the boiling sea.

The rising bubbles carried words, wry and raspy. "First Daughter."

Mekoa, the Deep Witch, previously the Island Witch, had a voice that was innately ominous. She only spoke through bubbles when she was sitting somewhere at the bottom of the ocean, a location she had frequented more often in recent years.

Hettie wondered if her mother had come to the Sedrian coast to check on her or if her powers had spread far enough to know what was happening here from as far away as the Paradisals. Neither would surprise her.

"I didn't realize she could talk to you from this far away."

"I don't think she could before. Seems her power is growing."

"That's mildly terrifying."

Hettie had mixed feelings about her mother. Sadness, anger, and respect warred within her. She leaned farther over the railing. "How's Fleana handling things?" Hettie had put her little sister in charge when she'd left the island for good.

Her mother continued to watch her from the blood turtle's eyes. "Better than expected, considering her age."

Deryl chuckled. *"If you'd been put in charge at eleven, you'd have been nothing but trouble, I bet."*

"I was put in charge at birth," she reminded him. *"Everything was fine when I was eleven. The Daughters' Coven wasn't filled with drama until Nuala started it."*

"She's a beast," she told her mother. "Given some rein, she'll have the entire island eating out of the palm of her hand in a year's time."

"She leaves me time to myself," her mother said.

Captain Pulley eased away from Hettie, drawing her attention. The tension aboard *The Lucky Lass* was palpable. Crew members stayed far back from the railing, casting fearful glances her way.

Hettie ignored them. She ignored a lot of things. Growing up as the eldest daughter of the great and mighty Island Witch, she was used to those stares.

"Need a hand while I'm here?" her mother offered. "These things aren't natural. They don't belong in the water. Or anywhere, from what I can tell."

"That's funny coming from her," Deryl said. *"Think she'll turn the fish-men into a new breed of glass shark?"*

Hettie could hear the revulsion in his voice.

Her mother conceived children by sleeping with corpses then reanimating the men as glass sharks, a previously mythical creature that parents told their children about to scare them into staying close to shore.

"I'd rather spare the world from whatever abominations would come from that romp in the surf. They'd probably rival Mother for sheer brutality."

"The sharks would probably eat one another." He gave a mental shudder Hettie could feel through their bond.

"That would *mean fewer glass sharks."* The mere thought of the beasts, one of which was Hettie's own father, turned her stomach.

"I'll handle them myself," Hettie assured her mother. Her magic had returned, full force. She could handle a few fish-men.

"Smart girl." The words were a murmur, hard to hear over the roiling bubbles. "If I taught you *anything* useful, it's that weakness leads to downfall."

Hettie gave the turtle a strained smile. "I've learned plenty of useful things from you. Some of those lessons were more painful than others."

The turtle studied her in silence until Captain Pulley cleared his throat behind her. The turtle ducked beneath the water and disappeared along with the bubbles, leaving the sea almost eerily smooth in its wake.

Hettie didn't turn around. "What is it, Captain?"

He cleared his throat again. "We could fight back the fish-men if they climbed aboard, but we're no use against them in the water. Even if we could lure them up from the depths, it won't help us get to shore." His words were hesitant. "Is there any way you can help?"

His careful avoidance of the word "magic" wasn't lost on Hettie. She held back a sigh. She couldn't blame him for being nervous.

In the Paradisals, her magic and her mother earned her reverence, which was distinctly different from fear. Hettie wasn't opposed to fear, but she preferred it from her enemies. Fear from allies could lead to its own form of trouble.

Trying to keep the disappointment from her voice, she said, "I'll see what I can do, Captain."

She listened to the shuffling of his boots as he withdrew.

Hettie already had a plan. She wasn't positive it would work, but it was a far sight better than returning to Garpoint. Half the soldiers would desert if something as simple as a burned bit of timber defeated them.

She scanned the ship, looking for the half-dressed man. Instead, her attention was drawn to a soldier watching her from beside the stairway to the aft deck. She was used to being stared at. Most of the ship's men and women watched her every move, though they averted their gazes when she looked their way.

This man's look was different—intense and predatory.

It made her hackles rise. Hettie paused to lock eyes with the man, wondering if he hated magic too.

He wore a tan shirt and brown trousers and stood out for more than just his raptor gaze.

The original Widows' Will consisted of soldiers from the five estates of Poll's Wander. This man's outfit didn't match any of the estate colors. Granted, some of the new soldiers were farmers from remote areas of Poll's Wander and beyond. A few were swamp hunters. Others were fishermen. Many had come from closer to Deep Knotting in northern Sedrios. Nearly all the soldiers were Pavinn, with medium brown skin, brown eyes, and black hair.

This soldier wasn't as pale as a true northerner, his brown hair and blue eyes clearly marked him as Andosh. He'd come from somewhere across the Beacon Sea.

"Why would an Andosh soldier sign up to join a Pavinn army?" she wondered. *"What stake does he have in this battle?"*

"Maybe he just wants to stab something," Deryl said. *"That's their primary hobby, isn't it?"*

Andos's mainland was almost always at war. Stabbing things was more of a continental hobby than a cultural one. One thing they weren't known for was playing well with others.

Mixing cultures had become common practice in the Paradisals. There, nobody cared what country you came from. If everywhere else hated you, the islanders were happy to have you. On the mainland, neighboring countries couldn't get along most days. Mix cultures and you were bound to have trouble.

"Then again, he did just see you talk to the ocean. And the ocean talked back. That has to be disconcerting."

Hettie chewed her lip. *"The Andosh like witches even less than the Pavinn."* While staring wasn't a crime, after the attack in Garpoint, she wasn't about to let her guard down.

The Andosh soldier was staring so intently that it took him a beat to notice she was studying him back. His eyes grew wide. He nodded cordially, turned, and disappeared behind a gaggle of female soldiers.

"Hey, maybe he's interested in you for other reasons. You're rather fetching in a murderous sort of way. He could be hoping to sing you a bawdy tavern song," Deryl said in a suggestive tone.

Hettie smirked and shook her head at how hopeful he sounded. *"I think you're the only one with a penchant for those."*

She made a note to ask around about the Andosh. For now, they had other problems to solve. Scanning the deck, she spotted the man in his skivvies sitting with his back to the center mast, pants and boots bundled at his side.

"Oy!" she called. "Still interested in being first to shore?"

CHAPTER 6

EVERYTHING IS FINE

Hettie

The soldier had zero interest in being first to shore. Or first off the ship, for that matter. Hettie's natural charm eventually convinced him it would be better for him to go than to stay.

"If you do this right, Quillum, you'll be just fine," Hettie told him.

"Probably," Deryl supplied.

"Probably," she agreed.

Captain Pulley came over.

"Stay in the rowboat and don't draw unnecessary attention," Hettie said.

"Won't the fish-men just climb into the boat?" the captain asked.

Judging by Quillum's terrified look, Captain Pulley wasn't the only one thinking along those lines.

Hettie would do all she could to make sure the rowers reached shore safely. They couldn't afford to lose the use of *The Lucky Lass*'s only rowboat. "It'll be fine." She waggled her fingers. "Magic and all."

Deryl chuckled. *"That's sure to put them at ease."*

"Hush," she scolded. She'd wasted far too much time trying to convince them to follow the plan. They'd rather stand around wringing their hands than put their trust in magic. The men aboard the ship were getting restless. It was only a matter of time before one of them did something stupid. They needed to get moving.

The captain cast a discreet look over the railing. Hettie thought he was checking for evidence of her mother until he muttered, "Magic didn't do Zacha much good."

He had a point.

Hettie gave the captain what she hoped was a reassuring smile. "You know what they say. Foolish brain, foolish bounty." She crossed her arms. "Let's avoid being foolish this time around."

The captain traded a dubious look with Quillum.

"Look, you've got three options," Hettie told him. "You can trust me, figure out your own solution, or go back to Garpoint and explain to all of Poll's Wander why you failed them. Your job was to get us from Garpoint to right *there*." She pointed to the ruined docks.

His gaze followed her finger.

"If being a pariah is your idea of a good time, by all means, let's give up. Otherwise, unless you've got a better plan, get out of my way so I can do your job for you." She hardened her voice. "We're wasting daylight."

"On the double," Deryl growled.

His frequent comments were getting on her nerves. *"You don't even know what that means."*

"I do too. It means hurry up."

"It implies speed in physical movement, not in decision making."

"Bloody seas, I just wanted to be a pirate for a minute. You ruin everything, you know that?"

"You ruin my patience. That makes us even."

She turned her attention back to Captain Pulley, who was stammering some kind of reply. She only caught the last of it, though his stiff posture and clipped tone told her he wasn't happy.

". . . job is to look out for my crew, but I'll do as you say." He walked off with his head held high.

She'd managed to piss off two men in the span of a few seconds. At this rate, the whole army would hate her by the end of the day.

A distant voice bellowed from afar. "What was *that*?" Servio had maneuvered his ship to the starboard side of *The Lucky Lass*, close enough to yell as if his input was wanted.

Hettie let out a dramatic groan. Even her sisters hadn't irritated her this much.

"Sounds like there's three men you've pissed off," Deryl said.

Hettie glowered at Servio, who stood on the foredeck of his ship. The morning light made his drooping jowls and pudgy waist look like a cross between a man and a sow. His thin white hair bordered on bald in places.

General Poll *Servio* was named after General Poll *Sedrios*, whose battle tactics from 250 years ago resulted in the country of Sedrios getting its name. General Sedrios had an army lieutenant who worshipped him and Servio counted himself lucky to be that lieutenant's descendant. With such a big reputation to live up to, Servio had earned an impressive record on the field. He'd fought to overthrow the Darrish empire half a century ago, as well as pitting himself against the Placid Waters Import Group after their attack on Arlea. Fighting against the Importers, who had enslaved the people of the Paradisals, would have earned him Hettie's respect if it hadn't been well known that Sedrios hadn't given a rat's tail about the islanders.

Servio was older than sin and had come out of two decades of retirement to relive his glory days in the guise of providing wartime expertise. Hettie just hoped he wasn't a liability.

"It was nothing," she told him, magic carrying her voice. It was hard to be dignified while shouting at the top of your lungs.

"It didn't look like nothing!" he called across the distance. "It looks like we're losing men before we even reach the enemy!"

"That's not entirely accurate. The fish-men *are* the enemy."

"Fish-men?" He snorted. He'd no doubt heard the tales and

dismissed them as fancy. "You decided to distract them by giving them easy kills?" he said bluntly.

Hettie scowled. "*I* didn't do anything. Some idiot decided to swim for shore. Look, we've got it covered." She tried not to sound testy, but damn it, she *was* testy. "I've got a plan worked out."

His grumbling carried across the water, but she couldn't make out the words, though that could have been because Deryl talked over him.

"I thought you brought him along for his expertise."

Hettie snorted. *"In battle. Not fighting fish-men."*

Captain Pulley readied the rowboat and Hettie had it lowered with five trembling men in it. Two rowed and three were armed and ready to decapitate any fish-men coming out of the water.

Hettie tied the end of a giant spool of rigging rope to the rowboat and sent the little boat off.

"If the rope is cut, turn back," she reminded them. "You'll have to tie your end to a boulder on shore." She'd done all she could to reassure them she'd be standing guard, but the boat still vibrated with their combined shakiness.

"They'll face off with horned men, but give them one that's part fish and they turn into a bunch of babies," Deryl said.

"The problem is, they can't see the enemy coming. I'm limited in how well I can track them without seeing them, too, so be quiet and let me concentrate."

She cradled the bottom of the rowboat with a shield, then gave it a magical push that nearly toppled the armed men crouched and ready for an attack. It had been difficult to control the force of her spells lately.

The men all managed to stay in the boat, which was good since Hettie would have had a significantly harder time protecting them in the water.

The rowers had only gotten a quarter of the way to shore when a half dozen figures swarmed up from the depths, arrowing straight for the boat. One tried to smash the bottom from underneath, but the shield held. This didn't surprise Hettie. The magic she'd stolen from her sisters pressed on her like she'd overindulged at a feast. Her shield was harder than stone.

Four other fish-men tried to climb aboard the little rowboat, but the swordsmen were ready, slicing off hands and through necks until only two of the six fish-men remained.

With Hettie's focus on the shield and the rowers too terrified to stick their oars in the water, the boat should have lost all momentum. It continued forward, though.

Hettie suspected her mother was aiding them.

"Maybe it's her way of apologizing for killing your lover," Deryl said cheerily.

Hettie had to remind herself it had been an accident. That hadn't made the loss any easier to bear, especially knowing her own refusal to see the truth about her family played such a huge role in his death.

Hettie kept an eye on the fish-men below while Captain Pulley hollered instructions to the nearby boats so they could board *The Lucky Lass* in an orderly manner. Some of the more creative folk on board had come up with a rig that would allow them to slide down the rope to shore.

"Mother," Hettie said to the water below. "Are you pushing the rowboat?"

Bubbles rose from beside the ship, and her mother's voice came plain as day. "You said not to help."

Her mother's waspish tone made her smile. Hettie could clearly picture the crinkles around her eyes as she glared daggers at everyone around her. "Thank you." She pointedly didn't specify for what.

A grunt of acknowledgement came in reply.

"How does she get bubbles to sound like her voice?" Deryl asked.

"I have no idea. Would you like me to ask her?"

"Definitely not. There's very little I know about how she does what she does, but what little I know is enough to give me nightmares for the rest of my non-life."

One of the fish-men rushed forward and launched itself out of the water at the little rowboat.

Hettie followed it, bending her magic to the task of slicing through its neck.

She'd learned in her previous fight that the fish-men's gooey bodies instantly sealed around severed blood vessels. Decapitation was one of the most effective ways to deal with them. She'd saved Elkin's life with that discovery.

The memory of him hit her again with a wave of emotion, almost crippling in its intensity. Gods, but she missed him.

She dragged her focus back to her work and managed to sever the fish-man's neck in mid-air. The head went soaring over the men. The body didn't make it that far.

One of the soldiers gave it a hearty stab. The limp purple body came crashing down on him and knocked him clean out of the boat.

"Good grief. These guys had one job. Stay in the boat." Hettie let out a low growl of frustration.

"In all fairness, that was your fault."

"Not helping."

The soldier in the water flailed in his leather gear, frantically closing the distance to the rowboat.

Underwater, another fish-man sped forward. Hettie realized, too late, she had let her shield slip.

CHAPTER 7

ROW! ROW! ROW!

Hettie

The fish-man closed in on the swimming man, but faster than Hettie could register, a huge shark came in and grabbed the fish-man's leg, dragging it down deep beneath the waves. The men were oblivious to their near miss.

Resetting her shield, Hettie scanned the water. The men aboard *The Lucky Lass* called out encouragement to those in the rowboat as they pulled their disarmed swordsman aboard.

The shark attack had been perfectly timed. This time, Hettie had no doubt her mother had orchestrated it. While she was grateful, the fact that she'd needed the help shamed her.

Hettie had been raised to take over as the leader of the Paradisals. That dream had died with Elkin, which was ironic. Ruling the island had been the one thing keeping her from exploring the world with Elkin. Now she had neither option.

Staying sane meant staying busy. She struggled to keep from

thinking about how useless and stupid Elkin's death had been. It was gutting. Years of promises had been severed like a snapped fishing rod.

"You might want to dwell on all this after the fighting is done," Deryl said.

Hettie scowled and checked her shield again. The calls from aboard *The Lucky Lass* had become a chant.

"Row! Row! Row! Row!"

Bolstered by their encouragement, the men in the boat rowed for all they were worth. The chanting turned to a cheer when they reached the rocky shore. The unarmed swordsman was the first to make his way up the jagged boulders. Helping one another, they all made it up, taking the rope tied to the rowboat with them.

They decided a skinny upright rock seated on a broad horizontal rock would make a decent landing platform. By the time the rope was secure, Captain Pulley had connected his end of the rope to *The Lucky Lass*'s main mast just above the crow's nest, creating a downward slope.

A line of soldiers lined up, ready to attempt what looked to be a dubious crossing.

"All right, men," Captain Pulley said, despite a quarter of the army being female, "we've prepared a demonstration on how to get up to the crow's nest. Pay attention so you don't bloody fall. At the top, we've fashioned a hook for you to slide down on. We'll pull it back after each one of you goes. God speed."

"Short and to the point," Deryl said. *"I like his style."*

"We'll have him give Servio lessons."

The demonstration was brief. The first soldier made the crossing at an alarming rate.

Deryl hooted. *"He's going to slam face first into that boulder."*

Hettie winced as he did just that, knocking himself out momentarily.

Captain Pulley cursed as the men from the rowboat dragged the unconscious man off the rock. They couldn't get close enough to catch the guy without getting kicked by a flailing foot or slammed into the rock themselves.

A crewman pulled on a thin rope to draw the hook back to the ship.

The captain hollered, "Use that blasted rope to slow them down at the end next time!"

The next volunteer took some coaxing, but his eventual crossing went better than the first man's. He still landed hard, but he kicked his feet up at the last minute and cushioned his blow.

One by one, the men crossed. Two other ships were tall enough for the same type of rigging, but nobody was keen on manning another rowboat. Instead, a rope was tied to a soldier's waist, and he was sent across on the hook.

Unfortunately, the weight of the rope managed to slow his descent until he was stuck hanging over the water. Determined to avoid a watery death, he pressed on, hand over hand, until he made it to the far side.

In the end, they managed to get two ropes attached to the boulders, each tied to the main mast of Jonathan and Vammi's ships, giving them a total of three paths to shore.

Hettie stood vigil, cutting down the occasional attack from lingering fish-men. It was hard to tell how many were around because they were spread out while her magic was focused on the immediate area.

Soldiers in the smaller boats boarded the larger ones and Servio ended up aboard Hettie's ship.

He came to stand beside her, watching a soldier down the rope with an undignified yell. "Why they put a witch in charge of this operation. . ." he muttered to himself just loud enough for her to hear. He raised his voice and added, "This is not the plan I'd have gone with."

"Nobody asked you."

"This does count as logistics for troop movement," Deryl said. *"If you're not going to hear him out, you really should have left him back at Garpoint. This way, you get all the suffering and none of the benefit."*

Hettie ground her teeth. He was right. She should have at least heard what Servio had to say. If the man could start off a conversation without immediately insulting her, it would be easier to give him a chance.

"This strands us on the other side. A key strategy for troop movement includes making sure you have a way back home."

"They'll get the dock rebuilt before we return. If not, we'll cross the mountains to the north. We're not stranded."

"The men are carrying a couple days' worth of food. You think that'll get them through battle, then over the mountains to boot?"

Dammit, he had a point.

"And what about the rest of the supplies? We have boatloads of equipment to take with us. Magic clearly doesn't improve your reasoning skills."

Hettie's temper flared. The man was insufferable.

Servio had criticized almost every plan they'd discussed in the weeks leading up to their departure. Every time they asked him what he suggested, he would deflect, saying he preferred to make decisions in the moment when he had real-time information. It was like he preferred not to plan anything at all and just wing it the whole time.

"If you had a better idea, you should have spoken up."

Servio blinked. "When was I supposed to speak up? I've been shuttled off to the side at every turn. Clearly, my input doesn't matter." He indicated his boat anchored next to hers, a reminder he'd wanted the leadership to travel together.

Hettie gave him a patronizing smile. "And yet you give it anyway. Did you have a plan to share or not?" Most of the men had made the crossing without much trouble, but it would be nice to have their supplies with them.

"It's a moot point now, isn't it?" he asked belligerently, his wispy white hair swaying like grass in the wind. "This is exactly why I suggested keeping all leadership aboard the same ship. If a problem arose, we could have talked it over together."

Hettie violently severed the head of a fish-man preparing to launch itself out of the water at a dangling sailor. "First off, you're not leadership. Jonathan is. So is Vammi. And we all agreed to be on different ships so that if problems arose, there would be someone to coordinate the men."

He threw his hands in the air and growled in frustration. "That's what the ship's captain is for."

The captain was in charge of the boat and the ship's crew. They were also in charge of the odd passenger, but the number of soldiers aboard far exceeded the standard passenger load for every one of the ships. It was ridiculous to assume the captain take charge of them all. One man could only do so much.

"What happens if one of our boats sink and it just happens to be the one with all the leadership on it?" This point had been brought up, but Servio didn't seem concerned with it. "The army can continue on without one of its leaders, but not without all of them."

"We'd all be on board with *you*, though, wouldn't we?" he said in a mocking tone. "Your magnificent witchy powers would save the day."

Deryl chortled. Hettie growled.

So many of the newcomers hated sorcery. They hadn't even given her a chance, the whiny pig-stickers. Servio was the most vocal one of all, and half his complaints were that nobody would give his input a chance, all while dismissing everyone else's input.

"What is it with you?" she asked. "It's clear you don't like magic. I'm not sure why you volunteered to be part of this war knowing I was coming along. It's not like you were invited."

Servio narrowed his eyes at her in a glare that would have been fierce for anyone not raised by the Deep Witch. "Maybe I'm not the problem. Maybe you're the one that should be staying behind," he said, waving a finger in her face.

She smacked it away. "I was here first."

"Oh there's a fine argument."

Another fish-man came in range of her senses, but it swam by the corpse of its fellow and beat a hasty retreat.

Captain Pulley waved timidly at them from a few feet away. The deck had emptied of soldiers, and it was her turn to make the crossing.

"If you don't like me being here, take it up with Jonathan." She headed for the rigging leading up to the crow's nest. She hadn't had a lot of practice climbing the ropes, but she made her way well, using magic to aid her. The last thing she wanted was to slip and look like a fool with Servio watching on.

When she reached the top, she was greeted with a piercing shriek. Ouri flew by on silent wings. She raised a hand in greeting, and he came in for a landing on the lip of the crow's nest. She crooned to him and stroked his head. "You can keep me company on my way to shore. It's as close as I'll ever get to flying."

"Not really," Deryl said. *"Sliding and flying aren't the same thing."*

"Nobody asked you."

"I know, but if someone had, I would have been glad to point out the distinction," Deryl said patiently.

A thick rope hung from a hook, knotted at the bottom to make a handy foothold. Hettie straddled the crow's nest, steadied the rope, and slid her foot through the loop. Looking down, she spotted Servio talking to Captain Pulley, who nodded along with whatever Servio was saying. They were probably agreeing on how tragic it was to have a sorcerer around.

"Move it, wench," Deryl commanded. *"I'm not getting any younger."*

"Technically, you're not getting any older either."

"True, but I am getting boreder."

"That's not a word." Hettie adjusted her grip on the rope.

"Sure it is. I just said it."

Hettie leaned forward, shifting her weight to the foot in the rope. When she released the crow's nest, she fell faster than expected. The bottom of her stomach dropped out as she zipped downward.

"Weee," Deryl called as they plummeted.

Ouri let out a joyful shriek and took flight, soaring above her.

The vibrations from the hook sliding over the braided rope numbed Hettie's hands, the ocean rushed up to meet her, and the wind whipped her hair out behind her. It was exhilarating.

She grinned fiercely. *"Weee, indeed."* She didn't shield herself from attack on the way down, but she was ready for it when it came.

"Danger," Deryl said gleefully.

The rope drooped before a short rise brought passengers to the landing platform. When Hettie was at the lowest point, one of the fish-men shot out of the water. It earned a boot to the face for its efforts.

Ouri let loose an outraged screech and dove to defend her, but the fish-man hit the water before he reached it. A second fish-man jumped, a hair too late to have any hopes of reaching Hettie. Ouri practically face-planted into it. With a squawk of delight, his sharp talons latched onto oozy flesh.

It flailed madly and Hettie worried it would injure Ouri.

A sharp warning came from Deryl. *"Pay attention."*

Distracted, Hettie nearly missed her drop. As it was, she had to turn sideways, slamming her shoulder into the rock hard enough to snap her arm bone. She sucked in a pained breath.

"You agreed not *to throw me into the ocean,"* Deryl said. *"It would be a shame to end up there on accident."*

"Poor you. I'd be the one listening to your tavern songs for the rest of my life." Hettie gave a mental shudder for effect, though her attention was still on Ouri, who was doing his damndest to keep the fish-man from reaching the water, though it was clearly too heavy for him to lift. He managed to mangle it pretty good before cutting loose at the last second when the fish-man hit the water.

The soldiers nearby had been watching and let out a cheer of approval. The swell of noise was like a tidal wave of sound in their mountainous surroundings.

Ouri heard it and screeched out his own response, climbing to soar over their heads.

Satisfied her bird was okay, Hettie went to work healing her arm. After a lifetime of practice, it was second nature.

"I feel sorry for that poor fish-man," Deryl said in a voice thick with false sympathy. *"He sure has fallen on hard times."*

"For Bukker's sake," Hettie said, invoking the name of the Pavinn gods' dog. *"Don't start making rock jokes. I'll never hear the end of them out here."*

Deryl let out a sigh of lament. *"Don't sing tavern songs. Don't make rock jokes. Don't talk like a pirate. You're on a one-woman mission to destroy fun."*

"Your version of fun and my version of fun are two completely different things."

"Okay, what's your version of fun?"

Hettie's reply was immediate. *"Anything not annoying."*

Deryl paused. *"So anything not fun is fun?"*

"Annoying and fun are not the same thing.

"I beg to differ," he said, clearly offended. *"Annoyance is the foundation of humor."*

A soldier helped Hettie off her landing spot. She joined the soldiers milling along a path leading deeper into the mountains.

Jonathan greeted her from his perch atop a low boulder. "Hettie!" he called, waving his arm in a manner wholly undignified for a man in his position. He climbed down from his perch to greet her. "I assume that ridiculous setup was your idea?" he said, nodding at the rope overhead.

"It got the job done, didn't it?"

His lips pursed in consternation. "Yes. Perhaps next time we can find a solution that doesn't involve stopping anyone's heart."

"That's what made it fun," she insisted.

"I beg to differ."

"I'm not the only one who thinks your definition of fun is skewed," Deryl said.

Hettie talked over him, perhaps louder than she needed to, since no one else could hear him. "You can beg all you want, but that was more fun than a growler in a barrel."

Growlers were large, tentacled fish that emitted an angry, buzzing sound to disorient prey. Whenever a fisherman brought juvenile growlers to shore, it was common practice in the Paradisals to stick one in a barrel full of water and let kids take turns squealing atop the buzzing seat.

Jonathan looked horrified. "Why on earth would you put a growler in a barrel? Wouldn't that make it angry?"

Reluctantly, Deryl said, *"Maybe don't use his definition of fun as a reference."*

CHAPTER 8
WHAT A BARNACLE

Hettie

Hettie climbed to higher ground, trying to get a view of the area. Everywhere she looked was more mountains except for the path carved through the rocky terrain ahead and the sheer drop to the ocean behind.

Jonathan pointed her in the direction of the man who had smashed into the boulder. Not only was his nose broken, but his cheekbone was cracked, along with two ribs. She healed him in short order, though the swelling in his brain from the blow was beyond her capabilities. Swelling wasn't an easy fix, even when limited to muscles. The brain was infinitely more complex.

Time would tell if he lived or died. The fact that he was conscious and able to speak was a good sign, though.

She moved on, healing soldiers with sprained ankles and other injuries. Some were clearly nervous about being touched by magic, but they gained a new appreciation for it when their wounds vanished.

Eventually, she managed to work her way over to Jonathan. "Where's Vammi?"

Jonathan's expression turned sour. "He's at the front of this disorganized mess," he said, waving his hands to indicate the milling soldiers.

Hettie motioned for him to lead the way, and he took off up the path.

Deryl chattered, though not to her as she'd been ignoring his commentary while she healed wounds. *"Hypocrisy is never ending, my friend."* A few moments of silence passed. *"Don't I know it. Do you remember that friend Miriam had? The pretty one?"*

Deryl was still able to talk to Gak through their magical connection despite the mountain range between them. Hettie couldn't hear Gak's reply since he and Deryl communicated independently of her.

"Yes, yes," Deryl said absently. *"Missing an ear. I forgot about that. She was still pretty without it. Now* she *knew how to have fun."*

Hettie said, *"See if he knows how to get your voice out of my head when you're talking to him."*

"Since you ignore me all the time, I'm going to return the favor," he replied, sounding snooty.

Through the crowd, Hettie spotted the emerald-green highlights of Vammi's uniform. Tall for a Pavinn, his curly headed mop stood several inches above the balding man he was talking to.

Vammi wore a strained look of patience. That was typical for people talking to Servio.

"We ran those Darrish right into the ocean at the Battle of Southfen long before you young pups were even born," the general said, shaking his head as if wounded by the fact that his current company was sorely lacking in battle expertise. He spoke loud enough for his voice to carry. "We lost a lot of good men that day and it shows."

Hettie snorted. *"What drivel. Does that saggy-fanged river-pirate ever shut up?"*

"I'm still ignoring you."

"It was a rhetorical question."

Vammi nodded politely. He caught sight of Jonathan and Hettie but didn't bring their approach to Servio's attention. His expression shifted, his eyes twinkling with mischief. It was a look he'd perfected, and one Hettie didn't doubt had gotten many a girl out of her underskirts.

"Lucky for us, we have your input along with our own Hettie Stormheart, Marsh Queen Extraordinaire." His eyes flicked up briefly to meet hers before focusing back on Servio.

Servio let out a guffaw. "Between the two of us, at least one of us should be helpful."

It was clear which of the two was which.

He reached out to clap Vammi on the arm hard enough to stagger him. "Back during the First Tyrranean Empire, Poll Sedrios worked with the Old Man. That was before the Old Man and all the rest of the sorcerers went into hiding, but the good general must have seen at least some benefit to having one around." He leaned in and spoke in a conspiratorial whisper loud enough to wake an entire encampment. "We both know Poll did the bulk of the heavy lifting, though, am I right?"

The expressions from surrounding soldiers ranged from disapproving looks to grins.

Servio's belly laugh carried farther than his words. He put up both hands, palms out as if in protest. "Now I'm not averse to working with a witch, but they're overrated in general, and especially in wartime. They're not trained in battle tactics." He waved a dismissive hand. "I'm sure they'd be helpful in healing minor wounds and such. But back in my day soldiers knew how to press on through injuries."

Several soldiers nodded along.

"War is won with blood," the general continued, shaking a fist for emphasis. "Coddling soldiers does more harm than good. Mark my words."

Hettie's smile was grim. "You might think differently when it's your guts on the floor."

Startled, he turned to look at her. Pompous as always, he said,

"Healing won't be necessary where I'm concerned. I've found it wise to avoid the sharp end of a sword."

"What a barnacle."

Hettie was mostly sure Deryl was talking to her, not Gak. Either way, she agreed. She stepped in closer to Servio. "You of all people should know swords can come from unexpected places."

"Advice you might want to take into consideration, witch. If you're not fighting, you have no place on the battlefield."

Hettie heard Jonathan inhale, ready to step in, but she held up a hand. "I didn't see you doing anything to keep the fish-men at bay."

He snorted. "Since when have fish been a problem?"

Many soldiers stared at him in silence. They had seen the fish-men. They'd been watching. Servio had been so convinced they didn't exist he hadn't even bothered to look at them. Too bad they hadn't attacked him on his way across the water.

"I've heard the stories," he said with a shake of his head. "They're obviously overblown tales unless I missed the swarm of jellied men climbing aboard to kill us all," he said in an overly sarcastic tone.

Moron. Hettie briefly considered throwing him in the bay to give him a better look. No doubt he thought their tales of Vincent's beast men were exaggerated as well. He'd find out the truth soon enough.

"We're wasting time," she said, turning to Jonathan and Vammi. "Everyone coming should be on shore by now. Shall we get them into marching formation?"

She was careful to word it as a question. The last thing she wanted was to sound like she was giving orders after she'd criticized Servio for trying to assume leadership status. Jonathan was in charge, and she was fine with that. It was hard for her to remember at times, though, considering her upbringing.

Jonathan nodded and the work of organizing the men commenced. They had anticipated the narrow mountain path. The soldiers had been drilled on what order to march in.

While the men moved into position, Servio made his objections known. "We have no business moving on."

Hettie fought to keep from rolling her eyes. "You're not part of this discussion."

Servio gave her a mulish look. "We need to focus on rebuilding the dock. The men can't possibly carry their gear the whole way. They'll be exhausted and overburdened on the eve of battle. What happens if we're attacked along the way?"

"The castle is just over a day's hike away," Jonathan said. "The men are fresh after standing around on ships for the past two days. They won't get exhausted in a day."

Servio slipped into his patronizing tone. "We don't have wagons. Do you suggest they fight with their packs on, or should they drop them and try not to trip while they're dodging sword thrusts? No wonder you lot are so keen to have a witch around. The number of wounds must be staggering with leadership this poor."

Hettie moved to smack him, but Vammi had anticipated her reaction and grabbed her wrist before the blow could land. "While pressing on isn't ideal," he cut in, "waiting for Vincent to ready his forces and drive us into the sea like the Darrish of old is not a solution. What else would you suggest? We need to keep moving or we'll be sitting hoop gulls. We can't wait for the docks to be rebuilt just so we'll have wagons and asses available."

"By my reckoning, we have enough asses," Hettie said dryly. She suspected Vammi's choice of words had been intentional.

Servio gave her a look that said he found her childish, which made her smile broaden.

"How did this joker become a famous general?" Deryl asked. *"He'd have trouble strategizing his way out of a cloth sack."*

"From what I can tell, his brilliant strategy would be to stay inside the sack."

"We've got a team of people building the dock already," Jonathan agreed. "The rest of us standing around are just going to get in the way."

A bleak-faced scout arrived to report a rockslide blocking the path beyond the next rise. "The boulders are too large for even a team of men to move," he insisted. "We're looking for another way around."

The news sobered the group, and they quit arguing long enough to press on to where a ten-foot-tall pile of rubble sat nestled in a low point between two rises.

Hettie scanned the mountains around and was glad to see Ouri perched on a peak, watching for trouble from overhead.

She spotted where the stone had broken loose from high up on one side where a dull gray bush had woven a jagged wall of vegetation. The roots could be seen peeking from the sharp crevices where it had burrowed in and weakened the rock.

"*Guess that rules out foul play,*" Deryl said.

"*Maybe,*" Hettie said, dubious. "*The poles from the dock were black.*"

"*What does that have to do with anything?*"

"*Think about it,*" she insisted. "*If the dock had been burned a long time ago, there would be growth and wear on the old posts. That fire was recent.*"

"*I still don't know what that has to do with the rockslide.*"

"*Someone had to come down here and burn it. I assume they made their way back to Stonehaven after. You think a rockslide just happened to occur between them burning the docks and us showing up?*"

Deryl let out a thoughtful "*Hmmm.*"

"The scout was right. This will delay us far too long," Servio said. "We need to send more scouts to look for other passages."

"You were just arguing for us to stay put," Jonathan reminded him.

"Fixing the dock is progress," he insisted. "This is busy work."

Hettie said, "They both limit our path of retreat and sever our supply chain. Why is one important and the other not?"

"*My guess is he can boss around a crew of dock builders, but rockslides are mundane. Pick up a rock and move it. No instruction needed,*" Deryl said.

"We can do both," Jonathan said. "I'll send my lead scout ahead. Nubal's nickname is Twig. He's excellent at his job, but he won't be much help moving rocks. In the meantime, we need to determine the best way to move these bigger pieces."

"I've got a plan for that," Hettie said.

If steep walls didn't border the rockslide on both sides, she'd have just pushed the boulders out of the way. As it was, there was nowhere for them to go but into the ocean or farther up the path.

"What are you going to do? Magic them away?" Servio asked.

"Why would I bother when I've got the might of a thousand men at my disposal?" Hettie asked. She turned to Jonathan and Vammi. "Line the men up along the path. Have them face each other. We'll pass the rocks down a line and toss them into the water. With luck, some of the boulders can be used to help with the new dock."

What she hadn't told anyone—what she barely acknowledged herself—was that she probably had enough power to level mountains. She'd hoped the pressure of her sisters' magic would dissipate, but it had grown incrementally over time until it was like trying to control a tidal wave. She had to focus on controlling it, meting it out in spells with the same level of care she put into adding volatile mixtures to her potions.

She pushed down her feelings of unease. The sun was setting, but the men lined up quickly. With more men than space, they could trade out as needed.

Taking charge Servio directed the men from the rockslide.

Passing the rocks along was choppy at first, but the men found a rhythm.

Hettie accompanied the largest rocks down the path, lifting with her magic to lighten the load. It was difficult to apply the right kind of pressure while the rock was moving, especially with her excess magic trying to escape her hold, but the steady cadence helped her catch on quickly.

Jonathan's scout, Nubal, returned to report, wearing a leather uniform in shades of brown and gray that blended in with the mountains. Nubal truly did fit his nickname of Twig. His uniform hung off his frame, making him look like a half-starved rat in a sack.

Jonathan had him wait until Hettie made it back from shore, despite Servio badgering him to get on with it.

"What have you found, Nubal?" Jonathan asked when they were all together.

Nubal's report was casual. The Widows' Will was prone to familiarity, a sign that they hadn't been an army for long.

Hettie could tell this irritated Servio, which made her smile.

"We found no other paths moving onward," Nubal reported.

"There are two clean-cut caves, cleared of brush. Scuff marks indicate they've been used recently by something resembling humans."

"Something resembling humans?" Vammi asked, amused. "What does that mean?"

Jonathan said, "He means the scuffs don't include gouges or scrapes, so it wasn't made by hooves and the marks are spaced out enough to limit the foot size to something similar to a human's, so no large cats or little mice."

Nubal nodded in confirmation. "We were also able to make out the top of a turret in the distance from up there." He pointed to the top of a peak not far from where they were, though Hettie couldn't see how he'd gotten up the sheer face.

"We're closer to Vincent's estate than we thought," Jonathan muttered.

"Great," Vammi said, clapping his hands together. "Let's finish moving this rock pile and be on our way."

"For once, I agree with you," Servio said.

"Your approval isn't needed," Hettie reminded him. Again.

He ignored her. "If we're this close, Lord Vincent is bound to know we're here. This rockslide was likely put in place to stall us while he readies an attack."

"We already thought of that," Deryl said. *"And of course he knows we're here. We were just yelling loud enough to wake the dead."*

"You think this rockslide was put here on purpose?" Jonathan asked.

Servio's face was set and his tone grim. "One thing I learned long ago is there's no such thing as coincidence in war."

"For once, I agree with him," Hettie said.

"But you're not going to tell him that."

"Gods, no."

Just as the last of the sun's rays dipped behind the mountain tops, a thunderous boom ripped through the mountains. Everyone nervously eyed the slanted rocky surfaces around them. The boom faded to a crackling rumble, like distant tree trunks being torn in half. A few dozen stones clattered down to land atop their pile.

"Definitely not a coincidence," Servio said dryly.

"More rocks to clear," a nearby soldier grumbled.

Several seconds passed before the last of the rumbles faded. The effect on the soldiers was palpable. They returned to passing rocks, hurried and skittish at the prospect of being buried under a second rockslide. Jonathan called the line to a halt in the failing sunlight after a fourth man dropped a stone, crushing his toes.

Hettie had it healed in moments. She rose to see Servio eyeing her suspiciously from a distance. She stared back until he turned away.

The soldiers made camp wherever they could in the narrow passageway. They filled the area from rockslide to ocean, some sleeping upright for lack of space, others finding flat spots on boulders higher up.

They'd moved enough of the rockslide to allow the more agile soldiers to clamber over it, but nobody was keen on dividing their forces.

When the men were settled, Jonathan sat by Hettie in companionable silence. The sound of a thousand men chewing dried meat and hard tack was louder than one would expect.

It wasn't until the eating had concluded and everyone was in their respective bedrolls that Hettie noticed the lack of ambient noise. There were no insects buzzing or birds chirruping, only the rustle of men as they tossed and turned in an attempt to find a comfortable sleeping position.

Hettie noticed things she'd missed during the daytime. The smell, for one. Beneath the sweaty, salt-encrusted odor of soldiers was a complex smell that came from the rock itself, like decaying citrus with leathery undertones. She wondered if mushrooms grew in this region of the Little Gods.

Elkin used to bring her strange plants from all over Andos, often ones healers kept on hand so she could use them in her potions. He'd tell her stories and keep her up far past her bedtime with adventures he wanted to take her on.

She took a deep breath, holding it until her thoughts clouded with dizziness before she exhaled.

"Do you hear that?" Deryl asked. *"Is that coming from* inside *the mountain?"*

When the buzzing in her head stopped, she could make out a distant shushing noise, like fine cloth sliding together, but more intense. The sound seemed to vibrate the entire mountain, subtle enough that she couldn't feel it unless she focused on it. After a few heartbeats, it stopped.

"Weird," she said.

The sound started up again. Hettie reached out with her magic. She sensed movement, and a lot of it, but the sound stopped when she got near it.

"Maybe it's underground insects, buzzing in harmony," Deryl suggested. *"A warning system to let Vincent know when enemies are approaching."*

It wasn't entirely unlikely. Hettie's sister, Aisley, could communicate with bugs. At least she could before Hettie stripped her of her powers. It would have been nice to have absorbed her sisters' skills as well as their raw magic, but power and skill were two different things.

Guilt and justice warred within her, knowing she'd left her sisters magicless. The idea of being so vulnerable terrified Hettie. Her brief taste of it in Garpoint had been profoundly disturbing.

Life outside the Paradisals had proven to be more dangerous than expected. Her magic was her safety. Oddly, it was also what made her a target. The press of her excess magic, usually uncomfortable, brought her peace.

Hettie shifted, trying to get comfortable. She listened for the sound in the mountain until her eyes grew heavy.

It never returned.

CHAPTER 9

BENEATH STONEHAVEN

Adyr

Once upon a time, Adyr would have flinched at the terror-fueled scream that echoed through the tunnels. Now he ignored it, his attention on the cage next to his. In it, his best friend, Bannot, lay curled up, a silent heap in the darkness.

After months of captivity, Adyr had lost hope of ever escaping the tunnels. He and Bannot would live in this gods-blasted hell until they died. If they were lucky, their death would come soon.

"When we first got here, all I wanted was a sword," he said conversationally in his creaky voice. He didn't harbor much hope that Bannot would talk. He'd started going days without talking. Adyr couldn't stop talking for more than a few hours. He could feel his throat closing in, shrinking from disuse the less he talked. "After a week, I'd have cut off my own arm just to sleep in a soft bed."

He waited, but Bannot didn't take the bait. Maybe he was asleep.

"Now, I just want to see the sky again." The words were a whisper. "I could die happy."

Adyr had accompanied the lords of Poll's Wander to Stonehaven. He'd been Lord Holden's personal bodyguard and right-hand man. Gods, that seemed like forever ago. Bannot had been Lord Guimont's stablehand, comfortable sleeping with horses.

That was before everything went wrong, before everyone was murdered. Sleeping in a stable sounded like a fantasy.

Now they were stuck in cages barely big enough for a grown man to sit in, down in one of the old mining tunnels that ran beneath Vincent's citadel of Stonehaven.

Waiting. They were always waiting. Listening for Cayon's footsteps.

Vincent was a murderer, but he was also a pawn. Cayon was the true ruler of Stonehaven, meticulous and ruthless.

Adyr relaxed as best he could in his upright position. His elbow touched the bar of the cage, and he pulled it in, wrapping his arms tighter around his knees.

Another scream echoed in the darkness. They grated on Adyr's nerves, though he knew it wasn't their fault. Few prisoners maintained their sanity, clinging feebly to the tattered remains of who they once were.

Adyr was the lucky one. He tried to remember that. But it was hard, sitting in the dark, surrounded by the unwashed bodies of his fellow prisoners. Adyr had come to rely on his hearing more than his vision. Not that it did him much good with the constant screams.

Cayon spent much of his time in the tunnels, experimenting with the Element. Mined from the nearby mountain, the Element had almost magical properties. Adyr didn't know much about it besides the effects it had on humans. He only knew that much by observing the results of the experiments.

Cayon had administered the Element to the prisoners from Poll's Wander, each through a different method. It had been boiled into broth, charred and snorted, baked into food, and compressed into little pellets drunk down with water. Each person was given their respective dose at the same time of day, every day, while Cayon observed and took notes.

Most people went insane. They bashed their heads in against their cage doors or clawed out their eyes or bit off their tongue and choked on it. Some became non-responsive and starved to death.

Bannot held shreds of his sanity together by sheer strength of will. For him, Cayon had mixed the Element with molten metal, shaped it into rings, then pierced Bannot through in dozens of places before welding the rings shut. Nose, eyebrows, belly, between each finger and toe, ears, jawline, back. The meat of his shoulders held the biggest of them.

This method allowed the Element to leech into the bloodstream slowly, so the changes were gradual. After several months, his face had become misshapen, the bones shifting and rounding to look bulbous in areas. His chest and shoulders had expanded to swallow his neck. The color had drained from his eyes, leaving them a ghostly white-gray. Scaly white horns grew from his face, just below each eye. His nostrils had widened until there was only a gaping, fleshy hole where a nose used to be.

If Adyr hadn't watched the changes happen, he wouldn't have recognized his friend. The abomination that remained had a guttural voice, incomprehensible to most, but Adyr understood him.

Anger overtook Bannot some days. A rage that couldn't be sated, where he smashed at the cage until he was a bloody mess. He would eventually break the bars and scrape himself up on them for hours as he thrashed.

By the third month, Cayon had put his cage within a second, larger cage. No measures were taken to protect Bannot from himself, only to keep him contained. Adyr would sing common lullabies and mournful bar tunes in those early days when the madness took hold, anything to calm his friend.

On good days, they would talk about Bannot's wife and child. His family would be wondering what had become of him. They must think him dead. Early on, they talked about returning home. As the weeks passed and the changes took hold, it became a sore subject.

By the fifth month, Bannot's hope had died. He hardly ever talked. When he did, it was to insist he would never return home. He was too monstrous, too unstable. He loved his family too much to see their hearts break at the sight of him. Besides, he would be a danger to them during his bouts of rage.

Adyr eventually stopped trying to calm him. When Bannot raged, Adyr did too, albeit quietly. He lost himself to dreams of stringing Cayon up by his hair and bathing him in the Element. He wanted the scientist to experience his own transformation, to let the horror dawn as his own future drained away, replaced by rage and madness.

For all his talk of grandeur, of changing the world, Cayon didn't experiment on himself. He was the control. The person to compare everyone else to. Adyr thought he was just as mad as the rest of them, only his madness came naturally. Tinkering with the Element daily surely hadn't helped. Perhaps it's what made him mad in the first place.

Vincent came down to Cayon's lair, though not often. He had changed too. He'd become a scurrying, paranoid shell of the man he'd once been. Adyr almost felt sorry for him until he remembered the night the lords had died.

Some days, Adyr wondered if he was the only sane one left. Or was he sane at all? He'd become obsessive about analyzing his own thoughts and behaviors, looking for signs of madness. This presented a unique problem. After what Cayon had done to their entire delegation, even the cruelest retribution seemed justifiable, for Bannot's sake, if not Adyr's.

While Bannot had received the most invasive treatments, Adyr had received the opposite. His cage was made of metal mixed with the Element. It didn't pierce him. It was just there, in close proximity.

Early on, he'd been terrified of sleeping. He'd wake with his knuckle resting on the bar. Or the back of his neck touching it. He'd begun wrapping his jerkin around his neck at night and sleeping with his arms crossed.

Two months passed, and he was unchanged. Cayon saw how he covered himself, so he had Adyr stripped. Bare-topped and bare-soled, he had no way to protect himself. He'd learned to take short naps sitting rigidly upright. The position left his muscles so tense they spasmed, locking up until it felt like knives were lodged in his back.

Some days it was hard to breathe.

Whenever his misery overcame his sensibilities and he considered leaning against the bars for relief, he would talk to Bannot.

Months later, he still hadn't lost his fear of the bars.

They were his prison.

His poison.

His life.

CHAPTER 10
CHITTON

Hettie

Hettie dreamed again of Elkin. Always Elkin. His smile, his accusing glare. His slow-motion fall through a sea of memories.

Her heart ached at the future she'd lost. She couldn't seem to breathe. Pain lanced her chest, sharp like a twisting knife.

Elkin's death had been weeks ago. When would it stop hurting?

Slowly through her hazy mind, she realized the pain wasn't just in her dreams.

A punch to her chest made her groan. Her eyes fluttered open to see a sharp yellow blade pointed at her face.

Hettie froze, adrenaline chasing the fog of sleep away until she registered the familiar, heavy weight on her.

Ouri stood on her chest. No wonder she couldn't breathe.

He spread his wings and hopped straight up. When his weight landed on her again, her already empty lung tried to expel more air. A coughing wheeze was all she could manage.

She reached up to wrap her arms around her feathered friend, more to keep him from trying to pound her into the unforgiving rock than out of love.

Irritated, she said, *"You didn't think this qualified for a danger warning?"*

"That's rich," Deryl said, sounding snotty. *"I warned you six times, ungrateful wench. You didn't listen. Shall I make it seven? Danger!"* he said in fake panic. *"A giant harpy is trying to cave in your chest. How you didn't feel that the first time he did it is beyond me."*

Hettie tried to calm Ouri, but he continued to flail about until she released him. He spread his wings and flew off. She sat up, rubbing her chest where his claws would likely leave bruises through her leather vest.

"That dream is going to be the death of you," Deryl said. *"And possibly a lot of other people if you end up losing control of your magic."*

Hettie did her best to keep a careful grip on her magic, doling it out for impressive feats that would have exhausted her before.

Deryl said, *"For the record you're still in danger."*

"Danger from what?" Senses alert, Hettie scanned the area.

"From an attack of sympathy. Jonathan's headed your way."

She heard the scuff of feet. Jonathan's voice came from the darkness. A few stars dotted the sky, but there wasn't enough light to see by. "Hettie? Are you awake?"

"I am now that Ouri's done trying to cave my chest in," she groused.

Jonathan stepped closer. She could just make out his figure in the darkness. "Oh. I thought you were having a bad dream."

"I was. Somehow he thought jumping on me was going to cheer me up."

"Or at least distract you from your misery," Deryl said. *"A bolder bird, I have yet to meet."* He chuckled to himself. *"Get it? A boulder bird?"*

"Your jokes are worse than my dreams."

"I'm just warming up. Wait until I hit my peak."

"I'll be in a fit of pique if you keep it up."

In the darkness, Jonathan crawled cautiously atop the rock next to Hettie.

"What has you up in the middle of the night?" she asked.

"Your screaming, most likely."

"I wasn't screaming."

Deryl snorted. *"Loud enough to wake the dead."*

Hettie flushed, grateful for the darkness.

"I couldn't sleep," Jonathan said diplomatically. "I'm feeling particularly on edge. Every time I close my eyes, it feels like someone is staring at me from inches away. It's unsettling."

"Here comes Vammi," Deryl said. *"We should have more parties in the middle of the night. It's much more fun that listening to everyone snore."*

Hettie cast night vision to see Vammi stepping over a figure sleeping nearby.

"For the record, I woke up from Hettie's screaming," Vammi said, grinning. "If you need strong arms to keep you safe, I have two of them."

Hettie scowled. Vammi's bedroll was halfway across camp. He'd heard her from there?

Before she could make excuses, Ouri let out an ear-piercing shriek.

"That, too, woke me," Vammi said.

Hettie barely heard him. Her attention was on Ouri, who swooped down at a rock face nearby. He looked for all the world like he was attacking the mountain. Something large swiped at him, and he banked hard.

Hettie stood, alarmed. Had her screams drawn the attention of something willing to attack an entire army?

Whatever it was could scale mountains. It was the middle of the night, everyone was asleep, and nobody but Hettie could see in the dark. They could be in serious trouble.

"He doesn't usually make so much noise at night," Jonathan said, looking up. Since he couldn't see anything but blackness, it was only a cursory glance.

"Wake the camp," Hettie said quietly.

"If he keeps screeching like that, he certainly will," Vammi said.

Jonathan waved him off, though Vammi couldn't see it. "What's going on?" he asked Hettie. "Is there danger?"

"Hey, that's my line," Deryl said, grumpy.

Hettie kept an eye on the rock face. "I think so. Wake them quietly. We need to be ready."

A flicker of movement caught her eye from above.

"You know, you could always just rely on my—Oh," Deryl interrupted himself sourly. *"Now there really is danger."*

So much for waking the army quietly. "On your guard!" she yelled.

Mumbling responses came from the sleepers closest to her. Before they were even fully awake, a huge figure slammed down with the force of a falling boulder.

A boulder with a head.

Hettie had a hard time making out the shape of it, even with her night vision.

"Handoon's feathered elbows," Hettie muttered. *"Is that a jumping rock?"*

The soldiers cried out in alarm. One had been partly crushed by the rock. He clutched his leg, screaming in pain. Those around him scrambled back from the boulder, unable to bring their injured companion with them, trapped as he was.

Confused men scrambled to their feet, looking around frantically for the enemy, but the screams were all they had to orient themselves. They were blind in the darkness and hadn't seen the rock move, so they'd assumed it had been launched into their midst.

A man and a woman backed into each other and began wrestling, each thinking the other was his enemy.

Vammi and Jonathan spread out, their eyes scanning the darkness. "What are we looking for?" Jonathan called.

"And is it armed?" Vammi added.

"It's a giant rock with eyes," Hettie called, magically enhancing her voice.

"So, less armed, more armored," Vammi said to himself.

"Did you say–" Jonathan cut himself off. "Never mind." He'd seen enough odd things to just accept her at her word.

The man and woman stopped wrestling each other long enough to center their attention on Hettie's voice.

Ouri let out a cry from far overhead, but a boulder wasn't something he was equipped to fight, and he knew it.

To Hettie's surprise, the rock creature unfolded. Jointed appendages that had been tucked in along the thing's body stretched out like big, stumpy legs that narrowed to dull points.

"It has a lot of legs," she told the army. "Like a giant spider guy made of rock."

"*Spider guy?*" Deryl asked. "*You've got to start coming up with better names for these things.*"

"*It's a rock with a round head and spider legs, what do you want from me?*" she asked, exasperated.

"*A little creativity for starters,*" Deryl said. "*Marshies because they live in the marsh. Fish-men because . . . Well, that's so obvious.*"

"*I'll stop it from killing people. You figure out what to call it.*"

"Good idea," he said, completely oblivious to her sarcasm. Or maybe just ignoring it. "*How about long legs? No,*" he contradicted himself, "*that's as bad as yours. Long nails? Oh! Maybe hang nails. No, wait, those are something different.*"

The rock thing let out a garbled, grating noise that almost sounded like speech.

"*Many-legged gargler?*"

Hettie let out a huff of exasperation. Deryl's immortality often gave him skewed priorities, but this was ridiculous even for him.

"*Agreed, that's too hard to say in a hurry.*"

Ignoring him, she studied the creature. She needed to stop it without hurting any more of their men. When it made another grating sound, she remembered the bracelet Liselle had given her. It was supposed to translate languages, but she assumed that was human language. Whatever this thing was, it certainly wasn't human.

"*The bracelet is a good idea,*" Deryl put in. "*Either it can help you figure out what this thing wants, or it won't come in handy until somewhere down the road, but knowledge is power, and you don't want to pass that up and risk lives just because you're scared to try something new.*"

"*I'm not scared. I'm just cautious.*"

"You'll never figure out what it can do if you don't try it out. That's not caution. It's avoidance."

She knew he was right, but dammit, she only had room for one voice in her head. What if this translator somehow put more of them there? Or did something worse.

The rock repositioned its feet, barely missing a woman who hadn't backed up far enough from the half-crushed man. Startled, the woman jumped, then hacked away at the stone stump of a leg. The creature was unfazed.

Hettie reached out with her magic, feeling for a heart. If the creature was a living thing, she could stop its heart and kill it where it stood. Before she could penetrate the outer shell of stone to find out what lay beneath, the thing spoke.

"Skarlna," it said in a grating voice, the garbled nonsense sounding significantly more like it was actually trying to say something.

"Bukker's tail, the chatty ton of rock can talk!" Deryl said. *"Chatty ton. That could be what we call it."* He made a thoughtful noise. *"Too on the nose."*

"Skarlna," the thing repeated. It made more noise, but Hettie couldn't understand it.

"Use the bracelet already," Deryl scolded.

Reluctantly, Hettie placed her hand over the bracelet and let her magic flow through it. She started with the smallest trickle she could manage and felt a tingle run through her arm and down her spine.

She wondered if the magic worked both ways. Did it translate her words for others? There was only one way to find out. She wasn't sure if the thing had ears, but she enhanced her voice anyway. "What is skarlna?" she asked it, the word tangling on her tongue.

"Instead of chatty ton, we could call it a chat-ton. Or chitton. Oooh. I like the sound of that better."

The thing paused, pivoting to face her. The shifting of its legs knocked over the woman hacking at it. She scrambled back, unharmed.

"Skalina," it said. The sound was as distorted as ever, though this time Hettie understood it was a name. Then it said, "Wife."

Hettie froze for a beat. Wife? Had the bracelet translated that accurately? The implications of a spider getting married were ludicrous. Was the translation wonky because the creature wasn't human?

"This thing has a wife?" Deryl asked.

"What would that even look like?" Hettie asked, bewildered. She imagined a feasting hall with spider webs draped along the ceiling as decorations.

"I was thinking about their wedding night. Maybe that's where the rockslide came from."

"Racha'o save me. Your mind always jumps straight for the ditch."

"Give back wife," the creature demanded.

The translation seemed to be doing fine with that part. "I don't have your wife," Hettie said. "You're the first of your kind we've seen."

"Are you talking to it?" Vammi asked.

"Witch," she reminded him.

"Right."

The man who had been screaming finally fell silent. Hettie hoped he'd passed out. That sort of injury was excruciating. She'd heal him later if she could, though she doubted her ability. Crushed limbs were complicated.

After staring at her for a long moment, the creature turned back to the crowd of soldiers. A few dozen yards off, someone had come up with torches. Those with light helped others get their own torches lit. Being able to see the creature only terrified them more.

"Hey," Deryl said eagerly. *"If you told me an hour ago that a talking rock spider was going to come crash into our camp, do you know what I'd have said?"*

"Little busy here, Deryl."

He ignored her. *"I'd have said, 'You gotta be chitton me.'"* He cackled.

"Wow."

"I know. I'm so good I impress myself."

Deadpan, Hettie said, *"And you wonder why I'm cautious about using artifacts. Your jokes are dreadful."*

Deryl gasped. *"Why would you say that? You are officially the biggest sore loser I've ever met."*

Hettie watched as the spider thing continued to scan the crowd. *"How can I lose? We're not competing,"* she said absently.

"Well, I'd explain it in line art, but I haven't got any hands."

"Sounds like a you problem."

Just then, the creature—the chitton, for lack of a better name—stepped forward, knocking over two people and crushing the leg of a third.

The screaming started again.

Hettie hadn't wasted her time. She'd managed to find something inside the creature similar to a heart, though it beat far slower than a human's.

"Skalina. Come home," the chitton muttered in its grating rumble. "The village waits."

Village? Did this thing come from a village of spider-rock people? Wherever it was from, it didn't seem to be hurting anyone on purpose. Killing it would seem premature if it hadn't been stepping on people.

In an attempt to get its attention, she magnified her voice. "Stop!" Her command thundered through the night air.

The chitton didn't seem to hear her. It continued on, crushing two more people.

She gripped the bracelet on her wrist. Maybe she hadn't run enough power through it and its translation effects had worn off. This time, she ran a good dose through and the tingle down her spine became a shudder. "Stop crushing people!" she demanded.

The chitton froze, its head swiveling in her direction. "Want wife."

"I told you, she's not here."

"Give wife."

Hettie wasn't sure if its tone turned mulish or if she imagined it. "Look, if I see your wife, I'll tell her you're looking for her, but you have to quit stomping on my friends."

The chitton's head swiveled down. It seemed to notice the screaming people for the first time. One of its legs had a woman pinned by the cloth of her tunic. It lifted its leg. "Wife?" it asked with its leg poised over the woman.

"That's not your wife," Hettie insisted.

"I smash," the creature said in its grating voice. "Find wife."

"You smash, you don't find wife. You die."

The creature seemed to consider that. Its head swiveled back to Hettie. "You find wife?"

"Yes," she said, trying to reassure it. She wasn't positive they fully understood one another with their choppy sentences, but the fact that it was listening to her was promising. "I'll look for Skalina. If I find her, I'll send my bird for you."

"Bird?"

"Yes. Bird." She raised her hands, summoning a ball of light in one and gesturing with the other. Ouri spotted the hand signal from overhead and let out an ear-piercing shriek that carried across the mountains. "If you hear that sound, come get your wife."

"Bird. Wife." It seemed to be reassuring itself.

Hettie hoped the chitton had enough brains in its thick skull to leave. Hettie felt sorry for it. The distress it showed over the loss of its wife echoed her own loss. She'd kill it if she had to. Hopefully it wouldn't come to that.

"Bird. Wife," it muttered again. Then it slowly picked its way atop what remained of the rockslide, careful to avoid stepping on any more humans, and clambered clumsily up the face of the mountain like a rock tumbling in reverse.

Hettie let out a long breath. She hoped it found its wife. Losing someone you loved was hard.

The camp quieted as the chitton disappeared into the darkness.

"Do what you can for the injured," she told the soldiers. "I'll start making the rounds." She'd already healed dozens of people before they'd left the shoreline. It was a good thing she had so much power. Even so, this expedition was going to wear her out.

"I'm wondering something. Your translation charm works for the chitton. How come you didn't understand Ouri just now?" Deryl asked.

It was an interesting question. Maybe Ouri's call wasn't meant to be words? Maybe it was just the bird equivalent of a yell? She had no better answer.

She pushed the question aside. There were men in need of healing. It was going to be a long night.

CHAPTER II

IN THE BEGINNING

Hettie

Hettie woke when something twitched by her left arm. Ouri stood guard over her. His tail feathers brushed along her arm, tickling her. He reached out and snapped his beak shut with an audible clack.

A gruff voice said, "To the nine hells with you, bird. Bah! Go do something useful and stop being a nuisance."

"There's only one hell," someone called.

Someone else snickered. "Not in Sedrios, there isn't."

An old Pavinn story told of nine wise men who met in a tavern to debate over what the Undergates was like. Each came up with their own version until the pirate king Racha'o walked in and told them they were all wrong, then bought them each a pint to ease their disappointment.

Some stories said it was seven men, not nine, and others swapped out Racha'o for Al Dagos, but everyone knew Racha'o was more likely to encourage a man to drink away his sorrows.

Ouri screeched again, and Hettie blinked in the shadowy predawn light to find Servio standing with his hands on hips, glaring down at the bird.

"What are you going to fend off that she can't protect herself from, eh?" he asked. "She's a damned witch. She doesn't need you."

Hettie closed her eyes again, fighting off a yawn. *"What is he blathering about?"*

"He came to wake you up, but Ouri wouldn't let him." Deryl's tone made it clear he was enjoying the spectacle. *"He nearly got his thumb removed for the effort. Lay still a bit. I want to see if he'll try to rouse you again."*

Ouri gave off a long, low raspy call that sounded like a rusty door hinge, though Hettie knew it for the warning it was. Servio, being unversed in Ouri's language, ignored it. He circled around to Hettie's foot and kicked.

Like a shot, Ouri's wings spread, and he lunged at Servio.

Hettie grabbed one scaly leg, holding the bird back as he snapped repeatedly at the boorish general.

Servio ducked, scurrying back with his arms covering his head. "That thing is a menace!" he hollered. "It has no place on this mission!"

"Neither do idiot generals," Deryl said.

"Don't take it so personal. He doesn't like anybody," Hettie said, trying to keep her grip on Ouri. While it was true, Servio trying to kick her awake didn't help.

"He likes me," Deryl said smugly.

"He doesn't even know you exist."

Hettie scooped Ouri's wings in and cradled him in her arms. "I'll thank you not to disrespect him," she told Servio, stroking the floofy amber feathers that framed Ouri's face and neck. "He's my companion, and he has more of a place on this mission than you do."

She'd only gotten a couple hours of sleep. Two soldiers had bled out before she could reach them. Four more would live, but never fight. She made sure they were stable before leaving them to be tended by their companions. At least they were close to shore.

Despite the lives she'd saved in the past, her failure to help those who needed it weighed on her.

Jonathan approached, drawn in by Servio's hollering. "She's right, General. You're a guest of the Widows' Will and a welcome one if you can keep to civil behavior. If you can't, you're a liability. I'd rather you turn back now than jeopardize our mission."

Servio pursed his lips in irritation at the scolding. "How is it we manage to lose men whenever you're left alone with them?" he asked Hettie. He'd slept down near the shore and missed all the action the night before. His absence during strange occurrences was becoming noticeable.

"I don't like your tone," Hettie said.

"And I don't like your body count."

She almost let Ouri loose on him. Instead, she made her eyes swirl like tidepools. The color drained from Servio's face, which was exactly the effect she was going for.

He swallowed hard. "It was the middle of the night," he said, struggling for civility and failing. "How did we lose men again? And don't give me this nonsense about a giant spider made of rock."

"How do you keep avoiding every dangerous creature we come up against? It's like you're hiding in back while the rest of us are on the front lines. I guess that's what generals do, though, right? Lead from the back?"

Servio's cheeks flushed, and his chest puffed up.

Jonathan put a hand on his shoulder. "Hettie did everything she could to save the wounded. She is the reason we didn't have more deaths."

While the words were meant to be comforting, it was a reminder that men *had* died despite her efforts. Hettie's eyes returned to normal. Suddenly, intimidating Servio didn't seem worth the effort.

"And I hate to tell you," Jonathan said, leading Servio away, "but there was indeed a spider. I saw it with my own eyes. I'll tell you more about it over breakfast."

Servio said something about fanciful bellyaching, but Hettie let it slide. He was Jonathan's problem for now.

The commotion had drawn more than a few stares. Hettie's gaze had them turning away. All but a familiar pair of blue eyes. The Andosh soldier studied Ouri with more than a passing curiosity.

"*Keep an eye on that guy,*" Hettie said. "*He seems too curious for his own good.*"

"*What do you expect when you wake half the camp in the middle of the night and then talk to a chitton in a strange language? I hate to break it to you, but he's not the only one that stares at you. He's just the only one that does it even when you're looking.*"

Hettie nudged Ouri into flight, then gathered her bedroll.

"*Don't get me wrong. It definitely adds to your mystique.*"

"*I might have too much mystique if half the camp is staring at me.*"

It took most of the morning to clear the rest of the rockslide. The chitton had knocked loose enough of the rocks that their work remaining from the day before was cut in half.

Though it took half as long, it felt like twice that. She pulled Vammi aside at one point and asked about the Andosh soldier with the staring problem.

"Ah, Tinto. He's a quiet one. Likes to keep to himself."

"He's not Pavinn, so what's he doing here?"

"Actually, he's half Pavinn."

That explained why his skin was darker than a typical northerner.

"Why do you ask?"

Hettie frowned. "He keeps staring at me."

Vammi gave her an appreciative look. "Of course he's staring at you. Everybody stares at you." His words took on a note of grandiosity. "You're mysterious and magnificent. A masterful Marsh Queen."

"Queen, eh?" she said with a wry smile. "Did you run out of words that start with M?"

He grinned. "We can call you the Marshie Monarch."

"No thanks. Queen is bad enough. Hell, I'm not even a Waywoman anymore," she said. Fleana would be a far better leader of the Daughters' Coven than she had been.

Vammi stepped in to wrap an arm around her shoulder and lay his cheek on her head. "May you one day see your true worth. You have a lifetime to become even more amazing, but in the meantime, if you ever need a friend to lift you up when you're feeling down, you call on Vammi."

His words were offset by the fact that his hand was slowly sliding down her back. Before he could grab a handful of leather-clad bottom, she elbowed him in the ribs. Hard.

A heavy grunt accompanied his grin. "You wound me," he said in an exaggerated groan.

"Not yet, I haven't." She narrowed her eyes and stepped toward him. "Let me fix that."

He danced away, laughing.

"I live vicariously through that man," Deryl said.

Hettie shook her head at his antics and went back to work.

"So you'd be reaching for my backside if you had a body?" she asked wryly.

"I'd be reaching for any backside in sight, even if it was yours," he said wistfully.

She wasn't sure if he'd meant that as a compliment or an insult.

Thanks to Servio's early-morning ruckus, Hettie couldn't stop yawning.

"I don't even sleep and you're making me tired."

"Sorry." Her mind-speak was clear despite the yawn that made her jaw creak. *"If you could remember that spell to banish exhaustion, that would be great."*

Deryl avoided discussing sorcerers from his past, but he frequently hinted at magical knowledge he was equally cagey about sharing.

"Just because it exists, doesn't mean I know it."

"So you mentioned it just to torment me? Actually, don't answer that."

Once the path was clear, the Widows' Will got moving.

Hettie's thoughts turned to the chitton. How had such a thing come to be alive? Was it one of Vincent's strange creatures or was it natural? There had been no sign of it after its departure. She wished she'd had more time to talk to it, but the lives of her soldiers were more important to her.

"Your soldiers?" Deryl asked. *"Interesting choice of words."*

"Not mine mine, but they were under my protection," she said. *"Not that it did them much good."* She was exhausted from lack of sleep and overuse of magic, so when her mood grew grumpy, she let it. Sometimes you just needed to wallow in your failures.

Her surroundings were as depressing as her thoughts. Thorny scrub brush and small, scraggly trees pockmarked the otherwise barren rocky terrain. The only larger trees around were occasional bell trees, but even those were the saddest looking specimens Hettie had ever seen, half the branches shriveled and gnarled.

"Looks like you won't be making any potions here," Deryl said. *"Not that you made any back in Garpoint."*

"True. I left all my supplies back home and haven't had the chance to purchase more."

"I find it interesting you still think of Storm Flower as home. You do recall being banished, right?"

"I wasn't banished," she said.

"Close enough."

Hettie scowled. *"Since we're talking about banishment, why don't you tell me about the sorcerer who banished you to the Murks."* It was a subject he'd been avoiding since she met him.

"No need to get snippy. You started it with your talk of potions. It's not my fault that's where the conversation led."

"Because you steered it that way."

"True," he conceded, *"but I stand by the fact that you started it."*

"And now I'm starting a new conversation," she said, as patiently as she could manage. *"You've been dodging my questions for months. Why are you so cagey about it?"*

"I haven't been cagey. I told you the first time you asked that I would tell you about it after I finished my tavern song."

"That's a stupid song."

He let out a huff of indignation. *"How can you judge it when you've never even heard it?"*

"The first verse was enough." The song predated Hettie's birth by at least a century, but she didn't have to be familiar with it to know it was going to be unbearably lewd. The first verse had hinted as much,

telling of a beautiful seamstress who turned away men's advances until a painter came along with hands skilled at ecstasy.

She didn't have a problem with lewdness itself, but Deryl could read her thoughts, and she didn't need to be conjuring up vivid images from his songs with him in her head.

She had boundaries, dammit.

Granted, she couldn't stop him if he was determined to sing it. The fact that he hadn't proved he respected her boundaries to at least some degree, even if he did insist on arguing the point at every turn.

"Honestly, I expected you to give in a long time ago," he said. *"Stubbornness is not an attractive trait."*

Hettie grinned. *"You're not the first to say so."* Before her common sense got the better of her, she forged ahead. *"How about,"* she said slowly, *"I promise to listen to your stupid tavern song in the future if you tell me about your past now."*

He perked up. *"Really?"*

"Yes, though I'm not saying how far in the future." There would come a day when she was so drunk she wouldn't remember the song by morning. If not, there was always her deathbed. *"Now tell me about this evil sorcerer. Were you the only person he's done this to? Come to think of it, how did he get your essence contained to your eyeball? Were you still alive? Did he cut it out?"*

"Whoa, slow down. I'll tell you about the sorcerer. I'm saving the rest for leverage. My history is all I have. If you want it, you have to earn it."

They reached the bottom of a descent and began heading up the next rise. Hettie was glad her home island had been mountainous. Many of the soldiers were used to flat ground and it showed in the awkward adjustment of their stride.

"One could argue carrying you around all day is payment enough."

"One could argue *that. One* would be wrong. *You have no idea how interesting the stories I have to tell are. For starters, the sorcerer who bound me was a woman."*

Hettie's brow scrunched. *"I could have sworn you said 'he' at some point."*

"I probably did. She was a man when I met her." Deryl paused to let that

sink in. *"Her name was Cerissa, and she was sneaky as a tundra snake with a heart just as cold. She wasn't against using gender bias to pull one over on a person. She had the habit of adopting whatever gender best supported the role she was playing. If she was infiltrating an army, she'd be male to avoid stray hands in need of a bosom to hold. If she was walking through town covered in blood, she'd be female since most men avoid bosoms when they're bloody. If anyone asked, she was a midwife with a story about a drunk husband who was paranoid about someone stealing his kid, so he insisted on being in the birthing room. By the time she got to the part where he accidentally knocked over an axe leaning on the wall, believe you me, they found somewhere else to be in a hurry."* He chuckled to himself.

"Innovative," she said in appreciation.

"Yes, she was. I didn't really appreciate it at the time, though. I was still mad about being bound to my eyeball instead of living with my wife."

"And your wife died before Cerissa did," she reasoned.

"Long before, assuming Cerissa died at some point."

Hettie paused until the soldier behind her cleared his throat. She resumed her upward trek. *"I thought you were bound to her until she died. How did you end up in the Murks?"*

"She severed the bond," he said simply.

"I thought you said there was no way to do that. That we were stuck together until I died."

"Well, unless you know the spell to sever the bond—and I'm guessing you don't—you are definitely stuck with me until you die. I also told you there's no way to transfer the bond to another person. I don't know if that's true or not, but neither one of us knows how to do that, either, so it's true enough for now."

Hettie thought back to her early days with Deryl. She couldn't blame him for keeping secrets when she'd clearly wanted nothing more than to get rid of him.

It was strange to think they'd only been together a season. Now, she couldn't imagine her life without him.

Of course, she'd felt the same way about Elkin.

Melancholy washed over her. She fought it back, focusing on her footsteps. Deryl gave her the space to breathe, but his presence was comforting.

CHAPTER 12

STONEHAVEN

Adyr

In the stretches of silence between prisoners' screams, when his mind could release its stranglehold on the present, Adyr existed in the past. Most often, he relived the day he'd arrived at Stonehaven, alongside the lords of Poll's Wander.

There had been signs. He'd seen them.

As they walked along the street that cut through the city sections —Lower Stonehaven, Upper Stonehaven, and Stonehaven Proper, where the castle sat—moments stood out to him.

An old woman, spindly and scowling, had spat at Lord Holden's feet.

One of Vincent's guards had moved fast. Too fast. He'd backhanded the woman so hard she'd spun in the air twice before landing in a tangled heap. Before anyone could react, in less time than it took to blink, she'd been on her feet in a crouch, lips pulled back in a snarl. She'd hissed at the guard, an ominous sound, then turned and ran off.

Vincent had shrugged off her behavior. "She's gone mad in the head from the plague."

"Plague?" This, from Lord Holden.

"Months ago. We had a village of folk tending the vineyards, but they all got sick. Went mad." He had waved a hand as if shooing a fly. "Killed mostly women and children, but it's passed now."

Uneasy looks had passed between the five lords of Poll's Wander. As Griff's personal servant and bodyguard, Adyr had found the situation unnerving. Unpredictable circumstances made it tricky to plan for eventualities. Luckily, Griff Holden was one of the most capable men in Poll's Wander and as good with a sword as Adyr. He was a man of the people, and they loved him for it. Adyr counted him as more than a leader. He'd been a friend.

Adyr's memory skipped forward, taking on a dreamlike quality. He was inside the castle. A hooded figure walked the corridors, his cloak moving in sinister, ethereal fashion.

In reality, it had moved like any other cloak, but his memory took on a life of its own. The red cloak, solid in color, took on a pattern, twisted by his mind's eye until it resembled the inside of a thousand mouths, as if the cloak itself were woven of screams.

Adyr could hear those screams.

He jolted awake to find his heartbeat pounding in his fingertips. Another scream punctuated the stagnant, subterranean air.

When it faded, he heard a different sound.

Measured footsteps echoed through the stone tunnels and Adyr listened for the swish of that cloak.

Cayon checked on his prisoners less often these days.

A thin shaft of light illuminated the far wall in front of Adyr. Cayon had reached his lair in the adjacent room. A clink sounded as the lantern was set down. The shuffle of paper followed. Cayon was reading from his journal.

Adyr hated how well he knew Cayon's habits: the sound of his actions, his footsteps, his breathing.

Above all, Adyr hated the desire to converse with the alchemist now that Bannot had gone quiet.

"How long?" Adyr asked, his voice a croak after months of so little use.

The shuffle of papers continued. "I told you not to disturb me when I'm working," Cayon said from the next room over. He didn't raise his voice. Cayon never raised his voice. He was calm and collected, always.

"How long did it take the villagers to realize there was no plague? That it was you poisoning them?"

Adyr had broached the subject before, which was how he knew Cayon started off by kidnapping a few villagers here and there. He'd thought nobody would notice. As if your neighbor disappearing was a regular occurrence in a remote community.

Cayon had explained away the disappearances at first, claiming travelers had spotted their bodies farther down the mountain, suggesting suicide. When that wasn't well received, he suggested they had fallen.

Adyr suspected the villagers knew the mountains like the back of their hands. One person accidentally falling to their death would be surprising. Several in a short time frame would be suspicious as hell. When enough of them kicked up a fuss, Cayon promised to dig into the matter. Instead, he poisoned their water supply.

"How long," Adyr repeated when Cayon didn't answer, "did it take the villagers to figure out you'd poisoned them?"

Cayon let out an impatient sigh. "Too long. By the time they figured it out, there was nothing they could do."

Adyr questioned that, as he did everything Cayon said. Perhaps they did figure it out, but with no other water supply around, they had no recourse.

"What about Vincent? How long did it take for him to figure out you were poisoning him?"

Cayon muttered something about idealistic fools but didn't elaborate.

If Adyr wanted conversation, he'd have to find a juicier topic. "Taken any new notes lately?" He stretched his back, pulling himself up as straight as he could without touching the bars before returning to his normal, semi-slouched posture. "Any new, macabre side effects from your black-hearted experiments?"

A page turned. Cayon ignored him.

"You've been studying this Element on hundreds, possibly thousands of people for months. What more is there to learn?"

Another turn of the page. Adyr was surprised when Cayon actually answered, though he seemed to be talking to himself.

"Humans aren't enough. I need something more."

"More? Ruining so many lives wasn't enough?" What more could he possibly want? What more was there?

Lost in his own thoughts, Cayon muttered, "More animals, maybe. Or sorcerers. That would change the equation."

Adyr shuddered. Gods help them if Cayon ever managed to get his hands on a sorcerer.

CHAPTER 13

TO SCOUT OR NOT TO SCOUT

Hettie

Hettie studied the layout of Vincent's citadel, listening to the wind moan its way through the chasm at her feet. The path they'd come in on opened to a large, mostly flat clearing, separated from Vincent's citadel by a yawning chasm that wrapped around the citadel in a semicircle. The citadel was backed by mountains, looming like the teeth of a hungry beast in the process of swallowing it whole.

Towering walls surrounded the citadel, blocking Hettie's view of the layout, though she could clearly see the castle on high ground at the back of the city. Men atop the walls worked, building it taller. The top half of the wall was clean cut. The bottom half, old and weathered. From the amount of newer rock, the men had been fortifying it for months.

Jonathan joined her at the edge of the chasm moments before Vammi and Servio arrived.

"This should be fun," Deryl said, entirely too eager.

Hettie had managed to avoid Servio all day, but it was time to strategize, which meant he would be giving his input. She struggled to remember this was why he was there. Before they could so much as greet one another, one of Vammi's Steppers pushed forward.

"Captain," he said, addressing Vammi before nodding a head in each of their directions. "We found a path up there." He pointed to a dip between two peaks to the right of the clearing.

Vammi raised an eyebrow. "And?"

The Stepper looked a bit green. "And we followed it, sir. It leads down to a little valley with houses and such. Every soul there has been long dead, though. Nothing but bones. Some stabbed. Others with broken necks. The entire village was slaughtered."

"Village," Hettie muttered to herself. *"Didn't the chitton say something about a village?"*

"I think so. Do you think this is the village he was talking about?"

"How many villages do you think are around here?"

"Probably not many," he admitted.

Servio looked thoughtful. "Going off on your own was a poor idea, but I'll warrant the information is good."

Hettie rolled her eyes. The Steppers were Vammi's men, and they didn't need a critique from a washed-up general.

Vammi didn't seem bothered by the comment. "If Vincent had another force out here killing villagers, it explains why he's fortifying the citadel."

"That's just it, Captain," the Stepper said, swallowing hard. "I don't think it was an enemy force."

Everyone paused in confusion.

"Why do you say that?" Servio asked.

The Stepper floundered for words. "It's hard to explain. You'd have to see it."

"Tell me what you can," Vammi said patiently.

It was clear the soldier was disturbed by what he'd found.

"In one house, two bodies are lying in one bed, each with a dagger in the other's heart and their hands still wrapped around the hilt, like they'd stabbed one another in their sleep. There were a group of people in a house around a dinner table all set up for a meal. From their positions, it seems they killed one other. They all wore matching rings with a kind of family crest on it." The man shook his head. "I don't think enemies killed them at all. I think they went mad and killed one another."

Hettie immediately pictured her sisters trying to stab each other. She gave her head a brief shake, trying to rid herself of the image. Vincent's forces were like enraged beasts. Madness leading to violence wasn't unexpected. Still.

Jonathan spoke up. "Perhaps the violent tendencies started in the village as some kind of illness that spread to Vincent's estate."

"Whatever happened to Vincent's men, it's gone far beyond a brain sickness," Hettie insisted. "Craziness doesn't make you grow horns and become the next best thing to immortal."

Jonathan nodded. "As you say. Whatever the cause, the people went mad. Perhaps Vincent needed to occupy them, so they didn't kill each other, so he sent them to Poll's Wander out of self-preservation."

Vammi rolled his eyes. "Don't make him out to be some kind of victim. He killed Lord Tuigasi and the rest before he sent anyone over the mountain to attack us. Slago's teeth, he even sent a letter announcing what he'd done. It was an eloquent letter. I read it myself."

"I read it too," Jonathan said impatiently. His disdain for Vammi showed through his careful mask of diplomacy. "It's possible that he invited the Lords over for help with this illness when his own people went mad and killed them. At that point, he would have assumed he wasn't getting help and decided to send his army off in the hopes that we would take care of them."

Hettie said, "That's a pretty big assumption, but it never hurts to consider new evidence. From the looks of it, his soldiers didn't kill the villagers. They went mad on their own." She considered the implications. "Your scenario would put a new spin on the letter he wrote. Instead of bragging, he could have been warning you."

Jonathan stood straighter, emboldened by Hettie's support. "Vincent could be building the walls higher to keep his people busy, so they don't get out of hand."

"Why bother? If they're that unstable, why not just kill them?" Vammi asked. "He has no hope for a cure. If he did, he wouldn't have sent them to Poll's Wander. Why not just poison them? Or better yet, toss them in the chasm? Why bother with fortifying the citadel?"

"Fortifying makes sense," Servio said. "They knew we were coming." He turned to point left along the edge of the chasm. "There are remains from a big bridge over there. Rubble on the far side lines up with it. Send your scout to see if the break is weathered or fresh. I'd warrant that thunderous crash we heard yesterday was that very bridge collapsing."

Jonathan's jaw tightened at the tone of command in Servio's words. "I've seen the rubble."

"Whether the bridge collapsed yesterday or a year ago doesn't matter," Hettie said. "It keeps us from crossing over to the citadel. It also keeps Vincent from getting to us, which is probably why he hasn't attacked us yet."

Jonathan nodded. "I'll send Nubal to search for another way in and put together a secondary party to look for more caves. Vincent's people mine the mountains here, so there must be tunnels. With luck, some of them will be useful."

Vammi frowned. "You don't expect the tunnels to lead into the citadel, do you?"

"We should be so lucky," Jonathan said. "Vincent must have another pathway out. Otherwise, he's stuck."

Vammi said, "I assume there's a path on the far side of the citadel leading to North Pass. A tunnel may give us access to it."

Servio grunted. "They may have expected you to come over North Pass. It's how they attacked you, after all. If they burned the docks, blocked the path with a rockslide, and blew up the bridge on this side of the citadel, what do you think they did over there?"

"He has a point," Deryl muttered sourly.

"It kind of sticks in your craw, though, doesn't it?"

Deryl grunted in agreement.

Jonathan sent a nearby soldier in search of Nubal. It took nearly an hour to locate the scout, who arrived with his hair plastered to his forehead, and his uniform rumpled.

"What on earth have you been doing?" Jonathan asked after taking in his sweaty, unkept state.

"Scouting," Nubal said.

Servio scowled. "Why were you off scouting when you hadn't been given an assignment, soldier?"

Hettie barked out a laugh. "What good is a scout that stands around with his thumbs up his nose until he gets a direct order?"

Sevio spoke in a honeyed tone, as if he were talking to a child. "Unauthorized scouting can alert enemies to our location and potentially prompt an attack."

"You just pointed out the collapsed bridge as proof they know we're coming," Hettie said.

"They know we're coming. That doesn't mean they know we're here now. Giving them our precise location is a foolish and unnecessary risk. Discipline is the backbone of any army." Servio turned back to Nubal, waiting for an answer.

Servio's glare had no effect on Nubal, who looked bored. Or maybe tired. Climbing over mountains all day had to be exhausting, especially for someone who grew up in the marshlands.

"We asked for you an hour ago," Servio scolded. "You're no good to us if you—"

"Leave him be," Jonathan cut in sharply. "Nubal is adept at his job. He works himself far harder than I would ever demand of him. I can't fault him for working *too* hard, can I?"

Servio opened his mouth, ready with a retort, but Vammi spoke over him. "We need a way across the gap," he told Nubal.

"Give the guy a break first," Deryl said. *"Maybe a meal."*

Hettie almost suggested as much, but Nubal perked up at Vammi's words. "There's a ledge carved into that mountainside over there," he said, pointing to the right, where the chasm turned sharply as it butted up against a sheer rock face. "I spotted that hours ago."

Everyone squinted into the distance. Hettie could just barely make out a line in the rock that might be ledge.

Servio muttered, "We weren't here hours ago."

Nubal almost hid another look of disgust. "You weren't. I was."

Jonathan traded a smug look with Hettie.

"You can only fit one person at a time on it, so it'll take a while to get the whole army across," Nubal explained. "They'll probably attack when they see you coming, so you'll want to plan for that."

Servio's mouth was set, though Hettie could swear she saw a hint of approval in his eyes before he turned back to Nubal. "Anything else? You didn't happen to find another bridge? Or a back pass through the mountains, perhaps?"

"Not sure," Nubal said, looking up to scan the surrounding mountains. "There are a couple tunnels that weave through the mountain, but I haven't been able to track any of them across the gap. Some of them head in that direction, but they're too twisty. Plus, there's animals in there. I hear them scurrying around."

Hettie doubted it was what she'd heard the night before. It sounded more like sliding than scurrying.

"Rats?" Vammi asked.

Nubal shook his head. "Bigger," he said. "A *lot* bigger."

"Then let's hope they're not rats." Jonathan shuddered. "I'd rather not meet giant mountain marshies if it's all the same to you."

"Did you see any of them?" Servio asked. "Find any droppings?"

For the first time, Nubal made eye contact with Servio. "Animals tend to do their business and move along. Animal quarters are filthy, especially when they're enclosed. These tunnels? They're spotless. Hardly any dust, even. Certainly no scat. No droppings of any kind."

Silence enveloped the group as they pondered that.

"What kind of animal doesn't poop?" Deryl wondered.

Hettie snorted. *"If it's alive, it poops."*

She contemplated the creature she'd heard. It was either something large or a lot of smaller things. Was it responsible for the clean tunnels? Did it live off scat rather than meat?

Deryl followed along in her thoughts. *"A giant, poop-eating rock creature. If it existed anywhere, it'd be here."*

Hettie looked at the men atop the citadel walls, small at that distance. Even so, backlit by the sun, she could see their outlines, jagged in some places, bulbous in others. She needed a closer look at the wall, along with the interior layout of the citadel.

Ouri had been flying overhead. He came down to perch atop a boulder thirty feet up.

"Are you thinking what I'm thinking?" Deryl asked.

CHAPTER 14
TOO MANY WALLS

Hettie

Hettie stood partway up the mountain, most of the way to where Ouri perched. She called the bird down to her.

"Use a double knot, just in case. I don't want to end up in the chasm. It would take you way too long to get me back out." Deryl gave a nervous chuckle.

"I grew up with pirates. I know what I'm doing," she insisted, dutifully tying Deryl's pouch to the amber hawk's bony leg. Ouri patiently nuzzled her head as she worked. *"But for the record, I'm not climbing down to get you."*

"Of course you would."

Hettie smiled, both at Ouri's nuzzling and Deryl's fretting. *"If you fell, I would. But you won't, because I know how to tie a damn knot."* She finished up. *"There. I even double-checked it."*

"Aww, you do care."

"If you fell, you'd probably distract me while I was climbing down to get you.

Then I'd fall to my death, and you'd be stuck in the Murks for the rest of eternity. Call it self-preservation."

Deryl hadn't said much about the Murky Realm. It was where his essence resided whenever he wasn't bound to a sorcerer. Shadowy things lived there, hence his name for it, but there wasn't much else he could say about it.

Figures weren't the only thing murky in the Murks. Time was distorted, as well, and he had trouble knowing if he'd been gone for a day or a millennium when he returned to his eyeball vessel.

"I like self-preservation. Maybe use a triple knot."

"It's secure enough," she said dryly.

She wrapped her arms around Ouri in a hug. On flat ground, he stood nearly to waist-height, but his rocky perch placed his head above hers.

"I need to get a better look at that castle," she told the hawk, sinking her fingers into his soft golden neck plumage. "Can you fly over it? Don't go too low and watch for danger."

Ouri cooed and crouched to rub his head on her chest, but she knew he heard and understood. Not only was he a fearsome fighter and agile as a weasel, but he was smarter than most humans she knew. He'd been a constant companion for most of her life and had been her closest confidant until Deryl had taken up residence in her head.

When she stepped back, Ouri let out a gurgling chirrup and took flight.

Deryl squealed in delight as he gained altitude.

"For being so old, you're surprisingly childlike."

"I will never get tired of this," Deryl said. *"And for the record, Gak says this is cooler than being the ruler of space and time."* His black pouch was a gift from Gak. Made of a strange, silky material with magical properties. When it wasn't invisible, it was opaque to onlookers while allowing Deryl to see out whenever he wasn't using the bond to see through Hettie's eyes.

He paused before talking again, this time to Gak. *"Well, even if you didn't say it, you know you were thinking it."*

Ouri winged his way over the chasm, and Hettie tracked his progress.

"So now that Hettie's finally letting me have fun, you've decided to take her place as the joy thief?"

Hettie said, *"He's just jealous. Pay attention. I need to know what you're seeing before Ouri drops down."*

"Fine," Deryl grumbled. *"I see walls. Big surprise."*

"What about outside the walls? See anything that looks like a supply line? Maybe they've collapsed the bridge south because they're getting supplies from up by Port Bibi. It may go through that village they mentioned."

He spotted the village immediately. *"There's a few dozen houses and a couple bigger structures to the northeast. That place makes your island look like a major city. No movement down there, though. No movement anywhere else either. I can't see anything that looks like a supply train. No wagons. Only one trail leading north, but nobody in sight. The only path from the village leads to where you guys are."*

The castle was essentially prepared for a siege but had no supplies coming from anywhere. Were they moving things through the tunnels? If so, from where? Egren? Daynce? Had they stocked up a year's worth of supplies early on?

Ouri swung a lazy circle around the castle, dropping lower as he went.

"How thick are the citadel walls?"

"Hard to tell from up here. The chasm drops down to approximately three-quarters of the way to the Undergates. There's some glowy dots down in there. And I mean waaay down in there," Deryl said. *"The wall builders are doing a crap job. There's no semblance of order to the height or thickness of it. It's only about three feet thick in some places and six feet in others. There's a spot where it's probably closer to ten feet, even though it overlooks a cliff."*

"Try to remember where the wall is both thin and accessible. I may end up having to break through it, though that'll take a lifetime without my sisters here to help." Hettie didn't relish the task. Their best bet might be to scale the walls. Knowing how savage Vincent's forces were, they'd lose over half their soldiers just breaching the exterior. *"It sure would have been nice for Gak to teleport us inside. I still think he could have been useful."*

Deryl let out a bark of laughter. *"He told you he'd be useless."*

"Yes, but he didn't tell me why. He dropped a mini army more than a day's walk from where we started back in Penelope. Why couldn't he help us get into the citadel?"

"He doesn't know the land or the castle's layout. Nothing obliterates an army like being teleported into a chunk of rock. Successfully getting us clear of Penelope was pure luck. It had been over a century since he'd traveled that land. He's lucky it hadn't changed all that much. He could have sent any one of you into a tree or dropped you hundreds of feet above the ground. The fact that nobody died is a miracle."

"But he's connected to you now, and Ouri can give you a great view of the land and the castle, so what's the problem?"

Deryl gave a heavy sigh of exasperation. *"The problem is my description isn't good enough. He can't see what I can see. If I tell you to throw a rock over a wall a certain distance and hit a target that's about thirty paces in and four steps to your right, would you be willing to bet lives you could hit it on the first try?"*

"I guess not," Hettie conceded.

"Although," Deryl said thoughtfully, *"getting over the wall is going to cause a lot of deaths anyway. A bit of trial and error would end up costing less total lives. If Gak took his best guess and failed, he could change his aim until someone survived. It probably wouldn't take more than a dozen tries or so, depending on his starting location."*

"I don't like the turn this conversation has taken." Hettie climbed higher up the rock face and found a nook to perch on while waiting for Ouri to return.

"Ah, well. It's a moot point anyway with Gak back at Penelope."

"Tell me about the citadel's layout," she said.

"Well, there's the wall that goes around the whole citadel, but inside that there's two walls that divide the city into three sections. Once you cross the chasm and get past the outer wall, you'll be in the first section, which is like a midsized city. The main street cuts through it to the first internal wall that leads to the second section. The houses look nicer there. Past that is the second internal wall with a gate leading to the castle area, which has a couple other buildings."

Hettie listened to his explanation with growing disgust. *"Abom-*

inable turd goblins drag me to the Undergates. You're telling me we have to get past three *walls?"*

Deryl chuckled. *"Arlea does have a sick sense of humor, doesn't she?"*

"I don't think we can blame this one on Arlea." The more she thought about it, the more irritated she got. Breaking stone was slow and grueling work, even with magic. They'd be sitting ducks. *"If we can even reach the castle, we'll be lucky if there's anyone left to stick Vincent's head on a pike by the time he's dead. Rusty elbows. We either need more men or another way in."*

"Yarp. It's suicide any way you cut it."

"Did you just say 'yarp?'"

"Yes. That's what pirates say." Deryl's tone was far more confident than it had any right to be.

"Not any pirate I've ever heard."

"Maybe you don't know as many pirates as you think you do."

Hettie's eye roll was practically a full body motion.

"You're going to fall off that rock if you keep that up."

"Good, it'll spare me from having to figure out how to get an army past those walls."

"You know what they say. When things go south, head north. Your bird is flying north, and I'm headed with him. I'm going to enjoy my flight while I can."

CHAPTER 15

PRE-WAR JITTERS

Hettie

Hettie explained the layout to Vammi, Jonathan, and Servio. When Servio asked how Hettie had come by her information, Vammi cut in, eyes twinkling. "She's a witch. She knows things."

It was a comment she'd made back in Garpoint during Vincent's invasion. It had been the only response she could think of to explain knowledge Deryl had given her.

Servio looked skyward. "Misguided faith will be the death of us all," he muttered.

"What's that supposed to mean?" Jonathan asked.

Hettie glared at Servio, waiting for an answer.

He stared them down until he realized they were actually waiting for an answer. "Witch or no, she's from the Paradisals," he explained. When all he got was looks of confusion, he threw his hands in the air. "Everybody knows the islanders have no spine. They were kowtowing to the Placid Waters Import Group for a hundred years, because they couldn't win a fight to save their lives. It's bred into them to be servile. They're sheep. To this day, the only reason they're free is because of Sedrians like me."

Hettie's mouth had been hanging open since he called her spineless. She snapped it shut. "The Sedrians are the ones who let the Importers enslave my people to begin with," she said through clenched teeth.

Servio pointed a finger of admonishment at her. "Let? If your people had put up a fight from the beginning, you wouldn't have been slaves at all."

"You judgmental bastard," she seethed. "I'll rip your heart out and choke you with it."

Servio ignored the threat completely. "If anyone has the right to be judgmental, it's me," he said in a pompous tone.

Jonathan raised a hand in protest and said, "Now see here—" but Servio talked over him.

"I was alive to fight off the Importers. You weren't even born until it was all over, so don't give me that sanctimonious argument about it being our fault. Anyone with freedom has it because their countrymen fought for it. You like to pretend you're special because you're a witch," he said, fluttering his hands as if her magic was supposed to be impressive, "but I wouldn't trust you to stand your ground in any battle. The second things get hard, you'll buckle. Mark my words."

Vammi let out a low whistle. "The second things get hard. You're going to wish you hadn't said that."

Hettie had gone quiet. Her desire to implode Servio's heart was overwhelming. Some sliver of logic in the back of her head told her she shouldn't. She would be feared more than she already was. It wasn't worth it.

Part of her knew it, but the magic pressed on her like a living thing. She could feel the pulsing of Servio's heart with her senses. The effort of controlling the magic stole her breath.

Servio paled, one hand coming up to clutch his chest.

"Hettie, don't," Jonathan said quietly. He knew what she could do.

He knew how she felt about Servio. He had to know how hard she was fighting to keep control of her temper.

Vaguely, she was aware of nearby soldiers who had gone quiet, watching their leaders argue.

They would fear her. Jonathan and Vammi would fear her. Her anger eased. She never wanted to see that look in their eyes. The one she got from strangers.

Vammi slung an arm across Servio's shoulder. "I think maybe you need a drink," he said brightly. He tried to lead Servio away, but the fool man only widened his stance.

"No," Servio said, shaking his head. Despite his sickly pallor, he refused to back down. "I'm fine."

Jonathan and Vammi traded looks.

Servio didn't seem to realize Hettie was the reason for his chest pains. Stubborn to a fault, he pressed on. "I stand by what I said. You come from a spineless people."

Hettie's voice was quiet and distant. "You fought the importers on the mainland. You did nothing for us on the islands." Her words throbbed in time with her pulse. "We freed ourselves. My mother did far more than you ever have to free our people."

He was right in part. Hettie hadn't been born until the conflict was over, but she'd been there to help pick up the pieces. She'd helped nurse her community back to health. They'd had plenty of spine once, until generations of families had had it beaten out of them.

To have this man call them spineless when she knew how hard they'd fought to gain back their independence and hold their heads high was galling. Not all fighting was done with a sword. Servio had never learned that lesson. He'd never been subjugated.

Even with his focus on physical might, he was misguided. The thought of Hettie's mother as spineless was laughable. She could drape his intestines around his neck with a thought.

What a buffoon. He was beneath her. A glory-hoarding cocksure malcontent who thought the Deep Witch was weak. He clearly had no clue what he was talking about.

Hettie shifted her focus and pinched a nerve in his spine.

He yelped and staggered with his hand bracing his lower back.

She barked out a laugh, short and mirthless. "You're a common-minded marshtrotter swimming with a shark," she said. "Speak to me like that again, and I'll remove your mouth."

Vammi grabbed Servio by the arm and hauled him away. "Let's see if the healer has something for your back."

Servio paused to turn back, raising a finger as if to make another asinine declaration, but Vammi forced him onward. "Not *that* healer. She's more likely to kill you than heal you," he said, still cheerful.

In their absence, the tension lingered. Hettie's magic ached for an outlet. She took long, slow breaths to calm herself.

Jonathan eyed the nosy onlookers. They turned away, giving her space.

Several minutes passed before she felt in control of her magic. She appreciated Deryl's lack of commentary. Even flying overhead, he must have felt her rage.

Once the pounding in her ears stopped, she noticed Jonathan was studying the citadel. "Planning your victory?" she asked.

He gave her a wry smile. "That's hoping for a bit much. I'm more concerned we'll lose."

She bumped him with her elbow. "Don't start counting the dead yet. We haven't even started."

"That's just it. We haven't even started yet and how many are dead already?"

When Servio had said the same thing, it had been an accusation directed at Hettie. She knew Jonathan well enough to hear what he wasn't saying.

He didn't blame her for the deaths. He blamed himself.

Jonathan had grown up with the soldiers of the Widows' Will. He knew a good many of them personally. If he lived through the battle and came home victorious, would it still feel like a victory knowing how many died under his leadership? How many mothers, fathers, husbands, wives, and children would he pass in the streets, knowing they lived every day without their loved ones?

The weight of responsibility was a heavy one, Hettie knew. When every death was a friend lost, the pressure could be crippling.

"I'm not fit to lead these men," he whispered. "You would do far better."

That was fear talking, she knew, but it echoed her own feelings. "I'm no leader. I could barely keep my own sisters in line."

"Yes, but they were your siblings. They're different. These men need someone strong. Someone to protect them."

She studied his downcast eyes and crinkled forehead.

"You don't see yourself clearly at all," she told him. "When Vincent's army attacked, you went up against men who don't feel pain and are ridiculously hard to kill. Scary men. You fought them to defend your home and your people. Without magic."

"Exactly," he said, as if agreeing with her. "Your magic makes you a far better leader."

"You don't understand," she said. "They don't need someone with magic to lead them. They can't relate to me. They need someone like you. A normal person willing to fight impossible odds for his friends. They respect you for that. My magic can help, but they fight for each other. They fight for Poll's Wander. They fight for you. Not for magic."

He stood a little taller. "That will have to be enough."

Hettie took his hand and squeezed it. "You're the perfect man for this job."

He squeezed her hand back. "I can do anything with magic on my side."

They shared a smile. "May the coins find our pockets."

"Don't go getting all sappy," Deryl said. *"Give him a hearty pat on the back and come untie me."*

She glanced up to see Ouri land on a nearby boulder.

"No sign of the chitton," he reported.

"Can't say I'm sad about that. Hopefully he found his wife, and they're happily scaling a cliff face somewhere."

Vammi sauntered up with a grin on his face, sans Servio. "The good general is a persistent one. Too bad he wouldn't know a losing battle if it smacked him in the face."

"Clam-licker of the year," Hettie agreed, glancing at Jonathan. The mention of losing battles erased his smile.

"I distracted him with talk of strategy. He insists we need to guard the ledge since it's our only way to the castle. If Vincent manages to destroy any portion of it, we'll be cut off for good."

"He's right," Jonathan said. "I was already planning to have it guarded."

"Don't bother," Vammi said. "I put him in charge of it. Guarding a mountain pass should be easy enough for a decorated general, even if he is big mouthed and chitter brained."

"That'll keep him out of our way," Hettie said. "I'd like to explore the tunnels Nubal found."

"Agreed," Vammi and Jonathan said simultaneously. They glared at each other.

"It'll be dark soon," Hettie said. "We'll take lanterns and two dozen men. If we divide them into groups of three or four, we can send them down separate paths together and cover more ground."

Jonathan nodded. "Each can carve a unique symbol into the paths they take so we can track who went where."

"Smart," Hettie said, sucking her teeth.

"We'll have to organize this group quickly," Vammi said. "When night falls, we should be at the tunnel entrance, ready to go in. We don't want lanterns visible to outsiders. That will tip Vincent off."

"Also smart," Hettie said, nodding. "We don't want him to know we're down there. If any of the tunnels lead to the citadel, he'll have them blocked off before we can find them.

"How long am I going to have to wait for you to untie me?" Deryl asked. *"Your winged rat is pecking at my pouch."*

She stifled a grin. *"Winged rat? I thought you liked him."*

"No, I said he liked me."

"Obviously not."

"Obviously not," Deryl mocked. *"Just get me off him before he poops on me."*

"Who is going on this mission?" Jonathan asked. "Hettie, of

course. I'm sure her magic will be useful in any number of ways. I'll be there with Nubal since he's most familiar with the passages."

"Woah, woah," Vammi said, holding up his hands. "You command the army. You can't go off on a side mission. What if something goes wrong? You want Servio to claim leadership?"

"I assumed you would lead," Jonathan said.

He shook his head. "The Steppers would follow me. The rest of the army *might*. It's not a sure thing. With the great General Servio regaling everyone with his victories, they may decide to follow him. Dividing the forces would almost certainly mean defeat. We can't risk it."

None of them could argue with that logic, though Jonathan didn't look happy about it.

Vammi put a hand on his shoulder. "Don't worry, friend. I'll keep her safe."

Jonathan gave Hettie a pained look. "I'll gather the men," he said sourly.

Vammi grinned. "Keep the fires warm for us," he called to Jonathan's retreating back.

Hettie elbowed his ribs in the same place she'd gotten him last time. "Quit antagonizing him," she scolded.

"I'm sorry. He brings it on himself." Vammi chuckled at her scowl, though he turned so his wounded ribs would be out of reach.

Deryl had begun humming a suspiciously bard-like tune.

"If Bukker had children," she muttered as she headed for Ouri.

CHAPTER 16
OF WIFE AND MEN

Hettie

Hettie followed Nubal up a path that would have challenged a cliff pig. Her night vision helped her see despite the shadows deepening into blackness. Nubal didn't seem to need the light.

Vammi and his group of Steppers weren't nearly so fortunate. They straggled along, tripping and cursing.

"*Is there a way to give others night vision?*" Hettie asked.

"*Probably. None of my sorcerers were interested in helping their fellow men, but if a person can be turned into a pig, I assume they can be given night vision.*"

"*But you don't know how,*" she clarified.

"*Of course not. You're the one with the magic.*"

She scanned the mountain for signs of whatever had been moving in it the night before. She'd warned the group before heading out. For now, the mountain was silent.

The clanking lanterns grew louder, as did Vammi's curses. He floundered up the last few steps and blew out a breath. "I need a drink, and we haven't even started yet."

"A drink of water?" she teased, holding out a canteen.

He snorted. "Who drinks water?"

The Steppers arrived on his heels, though they kept their grumbles to themselves.

Inside the tunnel, Nubal kindled a dim flame to life. The ceiling was low enough he had to keep his shoulders hunched and head ducked. The taller men in the group would have an awkward time navigating, but it was too late to send them back. They would need light to get back down the path and that would alert Vincent to their excursion.

A voice spoke from the rocky mountain above the tunnel entrance, startling them. "Find wife?"

Vammi and the Steppers gasped and drew blades.

It was the chitton. Hettie found she could still understand it, which meant the bracelet, once activated, kept working indefinitely. She ignored the soldiers, knowing their weapons weren't a threat to the creature. Despite her night vision, she had trouble picking out the chitton's shape. *"Where is it?"*

"I can only see as good as you can," Deryl reminded her.

"Then why do I keep you around?"

"To warn you of danger, which you don't appear to be in, for the record."

"Lucky me." She spoke to the mountain. "I haven't found your wife yet."

Something shifted, allowing her to determine the chitton's outline. One long arm, backlit by Nubal's lantern, waved in front of the tunnel entrance. "Wife?"

Hettie doubted a giant spider wife was inside the tunnel unless female chittons were notably smaller than males, but what did she know? "I don't think so, but I'll check."

The arm curled back into the chitton's body, and it hunched as if settling in to wait. "Check. Find wife."

So long as it didn't step on anyone, Hettie was fine with it standing guard. She raised her voice enough for the soldiers to hear. "Time to move, people." She entered the tunnels, which had a strange, rancid leather odor. She was just short enough to walk upright under the low ceiling.

Nubal waited a dozen feet in, hunched, but patient.

Vammi sniffed from behind Hettie. "It smells like a back alley after festival."

The play of torchlight on the tunnel walls highlighted the bands of gray, brown, and reddish rock surrounding them. Hettie's experience was limited to the slick, wet-walled caves of Storm Flower Island.

The stone of this tunnel was clean-cut and dry from the arid mountain climate. Hettie could practically feel her skin drying out. She missed the ocean already.

They lit their lanterns, one for every four Steppers, and moved deeper into the tunnels. Their footsteps echoed eerily, the sound magnified by the enclosed space.

Strange little alcoves were cut into the wall here and there, reaching from floor to ceiling, but only a foot or so deep. The lines were too straight to be natural. Hettie suspected they allowed miners to get out of the way when a cart passed, lugging rock.

Nubal stopped ahead, raising a hand for silence. The signal was passed down the line.

Hettie cast out with her senses. Hearts were easy to locate, and she found several up ahead. The nearest one was two dozen strides ahead, just beyond the torchlight. They didn't move. Surely, they'd heard the soldiers' footsteps.

"Unless they're deaf," Deryl reasoned.

"Why would they be deaf?"

"I don't know. I'm just saying it's possible they didn't hear us."

"Then why are they holding so still?"

"Maybe they felt the vibrations of our footsteps."

Many animals froze when they sensed danger. Especially those living underground. Hettie took advantage of their frozen stance, reaching out with her magic to feel their shapes.

They weren't human. At least, not completely so.

Though similar in general shape to a human, the nearest one was under four feet tall with thick, sturdy bones. It had fewer ribs, creating a shorter torso in proportion to the legs. The ribcage was wide, the shoulders twice the width of a full-grown man. The skull was average sized for the height, though instead of a smooth, spherical shape, the back of the skull was warped in a pattern much like the concentric ripples in water when you threw a pebble in it.

Hettie was fascinated. "Hello," she called softly.

"They could be hostile," Deryl cautioned.

"If there's a chance I can get them to tell us about the tunnels, I have to take it." Just to be safe, she shielded herself.

The strangers didn't respond, so Hettie crept forward into the darkness, leaving the light behind and letting the night vision take over. "Can you understand me?"

With her senses trained on the closest one, she saw its muscles tense as it poised for flight. "I just want to talk to you."

When the creature responded, it did so by taking off down the tunnel. It was remarkably fast, its furtive footfalls almost whisper soft.

"Slago's teeth." So much for having a pleasant conversation.

She couldn't risk the creature running off to warn Vincent of their snooping. Too many lives were at stake.

She reached out with her power and severed its hamstring.

CHAPTER 17
CRUEL MISTRESS

Hettie

You had trouble making friends as a kid, didn't you?" Deryl asked.

Hettie ignored the barb. She hadn't wanted to hurt it. *"If it had listened, this would have gone smoother."*

"Maybe it didn't understand you."

"I activated the translation charm. It works for the chitton. Do I need to activate it separately for this thing?"

"How would I know?"

Ahead, the creature made a series of jagged, chittering squeaks. Every sound it made was soft, almost muffled.

"It's so quiet."

"Not surprising," Deryl said. *"Sound carries in these tunnels."*

She approached cautiously, knowing a trapped and injured animal was more likely to attack than cower. She kept her voice low. "I'm sorry about your leg. I can fix that."

The creature let out a breathy hiss.

Hettie wondered if it understood her or if it was just reacting to her approach. She drew closer, intrigued by its appearance. Its skin was the same color as the stone around it. Beady black eyes glared at her from a brown and white streaked face. She had to trace the bones to realize it was curled in on itself, forearms braced on either side of its injured leg.

Hettie squatted a few feet away. "I'm going to fix your leg," she told it. "But if you run, I'll stop you."

It hissed again. She focused on the wound.

Healing was harder than it should have been. With her magical stores full to bursting, it was like trying to cauterize a dagger wound with a bonfire.

"You're going to have to blow off some magical steam before you explode," Deryl said.

"Good thing we'll be fighting Vincent in the morning. That was the whole point of saving it."

"I think you've saved more than is healthy," he said. *"At this rate, you'll vaporize the entire castle."*

"I'll try to avoid that. Half the reason we're here is to rescue anyone that needs it. The entire city can't be murderous."

"That's what you think."

When the leg was healed, Hettie held her hands out to her sides. "I just want to talk," she said.

"No talk. Go." The words came out in a low, reverberant sigh.

Hettie blinked. *"I guess the charm works."*

"I suppose full sentences are too much to ask for."

"We're not leaving until we talk to you," Hettie insisted.

The creature shook its head. "No talk. Go." The words were still a sigh, but more forceful somehow. Hettie couldn't tell if the word "go" was meant for her or it.

"Is everything okay?" Vammi called from back by Nubal.

"I'm fine. Stay back," she said, afraid his approach would scare the creature into running again.

She needn't have worried. It took the opportunity as soon as her head was turned.

Once more, Hettie reached out with her magic. She hesitated.

Severing body parts definitely seemed like the wrongest of wrong ways to establish healthy communication, but for the life of her, she couldn't come up with a better solution.

Wrestling with her magic, she tried severing the same tendon, but misjudged, snapping a leg bone instead. The sound of it carried, and she winced. *Bloody hell.*

The creature gave a pained groan but didn't collapse. It hopped on its good leg into the arms of another of its kind.

Hettie had been so focused on the one that she'd stopped scanning for others. There had been a handful before they took off, but a quick scan showed only the two remained.

For good measure, she severed a tendon in the second one's leg, taking care to do it right this time. It was easier without them running at full speed away from her.

Together, the two fell in a tangled heap with more quiet chittering.

"You're a cruel mistress." Deryl's sorrow wasn't convincing.

"I feel terrible about it, I really do, but it's like they have no concept of 'the easy way.'" If they were going to insist on the hard way, she would oblige them.

She made her way down the tunnel. "Are you in communication with Lord Vincent and his men?"

Her only reply was a strained, low-pitch whimper.

Vammi must have noticed she was further away and fumbled his way down to her. The rest of the Steppers stayed put, waiting for instructions.

"Didn't I tell you to stay back?"

He grinned into the darkness. "Funny. I thought I outranked you."

Hettie rolled her eyes, though he couldn't see it.

"Unless you're glaring at me," he amended. "In which case, you can outrank me. I might even let you discipline me." His sly look was directed at her left ear.

She fought back a smile and conjured a small ball of flame.

He blinked, his eyes finding hers. He caught sight of the two creatures on the ground. "What are those?"

Hettie turned to their legs but left them with partially wounded hamstrings this time.

"They look like toadstools," Vammi remarked when the two struggled to their feet.

Deryl barked out a laugh. *"He's right. Those comically broad shoulders and short little goat legs definitely give them a mushroomy figure."*

"If toadstools were carved out of rock," Vammi amended.

With the two creatures standing side by side, it was clear one was male and the other female. The male had a single stripe of hair running down his head and a short, clumpy beard that looked crudely hacked off. The newer captive was female. She was well-endowed with a full head of short, clumpy hair instead of just a stripe. Their hair was the color of rock. If there was clothing, it blended in with their skin and Hettie couldn't tell where one ended and the other began.

"Tell me about Lord Vincent?" Hettie asked.

"No talk. Go," the male repeated in his whispery voice.

"Did you understand that?" Vammi asked.

Hettie held up her wrist, her rune-etched bone bracelet clearly visible.

"Ah, yes. Glad to see it works. What are they saying?"

"They're telling us to go away. Or they're insisting they want to leave. I'm not sure which."

The two rock creatures grew agitated, whimpering like frightened mice. They turned to each other and began communicating in a disturbing manner that consisted of blinking, twitching, and soft noises that ranged from sighs to groans. The movements were so fast it was hard to follow.

"Are they conversing or convulsing?" Deryl asked.

"Beats me." Hettie was fascinated. She wouldn't have been able to tell it was communication if they hadn't taken turns between twitching sets. *"I guess that's one way to bypass the charm."*

"Maybe if you run magic through it," Deryl suggested.

Hettie tried that while maintaining her focus on the creatures. A wave of dizziness shot through her, gone before she could react.

"Hey," Vammi said, waving a hand at them. "Rocky toadstools."

They ignored him, continuing their conversation.

We must warn the others.

The words were in her mind, but different than when she spoke to Deryl. These words were more like a feeling. An understanding, similar to when Deryl gave a mental shrug, but more complex.

She won't let us go. This from the male.

It comes for us.

The female didn't specify what 'it' was, but Hettie understood it was something to be feared.

"We need to get to the castle," Vammi said loudly, as if talking to an old person with bad hearing.

"I'm not sure how much they understand," Hettie said under her breath.

They call it, the female gestured with a sense of urgency. *The others will be angry.*

"Let's find out," Vammi said, speaking deliberately as if the creatures were simpleminded. "Show us the way through the mountain or we'll drop you off a cliff."

Their eyes widened and their twitching and blinking increased to a frantic pace. Hettie could only make out snippets of meaning. *Monster. Death. Arrive.* Oddly enough, the soft sounds they made ceased completely.

"Are you getting this?" she asked Deryl.

"Vaguely, but I'm only getting the translation through you. The bracelet doesn't work on me directly."

"Look, guys," Vammi said more casually. "I know what kind of men Lord Vincent has at his castle. There's no way you get along with those tusk-heads."

His words did nothing to calm them. Their communication became so rapid they started vibrating across the floor.

"I don't think they like it when we talk. They're afraid of something," Hettie said quietly.

"They're probably afraid of Vincent," he said. "We're here to help get rid of Vincent's men for you. If you show us how to get inside the citadel, you'll never have to deal with them—or us—again."

The male paused long enough to turn to Hettie. "No talk. Go," he said in a strained whisper.

"No talk. Go," the female repeated.

They both froze, and Hettie could almost swear their expressions were pleading.

"These rocktoads are not very helpful." Vammi muttered as they continued their statue impressions for several seconds.

Deryl sniffed. *"Rocktoads. Honestly, he's just as bad at coming up with original names as you are."*

Hettie waved Vammi to silence. If Vincent had beast men stationed somewhere in the tunnels, maybe she could convince *them* to lead her to the castle.

In the sudden momentary silence, she noticed an ambient noise. Beneath the silence, somewhere between hearing and feeling, was a steady thrumming sound.

Hettie flared out with her magic, searching for the source of the noise. When she found it, she swallowed hard.

Something enormous was sliding through the bowels of the mountain. Larger around than a man was tall and long enough that she couldn't sense the whole of it. Over two hundred feet.

"Oh boy." Even Deryl sounded dubious.

Snake, worm, or monster, it headed their way at an alarming rate.

"Do I need to tell you you're in danger?" Deryl asked. *"Because you are."*

Hettie turned to Vammi. "Run."

CHAPTER 18
STONE DRAGON

Hettie

Together, Hettie and Vammi sprinted back the way they'd come.

"Run!" she yelled ahead to Nubal and the Steppers. There was no point in being stealthy. Much like an erupting volcano, their only chance was to get out of the way.

The tunnel entrance was too far. The beast was too fast.

Hettie already knew they would never make it.

"Danger. Lots and lots of danger," Deryl said tersely.

A pale blue glow emanated from the pouch on her neck. "What's happening to you?"

"I glow in the dark when there's danger."

He had glowed the first night they met when a shadow beast attacked her in her room. She'd forgotten about that. *"That makes you a target."*

"Don't blame me. I don't make the rules. If you ever run into Cerissa, you can file a complaint."

"Assuming we live that long."

"Good point. Run faster."

She reached the last place she'd seen Nubal and heard the pounding of footsteps ahead. When the only witch in your company told you to run, you *ran*.

A rocktoad prisoner pushed past Hettie, its gait jerky from the wounded leg. Hettie hadn't realized they were following.

"It's not like they're going to run the other way," Deryl reasoned.

The rocktoads had likely lived in the tunnels their entire lives. To survive, Hettie needed to copy them.

"I bet they communicate by twitching instead of talking to avoid getting that thing's attention," Deryl said.

That made sense. Hettie and her team had come tromping in, practically taunting it.

The second rocktoad passed them by. Hettie's view from the back made it hard to tell which was which as they ran in the flickering torchlight. Even the difference in hairstyles didn't define them since the rock-colored hair blended with the rock-colored skin.

"You know," Deryl said, *"by hobbling them, you've probably condemned them to death."*

"They run faster than I do." She was short enough to walk under the low ceiling, but barely. She had to be careful not to hit her head while running. The tunnel floor dipped and rose in places and it was all she could do to keep her footing.

Vammi ran beside her, ahead by almost a full stride. He reached out and gripped the shoulder of the first rocktoad as it passed. It pulled Vammi forward.

Hettie put on a burst of speed, which she found difficult since she had to crouch to avoid smacking her head. She caught up to the second rocktoad and copied Vammi's move. The rocktoad was strong and fast and barreled on despite her grip.

The vibrations of the beast turned to a steady hiss, growing louder at an alarming rate. It would be on them in seconds. Past Vammi's wildly swinging lantern, she could see more shadows from the light of Nubal and the other soldiers up ahead. The lights were all bunched together, which told Hettie they hadn't reached the surface. She'd known they wouldn't, but hope was stubborn sometimes.

She spotted an alcove ahead. The cut-outs weren't deep, but they just might work. "The alcoves!" she yelled ahead. "Hide in the alcoves!"

The Steppers kept running. Either their own footfalls or the thrum of the creature had drowned out her words.

Only one choice remained. She would have to fight the creature. Even if she could kill it, momentum would carry it forward. She would be crushed. Probably Vammi too. Still, Nubal and the rest might have a chance.

The worm-thing seemed to sense them. It sped up. How it managed to reach such speed in the confines of the tunnel was beyond Hettie, but time was up. She reached out with her power only to be slammed into from the side by her rocktoad. It had shifted its momentum so suddenly that it took her off guard.

Her feet tangled like rigging in high winds. She stumbled, cracking her head into the stone wall. Lights flared to life behind her eyes. She may have blacked out, though it was hard to tell. She lost her focus on her night vision spell, and everything went dark as the sound of the huge creature weaving through the mountain filled her ears. It sounded like waves in a tempest, but steady instead of ebbing and flowing. And it was *loud*.

As seconds passed, she became aware that her hand still gripped the solid, dusty shoulder of her rocktoad. How a creature of muscle and bone had come by skin like that, she had no clue.

When the spinning in her head stopped, she blinked, slowly registering the faint light from Deryl's pouch. It illuminated her position an inch from where the giant beast slid past.

They were pressed into an alcove.

She flared her senses, surprised to find Vammi and the other rocktoad squished into the alcove with her. The four of them were lined up front to back with her rocktoad in front of her and Vammi's rocktoad behind her.

The worm rocketed toward the tunnel's entrance but turned to wind up into the mountain rather than out into the open air. She hadn't known about the tunnel in the ceiling.

She studied the giant body with her magic. It had skin several inches thick and propelled itself along with appendages that looked like short, claw-tipped fins. Each fin had three claws with webbing in between. They were positioned in a spiral around its body that made a complete circuit about once every ten feet or so.

Over a hundred feet passed them by before the body narrowed. Hettie could just sense the tip of the tail in the distance. The easiest way to kill it would have been to go after its heart, which had passed her by while she was busy staring at stars. She let it pass unmolested.

"Man that was scary!" Deryl said. *"I haven't had that much fun since your sisters tried to suck the life out of me."*

His pouch no longer glowed. She'd been so focused on using her magical senses that she'd forgotten her vision was black. *"Again with the word fun."*

"You use whatever word you want. It was fun for me."

"Almost dying was fun?"

"Yarp. But only after I knew I'd survive."

She whispered the words to her night vision spell. *"Stop saying yarp. Nobody says yarp."*

"You just did," he said smugly. *"Twice."*

Beneath her hand, Hettie felt the rocktoad tense.

While Deryl seemed to think near-death experiences were enjoyable, Hettie did not. She was in no mood for games. "Don't try anything. I can stop your heart with a thought." She didn't raise her voice. "That goes for your friend, as well."

Vammi asked, "Did anyone else survive?"

The quaver in his voice brought Hettie up short. They'd brought nearly two dozen men into the tunnels. Vammi knew every one of his Steppers. He knew their families, their wives, their kids.

She searched the silent tunnel between the offshoot in the ceiling and the entrance to the outside. There was no sign of the men. So many lives, ruined in a blink. "No." The word came out in a whisper. Families had lost loved ones and didn't even know it. Husbands and wives were tucking their children into bed for the night, oblivious to the fact that their partners would never return. Her heart broke for them.

Clearly shaken, Vammi said, "That thing. What was that thing?" His shudder was picked up by her flared senses.

In a whisper so soft they almost missed it, the male rocktoad replied, "Stone dragon."

"A giant worm," Hettie explained. "It pulls itself along with little claw-tipped wings along its body. They call it a stone dragon."

"And apparently it eats entire contingents of men," Deryl chimed in.

Hettie couldn't bring herself to respond.

Vammi swallowed audibly. "We should leave before it returns."

"It'll probably be digesting for a while," Deryl said.

Hettie didn't like the image that conjured. "Agreed," she told Vammi. The stone dragon was long enough that it could have circled back for them, but her senses told her it had continued on a circuitous path away from them.

Interrogating the rocktoads was high on her priority list, but she wasn't about to do that in the tunnels. The problem would be getting them to leave the mountain with her. There was a good chance their eyes wouldn't adapt well to light. The camp below would have fires and lanterns ablaze.

She quickly healed their legs and fused the bones at the left knee together, locking it in place. They wouldn't walk in pain, but they wouldn't walk fast either.

A soft sound of protest told her they felt the change. "You two are coming with us."

CHAPTER 19

SURVIVORS

Hettie

The rocktoads protested only briefly before they stepped out of the tunnel entrance.

The chitton was waiting for them. "Wife?"

"Gah!" Vammi exclaimed, clearly on edge. "Why is that thing still here?"

Hettie sighed. "He wants to know if I've found his wife."

Vammi glowered in the general direction of the chitton. "The first rule of wooing a woman is 'Don't be creepy.'"

"I'm not sure that rule applies to spider women," Hettie said.

She gestured at the female rocktoad, wondering if the chitton understood sarcasm. "Does this look like your wife?"

The chitton hesitated. "Not wife."

"Darn," she said dryly. "I guess I'll have to keep looking."

The chitton agreed with her. "Find wife." It scurried away, legs clattering against the rocks as it went.

Vammi had lost his lantern, so Hettie led him down to camp. The rocktoads could see fine, but they moved slow.

Hettie almost unlocked their knees, but they were quicker than they looked. It was better not to risk it.

Hettie spotted Jonathan waiting for them at the edge of camp.

"Has he been standing there since we left?" Deryl asked. *"He's the leader of the entire army. You'd think he'd have better things to do with his time."*

Hettie's ragtag group was invisible in the darkness.

Jonathan didn't spot them until they were almost upon him. "You're alive!" he blurted, eyes wide. "Nubal came back twenty minutes ago claiming a giant beast had eaten you all."

"Nubal is alive?" Hettie asked. How had she not sensed him? "We thought it got him too. As far as we know, we're the only survivors."

Vammi sounded suspicious when he asked, "He was at the back of the group. He should have been first to die. How did he make it out?"

"Not gracefully." Jonathan said with a wince. "He tripped and was caught under the thing's mouth ridge. It shoved him along as it swallowed the rest. He said it went into the ceiling and left him behind a bloody mess. It's lucky he has long sleeves. He's bruised nine ways from a desert stone."

The leather scout uniform had probably kept him from being skinned alive.

Jonathan gave Hettie a relieved smile. "I'm just glad to see you alive. I was so worried."

"What about me?" Vammi asked.

"I could do without you," Jonathan answered without turning from Hettie. "I can always do without you."

Hettie worried about Vammi. He'd lost a lot of men, some of them close friends. She studied his face and spotted the moment he managed to push the pain down.

She'd done enough of that herself lately to recognize it.

"Next time, I'll stay here at camp like a coward, and you can be the one to look death in the face," he said with faux cheer.

Knowing what he'd been through, Hettie wondered how much of his perpetual cheerfulness was forced.

"By the time this battle is through, you won't be the only one with night-mares," Deryl said.

Jonathan clenched his jaw at the insult, but Hettie pushed the rocktoads forward. "Meet our guests. They live in the mountains. I intend to get more information on the stone dragon–which is what they call the giant worm–plus everything they know about Vincent."

Jonathan led them to a makeshift commander's camp near the center of the sprawling army.

Hettie didn't know much about armies in the field after growing up on an island, but she knew soldiers typically slept in tents. The Widows' Will had only been formed a few months ago. They weren't well equipped, and the burned docks hadn't helped. Everyone carried three days' worth of hard tack and slept on a bed roll in the open with their bows or swords next to them. Luckily, the hot, arid climate of the Little Gods made for perfect outdoor sleeping conditions.

Servio pulled a kettle from the edges of the commander's campfire and poured two mugs of something steamy. Tea, Hettie suspected.

Nubal sat on a rock with his back to them, but he stood at their approach and greeted them with a smile. At least, he tried to. The smile became a wince when it pulled on the raw scrapes that covered much of his face.

"You look like hell swallowed you whole and spit you back out," Hettie said.

"That's not far from the truth, when you think about it," Deryl commented.

Nubal just nodded. "I'm glad to see I'm not the only one who survived the night." He spoke carefully, not moving his mouth much. "You look to be in better shape, though."

Hettie traded a look with Vammi. Next to him, Jonathan stared at the ground. In light of his earlier conversation with Hettie, Jonathan could relate to losing men.

A woman bustled up to the fire, her tunic swaying along with her wide hips. She held a wooden bowl containing a dark paste.

"Let me see what I can do," Hettie said, crouching next to Nubal. His uniform was ragged and scuffed, worn clear through in places. In addition to his many scrapes, she found a ridiculous amount of bruising and mild internal bleeding. The scrapes were easiest to heal, so she started with those.

The healer watched Hettie closely as if to learn her secrets, inhaling in wonder as the wounds disappeared.

Deryl chuckled. *"Makes you want to stab him so you can really show off."*

Hettie moved on to the internal bleeding, which had mostly stopped. Bruises were complicated, but she did what she could by closing off the tiny sources of bleeding and spreading the blood out so it wouldn't pool.

Nubal thanked her profusely, though it had been a simple healing.

"You'd have survived fine without me," she told him. Her comment was ignored. It usually was.

"Watching you heal will never cease to amaze me," Jonathan said.

Hettie crouched by the fire, stoking it. Compliments for healing Nubal felt wrong after so many had died. She couldn't help thinking if she'd been more vigilant, she might have sensed the stone dragon earlier.

"Does that guy look like trouble?" Deryl asked.

A quick survey of the area within Deryl's line of sight revealed a soldier watching the rocktoads with a dour expression. He was far enough from the firelight that she could only make out a burly Pavinn with a round face and a downturned mouth, his dark eyes moody.

Hettie stood, drawing his attention. *"We lost men tonight. One of them may have been his friend."*

"Think they're blaming the rocktoads for that?"

"If they haven't heard about the stone dragon yet, they will."

A soldier standing farther back in the shadows put a hand on his friend's shoulder and pulled. The man broke eye contact with Hettie and disappeared into the darkness.

"Let's hope he doesn't go after the only people who know how to get through the tunnels. Violence isn't going to bring his friend back." They hadn't even made it past the first fork in the tunnel. They knew as little now as when they started.

Servio broke from the group gathered around Nubal and came to check his cups of tea. He handed one to Hettie. "Staves off shock," he said simply.

"Bet it tastes like sweaty armpits," Deryl said.

Hettie sniffed the cup to hide her smile. The earthy scent convinced her to take a cautious sip. It was strangely nutty with smoky undertones. She had to admit it was good.

Vammi and Jonathan herded the two rocktoads over to the campfire. They sat sideways and kept their eyes down, shielding their eyes from the firelight.

Hettie unfused the bones in their legs, indicating a rocky perch near the fire and gestured for them to sit. "Tell me more about this stone dragon."

They glanced at each other, blinking and twitching in communication. Hettie reached for her bracelet. It seemed to need a steady stream of magic to translate nonverbal language. Before she could activate it, the male spoke.

"Dragon nose," he said, breathing in deeply and deliberately. "Smell." He gestured at the humans gathered around. "Smell not stone."

He spoke just as quietly as in the cave. Hettie had trouble hearing him over the soldiers talking and the fires crackling.

"You're saying the dragon can tell when intruders are there because they don't smell like stone," she translated.

Both rocktoads gave a single sharp nod.

"But you do smell like stone."

Another nod.

Hettie hadn't noticed their smell, but if they smelled like the tunnels, that wasn't surprising.

Jonathan, Vammi, and Servio stood by, listening to Hettie's side of the conversation. Servio watched with narrowed eyes, as if Hettie were making up the ability to communicate with the rocktoads.

Hettie's attention was on the rocktoads' smell. She reached out with her magic to examine them. Their skin was similar to a human's beneath the caked-on rock dust packed into their pores. Arms, legs, hands, feet, face, ears, even the skin around their eyes.

"You'd think that would cause health problems," Deryl said. *"What do they do, roll in stone dust all day?"*

"Maybe," Hettie said. It would take a lot of time and effort to get the dust caked on so thickly and thoroughly that it didn't flake off. *"If the alternative is having a stone dragon come for you, I think most people would be diligent about dust bathing."*

"Come to think of it," Deryl said, *"that's probably why the snake has such thick skin. It rubs against rock every time it moves."*

"Good point. It certainly explains why the tunnels are so clean. I don't think it's picky about what it eats."

She focused her attention on the rocktoads. "You're not human. So what are you?"

Both rocktoads provided her with an identical series of twitches and sighs timed perfectly to coincide with each other.

"What's wrong with them?" Vammi asked.

"It's how they communicate in the tunnels to stay silent." Hettie supplied when the rocktoads glared at him.

"That's actually pretty smart." Vammi looked impressed.

"It's almost like they know how to survive in the tunnels," Deryl said dryly.

"Wait, so that thing tracks prey by sound *and* smell?"

Hettie shrugged. "Apparently."

Servio tossed his hands up. "How could you possibly know that?" he demanded. When the trio gave him a long stare, he said, "Never mind. She *knows* things." He rolled his eyes and grumbled under his breath.

Fighting a smile, Hettie turned back to the rocktoads. "I don't speak your language. What does Vincent call you?" At their look of confusion, she pointed to where Vincent's men could be seen, working by torchlight to reinforce the city walls. "The humans in the castle."

The female glared hatefully in that direction. The male answered, his tone making it plain he wasn't a fan of the name. "Sunless."

It was an apt name, for all they seemed to hate it. "I'm guessing rocktoad isn't any better than sunless."

"Rocktoad," the male said, sounding it out. His voice was deep and somehow solid. "Know rock. Not know toad."

Hettie explained, "Toad is short for toadstool." At their blank looks, she added, "Mushroom."

The rocktoads showed no signs of recognition.

"It's a plant. It grows in dark places."

The rocktoad nodded. "Rocktoad good name. Hard skin. Live in dark."

Vammi had chosen the name based on the little people's shape, not their ability to thrive in the dark, but if they liked the name, Hettie wasn't going to argue.

"Do you have individual names?" Hettie asked. "What should we call you?"

The rocktoads went through a series of twitches, each moving differently this time.

"What should I call you in *my* language?" she clarified.

They both briefly widened their eyes but made no other motion. She took it as the equivalent of a shrug.

Running magic through her bracelet, she asked them to repeat their names in their unspoken language.

The male's name gave her the impression of something firm and immovable. "Boulder?"

He seemed to recognize the word and nodded vigorously.

"Is that because he's the bolder *of the two?"* Deryl chuckled.

"You already used that one. You want original names? Come up with original jokes."

"I've been working on some new ones," he said, excited. *"A mountain climber walks into a tavern. Guess what he says."*

Hettie hadn't intended it as an invitation. Fighting back a groan, she said, *"Ouch, that hurt?"*

She could feel Deryl's shock slide through her. *"How did you know that?"*

"Really? That was your joke? Try something less obvious next time, flickerwit."

Ignoring his sputtered protest, Hettie focused on the female rock-toad. Her name gave the impression of vigilance and moral integrity.

Hettie couldn't come up with a word that worked. Sentinel, maybe? It sounded off, but she wasn't sure why. "How about Pillar?"

The female rocktoad considered the name, then nodded. "Pillar," she said, her voice lighter and more musical than her male counterpart.

Hettie gave her a genuine smile. "Glad you like the names."

Vammi leaned in close to Hettie. "You have a knack for making friends with underground creatures."

Liselle's bracelet had made her the de facto leader of interspecies relations.

"Fight castle?" Pillar asked.

"Yes." Hettie gave a grave nod. "Vincent attacked our home. We will attack his."

The rocktoads reached out, loosely clasping each other by the wrist.

Hettie wasn't sure what that meant. "What can you tell me about him?" she asked.

The rocktoads took turns answering, each word more hushed than the last.

"Evil."

"Bad."

"Torture."

"Make monsters."

Hettie's gaze drifted to the men atop the castle wall. She sighed. "That sounds about right."

CHAPTER 20

WORLD DOMINATION

Adyr

Adyr's eyelids drooped. Had he gone three days without sleep this time or four? Reality blended with memory, creating its own form of madness. He'd wondered if the presence of the Element made his memories so vivid.

His head wobbled as he tried to keep his chin off his chest. Sleep pulled him into the abyss.

The day his life changed, Adyr had accompanied the five lords of Poll's Wander to Vincent's feasting hall. They were led by an escort of armed men. A single long table sat to the right of the doorway, chairs facing outward to the large, open room where a traditional fighting square was drawn out on the floor. Besides the servants filling goblets, the only other person in the hall was a cloaked and hooded figure at the far-left wall.

Vincent strode in. He was a boulder of a man whose shaggy hair and long beard made him look like a black goat had swallowed his face and camped atop his neck, leaving only a set of brown eyes peering out.

"Come. Have a seat at my table." Vincent gestured to the far side of the room. Bowls of near-black grapes sat in bowls between place settings.

Adyr followed his lords, all of them on edge. They'd arrived only hours ago, but it was hard to miss the oddities indicating something was amiss. During the castle tour, every door had closed as they approached. Servants had scurried through the corridor. Armed guards were posted outside their chambers.

Adyr wasn't sure if they were being guarded or kept as prisoners.

Nervously, the lords took their seats. Adyr, ever watchful, took up station along the wall directly across from the table.

Four grown men and a child who looked to be around nine years old filed in and lined up near the hooded figure.

Adyr studied the newcomers. Their clothes were basic trousers and shirts. Of the grown men, three were unarmed and one was armed to the teeth.

The child wore two daggers strapped to his skinny waist.

Each of the men moved in a cagey, animalistic way. One man repeatedly clenched his fists while another paced along the back wall like a caged predator. Only the child was still. Unnaturally so.

Adyr shuddered in his dream. That child haunted him.

"Do you know what we mine here?" Vincent asked the lords.

Somewhere in the back of Adyr's mind, he tried to stop the dream, but it proceeded, heedless of his wishes.

Lord Rasmond said, "Based on what your merchants trade in Garpoint, I'd say mostly salt, silver, and copper."

Vincent grinned. "We mine all of those, but it isn't what we mine most. Not by a long shot."

One of the unarmed men let loose a loud growling roar.

"Do you mine angry men?" Lord Lorez asked nervously.

Vincent let out a belly laugh, smacking his hand on the table. "That's funnier than you know," he said. "We mine a different element. One that's unheard of."

"What kind of element?" Griff asked.

Vincent's grin grew, stretching his face. "That's exactly what I've brought you here to see. The element we mine has very special properties. We're only just beginning to discover what it's truly capable of. It turns men into demons." He gestured to the men standing along the left side of the feasting hall. "Into gods."

Adyr thought demon was the more likely descriptor. The fighters grew more agitated by the minute. While the one paced and the other clenched his fists, a fourth growled with increasing regularity, and a fourth fidgeted incessantly, a nervous series of motions on repeat, kneading his hands and scuffing one foot off the other.

The child remained still as a statue. Only his eyes moved, his gaze expressionless, as he studied the lords. They looked more like beasts than men. Certainly not gods.

The lords studied the men, as well. Vincent noted their interest. "I tell you in all seriousness that this element is the key to world domination. No exaggeration," he said, raising a finger. "With it, we can rule all of Andos."

Adyr almost snorted aloud. World domination? With a handful of jittery, drug-addled men? He suspected the old lady wasn't the only one mad in the head.

Lord Tuigasi sat at the far end of the table. He was usually content to coast through life, easygoing and unbothered. He seldom spoke out against anyone or anything, but he leaned forward to peer down the table at Vincent. "Whaaat?" he said, drawing the word out. Though he wasn't an idiot, he typically sounded like one. Even those who knew him were surprised on occasion to find he had a brain.

Vincent stared back at Lord Tuigasi, waiting for a more coherent question.

Griff nodded in his friend's direction. "What he said."

Frowning, Vincent continued with his pronouncement. "This element can alter the very essence of a person. It brings to bear the full potential of a human, mind and body." He looked down at his lap and fidgeted with his hands before admitting, "We're still trying to determine how to get specific results, but they range from an increase in physical strength to an incomprehensible boost in tactical analysis."

At the blank looks of his guests, Vincent waved a hand. "Here. It's best if I show you."

Vincent nodded at the cloaked figure across the room. "Cayon has assembled a handful of his best fighters. You're in for a treat tonight."

CHAPTER 21
OVER, UNDER, THROUGH

Hettie

ettie was true to her word. Once she finished talking with the rocktoads, she bid them farewell and let them return to their tunnels.

Their information was useful in a limited way. The oldest tunnels led directly to Vincent's citadel. The original mining camp had grown and expanded over decades until it had become the towering walled behemoth it was today.

The tunnels leading to the castle grounds had been blocked off years ago, but there remained one that would lead inside the citadel walls. The entrances were boarded up, but wooden slabs wouldn't be hard to get through.

The real problem was the smell of the humans, not to mention the amount of noise an army would inevitably make. They were sure to attract the attention of the stone dragon.

Using magic to cover their scent and mask their sound would be possible with a limited group. Hettie couldn't possibly mask the entire army, which was a moot point since the whole army disappearing would definitely tip Vincent off to the fact that they were in the tunnels.

The last thing they needed was to have the entire army trapped from both ends and the Stone Dragon on the prowl. Considering the feast it had enjoyed the night before, it was probably staying close in hopes of finding more bumbling humans to devour.

With her head full of planning strategies, Hettie couldn't sleep. Instead, she stayed up practicing a spell called Avid Preservation. She wasn't sure what it did. The description was obscure, but Deryl suspected it boosted defenses in some way. It sounded useful for battle.

The nuance of the language made Hettie sound like a toddler with a lisp. Deryl had not mocked her efforts at learning the spell despite numerous opportunities and Hettie appreciated his efforts at civility.

By the time she finally drifted off to sleep, she didn't dream for once.

"Hey, I thought of another joke," Deryl said as soon as she awoke. *"What happens on a rock climbing trip?"*

Hettie groaned, burying her head in her arm. *"You murder your companion for bugging you with lame rock jokes?"*

"No, silly. A fall!" He sounded far too pleased with himself. *"Get it? On a trip, you fall?"*

"Definitely murder," she muttered.

"Hey, what did the rock climber say after he fell?"

"Ouch? Didn't you already–"

"No, not ouch."

If she ignored him, maybe he'd go away.

"I don't have anywhere to go. I waited hours to tell you this joke while you snored. Now what did the rock climber say after he fell, dammit?"

Hettie let out a heavy sigh. *"That was harder than I thought."*

"No. He said, 'I'm feeling pretty low all of a sudden.' Honestly, though, yours was better," Deryl admitted begrudgingly.

It was still dark out, though the edges of the sky were just beginning to lighten. Hettie stood, stretched, and went in search of Jonathan and Vammi.

The camp was dotted with fires, stoked for the morning. Soldiers milled about, standing, sitting, eating, talking, or sharpening weapons as far as the eye could see and beyond, down the trail and around the mountain.

She could feel the shifting atmosphere as she walked past soldiers of the original Widows' Will—who smiled and raised a hand in greeting—versus new recruits. Some watched her with awe. Others with wariness. She knew which ones had taken Servio's preachings to heart. They gave her looks of disdain.

With the Temple of the Sky equating magic with devilry, most people were predisposed to be wary of her. She didn't need Servio stoking those flames.

Growing up on Storm Flower, she had always been in tune with the people. She didn't like feeling like an interloper. They were all on the same side. Battle had unified Poll's Wander. With luck, it would bring the newcomers together as well.

When she reached the commander's circle, she found it empty, the firepit cold. Nubal slept by a neighboring firepit, his face obscurely lit by the light of the low flames. The healer had applied a poultice for swelling that had dried to a deep purple gray, flaking in areas. It looked like desiccated bruises.

Hettie winced in sympathy. Despite her ministrations, he would likely be sore for a few days.

A pair of blue eyes caught her attention behind Nubal. The Andosh soldier was watching her again. Tinto, was it? He was tending the campfire. The dancing shadows made him look calculating.

Hettie debated talking to him, but decided they would soon see battle and men would die. Probably many. Possibly all. If he was one to fall, his stares would die with him.

"That's dark."

"I'm not saying I hope he dies. I'm saying I've got bigger things to worry about on the morning of an invasion. There'll be time to talk to him after we fight, assuming he lives."

Distant soldiers meandered into her line of sight, blocking her view of the man. When they passed, Tinto was gone.

In the wan light, her gaze was drawn to the castle. Ouri circled over it. Hettie had warned him not to hunt there. Vincent's men didn't behave like normal men and if one of them managed to hurt or kill her bird, she feared what she'd do.

The magic in her was already hard to control. If harm came to her best friend, she could lose her tenuous grip on her magic and end up killing every living thing on the far side of the chasm. The goal was to rescue noncombatants, including children—especially children. It had to be terrifying being a child surrounded by Vincent's beast men.

Three figures outlined against the backdrop of the castle caught her eye. Men stood at the near edge of the chasm, pointing at the castle: one rotund and broad shouldered, one lean and slouched, and one slender and rigidly upright. Hettie recognized their silhouettes and made her way over to them.

"Ah, Hettie, you're up," Jonathan said in greeting.

"You seemed to be sleeping well," Vammi said. "We didn't want to wake you."

"He means you weren't screaming," Deryl said.

"I know what he meant."

They were lucky they'd only heard it the once. She'd been having the dreams ever since Elkin's death. In Garpoint, she'd slept in a widow's house whose husband had died in the first fish-man attack. She'd lost a child that day too. She'd thanked Hettie for stopping the fish-men and offered her a room.

It had been her sister Angli who called in every shark for miles to attack the creatures. Hettie hadn't been the one to stop the creatures.

She took the room anyway.

The widow had never checked on her when she woke screaming in the night. She returned the favor when she heard the widow herself keening. It was never spoken of, something private. It was embarrassing to have the entire camp hear her.

"Right," she said brightly, eager to change the topic. "What's the plan?"

Everyone turned to look at Servio, already knowing he would press his opinions on them.

He didn't hesitate. His time to shine had come. "There are essentially three ways to get past a wall. Over, under, or through. Since their citadel is built on rock, we can't dig under it. I had a scout climb the mountain face to confirm that the walls are as thick as Hettie said."

Hettie ground her teeth. As if she'd lied.

Vammi slung an arm across her shoulder in solidarity. "You doubted her information?"

Servio gave them a bland look. "'I'm a witch. I know things' doesn't instill the same confidence in me as it does in you. I've found it never hurts to double check."

"Does the fact that she was correct boost your confidence in her?" Jonathan asked absently. He scowled at Vammi's arm resting on Hettie's shoulder.

"It boosts my confidence in the information. Let's get back to planning and put our egos away for now."

Hettie snorted. Servio's ego outshone them all.

He ignored her. "Normally with a wall this well fortified, it'd be easier to cut the supply chain and wait them out, only there doesn't seem to be a supply chain and our own supply chain is fragile." He raised an eyebrow at them as if the burned docks were somehow their fault.

"Actually," Jonathan cut in, "I received word this morning that the dock has been rebuilt. At least well enough to offload the basics. Food and supplies should be arriving tomorrow. They've killed three more fish-men and haven't had any problems since. I suspect the death of their fellows has provided the remainder of the group with ample warning to stay back."

"Or your mother is keeping them at bay," Deryl said.

"Doubtful if three got through."

Servio plowed on. "Regardless, they don't have a supply chain we can see. So my guess is Vincent has stockpiled food and will be comfortable picking us off over time until we retreat. Getting past the outer wall will only be the beginning. We have to fight through sections one and two, each with their own gate, before we get a shot at Vincent. Even with our own supply line somewhat intact, it's far from a sure bet."

"This is war," Jonathan said. "Nothing is a sure bet."

Servio nodded. "Which is why we need to either go through the outer wall or over it. Normally, I'd have made sure we had a battering ram, but there wasn't one available." He raised another eyebrow.

"There are big trees north of Poll's Wander," Vammi said. "If you had mentioned this earlier, we could have cut one down."

Servio scoffed. "You don't just cut down a tree. The wood is too fresh. You have to cure it for years before it becomes a proper ram." He paused as if waiting for Vammi to either look impressed with Servio's knowledge or abashed at his own lack of it.

Vammi just shrugged and motioned for him to continue.

Servio couldn't hide his flash of irritation, but he resumed laying out his plan. "As it stands, if we go through the outer gate, we'll have to get in close, which means getting pummeled from above."

"The door is metal," Jonathan said. "Hettie may be able to break the hinges from a distance."

"And if the gates at the two internal walls are wooden, she can burn them," Vammi said.

Servio's look told Hettie he didn't intend to rely on her skills. "Wooden doors are typically treated. They don't burn as easily as a house would. Magic might take out the hinges, but Vincent's men would pour out, and we'd be stuck between them and the chasm." Servio looked uncomfortable. "The Battle of Southfen taught me just how easy it is to shove an army back when you've got a specific place to get them to."

"So what do you propose?" Vammi asked.

Servio ticked off his fingers as he spoke. "You don't have battering rams; you don't have siege towers; you don't have ballistae; you don't have catapults. You're a ragtag group with very little experience in warfare and no training in strategy."

"It's almost as if he doesn't think we're up to the job," Deryl remarked.

"We may not be," Hettie admitted.

Jonathan spoke up. "We can't go under. You don't want to go through. So that means we go over. We've got ladders and a bigger army."

"Probably bigger," Vammi said. "Since the city is divided into three parts, it's hard to tell how many combatants they have."

"We can use that to our advantage," Hettie said. "We storm the citadel. Some of the combatants will be defending the castle, so we won't be fighting everyone at once, which increases our odds for success."

"We might win that way," Servio said dubiously. "But I've found it best to hedge my bets. Over, under, and through. I propose we do all three."

CHAPTER 22

WEED TESTING

Hettie

They laid out their plans. That evening, Jonathan and Servio would organize the troops, crossing the ledge with the bulk of the army. They would storm the front gate at dawn.

Hettie would go with Vammi and the Steppers through the tunnels to sneak up on Vincent from below. She'd voiced her doubts about getting everyone safely through, but Jonathan had a plan.

Hettie led Jonathan up to the tunnel entrance. "How sure are you this will work?"

"I really have no idea. My theory is based on sound science, so better than average, I'd say."

When they reached their destination, they set down their supplies. Hettie called into the tunnel for Boulder and Pillar. She suspected the stone dragon never left the tunnels. Just in case, she kept her senses flared.

"How did you learn about all this?" Hettie gestured to the bundles of plant stalks at their feet.

Jonathan shrugged. "Liselle has an extensive collection of books. One of them covers the plants of southern Andos. Initially I focused on those that grew in Poll's Wander, but eventually I branched out."

"I'm not surprised he spends his free time with his nose in a book," Deryl said. *"Learning about plants of all things."*

"Penelope's gardens were probably a good resource," Hettie mused. The Holden estate had two gardens with an array of flowering plants in the Holden family colors: blue, gold, and green. The green was easy enough, as were the yellows and orange that represented gold. Hettie had never seen so many blue flowers though. The only blue flowers on her home island were little wildflowers.

"I started that garden," Jonathan said proudly. "Some of them were shipped in from Egren and Arlea. I don't get much opportunity to study the plants in the mountain and desert regions though."

"So how did you come up with this idea?" Jonathan claimed the combined plants would produce a subtle scent that repelled predators that relied on their noses to hunt.

"There's a story in my botany book about ancient mountain dwellers," he said. "They trapped animals in caves by using this combination of weeds. It never says exactly what creatures they used it for, but one of the categories listed included large, burrowing animals. If we can get the rocktoads to place the bundles near a split in the tunnel and see if the stone dragon turns away, even with prey ahead of it, we'll know it works."

"I'll be the prey," Hettie reminded him firmly. She could sense the dragon in advance and use the alcoves.

Jonathan pursed his lips. They'd had this argument. He wanted the rocktoads to do the test, but they didn't smell like prey. Hettie would be a far better lure.

"If we're going to put a chunk of my army in the tunnels, we should test it properly," he conceded. He had initially volunteered himself, but as the army's commander, that was never going to fly, and he knew it.

It took an hour of calling before Pillar showed up. "Stone dragon," she said sternly. She stayed far enough back to avoid the light.

"Nice to see you too," Hettie said, hauling the plant bundles to Pillar. Jonathan followed, snorting at the smell of the rock, pungent and earthy. "We have an idea. We need your help."

"I help. You help," Pillar said.

Confused, she asked, "Help defeat the castle? That's what we're trying to do."

Pillar gently scuffed the floor with one foot, eyes downcast. "Help child."

Hettie blinked. She hadn't realized Pillar had a child. Or was it someone else's child? "A rocktoad child?" she asked.

Pillar gave a short nod.

"*Your* child?" Hettie asked.

Another nod, hesitant this time.

"She has a child?" Jonathan asked. Hettie waved him to silence. She kept forgetting he could only understand her side of the conversation.

"*This is what it's like when you interrupt my conversations with Gak,*" Deryl said. "*For the record, I never had a child. But from what I've heard, there's a lot of screaming involved in birthing one. That has to be tricky for a society that has to stay quiet.*"

"*There's far less screaming than the stories tell,*" Hettie said absently. "*It's hard to scream when you're in too much pain to breathe.*"

"*I'm grateful to be a man.*"

"*You're not a man; you're an eyeball.*"

"*Eyeballs don't give birth either, so I'm happy either way.*"

Hettie considered the issue of Pillar's child. If it was injured, she could likely heal it. Rocktoad bodies weren't the same as human bodies, but there were enough similarities, that she could probably put things right even without Pillar's body to use as a template. Hettie wasn't nearly as good with illnesses, but she could probably fix that too. It would just take time. Lots and lots of time. Possibly more time than she had.

Worse yet, some things couldn't be fixed. Hettie was all too aware of her shortcomings.

She almost asked what was wrong, but with their limited ability to communicate, even with the translation charm, she figured it was best to have a look herself.

"I will do my best to help your child," she said slowly. "I can't make any promises though."

Pillar nodded, apparently satisfied. "What need?"

Hettie lofted a bundle of weeds and explained.

Pillar sniffed the plants gingerly, then inhaled more deeply. She shrugged.

"It doesn't smell like much to us, either, but we don't hunt by scent. It takes a strong nose to detect these. We want to test it on the stone dragon. Can you help us find a place where the tunnel splits?"

Pillar nodded, heading deeper into the tunnel.

"That was easy," Deryl said.

Hettie agreed. *"Either she really hates Vincent or her child needs help badly enough to risk going head-to-head with the stone dragon."*

Hettie muttered the spell for night vision and waved Jonathan back to the entrance.

"Be careful," he whispered.

"I know," she said, waving at him more forcefully. One human was bait enough.

She followed Pillar, keeping an eye on the ceiling. The tunnel she'd missed the first time was angled to allow the dragon to enter without having to make such a sharp turn.

"That explains why I didn't see it last night."

"Can you sense tunnels with your magic?" Deryl asked.

"Living things are different. They're easier for me. I've trained myself to notice them. Rock is more complicated. I could locate tunnels, but it would be painstaking."

There was nothing to mark where two dozen men had died the night before. Even the discarded lanterns had been devoured.

She hoped the dragon got indigestion.

Pillar wound her way through the warren of tunnels, along several side branches, and through a hub where six tunnels met. Several turns later, Hettie thought, *"This mountain has more pathways than a good-sized village."*

At a crossroads where two tunnels crossed, they stopped. Pillar pointed down one tunnel. "Stone dragon," she said, indicating that's where she expected it to come from. She placed two plant bundles a few feet down two adjacent tunnels. For the dragon, the bundles would be to the left and straight ahead. If the test worked, the beast would need to make a sharp left-hand turn to avoid the bundles.

"Is this the point where I make noise?" Hettie asked, not bothering to keep her voice down.

Pillar's nod was nervous this time.

An alcove stood a few feet away. They would have plenty of time to duck into one when the dragon arrived.

Hettie raised her voice. "What's wrong with your child?"

Pillar winced at the noise, but she answered, still quiet. "Evil Man." She said it like a name.

Vincent. Her kid was in the citadel. "You need a rescue, not a healing." Crap. Healing hadn't been a sure bet. A rescue was even less of one. Her chin dropped to her chest. Nobody was safe in a war, captives least of all. There would be casualties, not all of them combatants.

Assuming she managed to find the kid alive, keeping it that way would be tricky. She opened her mouth to tell Pillar not to expect much.

Pillar had a tear running down her face. For all her stony demeanor, she clearly cared. She was a mother who wanted her child back from monstrous men, and she was counting on Hettie to make it happen.

Swallowing hard, Hettie nodded. "I'll get your kid back." She didn't say dead or alive, but she was thinking it.

"You're getting soft," Deryl said.

"Honesty isn't always useful." Sometimes it destroyed hope when hope was all you had left. Hope had power. Hope was where the impossible met reality.

"You have company," Deryl said.

Hettie's senses were focused far off in the distance, searching for the dragon's heartbeat or its subtle vibrations. That blinded her to the approach of someone behind her.

She spun to find a new rocktoad whose shoulders were so massive they seemed to swallow his chin. He looked from Hettie to Pillar and made a series of twitches. His eyes were flat and hard. His nostrils flared in response to their silent conversation. His twitches grew aggressive, and his soft noises were almost a harsh grunt.

Hettie could have run power through her bracelet, but she didn't want to drop her awareness even for that long. If the dragon came hurtling at them full speed, they'd need all the warning she could give.

Pillar's lip curled, and she gestured back angrily in reply to the grumpy newcomer's silent commentary.

They continued on in the quietest fight Hettie had ever witnessed.

"Would either of you care to fill me in?" she asked. Her irritation made her louder than usual, and her voice echoed down the tunnels. Hettie didn't much care. She was supposed to be making noise.

The grumpy guy flinched. "No dragon," he said to Hettie in a menacing whisper.

"Yes dragon," she said, purposely raising her voice. "I need to get to the castle with an army of soldiers so we can stop the evil men there." She tipped her head toward Pillar. "Besides, her kid is in there with the bad guys. Obviously *you're* not going to rescue it, so I'm volunteering."

At the edge of her senses, Hettie felt stirrings far below her. The nearest alcove was just past Grumpy. She didn't want to be stuck next to him when the dragon came slithering by.

Sucking her teeth, she stepped closer to Pillar.

"Leave child," Grumpy said.

"Did he just suggest abandoning the kid?" Deryl asked.

Hettie raised an eyebrow. "I can see why she came to me. You're about as worthless as a beached blackfin." She put a hand on Pillar's wrist, nudging her back.

Pillar ignored her first two nudges but then got the hint. She eased over to the tunnel next to Grumpy.

Grumpy stepped forward, as if expecting them to run away. His foot kicked the bundle of weeds on the ground, and he paused, bending to pick them up.

"I would leave that where it is if I were you," Hettie said.

The rocktoad sniffed the weeds suspiciously as he walked toward them. He stopped on the threshold between his tunnel and the stone dragon's. He twitched at Pillar, who did not communicate back.

"Warn evil man," she told Hettie, tipping her head toward Grumpy.

A light went off in Hettie's brain.

"He's working with the enemy," Deryl said, sounding scandalized. *"The sly bastard."*

"And at the expense of her kid. What a slimy loaf of rat vomit. I should kill him on the spot." She hesitated. Would Pillar get in trouble if she did?

Deryl's pouch began to glow. *"You're in danger. Maybe that'll solve your dilemma for you."*

Hettie nudged Pillar more urgently. She stepped back and quickly made her way to the alcove with Hettie on her heels.

Grumpy's eyes had widened at the glow from Hettie's pouch. He stepped into the intersection and stopped. Hettie could tell the moment he realized the dragon was coming. He hissed and threw the bundle down the wrong path before running back down the tunnel he'd come from.

The tunnel that no longer held dragon repellent.

"Fool," Deryl said, cackling.

"Time to see if these weeds work," Hettie muttered.

CHAPTER 23

THAT'S WHAT FRIENDS ARE FOR

Hettie

The stone dragon came hurtling through the tunnel. It almost smelled the weeds too late. Struggling to make the last-second turn, it caromed off the corner of the tunnel as it pivoted down Grumpy's path.

Once it turned, Hettie left her alcove to better view its passing. *"Man, that thing is fast."*

"No wonder it eats so much," Deryl said. *"It has to use a lot of energy getting around. I wonder how far it has to travel to get back to this area."*

"I have no idea."

When the stubby tail disappeared into the darkness, Hettie was surprised to see Grumpy sprint from an alcove he'd managed to hide in. He ran after the stone dragon, which was probably safest considering it couldn't turn around in the tunnels.

Pillar pointed urgently. "Stop. Warn evil man."

Hettie didn't hesitate. She reached out with her magic before Grumpy could get out of range and locked his hips.

Mid-stride, he fell on his face with a satisfying thud that could be heard over the distant hiss of the serpent's body.

Deryl cackled again.

Grumpy didn't give up despite having no chance of escape. He crawled along using his broad, powerful upper body.

Hettie locked his shoulder joints, timing each so his arms would be relatively close to his side.

She approached the grunting rocktoad with Pillar, who hooked a strong hand around his ankle and dragged him to an alcove. She shoved him in so he was neatly tucked out of the way in case the dragon came back.

He snarled at them under his breath. A lifetime of training kept him quiet despite his rage.

"Be grateful we moved you out of the way," Hettie told him. She turned to Pillar. "I can take him back to my camp. If someone finds him here, he'll tell them what we did."

Pillar considered for a long moment, but ultimately decided against it. She shook her head. "Stay."

Hettie shrugged. She couldn't fathom Pillar's reason for wanting him around. "He won't be able to move until I fix him. Just make sure no one finds him before the battle starts."

Grumpy grunted as he struggled to move. He blinked and twitched his face muscles. Hettie wondered how well he could communicate without the hand twitching to accompany it. His scowl made it clear he was threatening, not pleading.

Deliberately, Pillar turned away from him. "Come," she whispered.

Hettie collected the weed bundles and followed her back to the tunnel entrance.

Pillar stopped when the light from the entrance could be seen. She took the weed bundles and nodded firmly. Whatever happened from here on out, she was committed.

Hettie hoped she didn't get in trouble. If Pillar was detained by her people, it could derail their plans and cost them the war. Worse yet, it may cost Pillar her child's life. "We'll meet you here three hours before dawn. Take us to the citadel. We'll do the rest."

In her typical wordless fashion, Pillar nodded, turned, and left.

Hettie filled Jonathan in on their way down the path. He was giddy over his plan working. "I can't believe the stories were true!"

"He seemed a lot more sure it would work before we tested it," Deryl said.

"Not that it matters. We'd have tried anything if it had a chance of working."

"True. I guess the uncertainty is what makes it fun."

"There you go with the word fun again."

"Would you rather I tell rock jokes?" he asked sweetly.

"Why? Do you need better punchlines for them?"

Deryl blew out an irritated breath and went silent.

Hettie grinned, though soon she was lost in thought, running through their task list. It was going to be a long night.

In the end, she was right. It was a long night.

At midnight, Hettie anxiously watched as the first of the Widows' Will crossed the narrow ledge to the far side of the chasm in silence. Luckily, the stars didn't provide enough light to illuminate them, and they managed to go undetected.

Hettie turned her attention to Vammi and the Steppers, praying to Arlea their luck would hold. She couldn't rid herself of the fear that the battle would be lost while they were underground.

Hettie rubbed Jonathan's weeds over herself alongside the grim soldiers. They had lost nearly a quarter of their members to these tunnels and would go in with their eyes wide open.

Vammi ran through the plan with the soldiers.

Hettie added, "The rocktoad we'll meet up with tonight is Pillar. You won't be able to understand her, but I will. She's helping us because her kid is somewhere in the castle. Not all rocktoads are on our side. If you run into one, don't trust them not to warn Vincent's men, but don't fight them if you can help it. They've been mistreated by Vincent and his men, so they're scared of defying him. Stop them with non-lethal force if you can manage it, but don't put yourself at risk if they insist on dying."

She reiterated Vammi's previous orders. "For the love of Arlea, stay as quiet as you can. I can mask our noise, but not if you sound like a collapsing building. Pinch your neighbor if they're louder than you."

Everyone was ready long before it was time to go anywhere.

Hettie tried not to fidget. *"When people tell stories about adventure, they leave out the waiting part."*

"Of course. That part's boring."

"It's reality. It at least deserves a mention."

"I'd enjoy watching you pick rotten tomatoes out of your hair."

Hettie spotted Jonathan near the chasm. She left the camp, well-lit to draw the eye in the hopes Vincent's men wouldn't notice the soldiers lined up to cross the chasm.

When she reached Jonathan, she could hear Servio directing soldiers near the ledge.

"Has anyone fallen yet?" she asked Jonathan.

"No, thankfully. Let's hope our luck holds." He kept his eyes on the citadel wall, looking for signs of activity. "It's almost time." He exhaled, long and slow. "Do you think this plan will work?"

"As much as I hate giving Servio one more thing to brag about, I think it's a good plan. If we can catch them by surprise from underground, this battle could be over in less than a day."

While she'd convinced herself their chances of success were decent, Jonathan's doubts increased her own. It was a good plan, but not a sure plan.

"Nothing is sure in war," Deryl said.

"Some days it seems like nothing is sure but *war."*

"My father was a trader for the nobility," Jonathan said, shifting his weight. "It's how he met Liselle's father. Traveling around Andos, he'd seen his fair share of battles, though he tried not to get involved."

"Smart man," Hettie said.

Deryl grunted in agreement.

"Twice, he skirted a battlefield where tens of thousands of men lay dead. The fighting was still ongoing." He paused a beat, then shook his head.

Hettie expected him to say something about man's lust for battle.

"This battle is so small in comparison. I'm ashamed to admit I'm terrified. After fighting in Poll's Wander, I hoped I wouldn't be."

She almost laughed at his logic. "The day you start fighting is the day all notion of glory disappears. That first day, you're armed with stories told around campfires. You trade that in for experience that teaches you there's no amount of practiced swordplay that guarantees you'll live through the next opponent. Any moment could be your last. Terror is your body's way of keeping you alert when it counts. It's good for you."

"Way to cheer him up," Deryl said.

"I wasn't trying to cheer him up. I was trying to give him perspective."

They were only a few strides from the edge of the chasm. Hettie stepped closer to it, reaching out with her senses. Did the tunnels skirt the wall below? Had the rocktoads considered luring the stone dragon out to fall to its death?

"You don't seem terrified," Jonathan said quietly. "You're always so confident."

Hettie opened her mouth, but nothing came out. In Poll's Wander, she'd wanted to fulfill her duty and secure an alliance for her people. She hadn't been terrified until she was staring down Vincent's army. Even then, her fear wasn't of failing in her duties. She'd been afraid she'd never see Elkin again.

It was a fear she'd ended up confronting anyway. She was without her lover, without her home, and without her family. It wasn't like she had nothing left to live for, but there was certainly *less* to live for.

If the past few months had taught her anything, it was that you could survive a battle then die from an accident at home. Sometimes the living were in agony while the dead were at rest. Nothing made sense. Nothing went how it was supposed to. Good people died and bad people lived all the time.

Hettie was wholly unqualified to hand out hope on the eve of battle.

Still, Jonathan was her friend. Bringing up her own doubts would only drag him down with her.

"If only he had the same courtesy," Deryl said.

Hettie didn't begrudge Jonathan his doubts. What good were friends if you couldn't share your fears with them? "I was terrified when we fought at Penelope. Both times," she admitted, stepping back from the ledge to stand by his side. "I'm not terrified now, but I will be when the fighting starts."

He seemed surprised by that. "You have magic to keep you alive."

"Magic isn't a guarantee. I can die like everyone else."

A moment of silence passed, each of them lost in their own thoughts. Hettie reminded herself—vehemently—that she hadn't lost everything. She still had Deryl and Ouri. She had Liselle, Jonathan, and Vammi.

Strangely, her thoughts drifted back to the man in black who had watched over her while she slept in Garpoint. Having a stranger near while she'd been vulnerable was unsettling.

Jonathan continued to study the citadel. "I fear how the rest of us will fare against men like those."

The rest of us. Those without magic.

"We won't win this battle with magical might," she told him. "We lost at Penelope, because we didn't know what we were dealing with and most of the men had no fighting experience. We won the second time around. We got smarter. We had better tactics."

"Killing blows only," Jonathan said, repeating the mantra they had drilled into the Widows' Will before that second battle.

Hettie nodded. "And we had archers, more men, and fighting experience. The men in that citadel have no experience fighting a war. They're brutes, yes, but strength alone doesn't win a fight. There are other factors at play." She reached out to grip his forearm. "Have faith in yourself. Have faith in your men."

"I have faith in you," he said.

Hettie grinned. "As well you should."

Something in her quivered at the exchange. A part of her that whispered she was unworthy of his faith. Vincent's men were brutal. She could well be the first to die in battle. She could let her friends down. Send Deryl back to the Shadow Realm. Fail to rescue Pillar's child. Leave the world to Vincent's horrors. She could fail in any number of ways. Again.

She knew her thoughts weren't useful, but it was a struggle to push them from her mind.

A retching noise came from the darkness, and Vammi came to stand in the flickering edges of the nearest torch. "I have faith in you," he said, his tone syrupy and dramatic.

Jonathan glowered. "Eavesdropping is not an attractive habit."

"Leave him be," Hettie chided, though she was glad to see him. Vammi's inability to be serious for even a minute was a helpful distraction from dour conversations. He'd managed to derail the topic in a single sentence.

Vammi grinned, clearly happy to have gotten a rise out of Jonathan. "All of my habits are attractive habits. Women find me irresistible. If you need tips on getting one into bed, I can help."

"I don't need courtship advice from you," Jonathan said, tone scathing. "You're brash, domineering, and condescending. What's worse is you seem to think those are good qualities to have."

"That was spot on," Deryl said.

In a deluded sense of camaraderie, Vammi tried putting a hand on Jonathan's shoulder only to have it slapped away. Vammi held up his hands to indicate peace. "I'm just trying to help. The girl of your dreams is out there. I'll help you woo her."

Deryl said, *"Knowing Vammi, he'd demonstrate by wooing the girl himself."*

Jonathan's head rolled back in exasperation. "I would throw myself off a bridge before asking you for advice on women."

"The only bridge around has been conveniently destroyed," Vammi said.

Hettie could tell he was just getting started. He had a habit of goading Jonathan until he was trembling in rage. "Come on," she said, turning Vammi around and pushing him back toward camp. "Let him focus on the battle. It's time you and I head for the tunnels."

"I love tunnels," Vammi said, his voice pitched low.

Jonathan made a sound of disgust.

It took Hettie a moment to figure out why. When she did, she laughed. Vammi would have made a great pirate.

CHAPTER 24

UTTER MADNESS

Adyr

Locked in a memory-dream he couldn't escape, Adyr's stomach rumbled at the thought of food.

In his memory, Cayon spoke to the assembled fighters as servants brought a range of covered dishes into the feasting hall, placing a dish in front of each of the six lords.

The lids were removed to show identically prepared plates, each with a whole roasted chicken that looked appetizing but for the fact that the chicken heads were still attached, burnt feathers lining the neck. Beside the chicken sat an oversized bread roll sliced neatly in half to display a dark green paste inside.

Adyr's attention was pulled to the fighters, specifically the child. Presumably, each man would showcase their talents. What talent did the child possess that would put him in league with grown men?

The lords of Poll's Wander were likewise focused on Cayon's side of the room. Vincent noticed and seemed pleased in their interest.

"Cayon is a scientist. He's kept rigorous notes on his progress with the Element."

Cayon approached, his cloak billowing out behind him. Two of his men followed. Both were Pavinn, moderate in build and height. One was the fist-clencher. The other was the fidgeter.

The trio entered the middle of the marked arena. Cayon turned to address his men. "You will fight until there is a clear winner between you. Use restraint. No killing."

The casual delivery raised the hair on Adyr's arms. Cayon spoke like a mother telling her children for the thousandth time not to run on the stairs, yet fully expecting her caution to fall on deaf ears. Adyr eyed the lords.

Griff traded looks with Lord Rasmond. Lord Lorez sat between them, his head swiveling. Lord Tuigasi's normally vapid expression had been replaced by furrowed brows, and stodgy Lord Guimont watched the fighters, waiting to see how things went before forming a response.

Cayon cleared the marked fighting area and clapped his hands, signaling for the fight to begin. His hands barely touched before the men were moving.

In a flurry of limbs, the fighters crashed together, punching and kicking. Unlike children in the street, their attacks were organized and meticulous, each one dodging and landing blows with a methodical vengeance so intense Adyr couldn't tell them apart despite being a skilled fighter himself.

They circled one another twice amid an onslaught of strikes before the action faltered while each man struggled to gain a grip around the other's neck. Clencher gave up in short order, instead opting for a grip around Fidgeter's waist before lifting him bodily and falling backwards.

Several of the lords inhaled sharply at the expected impact of Fidgeter's face meeting the floor, but his hand, now free, met the ground first, pulling him forward into a sort of lunging run. His feet scrabbled over Clencher's chest. As soon as he was clear, he whipped around. Clencher had landed heavily on his back. As he sat up,

Fidgeter slipped up behind him to snake an arm around his neck, abruptly squeezing so hard Adyr expected to hear the spine crack.

"That's enough," Vincent barked. "I'd rather not lose one of my best fighters."

Cayon was already brandishing his double-clap to signal the end of the fight.

Fidgeter ignored it. The veins in his arms stood out as Clencher clawed at the arm locked around his throat, his mouth opening and closing like a fish out of water.

Cayon snapped a finger and the two guards at the entrance came forward. They pulled leather straps from around their waist. Each slipped a strap around a fighter's neck. They hauled the two apart.

Adyr wondered if separating them would kill them. Fidgeter never stopped struggling to hold on. Clencher lay still when the guard removed the strap from his neck. After a few seconds, he groaned and thrashed weakly, unaware that the fight had ended.

"Ah, good," Vincent said. His face lit up with a smile. "No harm done. As you can see, the Element has helped to increase their speed and heighten their instincts. They are absolutely deadly."

The fighter who had been prowling along the far wall was breathing heavily despite being a bystander. He was a squat, muscular fellow. Prowler strode forward, shoving aside the guard next to Clencher. Reaching down, he hauled Clencher into a seated position, head bobbing drunkenly. Prowler wrapped his arm around Clencher's neck, dwarfing it in his enormous biceps. He jerked.

The snap of a spine could be heard clearly throughout the room.

Everyone stared with their mouths agape.

A joyful grin bloomed on Prowler's face. He grabbed Clencher's head with both hands and twisted. More popping filled the room, followed by squishy sounds as meat and tendon were torn. He continued to twist until the skin looked like the casing between sausage links.

Lord Guimont spoke in his typical dry tone. "Yes, quite deadly. We can all see they're committed."

"Committed to insanity," Lord Lorez muttered.

Griff looked queasy.

Cayon hissed and pointed to the doorway, ordering the guards to leave.

One guard nervously prodded Prowler with a toe. Prowler gave Clencher's head a couple of yanks until it tore free, then tucked it under his arm and walked out looking delighted with his prize.

Blood from the headless man leaked from his corpse. A trail from the head marked Prowler's path.

"No matter," Vincent said. "I have more men. Which brings me to the reason for inviting you here." He turned a proud gaze on them. "My invitation extends to more than just a visit. More than just dinner. It's an invitation to rule the world."

"Utter madness," Adyr breathed.

CHAPTER 25

IT'S ALL IN THE TIMING

Hettie

Hettie scanned the deserted clearing. Firelight flickered across the camp, making the shadows dance.

Most of the Widows' Will had crossed the chasm, leaving only a handful of people tending the campfires, which were left burning to convince the citadel the army hadn't moved.

The Steppers lined up in pairs to make the hike to the tunnels easier. They would have to make the treacherous trek in the dark. By Hettie's estimate, they would make it to the citadel around dawn, when the main army would be fighting near the outer gate.

Motion in the firelight caught her attention. A lithe figure moved from one campfire to another. She held a lantern aloft, scanning bedrolls. Her deep purple outfit marked her for House Lorez. Her cropped sleeves and waist pouches indicated she was a messenger.

Hettie whistled to get her attention then waved her over.

She smiled when she drew close enough to recognize Hettie. "Marsh Queen," she greeted.

"You have news of the dock?" she guessed.

"Aye. But not good news." The woman tucked a strand of dark hair behind her ear. "There's been another rockslide. Bigger than the last. We have no hope of clearing it without your help."

Hettie frowned at that. "Did another chitton show up?" She was beginning to wonder if the creature burrowed holes high in the mountain.

The woman blinked. "Chitton?"

"A giant rock-spider thing," Hettie clarified.

"No, Marsh Queen. It happened yesterday afternoon. Nothing strange was spotted."

"Damn a wharf rat's moldy guts," she muttered. *"There's no way that was a coincidence."*

"Agreed," Deryl said. *"The timing is too perfect."*

The messenger said, "The dock is built and fully functional. We have all the supplies packed in wagons and ready to transport once the path is cleared."

"Fat lot of good that will do you. The fighting will be over by the time it gets to you."

It was unfortunate, but they had no way to get the supplies across the ledge to the castle anyhow. "Did anyone die in the rockslide?"

"None. Yesterday was spent staging the shipment by the docks. They were planning to leave at first light this morning. I tried to get here before the battle started so you'd know supplies won't be here until the path is cleared."

"It's a little late to stop things now." Hettie took a moment to breathe. The soldiers had food for the coming day. After that, they'd go hungry. It would do more harm than good to start the attack, make headway, then retreat. More men died retreating than facing a battle head-on. They wouldn't have the manpower to take the castle after a failure like that.

"Even if you pull back now, those castle walls are only going to grow more fortified and harder to get through," Deryl said.

He was right. They were going to have to gamble. Besides, they couldn't count on their trips through the tunnels to stay quiet. Eventually, someone in the rocktoad community would get word to Vincent. The tunnels were their single biggest advantage.

"I hate to say it," Hettie said, *"but I can see why Servio is such a fan of last-minute decisions. Things change so often that it makes you wonder why we plan anything at all."*

Taking section one would earn them food. The people in the city had to eat. They would have a stockpile somewhere. Hopefully not behind the second wall. Hopefully, the supply issues would spur the men to a quick victory.

Hettie waved Vammi over, and they discussed their options. He agreed with her.

"I love a challenge," he said. "This will make our victory even more grand. Bards will write songs about this battle. Mark my words."

"Let's hope we live to hear them."

"If you wanted songs about your exploits, you should have said so."

"Not from you," Hettie said. *"Never from you."*

"You're so mean," Deryl said, pouting. *"You're lucky I'm stuck in your head or I'd go somewhere else."*

Hettie smirked. "You're *lucky you're stuck in my head. Nobody else could stand you."*

She turned back to the messenger. "Jonathan should be down where the chasm meets the mountain," she said, pointing. "Tell him what you told me. We're heading out, as planned. Waiting will only cause more problems."

Timing was crucial. The Widows' Will would attack in hours. Any delay would give Vincent's men a chance to counter their forces. Hettie's group needed to infiltrate the castle during the early stages of fighting. If they were too early, the Steppers would be fighting the full might of the citadel alone. They would be crushed. If they were too late, the Widows' Will would be too far depleted before the Steppers arrived to turn the tables.

Everything hinged on a coordinated attack. Waiting would only hurt. The news just meant they *had* to take section one by the end of the day.

They got the Steppers moving and made steady progress. Pillar and Boulder were both waiting for them at the tunnel entrance.

"This kid we're supposed to find," Deryl said. *"You think Boulder's the dad?"*

"Not the time to ask," Hettie replied tersely. Focused on the coming battle and creating a safe passage through the tunnels, she had forgotten about the kid.

"Thanks for coming," she said, greeting the two stocky figures.

The rocktoads weren't big on casual conversation, so they nodded and tipped their head as if to say "Let's get moving."

Hettie muffled the sound of the Steppers by putting a shield between the soldiers and the empty space beyond. She couldn't do much about the vibrations of their steps and hoped the stone dragon wasn't close enough to feel it through the rock.

She cast a wide net, scanning as far out as she could. The dragon came within reach of her senses on two occasions, but it remained distant. The weeds were doing their job.

After over an hour of shuffling along, Hettie's neck and shoulders ached from modifying her walk. The tunnel ceiling was an inch past her head, but it dipped occasionally, and she was forced to slouch. The taller Steppers were perpetually hunched.

Hettie's magic was another source of discomfort. The built-up stores pressed at her. Using it passively for so long seemed to make it worse. She yearned to do something explosive.

She tried not to think about how much the pressure scared her. It seemed almost alive, and it wanted to obliterate mountains. The last thing she needed was to become a liability to her friends.

Eventually, the tunnels grew wider and taller. Low groans could be heard as the soldiers straightened their backs fully for the first time in too long.

Hettie suspected the taller ceilings were part of the original tunnel system dug out by humans. The rancid leather smell permeating the tunnels was less pungent.

Faint, muffled sounds of yelling could be heard in the distance.

Several tunnels branched out from theirs, but Pillar proceeded onward until their path turned right. The tunnel ended a hundred feet ahead at a ramp. "Out," she said, pointing.

Hettie had Vammi stay with the Steppers while she investigated.

Muffled yelling sifted through a wooden slab set in the ceiling above the ramp. It was distant enough she could tell the fighting wasn't directly outside. She suspected the door led to a side street or back alley.

"Sounds like the fighting is under way," Deryl said.

"We're not too early. Let's hope we're not too late."

Pillar gestured at the wooden slab. "Door."

"Yes. We'll take it from here, Pillar. Thank you." Hettie had no expectations for the rocktoad to join them. The sun was rising and a blind rocktoad would be no help at all. "I'll find your child," she promised.

Pillar nodded, casting a dubious look at the slab in the ceiling before turning to leave.

Hettie called to where Vammi waited. "Be ready to move."

A scan showed the door was thicker than expected. At least four inches of solid wooden beams banded together with iron. It was nearly as wide as Hettie was tall. Slits of dim light filtered through the cracks.

"How are you going to open it?" Deryl asked.

"By force. I'll make a shield and expand it upward until the pressure lifts the door."

"That's not going to work. Pushing upward will create an equal pressure downward. The ground is sloped, so your force is going to go sideways. Honestly, sometimes I forget how big the holes in your magical education are. You could fit a house in some of them."

Hettie knew how shields worked. *"I was going to level the ground first."*

"That'll take longer."

"Are you planning to offer a solution or just criticism?"

"Look, I know you've got rocky times ahead, so I'll help you out."

Hettie scowled. *"You're going to be a rock joke if you don't stop that."*

"You okay?" Vammi asked, heading toward her.

Irritated, she waved him back.

"No, really. I know this one," Deryl insisted. *"Cerissa blasted things apart all the time."* He described the spell, doing a poor job of relaying the hand gestures. She tried them without the words first until he said, *"Yes. Something like that."*

"It's a spell," she snapped. *"The difference between 'that' and 'something like that' can be disastrous. Is it right or not?"*

"Sure," he said, sounding not at all sure. *"At least to the best of my recollection."*

"You said you knew this spell."

His voice went up an octave. *"I did. I mean, well, I do. I do. You've got it right. Let's move on to the words."*

Growling, Hettie focused on the words, which weren't all that different from the spell for an expanding shield. Minor changes could make big differences when it came to magic, so she noted the nuances and committed them to memory.

She stepped back and focused on the door. The spell wasn't long, which made the unfamiliar hand motions harder to do since they were completed in tandem with the words.

"Don't forget to hook your pinky on that last swipe," Deryl reminded her.

The interruption had her stumbling over her words and the spell shot a vertical bolt of black light up through the door, leaving charred wood bordering a three-foot-square smoking hole. That hole was mirrored in the floor, where a new tunnel had been birthed from the unholy light. Hettie stepped forward to get a better look. Her night vision allowed her to see pretty far down into the hole, but she couldn't make out the bottom.

Deryl whistled. *"You should be more careful. You're going to kill someone botching a spell like that."*

"I'm going to make you a neck, so I can throttle it."

CHAPTER 26

WHAT'S FOR DINNER?

Hettie

Wisps of smoke drifted lazily above the gaping hole. Footsteps announced Vammi's arrival. Hettie watched him peer down into the hole, a dubious look on his face. "That is less useful than I was hoping for."

Hettie's eyes narrowed. "Next time you make the hole."

Vammi's disarming grin made it hard to stay mad. She sighed. "Get the men moving. I'll put a shield over it so they can climb up."

He knew her moods well enough not to argue. He gave a low whistle that carried through the tunnel. His men approached.

Hettie placed her shield and nodded for Vammi to climb out first.

He carefully put out a foot, feeling for the invisible shield. Satisfied he wasn't going to fall to his death, he stood with both feet on what appeared to be empty air and stared straight down. "That's unnerving." He pulled a thin cloth from inside his vest, unfolded it, and draped it over the hole. It covered the bulk of the opening. "Proof that there's something to stand on."

He drew his sword and raised his head, cautiously peering out the hole.

Surprisingly, nobody had come to investigate the beam of black light. The fighting had to be in full swing if that hadn't drawn attention.

When nobody stabbed Vammi in the face, he sheathed his sword. The street surface was level with his forehead, but he managed to pull himself out of the hole without difficulty.

The next soldier in line hesitated only briefly. He eyed his captain's cloth, then stepped onto it. He pulled himself up less smoothly. Vammi helped. One by one, the Steppers exited the tunnel.

When Hettie was the only one left, two soldiers reached down to hoist her up.

The putrid smell of unwashed bodies hit her nose as soon as her head was out of the hole. She'd forgotten the pungent smell of moldy goat milk that accompanied Vincent's men.

"Ye gods," she muttered. Breathing through her mouth, she took in her surroundings.

They were on a small road with houses lining both sides. One of the city walls loomed nearby. By the sound of it, the fighting was at least a few blocks away.

The houses were empty. Doors stood open with no signs of cowering citizenry. "Where'd everybody go?"

"Maybe Vincent has the women and children in the castle."

"You honestly think he's protecting the innocent?"

"I was thinking more along the lines of hostages. Or fodder, if we manage to get past section two."

One of the soldiers who had pulled Hettie out of the hole stood with her hands on her hips, broad shoulders dwarfing Hettie's. "I don't know about the people. The soldiers are taking cover in the houses so they don't attract attention while they wait for orders." Her voice was low and smooth like good brandy. She'd have made a compelling storyteller with a voice like that.

Hettie nodded. "Smart. Where's Vammi?"

She tipped her head at the house behind Hettie. "Captain's in there."

Just then, Vammi came out looking sick to his stomach.

"What's wrong?" Hettie was immediately alarmed. Vammi wasn't bothered by much. He was usually the one bothering others.

Instead of answering, he pointed inside with his hand over his mouth.

Curious, she went inside. The room held a table for four and a fireplace with a large cauldron hanging from it. A door led to a separate room, but three soldiers stood by the table with their hands pressed to the wood and their heads hanging low.

"This looks promising," Deryl said.

"Don't sound so excited." She had no idea what Vincent's people were capable of, but she was almost positive it would bring her new nightmares. "What am I looking for?" she asked the soldiers.

Without looking up, all three pointed to the cauldron. Hettie found it full of cold, watery stew. She sniffed the air, but the coals had gone out long ago and the smell of food no longer permeated the air. A large wooden spoon handle stuck out of the pot, so she stirred it, revealing brown lumps of varying shapes and sizes. *"Do root vegetables grow in the mountains?"*

"I'm more confused about the size. Why would you stick an entire turnip in the pot without cutting it up first? By the time the inside is cooked, the outside is mush."

"My mum took me to Kos when I was twelve," one of the soldiers said, sounding dazed. "She fed me testicles from a giant bingaro. I thought that was the most disgusting—" he dry heaved, unable to finish his sentence.

"What's a giant bingaro?" Deryl asked.

"It's a goat the size of a horse with so many horns it looks like it's wearing a crown. I saw a drawing of one once. I think they breed them in Kos."

The spoon bumped something hard. Hettie had to work to maneuver it to the surface. Two eye sockets peered up at her briefly before it fell back into the muck. Instead of digging it back up, she used her magic to feel it out.

A skull. Smallish. Human. Probably from a child.

For the love of Arlea. She had to fight to keep from retching herself. They were eating their children?

Further exploration found more bones in the pot. Severed fingers, cooked into wrinkly masses covered in thick sauce. Toes too. Cataloguing the bones helped keep her mind from dwelling on how the child got in the cauldron in the first place.

A pair of collar bones lay at the bottom of the pot, but she didn't find any of the long bones.

"Maybe those get sent to the castle," Deryl said. *"Fine dining and all."*

"They're starving," Hettie said aloud. Her voice was surprisingly even. "They're eating their own dead."

"Who says they died first?" a thick-necked Stepper at the table asked. His voice was deep, but Hettie could pick out the slight quaver that hinted at hysteria.

"Please let them have died first," another muttered, her eyes wide.

The male looked at his companions. "Is this what will become of us? Will they eat our dead?"

Vammi stepped into the doorway, though he stayed outside.

"Likely," Hettie said, opting for honesty. "When the only alternative is to starve, they'll eat whatever they can get their hands on."

Vammi shuddered. "There are no animals in the streets or in the houses. This is only one street, but I wouldn't be surprised to find there are none in the whole city."

"So much for stockpiling food. It's no wonder we didn't find a supply chain," Deryl said.

"What kind of hellish place is this?" the wide-eyed Stepper said.

"The motivating kind," Hettie said, looking each soldier in the eye. "This could have happened to Poll's Wander if Vincent had won the first battle. He didn't win then, and he won't win now. This is why we came."

Vammi nodded, standing taller. "This is a fight that will never again find its way to our families' doorsteps. They are starving and desperate, if they're not all mad. This fight ends here. Today." His words weren't filled with passion. They were said simply, yet the change in the men was visible.

They pulled themselves together and filed out of the house.

Judging by the looks on several of the faces outside, more than one house held cannibal stew.

Vammi made a hand gesture, and the Steppers began quietly filing into columns and followed a street that paralleled the wall.

With the battle under way, the wall builders had abandoned their posts. Vammi suggested they send someone up for a better look, but Hettie argued against it. There was no need to announce themselves to the enemy just yet. The whole point of infiltrating was to catch them by surprise and crush them between the two forces.

The castle could be seen at the far end of the city. Using it as a guide, they made their way toward section one. The Steppers had exited the tunnels on a side street in section two, not far from the gate.

Guttural shouts and the sound of running feet gave way to the clash of blades as they drew near the fighting. Past a row of houses, they could make out the main road, where a horde of soldiers gathered around a portcullis. The clamor came from those in section two, yelling through the gate to where the battle raged in section one. Apparently, the Widows' Will had taken the outer gate and fought their way clear through section one already.

"We're not too late, but we certainly aren't early."

"They're making great progress," Deryl agreed. *"We're missing all the fun. Figure out how to get in there and join the fight."*

Hettie motioned to Vammi that she was checking something out. She retreated down a side alley until she was out of sight. There, she pulled out the whistle she kept around her neck next to Deryl's pouch and blew it. The sound was inaudible to the human ear, but she knew it carried far.

Less than a minute passed before a piercing cry was heard overhead. Hettie blew the whistle again, standing in the middle of the alley and waving her arms slowly in the air. Ouri came rocketing down from above to land on the ground before her. He let out a "grawp" in greeting as he hopped over to her, wings half spread.

"Hello, friend. We're in a tight spot, and I need your help. Could you fly Deryl up for another look around?" She held up the pouch.

Ouri promptly rapped it with his beak.

"Stop that," she chided. "I'll wait right here and take him off as soon as you come down, okay? It'll be quick. One lap. That's all. Just don't go chasing food. I don't have a lot of time."

Begrudgingly, the amber hawk nuzzled Hettie's arm then held out his foot.

"I knew I could count on you." She kissed him on the head and quickly tied Deryl's pouch to his leg.

His one quick pass over the castle confirmed everything Hettie needed to know. The bulk of the Widows' Will fought near the portcullis with the rest of the soldiers spread out as they tried to clear the city. They'd cleared a path along the main road, but the portcullis would stop them short if the Steppers couldn't get it open.

"No wonder they made it into the first section so quickly," Deryl remarked. *"The guards are pretty equally divided between the first two sections of the citadel, so we were only fighting half his forces. Bad move on Vincent's part. He should have put more men at the first section then had them pull back if they needed to."*

"Nobody ever accused him of being a tactical genius."

"For good reason," Deryl said.

"While you're up there, do you see any rocktoads?" She had no idea how she was supposed to find Pillar's child in the middle of a battle.

"You think I can find a single person in this chaos? What does it even matter? You'd have to find a way to get to them before they got skewered and then figure out how to keep them alive until the fighting is over."

"Just because it's hard doesn't mean it's not worth doing."

"Either way, I don't see any rocktoads."

Once Ouri returned, Hettie went back to Vammi. The Steppers hid in nearby houses while they waited for orders. Either the people who lived in them had evacuated to avoid the fight or they were at the portcullis to join it.

"We're doing better than expected," Hettie told him. She relayed what she'd learned. "What can you tell me about the portcullis?"

Vammi said, "I can tell you Vincent doesn't have an army. He has a pack of bloodthirsty wild men, each struggling to be the last one standing."

Hettie blinked. "That doesn't tell me anything about the gate."

"They've jammed it," he said simply. "They aren't just keeping our forces out, they've locked themselves in."

"Interesting choice. I think I can use it to our advantage."

"Good. If they catch us here, we're sitting ducks. We don't have enough men to clear section two by ourselves."

"Right," Hettie agreed. "The Widows' Will is winning for now. Thanks to whoever jammed the gate, Vincent's forces won't be getting reinforcements."

"So we wait until our side comes to us?"

A roar caught their attention. They peered between the houses to where the crowd cheered at the gate.

Something slammed into the portcullis and a bony arm reached through. Holes in ragged long sleeves revealed dirt-caked skin. Judging by the clothing, it was one of Vincent's people.

A woman in the cheering throng lunged forward to grab the arm and sink her teeth into it. More people surged forward, fighting over the arm still attached to whoever was on the other side. Frantic, keening screams rose above the din of the crowd.

Every society had rules, codes of conduct that put everyone on even footing. Hettie could plainly see there were no rules in this place. It shocked her to see the masses viciously devouring a living person. It was mindless brutality that defied sanity. A little voice in the back of her mind told her she shouldn't be so surprised. She'd seen the stew. *Who says they died first?* She shuddered, and her stomach heaved.

Had Vincent been the one to order the sections locked back when the madness began? Had the city been doomed before the Widows' Will even arrived?

When the crowd backed up, the arm was gone, pulled back through the bars, presumably.

Hettie was too far away to make out details from the crowd, but she imagined blood dripping from their chins.

"Did somebody ring the dinner bell?" Deryl asked. Even he sounded a little queasy. Hettie could feel his disgust. It mirrored her own.

Behind her, Vammi retched.

CHAPTER 27
NO MERCY

Adyr

Adyr's fever dream was relentless. Feelings of helplessness burned in his gut as his traitorous mind played the memory as if he were standing in Vincent's feasting hall, even knowing as he did that the ending to his dream would only bring more nightmares.

After Prowler was removed from the hall, Vincent ran a searching gaze over the lords from Poll's Wander.

Lord Lorez was first to speak. "You're a madman."

Vincent blinked, turning to look down the table at Lorez. "You think I'm crazy?"

"Absolutely. Those aren't men; they're beasts," Lorez said, doubling down.

Lorez wasn't in the right mindset for diplomatic discussions. Griff stepped in. "I'm afraid I don't understand your talk of ruling the world," he sidestepped. "Perhaps you should explain in greater detail."

"Of course." Vincent regained some of his enthusiasm. "Don't you see? With soldiers like these, we could conquer any nation."

Two more guards entered, taking the place of those escorting Prowler and his new prize head. They went to work removing Clencher's body while the servants came in with rags to clean up the blood. Fidgeter skulked back to the wall where the kid and the growling guy waited.

Growler continued huffing, glaring at anything that moved. The child was motionless as ever. Did he even blink?

"Conquer any nation? We're not at war," Rasmond said.

"Even if we were, I wouldn't want to go to war with these men at my back," Griff said to further shut down talk of conquest. "I can see they're fierce and dedicated, but they aren't reliable in a fight. They would turn on their own men. They're uncontrollable."

"I can see what you're saying," Vincent said, patting the air as if trying to pacify a spooked horse. "And I understand your worries. To tell the truth, I didn't accept this plan immediately either." His eyes flicked to where Cayon stood. It was quick but telling.

Adyr didn't have to guess who came up with the plan for world domination. He wondered what had changed Vincent's mind but found he wasn't interested in the answer. Whatever it was, the lords would never be comfortable turning men into whatever these fighters were.

"As I said, the effects of the Element are different for each man. Not all of them are so out of control. Here, let me demonstrate." Vincent motioned to Cayon, who waved the growling man and the kid forward.

The two stepped into the arena. Growler was enormous compared to the kid.

Adyr felt the blood drain from his face. The child would be crushed in a fight.

"Whatever you're about to show us, I don't want to see it," Griff said firmly.

Tuigasi spoke up for the second time that night. "Yeah, I think we've seen enough."

Vincent's eyes were wide with excitement. "No, no, you have it wrong. You wanted to see discipline. Watch."

"That is not what we said," Rasmond objected.

Vincent ignored him.

Griff's voice was tight when he said, "If that child dies in front of me, your death will follow."

A garbled chuckle was his only response. "Fight!" Vincent bellowed. "No mercy!"

All the lords stood up, ready to step in and defend the child from the hulking beast of a man.

The boy seemed heedless of the danger. He was scrawny for his height, but his cold, unsettling gaze seemed to take in everything but the growling killer ten times his size towering over him.

With two daggers sheathed at his waist, the boy was comically outmatched. Growler had a sword at his hip and several throwing daggers strapped to his chest. He had a longer reach, even without his sword, and far more mass.

The lords meant to rush around the table.

They meant to give aid.

They didn't make it.

Adyr didn't even have the excuse of a table in his way. He'd hardly taken a step before the fight was over.

At Vincent's command, the child darted forward, impossibly fast. He ran up Growler's leg and leaped straight up. With one grip on a head full of hair, the boy jackknifed over the man's shoulder and onto his back in the blink of an eye. The move was so confidently executed it took Adyr a moment to reconcile the fact that a child had performed it.

Enraged, Growler pulled his sword. His movements were fast, but nowhere near fast enough. He stabbed with skill and precision, but wherever his blades were, the kid wasn't.

The kid pulled his little daggers and made a rapid series of motions Adyr couldn't follow. He was on Growler's back, then on the floor, under his legs, circling around him, then back in front. He flowed like water and seemed to defy gravity.

Blood drained from the man's wrists and soaked his clothing. His pants were sliced through at the backs of his thighs. His legs quivered.

Growler toppled to his knees.

The kid leaped lightly onto his shoulders and bent to run a knife down the veins along each side of his throat. A river of blood flowed down the man's shirt. As Growler crashed face first onto the floor, the kid dismounted, sliding to a halt a few strides from the table.

Adyr had never seen anyone move so fluidly, like the dance of a master swordsman. Only the kid *was* the sword.

At that distance, he could just make out the thin smear of blood along the edges of the kid's daggers. Through it all, the child's expression had never changed.

A tingle went up Adyr's spine. The child wasn't human. He was death made animate.

Vincent beamed at the lords. "See? If you're looking for discipline, we've got that. All I need from you is a few of your best fighting men. Say a dozen from each of you. We'll provide the dosing and training, and we'll monitor their progress. Cayon is a genius when it comes to creating the perfect soldier."

Adyr didn't have to look at his companions to know how they felt. Appalled. Disgusted. Incensed. What abomination from the armpit of the Undergates had been created? The monster standing before them had been a child once, innocent and youthful, with parents and maybe siblings. He'd had a whole life before him. What had they done to him? Adyr's heart broke for that little boy and his shattered future, just as it quivered in fear at what he'd become.

"If it is the last thing I ever do in this life," Griff ground out, "I will put a stop to this butchery."

CHAPTER 28

TOO MANY HOLES

Hettie

Hettie fought to keep her stomach under control. Her head felt stuffed with wool, and it was all she could do to breathe evenly.

She and Vammi leaned back against the house they were hiding behind. Made of rough-cut stones and expertly assembled, the house was topped by a thatch roof. Most of the city's houses were the same. Its construction told Hettie these people hadn't always been barbaric. They'd been a thriving community once, full of close-knit neighbors. Somewhere along the way, Vincent changed that.

Another cheer went up from the crowd. "We can't just sit here, waiting for the fight to come to us."

"Agreed," Vammi said, wiping his mouth along his sleeve. The smell of his vomit blended with the other disgusting scents of the city. "But if we manage to open the gate, we'll end up doing more harm than good. They outnumber us. By a lot."

"That's why we need to make a new gate. One just for us."

177

Vammi gave her a dubious look. "How are we going to do that?"

"We're going to go through the wall." Hettie chewed her lip while she thought through the logistics.

Deryl said, *"The wall is thinner between city sections than it is along the outside. You could break through away from the main gate."*

"How thin are we talking?"

"Only a foot or two. When I went up with Ouri, I spotted a tree on the other side of the wall. The branches made it hard to tell for certain, but it looked like the wall thinned out there because the tree was in the way."

"Stay put," she told Vammi. She followed the wall away from the portcullis, scanning the top of the wall for trees. She found it three streets over.

"That's the one," Deryl confirmed.

It was a bell tree, taller than most she'd seen and half-tucked behind a house. Hettie reached out with her magic to investigate.

"You're right, the wall narrows here. They would have had to cut down the tree or move the house otherwise. The tree's growth has weakened the wall over time." Hettie considered her best course of action. She wasn't great at breaking stone.

"You really need to expand your skill set," Deryl remarked.

"I don't see you doing anything."

"Hey, I just told you where the tree was. I'm being super helpful."

"Criticism isn't helpful."

"That's rich, coming from you."

Hettie let the comment slide. *"What if I do that black light thing again?"*

"You're counting on people ignoring that a second time?"

Valid point. It wouldn't do much good to blast a hole through the wall if Vincent's men swarmed it from both sides.

She was a healer, not a hole-maker, though between the two rock-slides, the tunnel door, and the now the wall, she seemed to be making holes more often than she was healing injuries.

"For what it's worth," Deryl said, *"they'll need plenty of healing by the end of the day."*

Luckily, she had plenty of magic to spare. Exhaustion would take her before her magic ran out. The press of it pulsed inside her. It was almost painful to contain, and she was having trouble thinking. She wanted to let loose and take care of the wall in grand fashion, but they were trying to be discreet, though she couldn't for the life of her remember why.

She closed her eyes, thinking through the spells she knew. She couldn't lift the rocks because of the mortar gluing them together, and she couldn't push at it because the wall weighed far more than she did. Fortunately, the house was next to the wall, and both were made of stone.

Hettie formed a shield bubble between the wall and the house and expanded it until stone gave way. Unfortunately, the house was the weaker of the two. "Son of a milk toad," she said, frustrated.

"Don't get your britches in a wad. Find a little hole in the wall and do the same spell from within it."

"That's a good idea."

"See how useful I am?"

"Except the shield would have to be smaller than my pinkie and there's no way I can make one that size. It'll just pop," she explained.

"Are you kidding me?"

"How often do you think I've practiced shielding grains of sand? My shields protect entire people most of the time. I'm not all that good at making them even when they're the preferred size."

"As sorcerers go, you're not very impressive."

The press of the magic swelled. She took a deep breath and tried to think peaceful, non-magical thoughts.

The sand beneath her toes on a warm, windy evening.

The gentle lap of the ocean as the sun sets in brilliant shades of orange and purple.

Elkin's special smile he seemed to save just for—

Her breathing hitched like she'd been kicked. *Don't think about Elkin. Don't think about Elkin. Don't think about Elkin.*

She cleared her mind and tried again, frantically searching for any part of her life that didn't include him. She thought of potions, brewing for hours, gathering supplies.

Elkin had been the only person to encourage her to make potions. Her mother had hated him for that.

"Hettie?" Deryl sounded worried. *"Hello? Witch lady. Ye of much magic. Are we taking care of this wall or what?"*

His interruption made her brain stutter. What had she been thinking about? Oh, potions. Maybe after they defeated Lord Vincent she'd shop for supplies.

"If we defeat Lord Vincent," Deryl said. *"That's looking less and less likely the longer you stand here like a hoop gull choking on a Salt-Blood turd."*

The imagery in his comment almost distracted her from the magic that pressed on her like she'd had a triple helping of cliff pig stew.

"Don't think of stew," Deryl said. *"It rhymes with spew, which is what the stew here will most certainly make you do."*

"Stew," she said aloud. "That's it."

"No, I said don't *think of stew. You're not listening."*

"You're right. I'm not, but that's beside the point. When I was young, Old Petey hired a cook. Stew was the only thing she knew how to make, but for some reason, her carrots were always hard."

"Did you notice I rhymed a minute ago?" he interrupted.

"Pay attention. I used to soften the carrots with a spell where I kind of massaged it from the inside. I haven't used it on carrots in ages, but I've done it a few times to pirates who came to the island with old scar tissue."

"What on earth does defeating Vincent have to do with carrots and scar tissue?"

"Not Vincent. The wall. It's a lot bigger than a scar, but it just might work."

"You've officially lost me."

Hettie stepped back, closed her eyes, and muttered the words under her breath. She moved her hands, capturing a portion of the wall the size of a doorway in her mind. Her fingers bent into claws as she squeezed the rock with her magic the way she did with the carrots and scars to break up their rigid internal structure. The rocks were much firmer than what she was used to, but thanks to her excess magic, she easily upscaled the pressure.

A grinding sound told her it was working. She felt the wall crumble into chunks. Satisfied, she released her power.

Or tried to.

Her magic bucked, straining to get out through the opening she'd given it. The effort to wrestle it into submission left her panting.

Once she had it firmly under control, she opened her eyes to see the rock had been reduced to dust. Not only that, but on each side of the new doorway, the dust had formed into four cylindrical cones, the points higher than Hettie's head.

Curious, she poked the nearest one with a finger. The stone dust was cold and gave way easily. She withdrew her finger, leaving behind a perfect round hole.

"Maybe not the best time for artistic pursuits," Deryl said. His emotions didn't feel nearly as flippant as he sounded. He was worried.

Hettie frowned. *"That wasn't my intent."* Beyond the wall lay a dirty street lined with rotten hovels. Clearly section one had been the first to decay under Vincent's rule. Maybe he'd locked the section gates to keep out the riffraff.

"I did manage to make a passageway in a secluded place without alerting anyone."

"That's true. I guess you have a point."

She chuckled, eying the four cones. *"I have four of them."*

"Maybe you should leave the jokes to me. That one was bad even by my standards."

"No more jokes from you. I don't have an ocean to throw you in, but there's a convenient cliff nearby." They both knew it was an empty threat. She'd nearly come undone the one time she'd thought she'd lost him.

Not the least bit dissuaded, he said, *"Think of all the jokes I could come up with down there. I'd be happy to tell you them in the middle of the night. Every night. Forever."*

Grumbling, Hettie made her way back to Vammi. She pointed out the entrance to Steppers as she passed.

Vammi was right where she'd left him. He spotted her and smiled.

With his attention on her, he didn't see the man come out from behind the house next to him. Two heads taller than the average Pavinn, the giant lofted a large meat hook. Enormous shoulders covered in brown fur seemed to dwarf his petite waist. Muscles bunched as he swung the hook like an experienced butcher, catching Vammi square in the gut, the impact lifting the captain to his toes.

Between one heartbeat and the next, Hettie's world stopped.

Not again.

She stood there stupidly, frozen for a single moment in time that lasted an eternity.

The man's orange eyes shifted, landing on Hettie. He sniffed the air, his lips rising to accentuate two bottom teeth that stuck up, reaching to just below his wide, flat nose.

When next she dreamed, that face would be featured in her nightmares.

She barely registered what happened next. Everything seemed to blur, moving with a dreamlike quality.

The man released the hook. Vammi fell with a thud and a groan, his hands clawing weakly at it.

A shout came from inside a nearby house and a Stepper came out. The horror on his face was a perfect picture of how Hettie felt inside.

Steppers flooded from the surrounding houses, pressing forward, unsure of what to do. Nobody could survive a wound like that.

Already, Vammi's eyes were glazing over, his vision distant and unresponsive. He would be dead in moments. Hettie would lose another person she cared about. She had so few.

Rage took hold of her, turning the world red like arterial blood. Deryl said something, but she couldn't make out the words past the roaring in her head.

Her magic swelled. This time, she didn't try to stop it.

A piercing crack filled the air and the stone beneath her feet shuddered.

CHAPTER 29

LOTS OF DEATH

Hettie

The butcher looked around, spooked. When his gaze landed on Hettie, his eyes widened, and his jaw went slack. He turned and ran, arms flailing in panic.

Hettie frequently made her eyes swirl like whirlpools to scare stupid people into submission. She had no idea what her face looked like now.

She was no longer in control. A distant bystander in her own body, she only dimly felt the magic pulsing through her, escaping in rhythmic bursts like the heartbeat of the universe.

She reached out with a thought and found the fleeing brute. She tried to stop his heart. She meant to crush it. Instead, it exploded, taking most of his torso with it.

The air around her grew still, a stark contrast to the growing howl of wind that echoed down the streets and through the houses, a tempest that shook the city.

Slowly, the crowd at the portcullis became aware of something not quite right in their world.

They stopped their cheering to look around in confusion.

The moan of the wind grew until it smothered the sounds of battle in section one. All the while, the air around Hettie remained still as death.

She drifted forward like a mist on a moonlit sea. Some part of her struggled, trying to wrest control of the magic. She lost ground with every pulse until she forgot why she struggled at all.

Deryl repeatedly called her from the distant mists of her mind. She couldn't focus on the words. The magic was too strong, an impenetrable shield keeping her from engaging. It felt alive.

A groan sounded at her feet where Vammi lay dying. Had she walked to him? She didn't remember moving. Her thoughts were evasive, like wet eels.

"Heal him!" Deryl shouted through the fog in her brain.

The magic agreed. She was a healer. What better use for it was there?

Reaching out with her power, she healed the wound, forcing blood back into their vessels, repairing displaced bits of muscle and flesh, all while forcing the hook further out of Vammi's body. It went far faster than usual. Faster than it should have. In a split second, the wound was closed, and the hook tumbled to the ground with a dull clatter.

Vammi was left panting and exhausted from the force of it.

Dimly, she noted his skin, pale and clammy, eyes glassy with shock.

The magic wanted more. More what? She wasn't sure, but she burned with the need of it.

"Stop!" Deryl shouted. *"You have to fight it!"*

Barely audible. Distant. Easy to ignore.

She stepped over Vammi, following the pull of the magic. The Widows' Will was in section one. This side was all Vincent's people, the monsters who ate human flesh, the cannibals and murderers, the crazed beast men.

Here, she could release her magic without fear of hurting the wrong people. She didn't know if her thoughts belonged to the magic or herself. And she didn't care. The portcullis wasn't far. She made her way closer.

Two men rushed her from the road, weapons held high. They knew she wasn't one of them. She suspected her eyes gave her away.

The first man had a flat, pig-like nose and a crooked horn jutting over his right eye. The other was missing a chin. His bottom teeth were angled so that his jaw cut sharply down to his throat. Both carried shovels that did them no good.

Hettie opened the pig-man's throat and froze the heart of the chin-less man in a block of ice.

Briefly, she wondered where she learned to freeze hearts.

She continued forward, every step resulting in the death of a dozen people. Hearts, arteries, tracheas, bones, they all came apart so easily. Human bodies were terribly fragile. And healing was so close to killing, two sides of the same coin really.

"Hettie, stop! You're killing yourself! You're killing me!*"*

The words took too long to register. By then, another three dozen people were dead. *"Deryl."*

His voice was desperate when it came. *"Yes. You have to stop! For me!"*

She cared about Deryl. Didn't she? Somewhere in the depths of her mind, she thought so. She tried to remember why.

The magic pushed at her, demanding to be used. It was so hard to think.

All the while, she kept killing. It was so easy.

"Don't send me back to the Murks! Please!"

His wail set off a reaction in her brain. Like the ghost of a butterfly she needed to catch. She paused to chase it through the windswept passages of her mind.

The magic tried to pull her back. There was so much more killing to do. Healing too, it whispered. With such power, she could probably heal death itself.

Elkin. She could heal Elkin.

She followed the magic, entranced, but she knew something was wrong. Something to do with the bodies falling all around her. Or was it the screaming? People fled, hiding anywhere they could to get away from her.

Slice, snap, wrench and three people collapsed.

It was too easy. She needed to make the killing more complicated. Instead of slicing vital organs, she tried stopping their lungs. That, in turn, stopped their heart, but it took longer. Much, much longer.

The magic fought her. It didn't want slow deaths.

Almost by reflex, she fought back. The last time someone took control of her magic, Elkin had died. Deryl had been close.

She dug a hole under someone's feet, moving bits of rock one particle at a time until the hole was big enough to bury him in. The man had hair that grew from his ears clear down to his shoulders. In he went, frothing at the mouth as he screamed obscenities.

"That's right, Hettie. Fight it. Keep going." Deryl's voice was urgent, but he no longer yelled. He was closer. She could almost feel him.

Two more people died before she could form coherent thoughts. Awareness flooded her mind. She was in Vincent's citadel, fighting to stop his atrocities, to vanquish his abominations.

She blinked. All around her, men and women lay by the dozens, dead to the last man. The living cowered behind houses, hooting and growling as they stared at her in fear and loathing. Their heartbeats called to her, a siren song.

No. This is wrong.

As terrible as Vincent's people had become, she was the monster to them.

Vammi staggered out from behind a house, pausing at the destruction she'd wrought.

He would see that the true abomination was her.

"Deryl?" Hettie was suddenly terrified he wouldn't answer. *"Are you okay?"*

"Yarp. For the most part."

The flash of annoyance helped stave off the magic's grip on her mind.

"You've got to keep better control though." His voice trembled. *"That was close."*

She stared in horrified fascination at what she'd done. Not that she'd killed—she'd done that in Poll's Wander, but never with a lack of awareness, void of conscience. This was something else, something inhuman.

She turned back to Vammi, nearly a hundred bodies between them. He looked stunned. She waited for his condemnation.

He threw his hands in the air and let them fall limp at his sides. "What the hell did we bring an army for?" He shook his head, then skirted the street alongside the bodies before picking his way across the shortest path to her. Nudging aside a heart with his boot, then bypassing a pile of intestines, he found his footing and stepped over one last body to reach her side.

Hettie was dumbstruck. What did one say after unwittingly murdering scores of people, even if they were the enemy? At least— she gladly noted—there were no children among the corpses.

"You want to finish up here?" he asked. "I could go for a beer."

She barked out a laugh, though it bordered on hysteria.

"Him and me both," Deryl said. *"If only I could drink."*

CHAPTER 30

KOTA'IMOGA

Hettie

A nervous shriek caught Hettie's attention. Ouri circling overhead, no doubt worried over her strange behavior. She lifted a hand to signal she was okay, though she wasn't at all sure that she was.

The wind had faded with her magic, and Vincent's men were growing restless. They inched from their hiding places.

"We should get out of here," Hettie said. They needed to get to the Widows' Will, but leading Vincent's men through the wall would hurt more than it helped. She grabbed Vammi's wrist and took off, leaping over the nearest corpse.

The cowering madmen took heart at their retreat. They swarmed from side streets to give chase.

"Danger." Deryl gave a resigned sigh. *"What a surprise."*

They hadn't yet cleared the last of the corpses when they heard a thunderous clacking, approaching fast.

Vammi slowed, his head swiveling toward the sound, but Hettie pulled him along. Whatever was coming, she didn't want to be in the open when it arrived. Several Steppers kept pace from a block away. Vammi must have told them to stay out of sight. The residents outnumbered them ten to one. Probably more.

Hettie and Vammi had almost disappeared down a side street when a voice called, "Skalina! Skalina!"

Hettie stumbled to a stop. She turned to face the chitton. It stood tall, legs extended as if it could see over the rooftops. It was the first time she'd seen it in daylight, and she realized how disturbing its skittery movements were.

Luckily, the chitton was a strange enough sight to keep Vincent's men back.

Ambling in a circle, the chitton spotted Hettie and scurried over, moving far faster than anything that large had a right to move. "Give wife," it demanded.

She held out her hands. "I haven't found her."

The chitton took one long leg and waved it around. "Bird. Give wife."

It took Hettie a moment to figure out it was pointing at the sky, shakily following Ouri's flight path.

As if in response, Ouri let out another cry.

"Crap," she said in realization. She'd told the chitton she'd have Ouri call out when she'd found its wife. Just her luck, it had been close enough to hear him.

"You better do something before it gets mad," Deryl suggested.

"I don't have its wife. What do I tell it?"

He gave an impatient huff. *"Do I look like a chitton expert?"*

"You look like an eyeball in a sack," she muttered before addressing the chitton. "I'm still looking for your wife."

"Where wife?" it asked.

She shrugged. She wasn't even sure what the wife looked like. "If she's here, she could be anywhere. Would she fit in a house?"

The chitton swiveled to face the nearest house. "Skalina?"

Vammi elbowed Hettie and jerked his head in the direction of the back alleys, urging her to escape with him. The Steppers waited a few dozen feet away, watching from side streets, ready to jump in if needed.

"Skalina?" When no reply came, the chitton reached out a leg and stabbed it through a thick wooden door as if it were made of parchment. It ripped the door free from the frame and sent it flying with a casual swipe. "Skalina?"

"Does it think she's hiding?" Hettie wondered.

"If that thing was looking for you, you'd be hiding too."

The chitton pressed forward, its bulky body crushing the front of the house in as it took a closer look. Satisfied Skalina wasn't inside, it turned and crossed the street to another house, crushing it just as easily.

The citizens grumbled and hissed from the sidelines. The chitton ignored them, moving from one house to the next.

"Maybe he can find Pillar's kid for us," Deryl suggested.

"That doesn't sound like your best idea."

A man rushed it, slamming a pickaxe into its leg. The flat blade ricocheted, lodging the pointy end in the attacker's forehead.

This seemed to anger the crowd. More men came forward, hoisting weapons ranging from garden tools to long wooden sticks. One man used half a barrel lid as an unwieldy bludgeon.

They came forward by the dozens to attack the chitton, who didn't seem to notice them in the slightest. It had no problem crushing the humans beneath its pointed, spidery legs.

"You're right. He'd get the kid killed for sure."

Vammi nudged Hettie again. This time, she followed.

With the mob distracted, they made it to the hole in the wall without being pursued. Hettie crossed through at a jog with Vammi on her heels. The smell particular to Vincent's men was even stronger in the first section.

"Well, that was close." The relief in Deryl's voice was audible.

"I don't think any of them followed us."

The majority of the Steppers were already waiting for them, lined up in front of the hovels. Hettie's killing spree had only taken a few minutes, and she was glad these men had missed it.

"I was talking about the kota'imoga," Deryl said.

"The what?"

The remaining Steppers followed Vammi through the hole. The run had put color back in his cheeks, though he was breathing hard. She hoped her aggressive healing hadn't caused unintended problems. If it had, they wouldn't be physical. His wounds were more expertly healed than anything she'd done before, though she was a little fuzzy on how she'd managed it.

Vammi strode to the front of his contingent. The blood-soaked front of his uniform—where the meat hook had been—earned him worried looks from his soldiers.

"Kota'imoga. Magic suck. It's complicated. The quick version is Cerissa took on an apprentice who got it. Geep didn't last long."

"Geep?" It was like he was speaking a foreign language. Had the magic scrambled her brain?

"Before you ask, that wasn't her real name, it's just what people called her."

"Her?" What did a woman do to earn such an odd nickname?

"What are you, a parrot? Stop interrupting. Geep learned a few spells and got a big head and at one point, ended up stealing the power of another sorcerer, similar to what you did with your sisters but messier. And deadly. Anyway it created some sort of magic whirlpool inside her. She went nuts and wiped out an entire village. Cerissa tried to help her control it, but she was too far gone. She ended up attacking Cerissa, who lost her patience right about then. That's when things got really bad."

Vammi barked out orders to his men, and they headed out at a jog straight for the portcullis.

Hopefully the chitton in section two would keep the crowd's attention so they wouldn't notice there were new troops in section one.

"The magic suck—kooty-whatever—is the whirlpool thing," Hettie said, trying to follow his explanation.

"Yes. Kota'imoga."

"Why am I just now hearing about this?"

"Geep took all the magic the sorcerer had available, then kept pulling from his magic source until he kind of melted from the inside. I was hoping it wouldn't do the same thing to you since you didn't kill your sisters."

"You thought a warning would be worse than ignorance?"

"I was keeping an eye on you."

Hettie jogged behind Vammi and his men. *"How'd that turn out?"*

"Okay, so maybe I should have said something. I figured you'd use a bunch of your magic in battle and be fine. It's what you kept telling yourself."

"That's before I knew there was a magical whirlpool that could take over my body and mind." For the first time in her life, her magic truly frightened her.

"For what it's worth, I helped you stop before you went too far."

"By 'too far' you mean more than a hundred bodies," she said dryly. *"How common is this magic suck?"* She suddenly saw why The Temple of the Sky had dedicated their entire organization to taking down sorcerers. She wasn't sure exactly how much destruction she could wreak if she put her mind to it, but it was a lot. She knew that much.

The magic still pressed on her. She hadn't expended much killing all those people.

"Not common. I've only ever seen it the once."

Three blocks from the main roadway, Hettie could see the fighting ahead. She spotted a serviceable sword forgotten on the side of the road and snatched it up. Until she figured out how to keep her magic in check, she'd have to fight the old-fashioned way. *"Is it curable? Or controllable?"*

"I assume so. Cerissa was ruthless. She'd have killed Geep from the start if she was a lost cause. The fact that she made the effort to get Geep to stop means more than you know."

Hettie nodded as she jogged along. *"Okay, so what did she tell Geep to do?"*

Deryl sighed. *"This is where I get less useful."*

"So on a sliding scale, we're talking negative numbers?"

He ignored the barb. *"Geep was busy laying waste to entire streets of people at the time, but Cerissa kept yelling for her to bubble the magic. Create a shield around it."*

Hettie blinked. *"A shield is a physical construct. Magic is intangible. Besides that, it's inside me. I can't . . ."* she trailed off.

After taking the stolen magic from her sisters, Hettie had decided they couldn't be trusted with that kind of power. She'd sealed up the place inside them where their magic regenerated. She'd essentially blocked it.

With a shield.

"Wait. Won't that just block off my own magic?" Hettie asked.

"Ehhh," Deryl said, sounding unsure. *"Maybe?"*

"Definitely negative numbers," she muttered aloud.

The street opened into a large space that looked like an ideal place to hold a market. With everyone in the city eating people stew, Hettie doubted they'd held a market in a long time.

The Widows' Will were stretched out over several blocks along the main thoroughfare. Despite having superior numbers, they were struggling. Vincent's people pressed in from both sides, bloodthirsty and wild.

A citizen battled a woman from the Widows' Will. Vammi stabbed him in the back. The Steppers spread out, eager to help turn the tables on Vincent's men.

Dirty, bestial people in rags fell upon the dead and dying, eagerly tearing into their flesh. They were mad with hunger and determined to fill their bellies, no matter the cost. One man had only a fresh stump left where his arm had been severed at the elbow. Blood flowed down his side, but he never paused his chewing.

Hettie's stomach turned. It wasn't just hunger making them mad.

A man in rags rushed her, pitchfork in hand. Hettie almost stopped him with magic. But at the last second, she held back. Instead, she hefted her sword, kicked the pitchfork aside, and stabbed him in the neck.

Without magic, it was going to be a long battle.

CHAPTER 31

HAVE A BREAD ROLL

Adyr

The tension in Adyr's body coiled tight as the dream reached its inevitable conclusion. He wanted to wake up, but his mind seemed devoid of any semblance of self-preservation, replaying the final scene in vivid detail.

Lord Guimont shook his head in disgust. "These experiments are an abomination. How can you stand yourself?"

Rasmond let out a huff that sounded like a half-sob, half-laugh. "You thought we would give you men? Are you kidding? So you could turn them into this?" He gestured at the boy standing before them, impassive and silent as death.

Vincent frowned at Cayon. "You may have been right. They're looking at it all wrong." He turned back to the lords. His tone was patronizing, as if he were talking to children. "I didn't see the whole of it at first either. You have to remember that soldiers die in battle. It's expected. Nobody fights a war without losing a few lives. Only the lucky survive. But with soldiers like this, the war would practically be over before it was started. Think of the lives this would save."

"There is no war," Tuigasi reminded him.

"Not yet," Vincent said, holding up a finger as if to make his point. "How long will that last? One has only to look at the history of Andos to know warfare is inevitable. There's no way it *won't* happen."

Griff cautioned, "There is a difference between defense against enemies and becoming one yourself."

Vincent sighed. "Forget about ancient history," he said, focusing on Griff. "Look at the wars in our lifetime. Sedrios helped overthrow the entire Darrish empire. There have been swathes of dead at every border. Egren, Verran, Stonewood, Arlea. Every neighbor has been entrenched in warfare within the past few decades. Even the Yellow Sea is full of warring tribes. It's folly to even entertain the notion that we're safe simply because there's a reprieve. This is the only time we have to prepare for the next onslaught."

He turned to the rest of the lords. "War is a sure thing. You know it, and I know it. Think of the peace we could create with soldiers like this," he implored. "Creatures of incredible power capable of defeating any army. Nobody would dare stand against us. There would be no war. We would have one world. One army. One ruler."

The warning bells in Adyr's head had been steadily building since they'd arrived in the feasting hall. He wanted to be on the trail home, leaving this godawful place behind. It wouldn't take much to convince the lords to order Bannot to saddle the horses.

"Let me guess," Rasmond said. "You would be the ruler."

Vincent opened and closed his mouth a few times, looking flustered, as if he hadn't considered how to answer that. "Well, I didn't mean one person. Think of it less like one ruler and more like one *rule*. All of us can agree on what we want the new world to be like, and we'd each do our part to ensure that outcome."

"How could we agree on anything when we already disagree on a fundamental level about *this*," Lorez said, gesturing at the disturbing child.

"Again, think of the lives it would save in the long run," Vincent said chidingly. "Between the desert and the marshlands, we have a naturally fortified corner of the world to grow our army. By the time anyone on the outside knows what's going on, we'll be too powerful to stop. Not even magic could thwart us. The Temple of the Sky has seen to it that sorcerers don't interfere on behalf of nations, so we're doubly safe."

"Oh I don't know," Lorez said. "They might just come out of hiding for this."

Cayon turned away from the feasting table, and Adyr caught sight of the look on his face. Predatory anticipation was the best way to describe it.

"We won't help you," Griff said plainly.

Rasmond said, "Never."

Guimont said, "Ever."

"Agreed," Tuigasi threw in for good measure.

Vincent finally seemed to register their determined looks. He shook his head. "I expected more from you."

Cayon spoke to the lords for the first time that night. His voice was surprisingly formal considering his hooded mystique. "Your short-sighted morality does the world no favors. We'll take the entire valley by force." He nodded to the kid. "Kill them."

The child leaped atop the feasting table like a marshie bursting from the ground. Little daggers flashed in his hands as he moved faster than a whipfish. Tuigasi was first to fall. Blood gushed from a wound at his throat. He hadn't even hit the ground before the next lord followed.

Lorez managed to fling his hands up, only to have both wrists slit deeply with one swipe of the child's blade. His other blade dove into the back of Guimont's chubby neck. From his abrupt collapse, Adyr suspected the blade severed his spine.

Rasmond stepped onto his chair, gaining a height advantage as the child advanced, but the child simply slashed at his inner thigh. Cursing, Rasmond stumbled off the chair and ended up with a dagger buried to the hilt under his jaw.

In the span of a single breath, four lords had been dispatched.

Adyr was already in motion, though he held no illusions about the four dead men. He could have been standing atop their table, and he'd still have been no use to them. They had died too quickly.

The child stood before Griff for three heartbeats, neither moving. Unfortunately, the lord was unarmed. They all were. They stood no chance against the demon child.

Adyr yelled, an attempt at distraction. The child paid him no heed, throwing his one remaining dagger from an arm's length away. It lodged in Griff's throat.

Adyr had only gone a half dozen strides. He ran on.

If he could not save his lords, he would avenge them.

In an act of stubborn defiance, Griff grabbed hold of the dagger and yanked it from his throat. He turned and threw it at Vincent with practiced accuracy.

Griff had regularly sparred with his soldiers. Sword fighting. Hand-to-hand combat. Knife throwing. He enjoyed it. He was good at it.

His skills meant nothing in the end.

His final knife throw landed directly in Vincent's chest, right where his heart would be. The blade should have killed him.

The child registered the attack before anyone else. He'd smoothly kicked a bread roll up from the table with one toe and flicked it straight into the blade's path.

Green paste oozed out from around the blade in Vincent's chest, mingling with blood.

Frantic, Vincent pulled out the dagger and laid a hand over the wound. Judging by the amount of bread roll smashed into the dagger's crosspiece, the four-inch round roll had been compressed to block over an inch of blade. The remaining bloodstained metal had likely gotten past the ribs, but it wasn't enough to reach the heart.

Adyr had never been so proud of his liege or so disappointed in an outcome. He wasn't sure if Lord Holden registered his failure before he collapsed.

Adyr hoped not.

CHAPTER 32

KILLING BLOWS

Hettie

Hettie fell into a rhythm of swipe, dodge, parry, thrust.

At some point, she ended up near Jonathan. They fought side-by-side. He had improved since their first battle together atop Penelope's walls. He'd grown more aware of his surroundings.

He didn't ask why she was using a sword instead of her magic. They just fought. And fought. And fought.

The Steppers renewed the army's vigor, allowing those who had been fighting since dawn to take a moment to catch their breath. When they'd killed off the last of the true fighters, Vammi pulled aside his Steppers and sent them to recruit others of the Widows' Will to chase down the mad citizens lying in wait for an opportunity to strike.

The city's first-section residents hid in the shadows of houses, only to pounce on soldiers once their backs were turned, trying to sink their teeth into a neck or an arm. Hettie found a man leaned against a house. A sword had sliced through his head. An ear and part of his skull were missing. Someone's severed arm lay in his lap. He ate it lethargically, unaware of the battle raging around him. His glazed eyes didn't register Hettie's approach.

Killing blows only. She removed his head.

The people were crazed, with an insatiable desire to kill. Fighting men or dying men, it made no difference. They attacked their fellow residents as often as they attacked the invading soldiers.

The sun was high overhead by the time they rooted out the last of the madmen from the distant corners of section one. They had hoped to rescue people. Instead, their morning was full of mercy killings.

"So much for benevolence," Deryl said.

Hettie was exhausted, her arms like jelly, though she knew the fighting wasn't done. What she'd seen of the people disgusted her. *"How do you corrupt an entire city like this?"*

"Brain melting parasite?"

"Let's hope not."

Three hundred soldiers guarded the jammed portcullis, ready to stem the tide from the second section if it opened. Servio was left in charge of them while the rest of the Widows' Will regrouped.

Soldiers trickled into the open market space, Vammi among them, his brilliant green uniform soaked in blood, more than just at the midriff. He came to stand by Jonathan and Hettie. "Today will not inspire bards to glorious songs of adventure," he remarked.

"A dirge, maybe," Hettie said. She'd forgotten how exhausting battle was. She was bone-weary, and they'd only taken the first section.

Jonathan gave Vammi a flat look. "You stayed out of the fighting because it wasn't glorious enough for you?"

Vammi's brow wrinkled in confusion. "I was fighting."

"No, Hettie was fighting. Alongside me. You were wandering around chopping off the heads of dead men," Jonathan countered.

Deryl sighed. *"Here we go again. What is it with these two? They're like an old married couple."*

Hettie discreetly delved Vammi, hoping her abrupt healing earlier hadn't caused issues she was unaware of. The tissue in the area was mildly swollen, but nothing that should cause him more than minor discomfort. Absently, she healed the scrapes and minor cuts he'd received in the fighting.

"They weren't all dead," Vammi said. "I was making sure they didn't get up and stab someone in the back. It's not something I usually have to deal with. But as you've said before, don't turn your back on them unless you're sure they're dead."

"You're a captain. You should be leading from the front. Besides, your men should be trained to deliver killing blows by now," Jonathan said.

"In the heat of battle, you don't always have the luxury of double-checking the wounded without getting skewered." Vammi's volume rose.

Jonathan's volume matched his. "Then assign one of your least proficient fighters to make sure the dead stay dead."

"All of my men are proficient fighters."

"Your actions would dictate otherwise."

While her nose had shut down in self-defense, Hettie's head pounded and the magic pounded with it.

She moved away from the bickering duo, skirted the men at the portcullis, and followed the wall to the right until she reached the makeshift entryway.

It would be best if she stayed on the other side, away from the Steppers and the Widows' Will. If the magic took over again, she'd end up killing her own soldiers.

Only in hindsight did she consider telling someone about what happened. Vammi had seen the aftermath. Had he seen her loss of control, or had he been recovering from his ordeal at the time?

The strange pillars of stone dust stood like sentinels guarding the hole. Hettie skulked down the streets, looking for a house with an easily accessible rooftop.

A few streets in, she found one with a barrel outside. She climbed up. *"I need to figure out how to control this magic, or it's going to destroy us all."*

"Be careful. I'd rather not be stuck in the mind of an unhinged sorcerer."

"Absolutely," she said, deadpan. *"If I went nuts and killed thousands of allies, I'd feel really terrible for you."*

"You should. Deranged killers do not make good company. And that's the best-case scenario. The kota'imoga would only kill you. I'd be stuck with shadow beasts for company until the next sorcerer dumb enough to bind themselves to me came along."

The barrel smelled like a moldy chamber pot. Hettie clambered onto the thatch roof, careful to test each step before putting her weight on it. She was one block from the main street with a row of houses between her and the crowd. An empty corral directly in front of her created a gap with a clear view of the people. They migrated past her view with twitchy, feral movements.

Hettie lay on her stomach near one side of the roof where the support beam underneath the thatch felt sturdy. *"You mentioned shielding. Should I give that a try?"*

Deryl gave a mental shrug. *"It's as good a place to start as any."*

Closing her eyes, she focused on the source of the magic deep within her and bubbled it off.

The pressure of the magic was immediately and drastically reduced. Slowly, her shoulders relaxed. *"That was easier than expected. I should have tried that weeks ago."* Walling it off had transferred the pressure to the shield.

"I just thought of something," Deryl said. *"Remember when your sister put a shield around a rock, then built up pressure inside so it would explode when she dropped the shield?"*

Hettie ground her teeth. *"You couldn't have remembered that thirty seconds ago?"*

"I could have remembered it three days from now. Be glad it was sooner rather than later."

He was right. Not that she was going to admit it. *"I don't expect to keep the magic bottled up forever. This isn't a long-term plan. What now?"*

"Don't look at me. Geep died before she got to this point. The upside is you're still alive to figure it out."

"Lucky me." Steeling her will, Hettie focused on the problem. She needed a way to let the magic out, but only a little at a time. She

needed a door she could open and close without having the shield bubble burst.

A crowd of men walked down the main street. She heard them before she saw them, their cadenced bootsteps a steady staccato.

A third of the city's citizens were barefoot. Another third were in makeshift sandals. Only a few wore full shoes and even those weren't very sturdy.

Hettie could tell by the sound that these men were better off than most of the citizens. When they came into view, she wasn't surprised to see they were armed better too.

A half dozen of Vincent's soldiers crossed in front of the corral where Hettie could see them clearly. They had proper swords and pikes, leather armor, and military boots. Expressions blanks, they paid no heed to the residents scurrying out of their way.

"Perfect target." Hettie opened a hole in the bubble of her magic. Either the pressure had built in the short time since she'd walled it off or the hole focused the magic and made it more powerful than normal. With no time to fine-tune her aim, her magic came out as an uncontrolled shot of pure energy. It blasted between two of the soldiers, sending them both flying with such force that their bodies punched holes in a house across the street.

Surprisingly, the remaining men didn't take notice. They kept walking as if nothing had happened.

Hettie let loose another burst and managed to direct it, blasting a wobbly line at the row of soldiers. They went flying into people, carts, and houses.

The first two soldiers climbed free of their holes instead of using the door. Blistered flesh showed through steaming armor.

"This is harder than it looks."

"Killing blows only," Deryl reminded her.

"I know, I know. I'm not used to fighting with wild magic." She had always had to force her magic to do what she wanted. It was a beneficial style for a healer, but not for a fighter.

She focused on one soldier's neck, opened the hole in her shield, and let the magic loose hoping the force would crack his spine.

Instead, it beheaded him, plus a little more. The shot struck just below the armpits, cutting clean through his body and gouging a line through the house behind him.

His arms dropped straight down, landing with a flop. The head and shoulders toppled slowly backward. The torso on legs was the last thing to fall.

"Your aim is terrible."

She growled. *"Remember when I said your criticism wasn't helpful?"*

Motion to her left caught her eye as someone snuck down the alley beside her. Leaning over as quietly as she could on the thatch roof, she glanced down to see a mop of brown hair in familiar clothing. It was the blue-eyed Andosh, Tinto.

Hettie scowled. *"What's he doing here?"*

"Did he follow you through the wall?"

Hettie scanned the streets behind her to see the Widows' Will two blocks back, stealthily spreading out. *"He should be with the others, not skulking around up here."*

Tinto prowled forward, oblivious to Hettie's presence overhead. He made it to the front of the house and looked both ways.

"Idiot," Hettie said. *"How close does he need to get? He's going to be spotted and alert the people that we're here."*

"We already determined stealth isn't his strong suit."

CHAPTER 33

VICTIMS, EVERY LAST ONE

Hettie

Hettie's last blast had killed one soldier, but it had alerted the rest to her location. They headed her way, spotting Tinto in the alleyway.

Tinto turned to run but stopped short. A child stood in his way, blocking the mouth of the alley.

Hettie could tell immediately the child was abnormal. Unsettling in his stillness, his posture was somehow both rigid and relaxed. From overhead, Hettie could only make out short black hair that framed his face.

Tinto must have noticed something was off. Even with enemies closing in on him, he seemed rooted to the spot.

"Fool man." Seething, Hettie focused on the soldiers working their way over to him. Her aim was true this time, and she took them all out with a swipe of magic across the neck that left five heads in the corral and five bodies on the narrow walking path next to it.

"Good thing they were all the same height. Your aim is getting better."

Hettie turned her attention back to Tinto, who stood sideways, trying to watch both ends of the alley at once. The strange child had disappeared.

The more Hettie thought about it, the stranger the child seemed. *"How many children have you seen in this city?"* she asked Deryl.

"None. They must have all ended up in stew pots."

Hettie's stomach churned. Had they really eaten every child in the city but one? How had he survived? *"Did the one here a minute ago make your skin crawl?"*

"I don't have skin, but yes, he was definitely unsettling."

She shifted her weight, and the motion drew Tinto's attention. His gaze traveled up the house. He flinched when he spotted her there not five feet away. She jerked her head hard in the direction of the Widows' Will.

Tinto took the hint and headed off at a dead sprint.

"I'm waiting for him to trip and fall on his face."

"He's headed the right direction. If he trips, he's not likely to get the wrong people's attention."

"He has my attention. I'm the wrong people."

A ruckus drew her attention to the soldiers she'd killed. Commoners robbed the dead of their weapons. Some fought each other over them, an endeavor that ended in three more people dead.

Hettie shook her head. *"At least they're not eating each other."*

Deryl chuckled. *"Remember when Vincent's men took Penelope, and we waited a week to take it back?"*

"So the shadow beasts could take care of them," Hettie said, remembering the creatures. Nearly impossible to kill, they'd made short work of Vincent's men during their brief takeover.

"This is just like that," Deryl said. *"If we just wait a bit, they'll kill each other off and make our work easier."*

"This wasn't the fight I came for. The entire city is overrun with homicidal crazies."

The too-still boy had been left to wander through a war zone. Maybe he'd seemed strange, because he lacked the bubbly energy of youth. Unlike most of the residents, his clothing was ragged and bloodstained. He'd learned to take care of himself and avoid the cookpot.

If he could stay alive through the battle, she might still be able to save him. With luck, he'd learn how to be a kid again in time.

The sound of a thousand boots marching in time interrupted her thoughts. Behind her, the Widows' Will marched forward. They lined the outer wall, spanning the entirety of the city's second section. With a coordinated attack, they'd be able to hit main street all at once and clear the city clean across in one fell swoop.

She sat up and watched them approach like a slow-rolling wave. She spotted Jonathan, Vammi, and Servio spaced out along the front ranks.

"Glad to see Servio's not just talk," Hettie said.

"After accusing you of being a coward to your face, that pompous swank-wagger can't afford to hang back. He'd never live it down."

After waiting at the jammed portcullis all morning, the residents were eager to jump into action. They met the army in a disjointed jumble, dirty and bedraggled enough to make the soldiers look like nobility among beggars.

The residents poured down the alleyways. In a move they must have coordinated beforehand, Jonathan, Vammi, and Servio stopped their soldiers just short of the final alleyways leading to the main road, forcing the residents to pass through bottlenecks, only to be cut down as they emerged on the other side.

They fell by the dozens, heedless of those ahead of them. They scrambled over their neighbors, hands outstretched, fingers curled into claws. Mad with bloodlust, they didn't bother to duck or dodge as they skewered themselves in an attempt to reach their target.

It was utter madness and heartbreaking on a scale Hettie couldn't quite process. Vincent hadn't just killed these people; he'd taken their minds and left them to fend for themselves.

She hadn't come to kill the residents, but she couldn't deny it needed doing. They were already dead, regardless of whether or not their hearts were beating, every last one a victim.

The onslaught continued. Soldiers pulled bodies out of the

alleyway as more came through. So many dead. So many left to be killed.

"This is an absolute slaughterhouse," Hettie said. *"They're so far gone they don't care if they die."*

"I wouldn't say that," Deryl said. *"People behind them are shoving them forward, so they don't really have a choice once they enter the alley."*

He was right. People entered, then had nowhere to go but forward.

Eventually, the flood abated. The Widows' Will pressed past main street with hardly a man lost, leaving close to a thousand bodies in the street behind them. It was surreal to see so many dead. Mostly men.

Brothers, husbands, fathers, and sons, Hettie watched it all from the rooftop with a heavy heart.

Ouri dropped in to keep her company. She absently stroked his head feathers, scanning the streets for signs of organized resistance. The devastation left behind was unreal.

In a way, Vincent had turned the Widows' Will into butchers. She was no exception, blessed Arlea forgive her.

In the wake of the army, Hettie climbed down from the roof, leaving Ouri behind while she picked her way through the carnage. It was only just past noon, and the battle was practically won. It felt like a qualified victory.

She pressed onward, one block, then two, trying not to stumble over bodies clogging the alleyways.

Ahead, Vammi stood on a roof. Below him, eight Steppers fought four men with enough hair on their arms and faces to make a decent carpet between them.

Vammi spotted her and grinned. "Jonathan is that way!" he called, pointing to the next block over. "Knowing him, he could use some help!"

Hettie doubted anybody needed help, not with the bulk of the resistance whittled down to rabble. She was glad to see Vammi in high spirits. It reminded her that her magic was used to heal far more often than to kill. It helped balance the disgust she felt at their liberation-turned-bloodbath.

With nothing else to do, she headed up the street. A few houses away, Jonathan backed out of an alleyway before lunging at something Hettie couldn't see. A moment later, a hand flopped out of the mouth of the alley floor. The sounds of sword fighting were distant, muffled by the stone buildings.

Hettie called out to him. "You've got them on the run!" At least, that's what she tried to call out. Deryl started talking the same time she did and something slammed into her head, scrambling her thoughts. The words came out as "You've goethemen—"

She fell, her head hitting the stone walkway. A metallic taste coated her tongue. She spit out a mouthful of blood, wondering what the hell happened. She couldn't think past Deryl screaming in her head.

When the ringing in her ears abated, she made out his warning. *"You're in danger! Get up before you get dead!"*

CHAPTER 34

YOU'RE DOING IT WRONG

Hettie

Hettie wasn't sure if she lay face down on the paving stones for a second or a day. It felt like the latter. Her head throbbed, and her body had turned to goo.

She groaned.

"Get up!" Deryl yelled, which did nothing to help the pounding in her brain.

"Darp," she said. She wasn't sure what was supposed to come out of her mouth, but she doubted that was it.

Someone stepped on her hand, and she felt the bones snap, though she didn't feel pain.

Scuffing feet danced in her periphery as two figures loomed over her, wrestling for a blade. A man with an elongated jaw lined in razor sharp teeth jammed an elbow in Jonathan's face. The blade went flying, landing an inch from Hettie's nose.

She stared at it, blinking stars from her eyes. Before her thoughts coalesced, she got a boot to the forehead.

"Shield yourself, dummy!"

Even when Hettie didn't know which way was up, she knew Deryl's nagging voice. Lucky for him, she was too disoriented to argue.

She managed to conjure a shield to cover her body. It snapped into place almost violently when she failed to remember the state of her magic.

Blearily, she watched Jonathan fight off the long-jawed man, who looked like a shark with far too many teeth bunched in multiple rows, practically spilling from his mouth. One cheek oozed pus through a hole with the corner of a tooth jutting through.

"Get up! Get up! Get up!" Deryl chanted. His pouch lay on the ground next to her head, the string still secured around her neck. She was lucky it hadn't come loose.

"Blrghh."

Impatient, Deryl said, *"At least open a vein in him or something. Jonathan's going to be dead in a minute, and you won't be far behind."*

Hettie tried to focus on the toothy man's neck, but all three versions of him swirled chaotically. She had the presence of mind to try healing herself first, which was easier. Even if the world refused to stand still, her magic swirled at the same speed and in the same direction as she did.

"Durgk," she said.

"What was that?"

Hettie ignored him. Her head felt stuffed with wool, and her limbs felt heavy.

The toothy man dropped into a fighting crouch. He said something, but his words were garbled by the long tongue lolling out from between his open maw. He leaped forward, his foot striking out, the contact punctuated by a dull thud.

One of Jonathan's legs bent at an odd angle halfway down the shin. With a startled grunt, he grabbed hold of the toothy man, clinging fiercely to keep from falling on his injured leg.

Toothy grabbed Jonathan's hand and squeezed, biceps bulging through the long sleeves of his shirt.

Hettie heard his fingers snap. She gathered her thoughts and focused her magic.

Jonathan slid to the ground, giving Hettie a clear shot. Just before she unleashed her magic, a flash of emerald-green announced Vammi's arrival. He darted in and stabbed a dagger in Toothy's crotch.

The man howled.

Hettie winced. *"Killing blow or not, that'll slow him down."*

"At least it wasn't the eye." Belatedly, he said, *"Hey, you can talk again."*

Toothy's torment was short-lived. While he was distracted, Vammi lopped his head off with a sword.

Hettie waved off Vammi's look of concern. He turned to assess Jonathan, who held one crumpled hand to his chest and clutched the thigh of his wounded leg with the other.

Vammi let out a frustrated sigh and knelt beside Jonathan. "You're a very special kind of stupid, aren't you? What made you think you could take that guy on by yourself?"

Jonathan's grimace turned to a scowl in a blink. He shifted his weight, trying to ease the pain of his broken limbs. "You of all people don't get to lecture me on acting without forethought," he said through gritted teeth.

Vammi's voice was flat. "Acting without forethought is more complicated than it looks. You, my friend, are doing it wrong."

"Have you considered maybe *you're* doing it wrong?" Jonathan shot back.

"I'm not the one with crippling injuries. If one of us is doing something wrong, it's clearly you."

Jonathan's breath hissed through his teeth, cutting off his reply.

Vammi placed his hands on his knees and tipped his head back to stare at the sky as if the gods were to blame for his current trial. "Forethought isn't as necessary as most people think, but when failure means death, you figure out a plan first, idiot."

While they argued, Hettie's vision cleared. She healed what she could and pushed herself to her knees. The house next to her had a conspicuous hole through the door, just the right size for Toothy's fist. *"Blessed Arlea. Did he punch me* through *the door?"*

"Yarp."

"That's not a word."

Vammi waved down a couple of Steppers, who helped lean Jonathan against a house across the street.

"You good?" Vammi called to Hettie, who waved him off again.

"You're still on the ground. Pull it together," Deryl said.

Hettie had one foot under her when she spotted the dark-haired child staring at her from behind a house two blocks up the street.

"I don't like that kid. He's weird," Deryl said.

"He's living in a secluded city full of monsters. It would be weird if he was normal." She beckoned the kid closer.

His eyes flicked to where Vammi and the Steppers fussed over Jonathan, so quick Hettie wasn't sure she'd seen it at all. Smooth as glass, the child walked to her. He had the grace of a dancer and seemed to float as he moved.

His plain gray clothes helped him blend with the surrounding stone of the city. Hettie wondered if that was intentional. It reminded her of Nubal's uniform.

When the kid reached her, he moved quicker than she could follow. One moment he was there and, in the space of a heartbeat, his hands flickered and he disappeared.

"Danger!" Deryl yelled.

Hettie only half paid attention. She scanned the roof nearby and thought she saw a foot disappear over the top. How had he moved so fast?

"You're bleeding out." Deryl's words snapped like a whip. *"Start healing."*

Hettie felt a warm wetness spreading across her chest. She glanced down to see her white shirt and red corseted vest soaked in blood. Her mind went into emergency mode, and she collapsed, focusing all her attention inward. She was surprised to find her neck had been cut. The cuts weren't large, not very deep, and only about two inches long each. The vertical slits followed her veins with a precision most healers didn't possess.

It was damned impressive.

The wounds were so clean she hadn't even felt them. That made them easier to close. A quick scan of her body told her she had wounds on each wrist as well. She healed those too.

Satisfied, she became aware of boots approaching. She opened her eyes to find Vammi crouching beside her. He placed a hand on her back.

"I'm fine," she said. *"Holy crap, did that kid just slit me like a holiday cliff pig?"*

"I told you he was trouble."

"You said he was weird. Not trouble. And you didn't warn me of danger until after he was gone."

"No, I didn't. And that scares the crap out of me. Did you see him move?"

"No," she admitted, pushing herself to her knees.

"Exactly."

"You've never had to see danger coming before."

"It's not about seeing. It's about intent. Just because you're standing next to a deranged killer, that doesn't mean they plan to kill you. If they decide you're a target, but they're not going to kill you until you're asleep in the middle of the night, you're still not in immediate danger. When they actively come for you, that's when the magic is triggered."

"That's why your warnings only come at the last second. Only this time it didn't come, even at the last second."

"Yarp. That means the kid decided to kill you—then actually cut you—faster than my curse could process. He was a blur, which was impressive, but he acted on his decision so fast it makes me wonder if he decided to kill you at all before it was done."

Hettie agreed. That was terrifying. Most kids couldn't decide what they wanted to eat for lunch. What kind of child murdered a stranger without a thought?

"Your curse is stupid. I assumed it was put in place to aid whoever cursed you, but if the warning comes when it's too late to do anything about it, it's useless."

"Sorcerers typically react quickly, plus they always have safeguards in place. Even if they die, they don't really die. You're a lot more helpless than Cerissa was. She'd have had her shield up."

Hettie hadn't felt the need once Toothy had gone down. *"Clearly, I should have assumed a child would try to murder me."*

Beside her, Vammi gasped. "What happened to you? You're covered in blood! That wasn't there a minute ago."

"I'm fine," she repeated, though a wave of dizziness washed over her from blood loss. She placed her hands on the ground to steady herself.

"So you keep saying." He turned to peer at where Toothy lay. "Did he stab you?"

Hettie slowly got to her feet, glancing down at the puddles of blood smeared into the stone at her feet. She'd bled a lot in the few seconds it took to heal herself. It was a testament to the kid's deadliness.

She was grateful for the above-average constitution her magic provided. Because of it, she was tougher and faster than normal, though not so much it was obvious to those around her.

Briefly, Hettie considered warning Vammi about the boy, but thought better of it. If the two crossed paths, Vammi would be dead before he could blink.

An uneasy feeling settled in Hettie's gut. What had they done to turn a young child into a demonic assassin? His actions defied nature.

In a flurry of wings, Ouri landed on the roof of the nearest house and let out a warble of concern. He tipped his head, watching her. He had likely seen her go down twice in the span of a couple minutes.

A flicker of gray up the street caught Hettie's attention. She pushed past Vammi and took off after it.

"What are we doing?" Deryl asked, his tone casually conversational.

"I think I just saw that kid."

"And now that you're healed, you want to give him a second chance to kill you?"

"No. I want to stop him." After a day of killing, the last thing she wanted to do was chase down a kid and decapitate him. She couldn't help thinking of her own younger siblings, though they were all girls. Unfortunately, this kid was not one of her sisters. He had proven himself ruthless and capable. She couldn't afford to let him go. *"I*

wouldn't bet against him being able to single-handedly finish off our entire army if he has a mind to."

Ouri called out, flying overhead.

She waved at him. "Follow that kid!" She pointed ahead.

Ouri let loose a classic hunting screech and left her behind in two wingbeats.

CHAPTER 35
ESCAPE ARTIST

Hettie

ettie ran past houses until they all blended together.

When she could run no further, she stopped with her hands on her knees and her lungs on fire. Dizziness washed over her in waves. *"Stay on your toes. I'm going to need a warning if that demon kid springs out of a barrel at me. Hopefully, your warning will come before the attack this time."*

"Don't worry. You won't get anywhere near him at this rate."

It wasn't the first time Hettie was grateful to be able to talk without wasting breath. Threats didn't sound nearly as sinister when you were wheezing. *"How about I drain a bucket full of your blood and have you do the running."*

He knew her well enough not to point out his lack of blood. Or legs.

Vammi sprinted out from between two houses and skidded to a stop beside her.

She hadn't realized he was following.

"You ran off like you had a pack of marshies on your tail," he said between breaths as labored as her own. He thought better of that statement and amended it with "Well, like a man would if *he* had a pack of marshies on his tail. We both know you'd be riding them, not running from them."

In Hettie's first encounter with a marsh pack, she'd managed to save a litter of marsh pups. She'd been friends with them ever since.

Hettie strode to the center of the street, searching the sky for Ouri. She spotted him off to her right, circling back toward the castle gate. If the kid planned to make it to the castle, he'd need a way in that didn't include walking through the front gate.

If there was another way in, Hettie wanted to know where. She waved for Vammi to keep up and took off for the third wall, which sat most of the way up a rise. For all that living on a caldera had built up Hettie's climbing muscles, it hadn't offered much opportunity for distance running. She was out of shape.

"Why are we chasing your bird?" Vammi asked.

"We're not chasing my bird," she said between ragged gasps. Why did he have to ask questions while they were running uphill? "We're chasing what my bird is chasing," she clarified.

Vammi's tone was overly patient. "Why are we chasing what your bird is chasing? More importantly, *what* is your bird chasing?"

"A kid that needs killing." She stumbled. He reached out to steady her. She slowed to a walk, avoiding the dubious look he directed her way. "How's Jonathan?"

Vammi took the hint to change the subject. "My men are guarding him. I doubt there's enough resistance left to worry about, but it can't hurt. He could use a healer though." The statement was carefully neutral.

"Couldn't we all." Jonathan would be in pain, but broken limbs weren't life threatening. She needed to take care of the kid first.

They kept running. Vammi's head swiveled as he peered down an alley. "We're only a block from the main street."

She grunted in reply. Scattered members of the Widows' Will made their way to the gate.

A shouted message came from up ahead.

Vammi stopped to listen. "The castle gate is open. Someone was trying to sneak out and a handful of soldiers surprised him. He ran back inside, but we kept the gate from closing."

Vammi didn't say it, but they were both wondering if it had been Vincent trying to escape. Going straight through an invading army seemed like an absurd plan. But when you lived in a mountain fortress with only one entrance and exit, options were limited.

"Wouldn't he have men guarding him?" Deryl asked.

"You'd think so. Unless they've all gone mad."

"That's a distinct possibility."

They made it another block before Hettie spotted the demon child. He came out of a side alley, casually gliding along like he hadn't just nearly killed the most powerful—and only—witch in Sedrios. Probably. With the Temple of the Sky chasing off sorcerers, most of those still alive were in hiding, so there was no real way to know if any were in Sedrios.

"You should probably be less obviously witchy once Vincent is dealt with," Deryl suggested.

Hettie tried to gain on the kid without catching his attention. He was slippery as a minnow and twice as fast. *"What fun would that be?"*

"Now you're catching on," he said enthusiastically. *"There's all kinds of ways to have fun."*

"Says the eyeball who can't die." The kid wove in and out of the crowds of soldiers, keeping Hettie from using her magic on him. She was still a dozen paces away when he turned and caught sight of her.

"You could cut off his feet from here. See how fast he runs then," Deryl said.

"That's barbaric. Plus there's too many people. I could miss."

"True. Besides, they'd probably think twice about teaming up with you if you went around chopping off children's feet."

"Doubly so if I accidentally chopped off their own feet."

"You can always heal them later."

"I'm sure they'd prefer to keep their feet connected to their legs."

The kid sidestepped to the nearest alley and leaped up using both houses as a springboard. He took three bounds and backflipped onto the roof, then took off at a sprint, leaping from one roof to the next. He was gone from sight in moments. *"How is he* not *falling through the thatch?"* Hettie wondered.

"What the hell?" Vammi said, keeping pace behind her. "I've never seen anybody move like that. Good luck catching him," he said, echoing Deryl's earlier sentiment.

They darted between houses, pushing past soldiers as they made their way to the gate. Hettie ignored the kid and followed Ouri's path overhead. She'd never keep eyes on the demon child. He was a ghost.

Vammi followed on her heels. "He's impressive."

"He is. It's a shame I have to kill him."

"Why do you want to kill him?" he asked between breaths.

"He slit my throat."

Vammi's steps faltered, and it was her turn to put out a hand to stabilize him.

"And my wrists. Faster than you can blink."

A low whistle met her words and the two jogged on. "That's why you're covered in blood."

She didn't get the chance to reply. They reached the gate and heard fighting on the other side.

The Widows' Will had cleared a path to the castle. The castle defenders had been driven back to each side of the courtyard. They were surrounded, outnumbered, and with their backs against the wall. From the snarls and yowls, Hettie imagined they fought like cornered animals.

Ouri circled the castle to the left and Hettie followed, picking up the pace once she cleared the throng of bodies at the gate. Ouri circled over a building near the back of the castle grounds.

Hettie tried to enter, but the front doors were barred, so she circled around back with Vammi on her heels.

She slowed to check around the corner before following the length of the building. Judging by the scattered hay and clumps of dried manure, it had been a stable in the recent past. The manure looked to be weeks old. Hettie wondered where the animals had gone.

"They probably ate them," Deryl said.

Hettie agreed.

At the back corner of the building, Hettie paused again.

Ouri cried out from overhead. Hettie glanced up to check the position of her bird just as Deryl snapped, *"Danger!"*

The building was taller than a house, but likely not tall enough to keep the child from scaling it. She scanned the roofline for movement.

The misdirection cost her.

A mountain of a man covered in scraggly black hair threw himself at her from behind the building. He crashed into her and Vammi both, the sour stench of rot and unwashed body hitting them nearly as hard. All three of them tumbled onto a pile of strewn hay.

Hettie tried to wrestle the man until the ground gave way beneath them.

They fell at least a dozen feet straight down only to come to a painful stop, precariously positioned at the edge of a ledge. The impact locked Hettie's muscles. A wave of agony washed through her. She lay stunned with the hairy man atop her.

Dark brown eyes peered at her through the mess, blinking owlishly.

She opened her mouth to speak, but registered Vammi's limp form sliding off the ledge next to her. She latched onto him, trying desperately to keep him from falling.

"Danger," Deryl said again, resigned.

Hettie was on her back with no leverage, so when the hairy man suddenly rolled off her, Vammi's weight yanked her off balance and over the ledge.

They fell another dozen feet. The jarring impact seized Hettie's lungs.

Those brown eyes peered at her from overhead.

It was the last thing she saw before her world went dark.

CHAPTER 36

A LIGHT IN THE DARK

Hettie

Hettie woke first.

Though the world was dark, she could see flickers of light above. A quick assessment told her an aching back would be the limit of her injuries. Her head was cushioned by Vammi's arm, which accounted for the lack of a split skull.

She couldn't tell if she'd been out for a minute or a day, but the brown eyed hairy man was gone.

By some miracle, she'd managed to maintain her magical shield in unconsciousness. The shield was a blessing and a curse. Without the discomfort of the pressure, she could focus more, but it made the magic harder to use. Whether she felt it or not, the pressure was still there and the minute she forgot that would be the minute she didn't account for it. The consequences wouldn't be pretty.

Unfortunately, trying to do magic deliberately while falling meant she hadn't done any at all. She was going to have to get better at casting in a pinch.

"Welcome back. Have a nice nap?" Deryl asked.

"How long have I been out?" She studied the dim light flickering overhead. Was that firelight? A torch? She couldn't see the actual flame, just the edges of the light it cast.

"Not terribly long. You didn't miss much. Sir Beards-A-Lot ran off as soon as you were out." While Deryl could see through his magical pouch, he often preferred viewing the world through Hettie's eyes. He didn't have that option when her eyes were closed.

With a few whispered words, Hettie cast night vision. The ledge they'd fallen from was a tunnel high overhead with a hole in its side that overlooked the room they had fallen into. They had initially fallen through the roof of the tunnel when it collapsed. Their second fall was from the lip of the tunnel into the room.

Hettie suspected the distant light was a lantern or torch tucked farther down the tunnel. Either way, the tunnel was too high up to climb to.

Hettie moved slowly. It was painful to sit up. Everything hurt. She suspected her entire backside was one giant bruise.

Her surroundings held a stone table on one side of the room with leather straps fastened to it in just the right place for a person's ankles and wrists. Thankfully, nobody was strapped to it.

"As vacation spots go, this one could use a little something," Deryl said.

"Like a cave in?"

"That would do."

A few small crates lined one wall and a portion of another wall extended out to create a stone bench. Hettie's nose wrinkled. *"Why a bench?"*

"It's not a proper torture chamber if it doesn't have room for spectators," Deryl said. *"Cerissa always loved an audience."*

A single doorway showed a stone corridor outside. They needed to get moving.

Hettie focused her attention on Vammi. A thorough delving showed his brain wasn't swelling, but he had a nasty lump on the back of his head. Luckily, there were no major injuries. His eyes opened as she wrapped up her delving.

"Oh good, you're awake," she said. "I wasn't keen on carrying you."

He squinted at the flickering light overhead. "Is that a tunnel?"

"Right. You can't see in the dark," she muttered. "This should be interesting."

He grinned up in her general direction, though his eyes were focused too far to the right. "You can lead me around like a toddler."

"Leading toddlers around is my top pick of exciting things to do when I unexpectedly fall into enemy torture chambers."

"What can I say? I do my best to make women's dreams come true."

She snorted. "You're incorrigible."

"Just like a toddler," he said. "Also, did you say torture chamber?"

She grinned and helped him to his feet. He didn't groan, but movement made him hold his breath. He was likely as sore as she was. He wobbled briefly, and she steadied him until his head cleared. Judging by the size of the lump on his head, he probably had a massive headache.

Hettie led him along slowly, in part because her own body was stiff. They made it to the doorway and out to the corridor, which was only wide enough for one person at a time.

Vammi walked behind her with his hands on her shoulders but after tripping on her heels, he shifted his grip to a handful of her hair.

Hettie would have given him her hand, but she knew she might need it if they found trouble. In her youth, she'd mastered her magic well enough to do most of her spells without hand waving and verbal speech, a feat Deryl found impressive. He'd convinced her to try them with words and hand gestures since she had to do those with the new spells she was learning anyway. Growing up, Hettie had thought it childish to use words and gestures. As it turned out, that way was easier and made the spells more powerful.

Hettie's hair hung to her waist. Vammi held it lightly, which gave him plenty of freedom while keeping both Hettie's hands available. Trouble had a way of finding her. If they came face to face with the killer child, they'd be dead before they even realized he was there, so she put a shield up to block the tunnel a foot ahead of her.

She had no idea which way would lead out and Vammi couldn't see past his own nose, so she simply picked whichever direction she could see down the farthest. As she walked, she branched out with her senses, hoping to find a stairway leading to the surface. She could map out organs in the body with precision, but that skill came from familiarity. You didn't look for the heart by searching the ankles. With tunnels, any passageway could be anywhere, plus the rock was dense and hard to penetrate.

"I swear we've crossed this intersection twice already. Am I going in circles?" She paused to gain her bearings.

"You're asking me? I can't see in the dark any better than you can. I have to use your eyes to see anything at all since you're the only one with night vision."

Vammi pointed over her shoulder. "Is that a light?"

She peered down the tunnel he indicated but couldn't make out anything. She shrugged, then remembered he couldn't see her. "I don't see anything."

"You can see fine," he reasoned, "so the difference between pitch black and almost pitch black probably isn't noticeable to you."

"Fair point."

He flicked his wrist, making her hair slap gently on her neck.

She snorted. "What am I, a horse?"

"This does feel a bit like reins," he said cheerily. "But a horse wouldn't sever my hand, so the comparison isn't entirely accurate."

She followed his directions until they rounded a corner to see a lantern flickering in the distance.

"Thank goodness," Vammi said. "Wandering in the dark with only a handful of hair to guide you isn't as relaxing as it sounds." He passed her, heading for the lantern.

"Careful. Someone might be down here." She released her shield and followed him. "That lantern didn't light itself. I don't need a torture table to tell me anyone down here will not be friendly."

He reached the lantern and paused, turning to her with a finger to his lips.

She listened. A tapping sound came from somewhere up ahead. It wasn't a steady tapping but there was a pattern to it, like rudimentary music. It reminded her of the dinners at Penelope, where the diners played interweaving melodies with their hands, feet, utensils, or anything else they could make noise with.

She listened harder and picked out the clink of glass.

Vammi left the lantern in place, once again taking hold of Hettie's hair. She led them onward, past the torch and back into darkness. Two intersections later, the sound was close. A scuff of a shoe came from a tunnel to their left. Carefully, Hettie peered around the corner to see a dozen feet of tunnel ending in a well-lit chamber. Along the wall were tables, bowls, tubes, and instruments Hettie had no name for.

They listened for a long time but heard nothing more.

"Someone was in there a minute ago," she said.

"There could be another exit."

Hettie crept forward. Vammi's steps were silent behind her, though she could feel his hand on her hair. The strange smell of moldy citrus and leather filled her nose, faint, but growing stronger as she drew closer. She suspected this tunnel connected to the rocktoad tunnels.

"Too bad we didn't know that before," Deryl said.

"We did fine without knowing it. I'm thinking this might be how Vincent escaped."

"You think he's gone?"

"Why would he stay? He's had plenty of time to get down here. He had to know he was losing hours ago."

"That's probably why that demon kid came to kill you. A last-ditch effort to slow the tide."

"Big mistake sending him after me. That kid could have taken out a lot of soldiers without me even knowing."

"Who says he didn't?"

Hettie hadn't considered that. *"Nothing we can do about it now. Let's just hope we still have an army when we get out of this stupid maze."*

She reached the end of the tunnel and surveyed the room beyond. A faint, acrid stench wafted out, different from the citrus leather smell.

Two lanterns illuminated a stone slab in the middle of the room, covered with bowls and utensils for grinding, scooping, and measuring. A complete healer's kit was laid out along with knives and a few oddities. Instruments Hettie had no name for lined the walls.

Two more doorways sat at the end of the room, one to the far left and one to the far right. The tapping noise was coming from the one on the right. Hettie snuck over to investigate, wrinkling her nose as the smell of excrement wafted out.

Vammi was more interested in checking out the instruments. He hefted a curved implement ending in a loop covered in jagged metal teeth.

Hettie peered through the doorway. The space beyond was either a very long room or a very wide tunnel. It curved at the far end, disappearing from sight. Lining the wall were cages large enough to fit a human, each separated by a stack of crates. The nearest cage held a figure curled in a ball and swathed in scraps of rough fabric. So much fur stuck through the scraps that Hettie couldn't tell if it was a mutated human or an animal wearing clothes.

She reached out with her senses to find whatever it was had died not long ago. The body didn't show signs of deterioration but had no heartbeat. A recent death.

Hettie said a quick prayer to Arlea. She could only imagine the torment it had endured. She hoped its soul would be judged kindly.

The tapping sound persisted. She eased to the far wall to get a better view of the cages. The tapping came from the fourth cage down, though the crates blocked her view of it.

A glance at the second cage told her it was occupied. A pair of eyes watched her from the shadows where a bony, naked man sat hugging his knees. His disheveled hair hung past his shoulders, concealing his face but for the nose and two eyes. Those eyes stopped Hettie in her tracks. His gaze was interested, but not intent. Alert, but not crazed.

Whoever the man was, he was sane.

Vammi darted into the room with his weight on his toes and a finger to his lips.

A moment later, Hettie heard a clink from the room with the

instruments. Someone had arrived. Or returned. Clearly they hadn't come from the room Hettie was in. They must have gone and returned through the second door.

Hettie locked eyes with the caged man. Would he give her away? Did he know she was trying to help?

Copying Vammi's gesture, the man slowly put a finger to his lips.

Hettie nodded and eased her way deeper into the room, but the man held his hand up to stop her. Judging by his expression, the idea of her moving alarmed him.

She put a hand on Vammi's shoulder. The tunnel room they were in was poorly lit from further down the hall. The room Vammi had just come from did little to illuminate their surroundings.

They all held still as the scuffing of feet and clinking of instruments continued. The mix of torture devices and scientific instruments they'd found made Hettie queasy. The person in the next room had locked up these people. Were they running experiments on the prisoners? Were they creating monsters or trying to cure them?

The terror on the face of the prisoner was enough to tell Hettie whoever it was didn't play nice.

Was the scientist bestial too? Was he as hard to kill as most of Vincent's men? Was he killable at all? Being in charge did come with perks. Hettie reached out to scan the person, hoping to find out what physical alterations he had. She was interrupted before she got the chance.

The creature in the first cage—the one with no signs of life— opened its eyes to see her standing three feet away. It let out a wail, reaching through the bars for her.

CHAPTER 37

MOURNFUL WAILS

Hettie

Vammi reached for the hilt of his sword, but Hettie stayed his hand, waiting for the person in the main room to come into view. Seconds passed and nobody came.

"Are you sensing danger?"

"If I had, I would have said so."

"You've been a little slow on the delivery today," she reminded him.

"Hey, I did fine with the chitton and the stone dragon. It's not my fault that kid moves faster than thought."

The prisoner's wail grew in intensity. It wrapped long fingers, matted with fur, around the bars of its cage and shook them so violently its body slammed against them. The outburst only lasted a few seconds before it collapsed in a heap, moaning pitifully.

Nobody came from the main room. When the racket died down, they heard humming with intermittent pauses punctuated by pouring or the tinkling of glass on stone as the person worked.

Hettie's heart raced. Her nerves were on edge. She struggled to calm herself.

"Apparently the screaming isn't new," Deryl said. *"Though I can't fathom how anyone could get used to that."*

Hettie glanced at the sane man in the second cage, waiting for some cue from him. She wanted a clear shot of the doorway in case the tinkerer entered, but Vammi was in her way and the man had motioned for her to stay put.

"How's the attack going?" the man in the cage asked suddenly, still watching her. His voice was even, though he spoke loud enough for the scientist to hear.

Hettie scowled. She opened her mouth to speak but the man put his fingers to his lips again.

"I told you not to interrupt me while I'm working," the tinkerer replied from the main room. Everyone waited in silence as the clinking resumed. After a long pause, the tinkerer spoke again. "Does this battle give you hope?"

The man in the cage didn't respond.

A sinister chuckle echoed through the tunnel. "There is nothing so weak in all the world as hope. You cling to it so desperately despite inevitable disappointment." He paused for a few clinks. "Hope is a curious thing. Worth studying, perhaps."

Who was this man? He spoke with authority and intellect, but she couldn't imagine a lord sequestering himself to an underground lair. Granted, nothing in Vincent's citadel could be called normal. What did she know?

"You think that's Lord Vincent?"

The caged man spoke again before she could reply. "The attack destroys your own hopes, does it not?"

The reply was quicker this time and less absent. "My hope is for knowledge. What I have gained cannot be taken from me, even if these irrational simpletons are willing to forgo world-changing discoveries for the sake of small-scale ethical dilemmas. They speak of things they do not understand."

"I think you underestimate the value of life," the caged man said. His eyes bore a hold into Hettie with their intensity.

How had he managed to stay sane surrounded by madness? She would have felt sorry for him if it weren't for his eyes. That gaze demanded dignity, not pity.

"This again," the tinkerer said, annoyed. "Leave the advance of science to those who have the guts to do what is required. If we left it to your lords—or mine, for that matter—we'd still be—"

His words were drowned out by another wail from the first cage. Head thrown back, its howl was long and mournful, encompassing more sorrow than Hettie could fathom. She had no trouble pitying that poor creature.

"If this guy has a lord, he's probably not Vincent." Hettie grabbed Vammi's hand and headed down the tunnel before the sound cut off. The sane man watched her from behind his bars. Was she imagining the panic there as she disappeared into the darkness?

Nearly twenty cages lined the tunnel, each with a huddled figure inside. A few of the caged figures stared out at her with hollow, defeated eyes. Her arrival didn't seem to spark any hope of rescue. They didn't even shuffle around to keep her in sight as she passed.

Hettie passed a light crag the size of her fist clinging to the wall. She hadn't realized they could get so big. The only other self-illuminating rock she'd seen had been in Penelope's basement.

The row of cages ended, but the tunnel continued into the darkness. Hettie was almost afraid to see what horrors lay farther down, beyond her sight.

If the tinkerer was responsible for altering people, he had likely altered himself. She'd have to be careful confronting him.

The wailing creature in the first cage seemed to fluctuate between dead and alive. It had no heartbeat, yet it screamed. If the scientist could create a being that defied death like that, why not take that ability for himself? If he was looking for immortality, he wasn't far from it.

Whoever the man was, she needed to take him down. She didn't want to risk leaving the prisoners locked in cages if she failed. *"I have to free these creatures."*

"Are you sure that's a good idea?" Deryl asked. *"They could be violent. Honestly, I'd be surprised if at least some of them weren't."*

She hesitated. *"I can't just leave them here to die. Besides, we'll need to let them out eventually. If they're violent, we'll kill them. Death would be better than staying like this."*

"If they put up a fight, it'll alert the scientist guy."

"I'll put up a shield. We'll open one cage at a time. If they end up trying to eat our faces, I'll kill them myself. Sound good?"

"I can live with that."

She blocked off the passageway with a shield to ensure the creature only had one direction to go: away from the scientist. She opened the first cage.

The shield ended up being unnecessary. The first creature heard the door unlock and immediately went to investigate. It pushed on the door, which swung open easily. After a moment of staring at the opening with eyes far too big for its face. It stuck an arm out and waved it tentatively. Baggy skin drooped from the appendage.

In a blink, the creature launched itself out the door and bolted headlong deeper into the tunnel in sheer desperation. The shield muffled the noise of its footfalls.

Hettie watched it go, hoping its future ended up better than its past.

Accessing her magic around the shield made the work clumsy, but by the third lock, she was quicker. The creatures in each successive cage watched their neighbor head down the tunnel. They didn't hesitate like the first one did.

Hettie shifted the shield with her as she went, nudging Vammi along. She released the next creature, which let out a screech of triumph as it disappeared into the darkness, long hair trailing behind it.

Hettie's shield didn't block noise well enough for that sound.

"So much for being stealthy," Deryl muttered.

Vammi drew his sword.

Hettie had known her luck wouldn't hold out for long. Wherever the scientist had disappeared to, he was bound to come investigate this latest noise. The keening wail had rapidly retreated down the tunnel, fading in the distance. The scientist would know it was loose.

Resigned, she left the rest of the captives in place and made her way to where the sane man waited in his cage. She hoped the scientists hadn't discovered immortality just yet.

Al Dagos favor me.

CHAPTER 38
AN UNEXPECTED RESCUE

Adyr

It was a strange feeling to have rescue so close at hand after captivity. It was already too late for the lords and their servants, save Adyr and Bannot. Their would-be rescuers had stumbled in right under Cayon's nose, a feat none would have dared to even try had they known him.

He recognized Vammi, captain of Tuigasi's Steppers, who were clearly part of the attack by Poll's Wander. Vammi's foolhardy antics had always paid off, luck of the gods be damned. Adyr was going to need that luck.

He didn't recognize the woman with him. She was handsome, with thick, long hair and eyes shadowed by the darkness of the room. Her confident demeanor and the fact that she was covered in blood, but moving freely told him she was capable. Clearly the blood wasn't hers.

She wasn't from Poll's Wander. Women there favored loose, flowing dresses to combat the heat and humidity of the swamplands. Her leather breeches and tight vest marked her as a foreigner.

He briefly wondered if she was from the castle, but nobody there would be down here without trembling in their stylish boots. Was she a random wanderer who joined the forces of Poll's Wander looking for adventure? Madness or stupidity seemed the most likely explanation.

Adyr heard the scuffle of feet scurrying down the tunnel. Was Vammi retreating? Smart move. They would be safer in the tunnels with the digger people than anywhere near Cayon. Hopefully Vammi would get word to the rest of the army that he'd found prisoners. Adyr had no illusions that he'd been recognized. He'd have said something, but—

Another set of scampering feet ran off down the tunnel. The sound was faint, but unmistakable. Had Vammi and the woman split up?

By the third set of scampering feet, Adyr's heart started to pound. There had been only two of them. A third set of footprints meant it wasn't the intruders running off. The only other living creatures in this room were prisoners. Did he dare hope?

Cayon was right. Hope was a dangerous thing. It could crush a man as easily as a falling horse.

The scientist had retreated to gather supplies from the little storage room off to the side. It led to an exit, Adyr knew, though he'd never seen it.

A double tap echoed far in the distance. Cayon was being summoned. Muttering under his breath loud enough for Adyr to make out, he retreated. The exit wasn't far. He would be out of earshot soon and Vammi would be safer.

Adyr glanced at Bannot, whose back was turned to him, as it had been for days. Early on, Adyr had been grateful Bannot had been in the stables during the dinner that ended their lords' lives. If only that luck had lasted in the weeks that followed.

By now, Bannot had given up hope. Adyr had too. Or so he thought. Vammi's arrival had stirred it to life with surprising ease and panic gripped him over the chance of it dying once more.

Hope wouldn't rekindle the same in Bannot. What life did he have to go back to, mutated as he was?

A sudden screech rent the air from farther down the tunnel,

trailing into the distance. It confirmed Adyr's suspicions, though how Vammi had managed to open the cage was beyond him.

A prisoner was free and well on its way to escape. Pressure built in Adyr's chest. It was happening. He would be free again! Free from the poisoned bars. He would see daylight again. He would sleep flat on the ground. Those little things were what he dreamed of.

He tried to focus on the present instead of dreaming of the future. It wouldn't do to get sloppy now. Joy was a dangerous thing.

Still, he couldn't help but think of running down those tunnels himself.

Quiet footsteps approached. Vammi and the woman returned, likely expecting a confrontation with Cayon. "He's gone. Called away," Adyr informed them. He was surprised to find his voice steady, if a bit creaky. His whole body seemed to hum with jitters. He wanted to push at the cage. To leave his gods forsaken hellhole and never return.

Vammi grinned and sheathed his sword. "Our luck holds."

Adyr gave the briefest hint of a smile in return. "Yours always does."

The woman stood just out of reach of the cage and muttered something under her breath. She flicked her fingers and the lock on Adyr's cage popped open.

He flinched, his eyebrows climbing up his forehead. "Sorcery?" This young woman, barely into adulthood, was a sorcerer?

Vammi scrutinized him. "Do I know you?"

Adyr was too distracted by the click of the lock opening. The sound echoed in his head. For the first time, Cayon wasn't there when his cage was unlocked. He reached out and pushed it. Despite the care he'd taken to avoid touching the metal, he didn't hesitate.

The door swung open. He closed his eyes and let out a shaky breath. Then his brain screamed at him to get out. Quickly, before some cruel twist of fate locked him back inside.

He climbed out as quickly as he could, but his body had lost muscle, and his movements were uncoordinated. Once free, he straightened slowly, long hair hanging in his face. The tattered remains of his pants, cut off above the knees, clung to him with months of caked on sweat and worse.

The sorcerer stepped over to Bannot's cage, peering inside at his friend's rounded back.

"Wait!" Adyr said, holding out a hand to her. "I need to explain something before you open that cage."

Vammi snorted. "This might not be the best time for stories. That man could be back any minute."

"That man," the woman said, nodding at the next room. "The scientist. Can he be killed?"

Adyr blinked, baffled by the question. "Of course. Anyone can die. Even you." Only gods were immortal, and even they weren't invincible if the stories were to be believed. "If you open that cage unprepared, your own death might happen sooner than you'd like," he warned.

CHAPTER 39

SOME WOUNDS DON'T HEAL

Hettie

Hettie wasn't sure how to take Adyr's words. It sounded like a threat. Falling back on her mother's example, she went with brevity. "Start talking."

The man from the second cage turned to the one in the third. "This is my friend, Bannot. I'm Adyr."

Vammi straightened in recognition. "Arlea's blessed skirt," he muttered.

Adyr let out an unsteady breath. "We came here with Lord Holden and the rest six months ago."

Hettie listened as Adyr relayed his story, summing up the death of the lords and his subjection to experimental torture.

Upon mention of the child murderer, Deryl said, *"We know that kid. He sure gets around."*

Hettie worried over the fate of the army. They needed to get topside before he slaughtered the lot of them.

"Cayon mentioned an army on his doorstep and—" Adyr's voice cracked, and he paused to clear his throat.

Hettie could hardly believe what he'd been through despite seeing the state of the prisoners firsthand. Adyr seemed to be the lucky one.

"Cayon's lucky he hasn't tried to catch you," Deryl said. *"You'd have murdered him extra bloody."*

For all that Adyr's movements were shaky, he had retained more muscle mass and had a better range of motion than was feasible for having spent so long in a cage. Perhaps the Element had bolstered his health. If his luck held, he would remain free of negative side effects.

When Adyr resumed, he had control of himself again. "Cayon isn't very talkative, but he ranted for days after the attack on Poll's Wander failed. We were hoping someone would counterattack, but with the lords murdered, we didn't think it was likely."

"Liselle has enough backbone for three men," Hettie said. "You can thank her when you get back. She assembled the Widows' Will."

"That's what we named the army," Vammi supplied. "It's the first combined army for the entire valley." He put a hand on Adyr's shoulder and gave him an encouraging smile. "Liselle will be glad to know you're alive."

Deryl said, *"Not that she needs a bodyguard when she's got a whole army."*

"He meant for sentimental reasons."

"Oh."

"What do you want to do with Bannot?" Hettie asked.

Adyr chewed his lip. "Free the others. Free him last. Let me talk to him first. He must stay calm."

Hettie eyed Bannot's back. His clothes were shredded, and he was covered in dried blood. Even through the double cage, she could see the dull silvery metal rings hooked through his skin. She surveyed the row of cages. *"These people have been through a special kind of hell."*

"Then I say we catch them and put them in these same cages to rot."

"Too bad they can't hear you. You could sing them tavern songs."

"Are you saying my songs are like torture?" he demanded.

Hettie chose not to answer. Instead she left Adyr to help his friend as best he could. Her magic could remove the rings and heal the wounds left behind, but the changes he described were beyond her capabilities. She wouldn't have a clue where to start on healing rage induced by madness.

The light crag seemed dimmer when she passed it the second time around. Or maybe that was just a reflection of her mood. She focused on the cage locks, working carefully with Vammi by her side. A magical slip up could cause the creatures inside more pain and suffering. That was the last thing she wanted.

Her work went quickly. In minutes, the cages were empty, their residents gone.

"I hope they know where they're going. I'd hate to think of them wandering the mountains until they died of starvation."

Deryl said, *"Or worse, getting eaten by a giant mountain snake. But hey, at least they'd die free."*

Hettie gave a gentle snort. *"Not much of a consolation prize if you ask me."*

When they returned to Adyr, he gave them a nod and stepped back from the cage.

Hettie wanted to ease Bannot's suffering as much as possible, but she wasn't sure how he would react. Afraid he might fly off the handle, she decided to do what she could while he was still safely contained.

Bannot hadn't moved. Hettie delved him, tracing his skin and bones to find each metal ring. She almost gasped aloud. He had over fifty rings in his body. The skin had healed over in some places. Others oozed pus. She worked carefully, removing the rings and closing the holes. She wasn't skilled with infection, but with it centered around the rings near the surface, she was able to push out the gunk and heal the wounds.

Bannot flinched at each ring that bounced off the floor of the cage but didn't move otherwise.

Hettie was dismayed by his Element-induced bone growth. It was too thick in some places and too long in others, bulging and folding as it grew. She couldn't fix that, so she moved on to his nose.

As best she could tell, the cartilage had disintegrated and been absorbed into the surrounding area, leaving a misshapen hole with a rigid border. If healing it was possible, she wasn't nearly skilled enough to do the job. She didn't even know where to start.

"I'm sorry," she said to Bannot's back. "That's the best I can do for now."

"Thank you," Adyr said, swallowing hard. He had flinched along with Bannot as the rings fell. "He's calm for now. We need to keep him that way."

Hettie grimaced. "The castle grounds are a battlefield. If you know of somewhere down here to hole up, you're welcome to stay out of harm's way. Just point us to the exit first."

Adyr shook his head. "We're coming with you. The tunnels are a maze. I haven't had a chance to explore them, but I know that much. I only know one way out of here. It isn't far."

He didn't say he wasn't about to stay in the dark underground any longer than he had to, but Hettie could see the panic on his face when she mentioned him staying below. She nodded in agreement and popped the locks on Bannot's cages.

With coaxing from Adyr, Bannot turned slowly, almost as if he were in pain. His face was a mess, his bone structure grotesquely mutated. His nose was so vacant it made Hettie wonder if he could smell at all. Assuming months of being trapped in a tunnel full of unwashed bodies and human waste hadn't dulled his senses out of sheer self-preservation.

Hettie knew what to expect after delving Bannot. Vammi wasn't as prepared. He went stiff at the sight and almost hid his muttered prayer.

"He's not even getting the full effect with it being so dark in here," Deryl said.

"Small blessings."

Adyr helped Bannot out of the cage. He lumbered a couple steps but remained stooped. A quick delving showed the bones of his spine were distorted, forcing him into a permanent hunch.

"That's gotta be miserable," Deryl muttered.

"Cayon kept notes," Adyr said. "We need to bring them. They may have information on how to reverse the damage."

"You can't fix me," Bannot said. The lower jawbone had thickened enough to impede his tongue, making his words garbled.

"Remember, we have a sorcerer now," Adyr said. "That's better than we ever dreamed of. Look at what she's done for you already. You're too close to give up now."

Vammi said, "You're in luck. Hettie is handy in a fight, but healing is her specialty."

Hettie elbowed him in the ribs and gave him a look that said 'I can't heal that, fool man.' She wasn't sure he could see it in the dim light.

"Maybe you can break that to them later," Deryl said.

Uneasy, Hettie scanned the main room for heartbeats and found none.

"Are you sure he even has a heartbeat?" Deryl asked.

Before she could process that, Adyr headed into the room. Bannot and Vammi followed.

Hettie paused to shield the doorway and release the shrieking creature in the last cage. As if it had been waiting, it immediately slipped out, quiet as a feather on a breeze. *"Sure. Now it decides to be quiet."*

"Maybe it was screaming to get out."

That actually made sense. Hettie left the shield up just in case one of the newly freed prisoners circled back. She'd drop it once they cleared out.

Adyr squatted to riffle through books lined on a shelf carved out of the stone table in the middle of the room. He picked out three thin journals and handed them to her. She tucked them into her bodice to keep her hands free. "Which way to the surface?"

Adyr pointed at the second doorway, which led through a short tunnel lined with crates to a bigger room with an earthen stairway climbing to a doorway that opened to sunlight. It had to be the exit.

Distant noises filtered in from outside. *"I can hear fighting,"* Hettie said. She'd half hoped the battle was over.

"I don't think that's fighting. It sounds more like screaming."

Hettie paused, listening harder, but the scuff of boots on stone made it difficult to hear clearly. Come to think of it, the yells seemed to be coming from farther back in the tunnels, not from the stairway.

A distant screech sounded and Vammi turned to her. "I swear I just heard your bird."

He was right. Hettie knew that screech anywhere. Before she could move, a familiar mountain of black hair came barging in, sprinting down the steps with Servio on his heels.

"Who is that guy?" Hettie asked. *"And why does he keep showing up at the worst times?"*

Servio brandished his sword, which might have looked intimidating if his belly hadn't been jiggling and his face hadn't been so red.

The hairy man stumbled to a stop when he caught sight of Hettie's group blocking his path further into the tunnels where he'd probably hoped to lose his pursuer.

Servio stumbled to a stop on the stairs when he saw the man was trapped. Both were puffing hard.

Bannot let loose a snarl that chilled Hettie to the bone. She turned to eye him.

He had gone rigid but for a quiver that shook his whole body with a subtle vibration.

Ouri screeched again, a panicked sound that distracted Hettie from Bannot. The call echoed through the tunnels, and she knew with a certainty it wasn't coming from outside. He was somewhere underground and closing fast. Hettie pulled out her whistle and blew, calling the bird to her.

"How did he get down here?" she wondered.

"He probably came looking for you."

A commotion by the stairs kicked up when the hairy man made a run for it. He didn't make it far. Servio's sword blocked his escape route.

"Vincent!" Adyr yelled. "Get back here, you bastard!"

Hettie's eyebrows climbed her forehead.

"That hairy lump is Lord Vincent?" Deryl asked.

She'd expected a vicious warrior, not a giant dog in desperate need of grooming. He hardly looked like a man. She wondered if Adyr was crazy after all.

Adyr said more, but the words were drowned out by a roar from Bannot, who wrenched himself free of Adyr's grip and ran headlong at the hairy man—presumably Vincent.

Panicked, Vincent fled back up the stairs, desperately deflecting Servio's sword with his bare hand.

Deryl hooted. *"Bet that hurt."*

Vincent had no time to inspect the sword wound with Bannot on his heels.

"What is going on?" Hettie said. *"Has the entire world gone crazy?"*

Servio stepped aside to avoid being trampled by Bannot, who barreled up the stairs with Adyr following close behind.

The entire scene of chaos lasted seconds. By the time things were quiet, Hettie heard what she couldn't with the previous noise: the sound of hide scraping rock.

"No," she breathed.

Ouri let out a third call, closer now.

With a deafening crash, the stone dragon burst through the side wall and into the room with Ouri trying desperately to stay out of its gaping maw.

CHAPTER 40

AVID PRESERVATION

Hettie

Hettie's previous encounter with the stone dragon didn't give her a full appreciation of its face. Teeth lined its mouth in rows that coated several feet worth of throat before disappearing into the dark abyss of its body. Its throat convulsed rhythmically, rippling in a constant swallowing motion.

In an attempt to avoid crashing headfirst into stone, Ouri had ended up hovering between the stone dragon's teeth as it plowed through the wall.

Hettie's heart jumped to her throat while her brain worked over-time trying to make sense of the scene. How in the void had Ouri gotten into the tunnels? For that matter, how had the stone dragon gotten there? The tunnels were blocked off. Had Pillar missed one?

The crash slowed the dragon, but Hettie was sure the enormous tube of mass would crash into the far wall and take Ouri with it. Her oldest friend was going to die. She could feel it in her bones.

Time stood still as Hettie wasted time wishing she'd killed the dragon when first she laid eyes on it, before it had eaten Vammi's Steppers. She'd had the power. She wasn't against using it for death. Especially when letting the beast live meant the death of her dearest friend.

Her family. Her island. Her people. Her love.

She'd lost far too much to lose him too.

Hettie flared her senses, seeking out the beating heart of the dragon. It took more time than she had, but she was in luck. The dragon's gaping maw stopped a foot short of the opposite wall. It didn't crush Ouri into the stone.

Flapping wildly to get clear, Ouri launched himself sideways.

The dragon was too fast. Its mouth snapped shut, catching one wing in its jaws, along with half of Ouri's body. The bird's alarmed screech choked off so suddenly the entire world seemed to go silent.

Hettie felt the impact like the severing of fate. An entire future—one with Ouri in it—disappeared in a flash. In that crystalline moment, memories flowed by in a blur.

The day she found a baby bird, motherless and lost in the trees.

Running through the wooded mountains.

Lingering on the sun-warmed beach.

Chasing cliff pigs through the streets of Port Placid.

Saving her toddler sisters from kidnappers.

Sailing to a new land for the first time together.

Meeting the marshies.

Fighting the fish-men.

More memories than one lifetime could hold. This was where those memories came to a violent, abrupt end.

Her heart stuttered from the pain. It seized in her chest for one exquisitely pivotal moment before the carefully crafted shield around her magic shattered.

A concussive blast radiated from her, knocking everyone in the room down.

The stone dragon gave a high-pitched squeal of pain, thrashing about with Ouri still clenched in its merciless jaws.

Hettie didn't realize she was speaking until the words left her mouth. The spell for Avid Preservation had done nothing for her during practice, but with her power flooding the air, her will seized it, twisted and manipulated it until it became a force of unholy wrath.

The words that had escaped her in practice poured out with compulsion, her fingers moving in time with the spell.

She channeled the magic into Ouri, avidly willing him to be preserved. In the end, she wasn't sure if the spell worked as intended or if her determination wrangled the magic into doing what she wanted. All she knew was, in that moment, she was Ouri's only hope.

A bar of golden light shot from her hands directly into the bird's limp body. It soaked into his amber feathers, bringing them an ethereal glow of black-tinged gold. Veins of crimson fire streaked through every feather, spreading to encompass all of him, pulsing with light.

Ouri grew with each pulse until he was three times his normal size, enormous in the underground chamber.

With a croak, his head came up to peck madly at the dragon's rounded head with the force of an axe.

The dragon jerked back in surprise. Tough hide, meant for scraping rock, was no match for Ouri's golden beak, lined in flickering black flames. He gouged chunks of flesh from the worm until it opened its mouth and released him.

"Holy hells! It worked!" Deryl yelled. *"I can't believe you pulled that off!"*
Hettie barely heard him.

The triple-sized fiery hawk of vengeance attacked with everything he had. Skirting the dragon's head, Ouri circled to its neck to rake claws big enough to wrap around Hettie's head through its thick hide, scoring deep lines that oozed blood. The huge serpentine body writhed as if trying to back into the tunnel where the razor-tipped teeth were the only thing exposed. It reared, slamming its head into the ceiling, raining dust down on the room's inhabitants.

With wings so huge he couldn't fully extend them, Ouri moved with the dragon, gouging again and again into the worst of the wounds, as if he'd decided to take up tunneling himself and found the dragon's body to be a great place to start practicing.

Hettie shielded herself to keep from getting bowled over by the fiery feathers, dragging Vammi with her as she retreated to the staircase where Servio cringed, wide eyed at the scene before him.

He wasn't the only one amazed by the magnificent bird.

Hettie's heart doubled to see Ouri in a physical form that matched how she thought of him. Most people saw him as just a bird, if a very large one. He was so much more. His intelligence rivaled that of many humans, and his predatory instincts made him a ferocious fighter.

More than that, Ouri understood her. He joined her in adventure and comforted her in loss. He had been there for her through years' worth of trial.

She was more than happy to return the favor.

Despite Ouri's efforts, he wasn't close enough to the dragon's vital organs to kill it. Those were tucked further down the body, just inside the tunnel where he couldn't reach. Their fight would likely cave in the walls before it came to an end.

Hettie didn't mind the loss of Cayon's workspace, but she didn't want to injure any captives that might still be in the tunnels.

She found the dragon's heart again. It took more effort than she expected. Avid Preservation had diminished her magic reserves, leaving her more depleted than she'd ever been. She was panting by the time she found the beast's heart and sliced it open.

In seconds, the dragon's motions grew lethargic. After a full minute, it shuddered and lay still.

Ouri gored it two, three times, then let out a strangled *grawp* and stepped back from the mutilated flesh. He looked around, his rapid motions telegraphing his agitation. He had almost died. Possibly *had* died. And now he was big enough for Hettie to ride on.

He'd been with Hettie his whole life and had seen her do a lot with her magic. He had only ever been on the receiving end of it when she healed him. This was a new experience and it clearly alarmed him.

Hettie called softly to him.

He turned awkwardly, his tail feathers scraping the wall. She kept her shield up but held out a hand to him. He tried to hop to her, smacking his head on the ceiling hard enough for chunks of stone to come down before tripping on the landing to sprawl at her feet.

It was a good thing Hettie had her shield up because his beak was half the size of her head and it cracked audibly against the invisible barrier.

She crouched by his head, releasing the shield. "You're okay," she cooed, stroking the floofy feathers lining his neck. "You're going to be fine." Her hands trembled. She buried them in his mane, leaning down to breathe in the scent of him, wind with musky undertones. And, currently, stone dust. "I thought you were dead, and I couldn't let you go. I'm sorry you're so huge. I'll figure out how to put you back."

"I don't think you need to. He's smaller than he was a minute ago."

Hettie studied her friend. He did look smaller, but it might have been his dormant position. With his wings out and his feathers flared, he always looked larger than he was. She wasn't convinced until she noticed his glow dimming. Slowly, the black flames receded into the nooks of his feathers, fading into shadow.

Vammi stood halfway up the stairs by Servio. "Never a dull moment with you," he said, grinning. He cast a look up the stairs. "I'm going to check on Adyr and Bannot. Are you good here?"

Hettie nodded, her focus on Ouri. The spell left her comfortably drained for the first time since she'd taken the power from her sisters. *Since the night Elkin died.*

She shied away from that thought.

Delving into Ouri, she observed the changes in him. While he was essentially the same proportions, every bone, feather, and muscle fiber was coated in a fine invisible substance not unlike a shield. As he shrunk back to his normal size, the shield thinned and disappeared.

"I've seen some pretty intense magic in my day and even I'm impressed by that spell," Deryl said.

The spell had made him bigger and stronger, protected him, healed his injuries, and possibly brought him back to life. *"I don't know if I'd be able to cast it again. I couldn't during practice. This time I just sort of cast it on instinct."*

"If you've done it once, you can do it again. We'll practice more."

"I don't know. It may take more magic than I naturally have. Now that I've used up the extra stores, I should end up back at my usual level, right?"

He gave a mental shrug. *"Remember how the only other person I know with kota'imoga died?"*

Ouri calmed as he shrunk, scooting closer until he was practically in Hettie's lap. He nuzzled her with his beak and gave a chirrup before shaking himself and preening his feathers as if to make sure they were all still there.

"See? Good as new," she told him.

He pecked at her belt, hoping for a treat. She hadn't brought any. "We're mid-battle and our food is rationed," she reminded him.

He chirped in disappointment and turned to eye the stone dragon. He flapped over to the great worm and gave it a tentative peck.

"He's not going to eat that, is he?" Deryl asked.

Ouri pecked once, twice, then began tugging off strips of flesh in earnest.

Hettie smiled. *"Maybe the transformation made him hungry. If that's the price for escaping the jaws of death, I won't complain. He can eat the whole damned thing."*

"I guess in times of war, when things get rocky a good meal is hard to come by."

Hettie groaned.

CHAPTER 41

NOBODY SIGNED UP FOR THIS

Hettie

Hettie left Ouri to his meal. She headed for the exit.

Servio was standing halfway up the stairs with his eyes popping out of his head. "General?"

He blinked as if coming out of a daze and gave his head a vigorous shake. His gaze was locked on where Ouri had most of his head buried in the dragon's deepest gash. "I didn't know sorcerers could . . . I mean, that was . . . How did you . . .?" He trailed off.

"Sometimes we're useful for more than healing scratches."

His gaze finally fixed on her. "I didn't believe you. About the men."

Hettie frowned. "The men?"

"The men here. The way you lot talked, I thought you were exaggerating. Horns? Extra teeth? Enough hair to look half dog? Men with transparent purple bodies and fins?" He snorted. "Preposterous."

She could see where he might have thought they were all a little nutty themselves.

"You sounded like children frightened of your own shadows." He opened his mouth, then paused to glance at Ouri, who had his shoulders and one foot inside the gaping wound. He swallowed hard. "My words fail me." He shrugged helplessly. "I didn't sign up for this."

"None of us did. But we're still here. And so are you." She clapped a hand on his shoulder. "That says a lot."

She left him to ogle her bird. When she exited the staircase, she was thirty paces from the stable.

"There's the hole you fell down," Deryl remarked. *"And to think it was right there this whole time."*

Hettie sighed. A quick scan of the area told her most of the fighting was over. Despite the low humidity, the air felt hot and oppressive after their day of fighting.

Soldiers milled about near the front of the castle. The Widows' Will had been victorious, but the soldiers weren't celebrating. Hettie couldn't blame them. The fighting had been a depressing affair.

With the child assassin on the loose, she was relieved to see their army intact.

A ripple went through the mass of soldiers just before Vincent shoved his way through a gap in the crowd, running straight for the front gate.

Hettie hadn't gotten a good look at him earlier. This time, she made out the discolored undergarments covered in dirt and sweat stains, nearly covered by the masses of fur along his arms. From the bulge of the clothing, it covered his torso, as well.

Bannot gave chase, knocking two soldiers to the ground in his pursuit.

Vincent grabbed a stray soldier and flung him in Bannot's path. Despite his hunched posture, Bannot kept up, leaping over the splayed soldier with surprising agility. He caught up to Vincent a few strides later and took him out with a flying tackle.

Adyr and Vammi pushed their way through the crowd and closed on Bannot, whose fists pounded repeatedly into the fallen leader who curled in on himself for protection.

The pair had gone down not far from Hettie. She shielded Vincent before Bannot could kill him.

"Why are you protecting him?"

"Because I want to talk to him. He doesn't deserve to die like this, pummeled into oblivion by a crazed prisoner."

"He deserves far worse than that," Deryl said.

"Exactly."

Vammi and Adyr arrived, puffing from their sprint. They watched Bannot's fists hammer down until blood from his hands smeared the outside of the shield.

"He does realize Vincent isn't moving, right?" Deryl asked.

"If so, he doesn't seem to care." Hettie wasn't sure if she should stop Bannot or let him continue. If he was unstable as Adyr suggested, it was better his rage be focused on Vincent than anyone else standing around.

"He's not going to be happy when he finds out you've shielded Vincent," Deryl said.

"He'll get over it."

"That would've been an anticlimactic ending for a man who assassinated every lord of Poll's Wander and then invaded, all while corrupting his own people."

Hettie nodded. Adyr had mentioned that Cayon's experiments included Vincent. As far as he could tell, though Vincent hadn't been notably affected when he'd had the lords murdered.

Bannot's blows finally slowed as his rage wore off. Vincent was hardly visible beneath the smears of Bannot's blood.

Vammi leaned over Bannot's shoulder to get a look at the damage. His eyes flicked up to meet Hettie's when he saw the shield.

Hettie shrugged. "Jonathan will want to talk to him."

"What is this?" Bannot said, noticing the shield for the first time. He reached out a hand to swipe at the blood, which smeared cleanly against the glassy outer surface.

Vammi eyed him warily.

"You could always lock his joints like you did with the rocktoads."

"I could," she agreed. *"But making him a prisoner in his own body should be a last resort. He's been through enough."*

"If you say so," Deryl said. *"I think it would be funny. Think of how mad*

he'll get, and he won't be able to move. In the grand scheme of things, that's not even going to register on the scale of torment he's seen."

"I'm going to assume you're joking."

Deryl was silent for a long moment. *"Mostly,"* he hedged.

Bannot glared at Hettie.

"Jonathan leads the army that rescued you. It's only reasonable to let him talk to Vincent before you kill him."

Adyr didn't look particularly pleased about that plan. Neither did Bannot, for that matter.

"I will kill him," Bannot growled.

"I doubt Jonathan will argue," Hettie said placatingly.

Adyr continued to scowl at Hettie but nudged his friend. "Vincent is captured. Let's make sure Cayon doesn't disappear. He's far more dangerous."

Bannot allowed himself to be led away.

Hettie waited until they were a distance away before pointing out six men. "You lot take this hairball and keep him under guard. Nobody is to touch him until Jonathan gets a chance to talk to him."

Jonathan needed a good healing before he was up to questioning prisoners, but she'd get around to that. Like Adyr, she wanted to track down Cayon first.

The six men stepped forward to grab Vincent. Hettie released the shield over him. The blood smears fell to mat his hair.

When the soldiers pulled Vincent to his feet, he whimpered, holding the hand he'd used to push away Servio's sword.

A quick delving told Hettie the tendons in his palm were severed. She didn't bother to heal it. He'd caused plenty of suffering. It would do him good to experience some of the same.

The soldiers led him away. His whimpers turned to a keening wail, and he rocked in their grip, an agitated motion. "He'll kill me. They'll all kill me," he said in a reedy voice.

"You should have considered that earlier," Hettie muttered.

"They're crazy!" Vincent screeched. He threw back his head and laughed, the sound grating on Hettie's nerves. "We're all crazy! The world is mad!" He kept cackling and gibbering until she could no longer make out his words.

"Good riddance," Vammi said, watching in fascination.

The remaining soldiers slowly began to disperse once the drama was over. Hettie took note of two soldiers in particular. They ignored the crowd, watching her instead.

She found it especially odd that they weren't together. Instead, they were diagonally separated by a few milling soldiers, seemingly unaware of each other.

The one closest to Hettie was the Andosh soldier. *"There's Tinto. I've been meaning to talk to him. The one in back looks familiar, but I can't place him."*

Deryl piped up. *"That's the same guy who was glaring at the rocktoads at the campfire,"* Deryl said. *"I recognize him by his earlobe."*

Hettie saw that his earlobe had been sliced at the midpoint. The injury was old and healed with a gaping horizontal slit dividing the top half of his ear from the bottom. The people next to him started moving, following the crowd, and he was pushed along.

Before Tinto could disappear too, Hettie pointed at him and barked, "You! Come here."

Despite blatantly staring at her, he seemed surprised she'd noticed him. He cast a furtive look at the soldiers around him, swallowed hard, and stepped forward with his shoulders hunched.

"He looks terrified," Deryl said. *"This'll be fun. I haven't seen a grown man wet himself since my first sorcerer."*

"And you're not going to see one today." She knew his argument before he made it. *"I get to decide when to make men involuntarily pee."*

He gave a sigh of longsuffering.

"Tinto, right?" she asked brusquely.

The soldier ran a nervous hand down his uniform and straightened his spine. "That's me." His gaze stayed firmly locked on Hettie's throat.

"Where are you from?"

He blinked. "What do you mean?"

Hettie scowled. "I mean you're not from Poll's Wander. Where. Are. You. From?"

Tinto's mouth opened and closed in a rather good impression of a fish. "I don't know. Here and there?" He said it like a question. "I like to travel."

Vammi tried to muffle a snicker.

Hettie fought to keep her irritation in check. *"That was supposed to be the easy question."*

"Maybe geography isn't his strong suit."

"You've been watching me," Hettie said, cutting off Tinto's stammering attempt to spew out something resembling a coherent answer. "Why?" Before he could start blathering again, she said, "And for Bukker's sake look at me. Stop staring at my neck."

Tinto's mouth drew into a thin line. "Never look a sorcerer in the eyes." The words came out automatically, with a surety that came from practice.

Hettie stared at him. "Who told you that?"

A flicker in Tinto's gaze said he was considering his answer. "Everybody knows that."

"Really? Because I'm a sorcerer and I've never heard that." Granted, she was from the Paradisals, so there was a great deal she didn't know about sorcerous superstitions across the mainland.

Tinto shifted his weight like his body was about to bolt without checking in with his brain. His voice had a quaver to it when he replied. "Have you spent much time in Mirrik? Everybody in Mirrik says sorcerers can hypnotize you with a glance."

Hettie looked at Vammi, who shrugged. "Never been to Mirrik."

She turned back to Tinto. "I can do plenty of things and none of it requires eye contact. Why have you been spying on me?"

"Spying?" His voice rose in pitch until it cracked. "I wasn't spying. I've just never seen magic before. We don't have sorcerers in Mirrik."

"But they tell you not to look them in the eye?" she asked, raising an eyebrow. "Must be a holdover superstition from before your Temple killed them all off." Hettie kept her tone flat.

"Some of them left on their own," Tinto said. "Besides, can you blame them? The whole reason the Temple got started was because sorcerers kept using Mirrik and Brunland as pawns. The Red Lady double-crossed her own country the day after they gave Norrik the boot."

Andos had a complex history that was hard to keep track of, but even Hettie had heard that particular tale.

Hettie snorted. "Points for honesty. I'll return the favor. I don't like how you've been staring at me, so know this. If a Temple assassin comes after me, you'll be the first person I hunt down."

Tinto's mouth dropped open. Forgetting himself, he looked her in the eyes for the first time. "That's not fair! You're in the middle of a battle. People are already trying to kill you."

"You are covered in blood," Deryl reminded her.

She'd forgotten about that. Still, with the battle all but over, it was a moot point. Before she could say so, Vammi spoke up.

"He's got a point. That demon child kind-of murdered you once today already."

Tinto's eyebrows tried to climb up into his hairline. He mouthed "kind-of murdered" to himself.

"That reminds me," Hettie said darkly. "We've got some people to look for. And that kid is at the top of the list."

CHAPTER 42
KIKKA BARK

Hettie

Hettie and Vammi met up with Servio for an overview. Minimal lives had been lost on their side. The opposite could be said for Vincent's, whose entire population had been obliterated.

"Cheer up," Deryl said after they'd searched the castle for an hour looking for Cayon and the child assassin. *"Nobody's been found with slit wrists, so the kid was only after you, and he failed. Cayon's gone. The kid's gone. We won. Let's go home."*

They had won, but at what cost? An entire city was lost. Thousands of people.

Hettie paused at one of the castle's open-air windows, surveying the city below. Crushed houses and clusters of bodies were visible even at that height.

She thought back to the stories of her mother fighting the Importers. Had the streets of Port Placid ever looked so bleak? If so, she was glad she hadn't been around to see it.

The chitton caught her eye. It was perched halfway up one of the castle's turrets, surveying the city as well. The sight of it sitting there all lonely, looking for its wife magnified Hettie's feelings of failure.

How long had the people's city been living like that? Was it too much to ask for anything to turn out right? Everyone had died and even the chitton couldn't get a happy ending.

Hettie wanted justice for these people. She didn't feel guilty for killing them—regret, but not guilt. Ending their suffering had been a mercy. Someone needed to be held accountable for their suffering, but both Cayon and the kid had disappeared like shadows in the mist. They had Vincent, but he was more than a little out of his mind already.

Cayon and the kid weren't the only people Hettie had been hoping to find in the castle. She'd been sure at least a few poor souls had been tucked away somewhere. Locked up for whatever purpose. She'd hope to save more people like Adyr.

She couldn't use Bannot as an example. Or any of the rest she'd freed from cages. "Rescued" wasn't really a word that applied. They'd been changed so drastically that they had no life to return to.

Death might have been kinder.

The castle had no dungeon, surprisingly enough. The tunnels held several more rooms with empty cages, but no prisoners. Pillar's child remained unfound, and Hettie was not looking forward to breaking the news to her.

No rescued child. No Cayon. No demon child. When she'd told Adyr she was looking for the child, he shuddered. "I haven't seen him in months, but I still have nightmares about him."

"Considering what he's been through, that says a lot."

"I can't blame him. I may end up with nightmares of my own."

"If that kid wants to feature in your nightmares, he's going to have to get in line."

She pictured the kid patiently waiting in line behind a sign that read "Nightmares." She'd gladly face him a thousand times if it meant she didn't have to watch Elkin die.

The chitton spotted her and skittered over to her tower. "Wife?"

Hettie mentally added 'no chitton wife' to her list. "No wife. I'm sorry."

The chitton slumped, the gesture surprisingly accurate in reflecting how she felt.

"Keep looking," she told it. "She's out there somewhere."

After a moment, the chitton slowly pulled itself up. "Find wife," it whispered. Then it skittered away, disappearing around the corner of the castle wall.

Vammi appeared from down the hall. "I'm going to see Jonathan. Care to join me?"

She almost groaned in disgust. She'd left their commander injured in enemy territory. It had felt necessary at the time. Considering how things had gone, she'd have been better off staying behind with him. "Absolutely. I need to heal him."

"I left the Marner brothers in charge. He's in good hands."

The Marner brothers were the twin sons of Lady Tuigasi's healer. They'd assisted the Daughters' Coven after the Battle of Poll's Wander. They weren't healers, but they were competent assistants.

It took several minutes to get through the bottleneck of soldiers at the gate. Nobody wanted to be in the cursed city after nightfall. The press of bodies made it difficult to talk with Vammi until they were through the gate.

They found Jonathan where they'd left him. His typically tidy appearance was disheveled. Sweaty and tousled, he looked like he'd been in a tavern brawl. Despite that, he seemed to be in good spirits with an uncharacteristically goofy grin on his face. He beamed up at them when they approached.

"Sorry for leaving you like that," Hettie apologized. She held her arms out to display the blood smeared on her legs, boots, and chest while she explained about the child assassin.

"That's most terribibly disfortunate," he said, frowning at his own word choice. "Nonfortunate?"

The Marner brothers snickered. "Unfortunate," one of them said helpfully.

Hettie rolled her eyes. "Bukker's soggy toes, what did you give him?" she asked the two round-faced soldiers.

"Ground kikka bark," one said, grinning. "He didn't even get that much."

"What is kikka bark? Is it from a tree?" she asked.

The other brother nodded. "They probably don't grow on the islands. The kikkapountas tree has a loose, thick outer bark that can cause nausea and hallucinations. That outer part's a dull brown. If you peel it off, there's a layer of smooth red bark beneath. Grind it up and you get a potent painkilling sedative."

"Vammi," Jonathan said with a bit of slur to his voice. "I was talking to my friends here and it turns out you're a really swell guy."

"Swell guy," Vammi repeated slowly, as if he'd never heard the antiquated phrase before.

"Yes. I think I've had you all . . . of you wrong." He stumbled over his words but pressed on. "Servio too. Did I tell you how he got us over the wall? He came up with ideas I would never have thought to try. Why, that bit about the distraction while we carved under the wall was brillia . . . brill . . . very good." He made little hopping motions with his hands. "The good general is always thinking three steps ahead."

Hettie and Vammi traded amused looks while Jonathan became absorbed in the hopping motions his hands made. He mumbled about hammers and wedges, oblivious to their mirth.

"How does your leg feel?" Hettie asked when his hands finally dropped to his lap.

The leg had been straightened to some degree, but it was clear where the break was.

"You know, it's mostly okay as long as I don't move. Or breathe. The breathing is harder to not do though."

Hettie bit her lip to keep from laughing at him. "How about I fix it?'

Jonathan gave her a wary look. "It doesn't feel very good if you move it."

"I'll just look at it first." She pulled out Cayon's journals. "In the meantime, see if you can make sense of these."

He took them eagerly and opened one. "What are they?"

"Journals from the mad scientist who used this city for his experiments and managed to turn men into monsters."

"Like alchemy, but with people." He opened the oldest looking journal, and his face grew studious as he flipped through the pages rapidly, spending only a few seconds on any page.

Deryl made an appreciative gesture. *"I don't think you could have invented a better distraction for him."*

Hettie focused on healing Jonathan's leg, which was easier now that she wasn't drowning in excess power. In the hour or so since she'd used it to save Ouri, it had almost returned to her natural levels.

She motioned for the brothers to help position the leg better for faster healing. They didn't need instruction.

Vammi held Jonathan's shoulders down, though he seemed so entranced with the journal he barely noticed the work being done on him. The kikka bark surely helped.

When the job was done, Hettie had to ask Jonathan how he felt three times, then take the journal from him before he registered the question and answered.

"What? That's fascinating," he said, trying to take the journal back.

Hettie held it out of reach. "How are you feeling?"

"I'm fine. That was written by a woman nearly a hundred years ago. She came with a small contingent of miners who started the first mining tunnels in the area." His slur was gone, and he spoke with intensity. "The deeper they dug, the more they were affected by something in the mountain." He sat up, growing more animated as he talked.

"Wow. Forget kikka bark," Deryl said. *"Just give him a book and commence amputating limbs."*

Jonathan was still staring at the journal in Hettie's hand. "They grew paranoid of things lurking in the tunnels. They were convinced the gods had blessed them with strength and night vision, so they grew wary of the light. Large snakes appeared, living off rats in the mountain. Over time, they got bigger, and the people learned they were attracted by noise. They developed their own hand language so they could communicate silently."

The muddling effects of the kikka root seemed to have worn off. It was like he'd stored up energy during his period of rest and it was coming out in a rush.

Hettie agreed with him, though. The journal sounded fascinating.

"At one point, a new group of people came to inspect the mines, but they left after meeting the original miners. The newcomers told them they'd gone mad, and they obviously *were* mad, but they didn't realize it."

Jonathan reached again for the journal and Hettie handed it to him.

"Are you saying that journal tells about the origin of the rock-toads?" she asked. It sounded like a campfire tale.

Vammi said, "They had to come from somewhere. Knowing what we do about the Element, I wouldn't discount it."

"That's not the strangest part," Jonathan said as he flipped back to the page he'd been on. "It appears their madness affected their memory. The handwriting never changes, but it seems to cover a lot of time. Eventually, the entries make it sound like the writer believes their people had always lived in the mountain, and they had never seen outsiders."

Vammi began reading over Jonathan's shoulder. "Perhaps the journal is passed down through the generations."

"It never indicates a shift. The writer talks about the same people throughout the story. As crazy as it sounds, I think it could be the very same people that live there now. Let me show you what I mean."

Soon, both men were entranced in reading.

CHAPTER 43
MANY FORMS OF SUFFERING

Hettie

The general consensus was that the rocktoad journals did appear to be written by one person over an inordinately long period of time. Long enough for a group of less than a hundred people to dig miles and miles of tunnels. Hettie couldn't be sure it was the same rocktoads she'd met without identifiable markers though.

When the sky grew dim, they made their way out of the citadel. They exited the city to find nobody wanted to cross the ledge in the dark. As a compromise, the soldiers gathered in the clearing between the outer walls and the chasm.

The general air of melancholy improved as the night wore on. Many had been under the impression Jonathan had fallen to battle. More respected and beloved than he knew, it had taken an additional toll on morale. Now that Jonathan was safely among his men, all seemed well, and talk turned to families and friends they would soon see again.

Hettie made her way through camp, healing the worst of the injuries. She would handle the rest in the morning while the healthier soldiers went across the ledge. It had been a long night and, magic or no, she was exhausted.

Servio organized the soldiers. Together, they built a huge bonfire that lit the camp. They burned tables, chairs, empty barrels, and anything else they could find in the first section of Stonehaven. The flames warded off the shadows.

Word of the Element had spread, and the steady drone of paranoid discussion carried in the night air.

Runners were sent to summon Vincent, who had been escorted to a boulder-rimmed guard post just outside the gates. Everybody had taken to calling him Vincent. The "lord" had been dropped. He was deemed unworthy of the title.

Hettie almost groaned in relief as she sat with her back against a cool rock, back a ways from the blazing bonfire. She pulled out one of Cayon's journals to read while she waited. In the second of the three journals, Cayon had written with excitement about the results of a recent experiment. He had presented his findings to Lord Vincent only to get a lecture on ethics in return.

Cayon had demonstrated the abilities of three of his subjects. The first had gone nearly a month without sleep, the second had grown sharp thorns all over her skin, and the third was able to bleed endlessly because his body regenerated blood as fast as it was lost. "The potential for future discoveries is astounding," he wrote, clearly fascinated.

Vincent had agreed the abilities were incredible, but he was concerned they were unpleasant for the subject. Disgusted by the methodology, he asked how many people had suffered worse fates than the three on display. Cayon refused to answer, insisting Vincent "focus on the potential."

"That doesn't sound like the Vincent we know," Deryl said.

"I'm beginning to think we don't know him at all."

By the end of the entry, Cayon felt justified in adding bits of the

Element to Vincent's food. He could change the world with over a thousand subjects to study. He just needed to get Vincent on board.

Hettie muttered, "Crazy what you can do when you're not weighed down by pesky things like empathy."

Adyr and Bannot walked through camp. Adyr had gotten a shirt and a new pair of pants somewhere. His long hair was tied, a tangled mess at the back of his head. He'd washed his face, which only served to highlight the sharp cheekbones and bags under his eyes. His wrinkle lines made him look much older than he probably was.

Jonathan spotted them and scrambled to his feet. "Adyr! It really is you!"

Adyr clapped Jonathan on the back. "I missed you more than you know."

"Great gods, man, look at your face." Jonathan reached out to lift up a long clump of hair that had fallen free from the string Adyr had tied it back with. "And your hair." He let the clump fall. He stared at his friend in horror. "You've been here captive this whole time?"

Hettie knew Jonathan well enough to know he would feel guilt over not bringing an army to rescue his friend earlier, never mind that he didn't even know he was here. Where Cayon lacked empathy, Jonathan had too much. It was crippling at times.

"It's okay," Adyr said quietly, showing he knew Jonathan well too.

"No, it's not."

"No, it's not," Adyr agreed. "But the fault doesn't lie with you."

As if by joint agreement, Adyr, Jonathan, Vammi, and Bannot sat. They stared at the fire for a long while, each lost in their own thoughts.

The silence was broken by Jonathan. "You really need a shower."

Adyr threw his head back and laughed.

"Both of you smell as bad as you look," Jonathan insisted.

"Practical as always," Adyr said, wiping his eye. "To think I almost missed you." He clapped a hand on Jonathan's shoulder and shook him good-naturedly.

Jonathan almost fell over, which made Adyr laugh again. "I've been stuck in a cage all this time. You've been training an army. How are you in such poor shape?"

"Count on you to focus on fitness," Jonathan said, grinning.

Hettie watched it all from outside the group. They bickered like family. It made her miss her own.

"You know," Deryl said, *"I'd argue you're as much like family to Jonathan and Vammi as Adyr is."*

"They grew up together."

His response was slow in coming. *"It doesn't take a lifetime to form a family."*

She'd known people who got married when they'd only known each other a week. *"I suppose you're right."*

Adyr laughed at something Vammi said. It was good he'd gained back the family he'd lost. Most didn't get that chance.

Pillar certainly wouldn't.

Deryl could probably relate. His wife had been taken from him, and he'd never gotten her back. He'd never had any kind of family after, as far as Hettie knew. Granted, there was a lot she didn't know about his past. "Tell me more about your time with Cerissa."

"After we go through the journals," Deryl hedged. "The one you've got sounds like Cayon's early days. See if the other one tells more about what happened later."

She hefted the last journal, which was smaller than the other two. It was a reference guide of sorts, written in Cayon's neat handwriting.

Limited exposure to the Element via any method yields unsatisfying results.

Intermittent, noninvasive, long-term exposure provides minor change that takes months to manifest. Sometimes years. When using noninvasive measures, exposure must remain constant.

Intermittent, invasive exposure has been more promising. Results can be seen within two to five weeks. More invasive procedures produce more dramatic results and effects can be fine-tuned by adjusting the frequency of exposure. The type of effect, however, is unpredictable.

Below the statement was a chart showing durations of exposure to non-exposure and the length of time it took for the body to heal from the damage. Beneath the chart was a sentence in fine script.

Note: Changes of bone structure do not revert to normal once treatment has stopped.

Hettie read on. It was morbidly fascinating.

According to the chart, Adyr's type of exposure typically resulted in minimal changes, all of which were likely to heal naturally over time.

From what Hettie could tell, most of his ailments were the result of being cooped up so long. He'd lost weight and grown weaker. He may have been less mentally stable than when he went in, but that wasn't unusual for someone who had been locked up in a tunnel and experimented on for months.

"He was lucky," Deryl said.

"I'm not sure that word applies to anyone under Cayon's care."

"Well, comparatively, anyway."

Hettie wasn't sure comparisons were relevant. If you suffered trauma, did it matter if someone else had it worse?

Hettie returned to the first journal, flipping ahead. By the time she finished it, she was even more disturbed.

Based on the range of results producible from the Element, it is feasible to produce more dramatic results. With the right starting specimen, a combination of long-term exposure methods could yield a soldier so resistant to pain and death that they might become unkillable, as well as resistant to aging, as the journal of the Sunless implies.

The ultimate question haunts me. Is immortality within reach? If so, would using the same methods on a sorcerer yield a god?

Hettie shivered at the implications. The Sunless. The rocktoads had told her that's what the humans called them. Had the old journal given Cayon the idea to experiment on people?

She had no idea if he could come up with something that resembled godlike powers, but the number of lives ruined in the attempt would be mindboggling.

"The dates where he mentions Vincent's complaints correspond with the attack on Penelope," Deryl said.

"Which means he never left Stonehaven. He sent a look-alike in his place."

"A look-alike from before he became a giant walking hairball."

"I wonder if it was Cayon's idea to keep him here."

"Probably. Vincent was part of the experiment, so he'd want to note any changes." Deryl was silent for a long while before saying, *"Did you notice he never mentioned the suffering of the prisoners?"*

For Hettie, the wailing, tapping, and moaning had been hard to ignore. Cayon hadn't seemed to notice it. Like he had trained himself to ignore anything but the results he wanted.

"That was all while they were sitting in cages," Deryl said. *"Can you imagine the screams while he was stabbing them with metal or dripping poisoned water in their eyes?"*

The mental images she conjured were interrupted when Servio approached. His uniform was mussed and torn in a couple places where it looked like he'd run into a blade of some kind. One tear had a blood stain, though Hettie couldn't tell if it was his.

He held two cups of tea and extended one to her.

She took it and sipped, letting the smokiness erase the faint taste of bile in her throat.

Servio cleared his throat and shifted his weight, looking awkward. "Excellent job today."

"Excellent is a stretch," Hettie said. "Today was downright depressing."

"War is always depressing," Servio said. "Every time. There's a sense of victory in taking down the commander of an army, but the soldiers are there for a paycheck or because they were pressed into service. Killing them only ever feels like a slaughter." He sounded as tired as she felt.

Hettie snorted. "Too often, leaders are cowards. They'll put the lives of others at risk, but not their own." She'd been raised with a different model. Her mother did the bulk of the fighting herself.

"She fights from the bottom of the ocean though," Deryl said. *"It's not like she's in danger."*

"Yes, but neither are her people."

"At least nobody alive really knew them," Servio said, gesturing to the towering walls behind them. "It saves a lot of heartache."

His words irritated her. Especially after reading of Cayon's heartless pursuit of inhuman soldiers. "Shouldn't somebody mourn their passing?"

He sighed. "Women's feelings have no place in battle."

Hettie almost threw her tea in his face. "Women's feelings?" she said, disdainfully. "It's not women's feelings to mourn the dead. It should be everybody's feelings."

"True," Servio said calmly. "Note I didn't say you shouldn't have them. Just that they aren't useful." Before she could give a retort, he held up a finger to stop her. "The term wasn't meant to be an insult. Women are typically more caring than men." He sat on the ground beside her. "After a life of war and killing, I'm convinced the world can use as much caring as it can get. It's simply one of the least useful feelings to have on a battlefield. They lead to distraction and ill judgement and can get you killed faster than you can imagine."

Hettie wasn't mollified by his words, but she had to admit they made sense. She'd let her guard down with the demon child. Wanting to rescue him wasn't wrong, but she should have been more cautious.

"I was promoted to general long ago," Servio said.

"It didn't take him long to get back to boasting, did it?" Deryl said dryly. He and Hettie had both grown sick of his stories.

His tone was subdued this time though.

"Another general had gotten sick. He grew worse every day. By the time he died, he was bleeding from every orifice."

"That sounds pleasant," Deryl said.

"A new general was brought in. He promoted me to lieutenant. A month later, he grew ill as well. His death was quicker. It took four days for his eyes to bulge out of his head. Nobody knew what killed him either." Servio gave a mirthless laugh. "There were rumors the position of general was cursed."

Hettie couldn't make out the point of his story. "You're saying what? Everybody dies? Life is unpredictable?"

His gaze was steady when he met her eyes. She could have sworn she saw sadness behind them.

"Companionship is a rare thing for a career soldier," he said.

Deryl said, *"He's making less sense than usual."*

"I had an ongoing relationship with the camp healer. It turns out she wanted to marry and intended to pave my way to greatness."

Hettie put two and two together. "She poisoned the two generals."

Servio shook his head. "Magic." The words were bitter. "I didn't even know she was capable of using it." They sat in silence until he said, "I would have married her. Instead, I had her beheaded for murder."

Deryl whistled. *"No wonder he hates you. Judging all magic users by the actions of one is pretty ignorant though."*

"Look who's talking."

"Hey, I've been bound to more than one sorcerer, and they've all been monstrously vile."

"I've been trying to prove myself as a general ever since," Servio said with a sad smile. "I know I come off all wrong. I don't mean to. It's ingrained in me at this point."

"You're renowned for what you've done in the past. Do you still feel like you need to earn your position?"

"Yes. I will never feel otherwise, because I never should have had it in the first place."

For once, he wasn't being condescending and snide. Hettie was surprised to find that he was almost likable when he was being honest and humble.

"Today," he said, "with these people—these animals—you didn't hesitate. You were prepared for battle." He didn't look at her, staring into the fire instead. "I wasn't. This place terrifies me."

"I'm not immune to being terrified," Hettie said.

"Your nightmares." Servio took a deep breath. "I see how you faced today's battle. I can't help but wonder what could possibly wake you screaming in the night." He glanced at her, eyes haunted. "There are rumors that come from the Paradisals. About the Island Witch."

"She goes by the Deep Witch now, since she lives underwater."

Servio's eyebrows rose, and his eyes widened. "She lives under . . ." He blinked. "And the rumors?"

Hettie wasn't sure which rumors he was talking about, but chances were good they weren't exaggerated. "Likely true. If I had to guess, the rumors are only half of it."

Servio was quiet after that.

CHAPTER 44
JOERI

Hettie

Vincent's hysterical babbling could be heard long before he made it to camp. Escorted by a handful of soldiers, he drew stares, though Hettie wasn't sure if it was the astounding amount of body hair or the mad laughter punctuating his ramblings that drew more attention.

"As terrifying tyrants go, he's not very intimidating," Deryl said.

Vincent approached with rapid, jerky motions. It was easy to believe he'd been twisted, just as his people had. She could have dismissed his behavior as good acting, an attempt to avoid punishment, but the body hair could only have been produced by the Element.

In light of Cayon's journals, Hettie almost felt sorry for Vincent, but even if he was just another of Cayon's victims, he was the leader of Stonehaven, and Cayon had been his responsibility. Vincent had been aware of the experiments and failed to stop Cayon.

Looking at his matted hair and clear displays of mental instability, Hettie wondered if maybe he'd suffered enough.

He was pulled to a stop near where Hettie stood around the main campfire with Jonathan and Servio. Vammi had taken Adyr and Bannot to get rations, a bath, and whatever else he could think up to keep them away. The last thing they needed was Bannot flying into another rage.

The guards formed a loose circle around Vincent, and the three leaders joined it. A muttering, shuffling mass of bodies pressed in around them as every soldier within hearing distance crowded in to listen.

While the day hadn't brought many deaths among the soldiers, when combined with the previous battle of Poll's Wander, almost every member of the original Widows' Will had lost a friend to Vincent's tyranny. On the chance that one of them might take justice into their own hands, Hettie put a shield around Vincent.

She spoke over the murmuring crowd. "I've read Cayon's journals."

Vincent twitched, distracted by something in the sky. Ouri, perhaps? Or was he flinching at shadows?

Hettie hadn't had the chance to brief Jonathan on the journals yet, so she summarized as she spoke to Vincent. "Cayon couldn't convince you to join him, so he started drugging you."

Jonathan raised an eyebrow at her. The mutters of the crowd grew louder.

Hettie asked, "Why didn't you stop him when you had the chance?"

Vincent spun in a half circle, jerking like a puppet as he scanned the crowd. His head wobbled drunkenly, and his body hair seemed to ripple along with his movements where it stuck through his tattered clothing.

"Joooe-riii." Vincent let the word draw out for a couple seconds like a moan. "Joooe-riii."

"What are you doing?" Jonathan asked.

"Who or what is Joeri?" Hettie asked at the same time.

"Joooe-riii," Vincent said. "Cayon and Joeri." He spun to face Hettie. "Both. They'll both rule." He grinned, eyes wide. "They'll rule in madness." His ensuing cackle made Hettie's hair stand on end. "We're all mad now!"

The soldiers stared on in fascinated disgust as Vincent continued ranting.

Hettie stepped forward, dropped the shield, and grabbed a fistful of his neck hair. She slapped him hard enough to make him see stars.

He blinked his owlish brown orbs at her, and she made her own eyes swirl like tidepools in return. "Who is Joeri?" Her voice came out low and rumbly like a thunderstorm low over the ocean.

Her approach subdued Vincent. His manic grin faded, and he swallowed audibly as sanity returned. "Joeri is the benefactor." He raised a hand and pointed north.

Since he was cooperating, Hettie released him. She let her eyes and voice return to normal. "Tell me more."

He opened his mouth. But his whole body spasmed, and he let out a grunt. He stood still for a few heartbeats before his legs buckled. He collapsed, landing limply, and didn't move.

Hettie stared. *"Is this his plan to get out of talking? Play dead?"*

"It's not a very good plan unless he's going to stay that way."

Convinced it was trickery, she held out her hands to keep the guards at bay before delving him. It didn't take long to figure out his heart wasn't beating.

"That's a lot of blood," Deryl said. It seeped in a spreading puddle around Vincent. *"If he's playing dead, he's really good at it."*

Hettie was baffled. Had he arrived injured? She went to heal him only to find his insides shredded. Two puncture wounds marked where daggers had been inserted just below his ribcage on each side. From the looks of things, the daggers had been twisted back and forth until there was nothing but mush left. There was no way Vincent could have walked into camp like that.

"What's wrong with him?" Vincent asked. By the alarm in his voice, he'd noticed the blood too.

"I'll give you one guess at who could have caused that kind of damage in the middle of a crowd in under a second's time," Deryl said.

"Dammit." Her mind reeled. "I shouldn't have dropped my shield." Her blood ran cold at the thought of the child assassin being so close. Belatedly, she shielded herself.

It was pointless to scan heartbeats. There were too many around. She looked over the crowd, already knowing she wasn't going to see the kid coming.

"If you were his target, you'd know it," Deryl said. *"Cayon probably sent him after Vincent."*

Hettie tried to organize her racing thoughts. *"Or this Joeri guy. The question is why? Does he blame Vincent for losing the battle?"*

"I'll bet you three mugs of ale and a tankard of cheese it's because Vincent is a liability."

Hettie paused. *"Vincent was barely coherent. And really? A tankard of cheese?"*

"You guys don't do liquid goat cheese? It's really good. Especially with crushed berries mixed in. Back home, Ottofay used to run a tavern that sold it. Anytime a customer got stupid drunk and unruly, they'd be forced on stage to entertain the other patrons. The barmaids had a special batch of goat cheese they brewed with pepper flakes in it. After the unruly drunk finished entertaining them, the crowd would vote on how much spicy cheese he had to drink." He sighed wistfully.

"You drank it too," Hettie guessed.

"All the time."

One would think abusing paying customers was bad for business, but Hettie knew better. That sort of thing often drew in a crowd. There were always people like Deryl who adamantly refused to learn from their experiences.

Jonathan leaned in closer to Hettie. "What happened?" he asked in a tight voice.

She'd explained about the kid when they were still in the citadel, so it didn't take long for Jonathan to get the picture.

"You weren't joking when you said how fast he moved." Jonathan scanned the crowd.

"Post sentries. Keep the fire going. That kid could take out our whole army in an hour if we aren't careful. Hopefully he was just after Vincent."

They waited for Adyr and Bannot to return. They explained what happened and asked if either had heard the name Joeri before. Neither had. Bannot wanted to be the one to throw Vincent into the chasm. If it gave the man closure, nobody was going to object.

Soon after, the camp settled down for the night.

Hettie doubted anyone slept well. They were all grateful when morning came. Crossing the chasm was a slow process that took most of the next day. Thankfully, it was uneventful.

Hettie stayed behind to heal the last of the injuries. She was one of the last to cross in the late afternoon when the sun's slanted rays no longer penetrated the chasm's depths. Midway across, she looked into the darkness where a thousand tiny lights winked in and out of existence. Light crags, she guessed.

Staring into the abyss made her feel like she was falling. Someone had strung a rope along the wall with intermittent anchor points, and her knuckles hurt from gripping it so tightly.

Witch or no, she couldn't fly.

Ouri called a greeting from overhead. He seemed no worse for wear after eating the stone dragon. Movement high up on the cliff face drew her eye. The hairs on the back of her neck stood up. She scanned the mountains until she spotted a shadow moving.

Sun glinted off dark hair. The silhouette of a thin form was briefly visible, backlit by the sun before it disappeared over the top of the outcropping. Hettie broke out in a cold sweat. *"If he's not here to kill us, why hasn't he left?"*

"You'd think a child would have somewhere else to be," Deryl said.

She wasn't sure the term "child" was apt but didn't argue.

A soldier cleared his throat behind Hettie, who was holding up the line.

She ignored him, reaching out with her senses. If she could stop the assassin's heart from a distance, it would be the safest way to take him down. She wouldn't dare send soldiers after him. He was far too quick and clever with those knives, and that was assuming they could get to him.

She tried to ignore the flutter in her stomach. Regardless of his deadliness, he was young and he'd had no say in what he'd become. It was impossible not to think of her younger sisters every time she thought of the boy.

Despite her efforts, she couldn't find him from that distance. With a growl of frustration, she continued across the ledge. On the far side, she found Vammi and Jonathan discussing plants of all things.

"Is he boring you, Vammi?"

Vammi shook his head. "It's strangely fascinating. He's like a scholar but only in the most useless ways."

"Plants are far from useless," Jonathan insisted. "They kept the stone dragon at bay in the tunnels, didn't they?"

He gestured to Jonathan. "Carry on. What was the one with the heart-shaped leaves called again?"

Before they could get back to their discussion, Hettie told them she was off to see the rocktoads.

"Want company?" Jonathan asked.

She shook her head.

"It'll be dark soon," Vammi said. "You'll slow her down." He motioned impatiently for the lecture to continue.

Hettie left them to it, grateful to make the journey alone. It gave her time to think.

How did you tell a parent their child was gone? That they had either been experimented on, killed, or made into stew—maybe all three.

By the time she reached the cave entrance, she still didn't know what to say.

The last rays of the sinking sun disappeared behind the peaks to cloak the land in dusky shadow.

Night vision gave Hettie a good view of the distant ledge to the citadel. She wanted nothing more than for centuries to pass while it fell into ruins, never to be inhabited again. It had become a place of evil.

She reached out with her magic to weaken the ledge. At that distance, and with her magic depleted by Ouri's transformation plus the many healings, she could barely touch it. After several minutes, the most she could do was crumble parts of it until it was impassable. It was enough.

The scuffing of feet came from behind her as figures emerged from the tunnel.

With a heavy heart, she turned to face them.

CHAPTER 45

SURVIVORS

Hettie

Dozens of rocktoads filled the tunnel as far back as Hettie could see. Every one of them wore a smile that stretched their cheeks. Even Pillar, who led the group.

"Are they hoping you've got the kid hiding in your shoe?" Deryl asked.

Hettie was just as confused. She clearly hadn't brought back Pillar's child. Her failure should have been obvious.

If they'd been monitoring the battle though, they would know Hettie's side had won a sweeping victory. Clearly they hadn't assumed the worst.

Their joy made Hettie want to curl up in a ball and disappear. Pillar's in particular. Hettie would be smashing that happiness like a bug underfoot. She really didn't want to have this conversation, but her mother didn't raise weak daughters.

Pillar spoke before she could get any words out. "Stone dragon dead." The words were still quiet, but much louder than her previous whisper. Her eyes sparkled, and she bounced on her toes.

Hettie blinked. "Oh." That was certainly a reason for them to celebrate. Hopefully it would take the sting out of her news. "Yes. Well sort of." Ouri had been the one to kill it.

"Take the win," Deryl advised.

"The stone dragon is dead," Hettie confirmed. "Your tunnels should be safe."

A wave of hand signals rippled through the crowd. Clenched fists held high, opening to splayed fingers in a "bursting" gesture. It felt celebratory.

Hettie cleared her throat, uncomfortable. They probably didn't get to celebrate often, and her news would be like a bucket of cold water for Pillar. "About your child."

Pillar reached forward, taking her hand. Her dry skin rubbed a fine layer of dust onto Hettie's palm. "Child home. Child safe." Pillar squeezed, her grip making Hettie's bones ache.

Hettie registered the tone of gratitude first, then the words. "Wait. Your child is home?"

Pillar's words tumbled out, her excitement overcoming her. "Home. Free cage. Free children." She stopped talking long enough to wave to someone a few rows back. Another rocktoad pushed forward, with long hair and a stumbling gait that looked painful.

Hettie couldn't tell which of the pitiful creatures she'd rescued it was. They'd all been huddled in cages. As Pillar's child hobbled closer, Hettie could see her skin wasn't nearly as caked in rock dust as usual. Almost by reflex, she reached out with her magic to find muscles and joints deteriorated from lack of use, but no major damage.

For being one of Cayon's prisoners, she was surprisingly unaltered.

"The journals claim the rocktoads have been living in tunnels full of the Element for decades, if not centuries. They've probably built up a resistance," Deryl said.

The child made the hand burst motions, smiling all the while.

Hettie wore a matching grin. She'd thought she'd failed in saving this child. The flood of emotion was overwhelming, and she swallowed hard before she spoke. "How did you get home?"

A gruff voice said, "You free them. They know home."

Hettie peered into the tunnel, searching for the voice. Several rocktoads bent to lift something. Some moved out of the way to make room for the ones carrying the load. A clustered group came out of the tunnel, carrying their load. One of the bearers was Boulder.

To Hettie's surprise, they carried Grumpy out and laid him at her feet. His hips and shoulders were still locked, though he was smiling instead of scowling. Or maybe it was a grimace. Hettie couldn't tell.

She raised an eyebrow. "They took off your gag."

Grumpy gave a short nod. "Pillar not want me warn Cayon you coming."

He spoke her language well for a rocktoad. "You were working for him." She couldn't keep the hardness from her voice at the thought of him turning against his own.

"Yes. No. Cayon take *me* child first. I work so he not hurt me child or her child."

Hettie mulled that over. She could understand how desperate he must have been. He and Pillar were working for the same result, they just went about it in different ways. Grumpy tried to please Cayon. Pillar tried to overthrow him. In hindsight, hers was the riskier maneuver. Luckily, it paid off in the end.

Hettie was still coming to grips with the news that her child had made it home safe.

"Is your child okay?" she asked Grumpy.

He nodded brusquely. "Child okay." He looked intently at the rocktoad standing next to Boulder. Hettie noticed for the first time that this rocktoad also had little in the way of dust caking his skin. He knelt to put a hand on Grumpy's shoulder.

Hettie took a moment to unlock Grumpy's limbs. He sat up slowly in stiff, jerky motions.

"You set us free from the cages," his child said. "The stone dragon came. It died. We were trapped in a side tunnel." His words came out hesitant, as if he had to think of how to speak in complete sentences.

Hettie had been afraid the thrashing worm had killed the freed prisoners. She was glad to know they'd managed to duck into a hidey hole somewhere. "If you were trapped by its corpse, how did you get free?"

Grumpy's child spoke to Pillar's child using hand signals. Pillar's child stepped forward, holding up a hand. Nails, sharp and tapered like dagger tips, protruded from each finger. Dark discoloration marked the cuticles. The angled sides were too straight to be natural. Hettie wondered if she had sharpened them on the stone walls.

Pillar's child spoke in a soft voice. "Dig. Bring others home."

"Others," Hettie said. Had they brought all the freed prisoners here?

Pillar's child turned to face the tunnel entrance. All the rocktoads in the vicinity followed suit. A lot of shuffling went on inside the tunnel. A new rocktoad emerged, taller than the rest, and older, though Hettie couldn't pinpoint how she knew that. Behind it followed a string of children.

Hettie's mouth dropped open when she realized they were human children.

Dirty and dressed in tattered clothes, they ranged from around ages five to fifteen. With the difference in heights, it was hard for Hettie to count them, but she estimated there were nearly twenty of them in total.

"Those kids were not in the cages we opened," Deryl said.

"No. They must have been locked up somewhere else. The prisoners we freed rescued them."

"Aren't they lucky. Do you think they want to hear a joke?"

Hettie watched the children stumble forward, clinging to each other in small groups. Two girls in front had telltale signs that they'd come in contact with the Element. One had eyebrows far too long to be natural, reaching down past her cheekbones. Another had a little horn growing beneath her chin.

Hettie just barely managed to keep from bursting into tears. It had already been terrible to think of rocktoad children locked up in those underground tunnels, alone, tortured, and devoid of hope. She'd lost all hope of bringing home survivors. Her heart ached unbearably to think of what the children had endured. The youngest was still so small.

"My heart," she whispered.

She'd been convinced their rescue mission was a failure. They'd been too late to save anyone but Adyr and Bannot, who would never be the same. Shutting down the citadel was the best they could do, and it had cost the lives of nearly everyone who lived there.

Watching the tortured, terrified children, Hettie decided all the deaths were worth it. If they had done nothing but save this frightened gaggle of kids, it was worth the trip. She liked to think Vincent's people—had they been sane—would have been grateful for that.

CHAPTER 46

HOPE FOR TOMORROW

Adyr

Adyr had left his prison bars behind. He and Bannot were finally free. He should have been happy. Everything should have been good.

Everything was not good.

It was more than the looks of disgust and pity from nearby soldiers. It was the way Bannot sat quietly staring into the fire. It was the way he'd grown quiet in the weeks before their rescue.

Adyr could handle the rages. It was the pensive silence that worried him. Their newfound freedom should have changed that.

"What are you thinking, friend?"

The quiet stretched. Bannot gave a short shake of his head. "I don't know how to say goodbye."

Adyr fought the spike of anger and disappointment that boiled in his guts. They'd made it so far. By gods, Bannot was not going to die on Adyr's watch. "I won't let you kill yourself. Your family needs you. They've been waiting months to see you. Under the right circumstances, months can feel like an eternity. You know that better than anyone. Don't make their wait be in vain."

Bannot was shaking his head in earnest before Adyr had finished speaking. "I can't return to my family. Look at me." He sighed, and it sounded like a growl. "I'm hideous, and I'm volatile." His voice dropped to a whisper. "I have nightmares about going home. It terrifies me how certain I am that I'll be the one to kill them. In my dreams, I can feel my hands around my own child's throat. I can't let that happen."

When they were caged, it had been easy to argue with Bannot, to insist it would all work out. Now that they were free, he found the words didn't come so easily. If Bannot went home, he might very well kill his family. Adyr had seen enough of his rage to know that. "What will you do?"

Bannot chewed his lip. "I need a favor. A big one." He didn't wait for Adyr to agree. He knew his friend would do anything he asked. "Take care of my family. I can't be there for them, but you can. Do this for me."

"You're not going to kill yourself," Adyr reiterated.

"No," Bannot agreed.

"Then what?" He needed Bannot to convince him death wasn't the option he focused on. He'd focused on it far too often during captivity.

"Cayon is still out there."

Adyr saw the request to care for his family in a new light. Bannot wanted to go after Cayon and knew Adyr would have accompanied him. Bannot wanted to go alone.

"He's in the wind. You'll never find him."

The silence grated on Adyr's nerves.

Eventually, Bannot spoke. "I know where he is. A scout spotted him. A man in a pale gray cloak. He thought it was just a fleeing citizen."

Adyr closed his eyes. Cayon's cloak was deep red, but it was lined with silver satin, easy to flip inside out. "Where?"

"Riding a horse down the pass beyond the valley."

Past the village he'd poisoned. And on a horse, no less.

The latter was too much. It had to be Cayon. Nobody else would have access to a horse. He'd probably taken it out through the tunnels days ago and hidden it somewhere in the mountains.

"That path leads to the Yellow Sea. The desert will kill him." It was Adyr's last resort, but he knew the battle was already lost.

"You know I can't leave that to chance," Bannot said quietly.

Adyr chewed his lip. "I'll come."

Bannot shook his head, as Adyr knew he would. "It's safer if I do this alone. I need you to take care of my family."

Adyr paced, leaving Bannot to stare at the fire. He didn't want to let his friend go off alone, but he could sense the finality of his decision. Bannot would not be swayed.

The frustration ate at him.

A blue-eyed Andosh cut through their campfire. Vammi had mentioned him. Apparently, Hettie had found the man suspicious. What had his name been?

Tinto.

Adyr owed Hettie his life. It was a debt he would likely never be able to repay. Since he couldn't aid his old friend, he could at least aid a new one by making sure Tinto wasn't a threat.

The man disappeared into the darkness. Adyr followed.

He had been a proficient fighter. His months of captivity had weakened him, but there were ways to get the upper hand without strength.

Adyr snuck up behind Tinto and grabbed him by the throat. With one leg outstretched, he twisted at the hips, pulling Tinto off balance. Tinto ended up in a half backbend, legs splayed in an attempt to keep from falling. Adyr held him in that position.

Tinto's struggles were brief and uncoordinated.

"What harm do you mean Hettie?" Adyr's words came out harsh, and he realized he was taking his frustration with Bannot out on Tinto.

"What?" Tinto squeaked, his voice raspy from the grip on his throat. He searched Adyr's face in the dim outskirts of the flickering firelight and recognition dawned. "You're that prisoner."

Adyr shook him. "The witch. You will not harm her."

Tinto's eyes widened in panic. "Like I said, I wasn't spying on her. I just never seen magic before."

"Lies." It wasn't a question or even an accusation. It was a statement of fact. "Tell me why you're here." Before Tinto could answer, he said, "You have one chance to answer truthfully before I snap your neck and throw you into the ravine. Nobody will miss you."

Tinto trembled in fear. "I came for my father," he said. His voice only quavered a little.

"What does your father want with Hettie?"

"He thinks she's evil," Tinto breathed.

Adyr huffed in disgust. "He's with the Temple of the Sky." Again, it wasn't a question.

Tinto nodded vigorously. "He is. But he's not a bad man."

"He is in my book. I've seen enough horrors to know good people from bad. Magic or not, Hettie is a good person. I'll kill anyone who comes against her."

"Agreed," Tinto said earnestly.

Adyr had been about to make him wish he'd never joined the Widows' Will, but he paused at the sincerity in that word.

"I agree," Tinto repeated. Words tumbled from him. "My father thinks she's evil, because the Temple told him so. Said sorcerers were devils come straight from the Undergates. I heard it myself a hundred times." He licked his lips. "My father thinks I'm a screw up, see? Says I can't do much right. I just wanted to make him proud."

Adyr held no pity for the man. "You thought bringing him Hettie would put you in high esteem."

"Yes. I been trying to figure out how to capture her without getting my brains boiled. I was planning right up until she saved my life. Took out brutes that would have killed me in an instant." He slumped, his weight dragging on Adyr. "My old man was right. I screw up a lot. The witch spotted me on day one. *And* day two. She's not stupid. She knew I was up to something, but she saved my life anyway. She could have let me die, easy. She wouldn't have even had blood on her hands."

"So now what? You're content to let her be?" Adyr scoffed.

"I been trying to think of how to break the news to my dad. I told him I was going to hunt down a witch. He laughed in my face, of course. Still, he taught me to use my brains."

Adyr snorted. "Sounds like your dad doesn't know much about using brains."

Tinto's back straightened at that. "My daddy's no fool."

"He believes what a bunch of zealots tell him."

"You can't fault him for that," Tinto insisted. "Ain't no sorcerers around anymore. They all left. The Temple's supposed to be the authority on magic users. They say magic's evil, and we believe them. There's nobody around to say otherwise. How are we supposed to know?"

"By seeing one for yourself," Adyr said dryly. He loosed his grip on Tinto's neck, letting him fall to the ground in a heap. He didn't seem like much of a threat.

Unless he went spreading tales of Hettie's magic use. The last thing she needed was to have the Temple coming down on her head. That would be just as bad for Poll's Wander. The Temple went after anyone who even associated with sorcerers. The Widows' Will had taken on Vincent's men, but taking on the Temple was something else altogether.

"Look," Tinto said. "My father didn't raise a fool. I've seen her work. I see she's got friends. People who care about her. People who'd die for her." He gestured at Adyr. "She saved a bunch of people and healed a bunch more. Temple folk would have said she's taken command of the animals, but I seen that bird of hers. It straight loves her. What kind of person gains the love of a lion hawk of all creatures. Or amber hawk. Whatever you call them down here." He let out a humorless laugh. "When you've been told one thing and your eyes tell you something else, it doesn't take a genius to figure out something's wonky."

Adyr chewed his lip in thought. Tinto sounded sincere enough but letting him go was still risky. It would be safer to kill him.

It bothered him, though, to take one more life. Hadn't there been enough killing? Besides, shouldn't Hettie be the one to decide how much of a threat Tinto was? Adyr would tell her and let her decide. He didn't know her well, but he was almost positive she'd let him live. She'd already known he was up to something. She even suspected he was connected to the Temple. All she'd done was give him a warning and let him go.

His silence must have worried Tinto, because he spoke up.

"I plan to return to the Temple if you'll let me. My father will wonder if I really did find a sorcerer if I don't return. I'd rather go back and tell him I couldn't find one."

He didn't seem too excited about that course of action.

A pair of soldiers wandered by, so they waited in silence until they passed.

"You would have him think you screwed up again?" Adyr asked.

Tinto shrugged. "That's nothing new." His sour look turned to resignation, then to thoughtfulness. "I don't know that I can stay with the Temple now that I know sorcerers aren't evil. I mean, I assume some sorcerers are evil, but clearly all of them aren't. I'll say I couldn't find any, because they've done such a good job getting rid of them. It's near enough to true. It's been ages since anybody's reported actual magic anywhere. It's all just been rumors."

"You won't try to convince them sorcerers can be good?"

"No. I wouldn't have believed it without seeing it. They won't either." Tinto's back straightened. "My dad won't miss me much if I decide to go my own way. Settle down somewhere. Raise a family."

Adyr stayed silent. The man was doing a fine job talking himself in the right direction.

"I used to be scared of being a father." Tinto laughed to himself. "I thought, what if I'm bad at it? What if I turn my kids into horrible people."

"And now?" Adyr asked.

Tinto ran his gaze over the fires dotting the landscape. "I can't do no worse than what's happened in these mountains. As big of a mess as this was, there's still good in the world. There's still hope for a better tomorrow."

"Hope." Adyr's voice was hoarse. "Is a very hard thing to kill."

Tinto nodded again. "If there's hope for these soldiers after the things they've seen, then there's hope for me too."

"And for your children."

"And for my children," Tinto repeated.

"Which you'll raise far from here."

Tinto cast him a nervous glance. "Which I'll raise far from here."

"Because if trouble from the Temple comes looking for Hettie, I will personally find you and murder you in a way that will obliterate the hope of your entire generation."

Tinto paled. "Yes, sir." He inched away from Adyr.

Adyr hid his smile. "Best of luck on your journey."

"Thank you, sir," Tinto replied in a small voice.

The silence that followed stretched out. Tinto continued to inch away from Adyr until he felt safe enough to turn and run.

Adyr watched him go, satisfied the issue was settled. The Temple wouldn't be coming for Hettie. At least, not today. Who knew what the future held.

CHAPTER 47

IT'S GOOD TO BE DIFFERENT

Hettie

Before Hettie took the children back down the mountain, she charged the rocktoads with defending the area. Vincent's people were gone. Cayon had no more subjects to experiment on and the rocktoads would be able to overpower him alone. Hettie warned them she'd crumbled the last passageway to the citadel. The tunnels were the only way in.

For their part, they were eager to comply with her request. Their children had paid the consequences of Cayon's ambition. They wouldn't be quick to trust newcomers.

Satisfied, Hettie shepherded the children down the path.

Hettie used her magic to light their way, but the journey back to camp was slow. The children had to rest often. Being caged had atrophied their muscles, but Hettie was patient with them. Most had no shoes, so she kept herself busy weaving multiple spells at once, shielding as many feet as she could while maintaining her ball of fire overhead.

None of them had objected to going along with her once Pillar's child assured them it was okay. Strangely, they didn't bat an eye at the floating fireball. The little girl with the horn on her chin clung to Hettie.

When they stopped for a rest, the girl huddled into Hettie's side, smiling shyly up at her. "You're different, like me," she said. At around eight years old, she was one of the youngest of the group.

"Everyone is different. Sometimes you can see the difference and sometimes you can't, but it's there," Hettie assured her.

The girl with abnormally long eyebrows inched over to join them. "Different like me?" She looked closer to age ten.

Hettie shrugged. "If they were like you, they wouldn't be different. You'd both be the same."

"You can make fire," the first girl said.

"And invisible shoes," the second girl said.

As they talked, the rest of the kids crowded closer on the narrow path. Hettie felt like she was in the nursery with her little sisters. They asked her name, and she asked theirs. She taught them what "unique" meant, and they took turns listing how they were different from one another. By the time they got moving again, the kids were in high spirits.

"You're awfully quiet," she said to Deryl during one of their stops.

"Am I? Sorry. Gak has been telling me stories about some of the strange people he's run across."

"As a human or a portal?"

"Hmm? Oh. Portal. He can barely remember who he met as a human, it was so long ago."

Deryl grew quiet and Hettie assumed he'd gone back to listening to Gak until he said, *"You're quiet yourself."*

"I'm thinking about what to do with a couple dozen traumatized kids." She blew out a breath. *"We'll take them to Poll's Wander, obviously, but what then? Where will they live?"*

"Liselle will find homes for them."

Hettie smiled. *"Knowing her, she'll probably invite them all to live at Penelope, then spend the next decade wondering what she was thinking."*

"You know," Deryl said, *"that's not a bad idea. At least they'd all be together."*

Hettie had been thinking the same thing. She wasn't sure how long the children had been imprisoned, but they'd endured a terrifying experience together and clearly had no family to speak of. If they were split up—even to good homes—nobody would understand them the way they understood each other. *"Liselle is leader of Poll's Wander for now. I doubt she could continue organizing recovery efforts if she had a bunch of kids to take care of."*

Deryl grew thoughtful. *"That's true."*

"Even if others were put in charge of them, children are loud and curious, and they get into everything. It's part of what makes them a joy to be around."

"Liselle would have to clear out her artifacts. Some of them are dangerous."

Hettie pictured Fleana, who was always getting in trouble as a kid. She'd been wild as the wind and Hettie's favorite sister. She'd probably grown up a lot in the past few weeks since Hettie put her in charge of the Daughters' Coven.

She felt a stab in her chest every time she remembered they would never again run and play on sunny beaches together or climb the mountain paths of their island home.

"Stop that," Deryl said. He hated when she got mopey.

"Sorry."

"If it's exploring you miss, we can fix that." His voice grew excited. *"Things here are pretty much wrapped up. We can go see the world."*

Hettie made a noncommittal sound. She'd always wanted to see the world, but she'd wanted to see it with Elkin. It seemed a lonely prospect without him.

Beyond an outcropping of rock, the clearing came into view below. It was alive with bright bonfires, twice as many as they'd had before.

By the time Hettie reached the bottom of the path, she spotted Jonathan, Vammi, and Servio waiting for her with a pile of bedrolls and an abundance of food and water. They had clearly seen Hettie's light and the children it illuminated.

"Where did all that come from?" Hettie was pretty sure they'd been almost completely out of food that afternoon.

Jonathan beamed at her. "It seems the supply chain is at least partially intact."

Hettie's eyebrows rose. "They cleared the pathway?"

"No, but they did manage to create a chain of men who passed the supplies along, allowing them to bypass it. At least with food and water. Any of the bigger supply items are still stuck on the other side."

"Not that we need them at this point," Vammi said.

Servio nodded. "The ability to overcome obstacles is the key to success for any army."

For once, his tactical spoutings didn't sound like so much rubbish to Hettie.

Deryl chuckled. *"Turns out he's not so bad when he's not being a pompous braggart."*

The three men surreptitiously eyed the children huddled by the rock face behind Hettie.

Vammi leaned in close to Hettie. "From Stonehaven?"

One of the children piped up. "We're from the village, not the city."

It was Ezzir, the youngest boy in the group at age six and the most talkative of the bunch. He was also the farthest from Vammi. Far enough Hettie wondered if he had Element-induced hearing enhancement.

When the adults turned to look at him openly, he continued in that rambling conversational way young children had. "Lord Vincent used to visit us with treats from the castle kitchen." His face fell. "But then everyone started disappearing. And then dying. Lord Vincent took us to live in the castle. Only one night a soldier came and took me down in the tunnels and locked me in a cage. I didn't like it there."

Brinny, a seven-year-old girl, spoke up. "We wanted Vincent to come rescue us since he's a lord, you know? But one day we saw him and realized the bad man got him too. He wasn't locked in a cage, but he was different."

"He was hairy like me." This from Rumi, the girl with the long eyebrows. "Only his hair was all over." She waved her hands to indicate her whole body.

"It must have been terrifying to realize even the grownups aren't safe from the bad guys," Deryl said soberly.

The kids fell silent. They huddled by the wall, their eyes razor focused on nearby soldiers eating food. They needed food.

Dinner wouldn't be fancy, but considering what Stonehaven's residents were eating in the end, the children weren't likely to complain.

CHAPTER 48
VALICOR

Hettie

Word spread through camp. Dozens of people volunteered to tend the children. Many missed children of their own. The group was herded off to dinner.

"Looks like the day has been salvaged," Deryl said. *"Now we can relax and plan our next adventure."*

Hettie made her way to the leaders' camp. *"We're not completely done. I still have to clear that rockslide tomorrow."*

"That's tomorrow's problem. Tonight, we dream."

It would be nice to dream of something other than Elkin's death. Her dreams had been blessedly blank the past two nights.

"Not that kind of dream. I meant dream up adventures. Besides, talk to Servio about tea if you want another dreamless night."

Hettie stopped short. *"What does Servio's tea have to do with dreaming?"*

In a carefully neutral tone, he said, *"He puts something in it to help you sleep better."*

Even if she hadn't been drugged in Garpoint, the fact that it was Servio giving her unknown substances put her hackles up considering how poorly they'd gotten along for the majority of the journey. *"You knew this and didn't tell me?"* she asked, clenching her fists.

"I'm telling you now. Besides, there was no harm done. If a healer had given it to you, you'd have been fine with it."

"Because a healer knows what they're doing. Servio's not a healer," she said firmly.

"Not in the comprehensive sense of the word," Deryl admitted.

"What does that mean?"

"It means his expertise in healing is limited to specific ailments. Like those brothers who took care of Jonathan. They aren't healers, either, but they're obviously familiar with kikka bark."

"They were trained by their mother, who is a healer. I doubt Servio has any training whatsoever in the use of whatever he puts in his tea."

"Did you really suggest a general who's been through numerous wars has never asked a healer how to get his traumatized soldiers to sleep well? Soldiers who are much more likely to die if they're sleep deprived? Or are you assuming soldiers in battle don't have nightmares."

Hettie scowled. *"I can't verify anything if I don't know about it. Who knows where he's getting his ingredients?"*

"You're right. I'm sure he just picks random plants as he marches across the land. Even here in this barren land of stone. Honestly, Hettie, where else does one get specific herbs besides a healer?"

He didn't actually say she was being unreasonable, but it was obviously how he felt. She sighed. *"When did you find out about this?"*

"Last night. Jonathan came to check on you. He ran into Servio, who told him you should sleep well. Something about his tone and the way he glanced at your cup had me putting it together."

"What if something had happened at night and I didn't wake up?"

"It doesn't put you to sleep. You were up for hours after drinking it both nights. Besides, one of the soldiers standing guard tripped in the middle of night. He cursed under his breath, and you sat up like a bolt and glared him down."

She vaguely remembered that. And she felt more rested than she had before the battle started.

"Trust me, you're much harder to wake when you're dreaming than when you're not. Ouri had to practically eat your face to get you to wake up that first night."

Hettie rolled her eyes, but she couldn't fault his logic. *"You've put some thought into this argument."*

"Because I knew you'd bite my head off when I told you."

He'd been right. She had.

Vammi waved at her from a nearby bonfire, and she headed over, eying the wineskin in his hand.

"You've been impersonating a rock for a while. Everything okay?" he asked.

It was easy to lose track of her surroundings when she talked to Deryl. "Of course," she said. "Everything is turning out better than I expected. I'm glad we were able to help those kids."

"Agreed." Vammi motioned to where Jonathan sat near the fire. "He won't stop making plans for the children, even though he knows Liselle will be deciding what to do with them."

Jonathan raised an eyebrow. "This isn't a simple decision, it's over a decade of childcare. Even if we don't have the final say, we can at least come up with ideas to streamline the process."

Hettie smiled. "You're a good man, Jonathan. If Vammi doesn't want to brainstorm with you, I will. Tell me what you've got so far."

He gave her a grateful smile, then listed a handful of good families that might be willing to adopt the children in pairs. "Poll's Wander could have a donation center to help pay for extra costs. It won't take much to convince Liselle to pay for the rest."

"Knowing her, it'll take more work to convince her *not* to pay for it all."

"Agreed," Jonathan said ruefully.

Vammi muttered, "You're going to need a lot more than a handful of families."

"He's right," Hettie said. "Besides, I was thinking bigger." She explained her thoughts on keeping the kids together. They would overrun Penelope, so that wasn't a good option, but they needed somewhere to call home.

Servio joined the group in the middle of her explanation. All three men looked impressed—or maybe daunted—by the staggering scale of her proposal.

"It's true, they can't stay at Penelope indefinitely," Jonathan mused. "It's simply not a suitable long-term plan."

"So make it a temporary solution," Servio said. "Build them a place that *is* suitable."

"Put the kids to work building it. That'll keep them busy," Vammi muttered.

"I was thinking along those same lines," Hettie said.

Jonathan looked appalled. "You can't have children building a home. Certainly not one that size."

Hettie waved him off. "Trust me, kids are more capable than you think. Instead of just asking for money, we'll also ask for skills, supplies, and time. People can donate to get the children's home up and running and the children themselves can help in whatever way they can. That way, once it's built, it will feel like it's really theirs."

"Who will be in charge of all this?" Jonathan asked.

"Don't say what I think you're going to say," Deryl groaned.

"I will," Hettie said. "At least, I'll head up organizing it."

Deryl groaned some more. *"What happened to adventuring?"*

"You don't *think this is going to be an adventure?"*

"Okay, then what about exploring?"

"How long does it take to build a building? A few months? We'll be exploring the world in no time. This way, we'll have a home to come back to between adventures."

"You lost your family, so you want to make a new one with a bunch of trau-matized toddlers. How is that a good idea?"

"They're not toddlers," she argued. *"And how is it* not *a good idea? The kids need stability. Until they find someone to take the job permanently, who else is better qualified to lead a gaggle of unique kids?"*

Deryl went quiet. *"You have a point."*

Vammi and Jonathan stared at her for the two heartbeats it took for her conversation with Deryl to wrap up.

"You're going to stay in Poll's Wander?" Jonathan asked. He sounded surprised but looked pleased.

Hettie nodded. "For now, at least."

"Then I volunteer to help too," Vammi said a little too loud.

Servio raised an eyebrow. "But you're the captain of the Steppers."

His wince reminded Hettie of the men he'd lost. That pain was still fresh. Burying himself in a new project would be a nice distraction after he visited the families of the fallen.

No wonder he'd been drinking.

As if reading her mind, Vammi gestured to the camp. "They'll be enjoying their families in the coming weeks, not playing with swords. They can guard a castle at peace just fine without me." He grinned at Jonathan. "Whatever you need. As long as it helps my good friend Hettie."

"And the kids," she reminded him dryly.

"And the kids," he agreed.

Servio scratched his forehead. "I have far more experience with soldiers than I do with children, but I wouldn't be opposed to stopping by a few times a year to give them a history lesson or two."

"*By that, he means regale them with war stories,*" Deryl said.

"Don't put yourself out," Hettie told the old general.

"Oh don't worry." He gave her an impish grin. "It won't be any trouble at all."

"We can call it the Home of the Widows' Young," Jonathan suggested.

"Too long," Vammi said. "How about Radiance or Sunlight, since they're out from underground?"

Servio looked unimpressed. "I guarantee you they don't feel radiant."

"Not yet," Vammi agreed. "It's something to strive for though."

"Radiance might be a stretch. Something akin to Serenity might work better," Servio suggested. "With luck that'll be achievable."

"That's not going to cut it," Hettie said. "They've been through a lot. At a minimum, they've lost their parents and been imprisoned and terrorized. There's no amount of radiance or serenity that's going to block that out. Even as a healer, there's not much I can do for them. They've got a long way to go before they reach anything approaching happiness or peace."

She chewed her lip, thinking of her nightmares and the daily efforts to keep from succumbing to misery from Elkin's loss. "They're going to have to fight in those darker hours."

"What about Valicor?" Deryl suggested.

"What's valicor?"

"I remember it from one of Cerissa's books. It was an antiquated word, even back then. It means something like petrified will. Like a state of being where a person's willpower has become hardened until nothing can shake them. Think stubborn, taken to the extreme."

"Valicor." Hettie smiled, listening to the sound of it. *"I like it."*

"What's that?" Jonathan asked.

"We're naming it Valicor."

Vammi and Servio gave her blank looks, but Jonathan perked up. "Valicor? Like stone willpower?"

Hettie nodded. *"Stone willpower. Even better, considering they come from the mountains."*

"Of course he would know obsolete words," Deryl said, disgusted.

"Stone willpower?" Vammi asked. "What does that even mean?"

Jonathan ignored him to ask Hettie, "Where did you come across that word? It hasn't been used for hundreds of years, and it wasn't common even in its prime."

"It wasn't even common in its prime," Deryl mocked. *"Know-it-all."*

"I'm a witch," Hettie said, her smile turning sly.

"You wound me, Hettie. I don't get any credit around here."

"What am I supposed to say? My eyeball told me? Claiming witchy knowledge is basically my way of giving you credit."

"She knows things," Vammi crowed.

Servio frowned. "You keep saying that like it's an answer."

"To us, it's a fine answer," Vammi said. He was getting louder the more he drank.

"Have a little faith, General," Jonathan added. "After all, she did know the word."

Servio adopted a look of long suffering. "And I suppose the fact that she's a witch is indisputable."

The group chatted amicably, and Hettie mentally organized the list of tasks needed to get Valicor up and running. Her thoughts were interrupted when Jonathan began humming next to her. As she listened, she became aware of a rhythm rising from pockets of nearby soldiers. Gentle thumps and taps and intermittent stomps.

Hettie smiled. She could pick out the groups of soldiers from Penelope by the complex beats they made. It shifted as it went, changing tempo and tune. It was a ritual of sorts that Penelope's inhabitants performed at every meal. It felt like camaraderie. Like togetherness.

Like family.

Hettie hoped the children were enthralled by it like she had been her first time hearing it. Hopefully they would pick up the habit at Penelope. It made her smile to think of them making it a tradition at Valicor.

"*Good idea,*" Deryl said. "*I'll teach you a few tavern songs and you can pass those along too.*"

"*I think they're a little young for your tavern songs.*"

"*Come on. Music is good for the soul.*"

"*It is. Just not your music.*"

He grumbled a bit, but then brightened. "*Hey, I've got some new jokes to tell.*"

"*As long as they're not rock jokes.*"

"*No, no,*" he insisted. "*No rock jokes. Since we're naming their home Valicor, I figured rocks weren't fitting.*"

Hettie felt a moment of relief until a nagging suspicion started. Stones weren't any different from rocks.

"*Laughter is good for the soul too,*" Deryl said. "*Some days it's the only thing that* will power *you through.*"

"*Use those sparingly,*" Hettie advised. "*We're not that far from the chasm yet.*"

CHAPTER 49
WE'RE NOT IDIOTS

Hettie

That night, when Servio offered tea, Hettie took it without complaint. "What do you put in this?" she asked.

"Oh a bit of this and that. It's my own special brew," he said with a smug smile.

"Which bit of this or that keeps me from dreaming?"

His smile froze. He eyed her warily. "You know about that?"

She smiled.

"Yes, yes, witches know things," he muttered with a dismissive wave of his hand. "Drivenseed soaked in honeyfin juice, which is then dried and crushed."

She'd heard of drivenseed, though it didn't grow on Storm Flower. If she remembered right, it was good for calming hysterics. *Any clue what honeyfin juice is?*

"Never heard of it."

Too bad. After using the "witches know things" line on him so

303

often, she hated to admit when she didn't know something. She relented. "What's honeyfin juice?"

Servio raised an eyebrow as if expecting her to spontaneously answer her own question. "The honeyfin is a fish from Coldspine. It has glands that shoot out a cloudy, honey-colored substance to confuse predators."

"Interesting." She sipped her tea. "If the drivenseed calms the mind, what does the honeyfin juice do?"

"On its own, it causes partial short-term paralysis, but combined with the drivenseed and dried, it blocks strong memories during sleep."

"Short-term paralysis? That's not alarming at all," Deryl remarked.

Hettie wasn't too worried. The potions she made often consisted of ingredients that behaved differently when raw, cooked, or mixed with other ingredients. Potions were an art.

"You might want to offer some of that to Vammi," Deryl suggested.

"Why?"

"You haven't noticed he keeps his back to walls whenever he can? When he can't, he shifts around a lot so he can keep track of what's behind him."

Hettie hadn't noticed that, but then she'd been distracted lately. *"When did this start?"*

"I noticed it while we were still in section two. I think that guy with the meat hook took him off guard. He's spooked."

She took another sip, mulling that over. Vammi had nearly died. It was no wonder he was on edge.

"Keep an eye on Vammi," she told Servio, explaining what had happened.

"Near-death experiences have that effect," he said, nodding. "I'll watch him."

Strangely enough, she trusted him on that.

Instead of sleeping by the commander's fire, Hettie opted to sleep near the children.

"I wonder if the kiddies know the demon child," Deryl mused.

Hettie hadn't thought of that. *"Let's hope not."*

His words stuck with her, though, and she had trouble falling asleep, which only further convinced her that Servio's tea didn't do anything to force her to sleep. She hated to admit it, but she was impressed by how accurately his concoction hit its target. One wrong step in potion making meant side effects that often outweighed the benefits.

She couldn't wait to get back to Garpoint so she could borrow Jonathan's plant books. The mainland held endless opportunities for potion making. She started making a mental list of ingredients and equipment.

She fell asleep halfway through, but woke to Deryl's voice some time later.

"What is this guy doing?"

Hettie opened her eyes just as a fistful of powder landed squarely in her face.

"Oh! I'm so sorry!" a man said in a frantic whisper. "I'm so clumsy."

Hettie couldn't see past the powder, which stung. She tried to sit up, but a hand—presumably the man's—pressed her shoulder down.

"Here, let me clean you off. I'm such an idiot. I just wanted to take home a handful of rock dust, you know? For when I'm telling my grandkids about the battle one day. Only now I've gone and dropped it in your face like a fool." He wiped gently at her forehead and cheeks, brushing dust off with his fingertips while he chattered.

Hettie didn't recognize the voice. He seemed friendly enough, if bumbling.

"What time is it?" she asked Deryl, still groggy.

"It's the middle of the night. Why the heck is he scrounging around for rock dust at this hour?"

That was a good question. *"Night guard?"*

"Maybe. Something's weird about him."

Hettie's thoughts were growing fuzzy, and it was hard to concentrate on his words. She meant to ask what was wrong but couldn't seem to form the thoughts.

"He sounds apologetic," Deryl said dubiously. *"But he looks kind of eager. You might need to—Hettie!"*

He barked her name, but it echoed in her head, receding at an alarming rate until only silence remained.

She wasn't sure how long she was unconscious, but she knew it wasn't nearly long enough. She woke to an incessant pulsing in her head. She would have tried to go back to sleep if Deryl hadn't been singing.

"Danger, danger, danger-danger-dangeeeer." He sang to a tune Hettie didn't recognize.

"Gods, please stop."

"You're awake!" he crowed. *"I've been trying to get you up all night. The sun has been up for almost an hour."*

"If bleating like a cliff pig birthing a coconut was your attempt to wake me, it's no wonder my head is pounding." The fuzziness of the night before fled, leaving her to experience her mental torment with crystalline clarity. Additionally, a shooting pain ran up her left arm, which led her to the discovery that her arms were tied in front of her.

"Don't blame me. It was that powder they knocked you out with."

"Yeah, about that. You could have warned me earlier, Captain Useless."

"I warned you as soon as I could," he insisted. *"The magic only tells me when you're in imminent physical danger. It didn't so much as flicker. The only danger was of getting a really good night of sleep. Even now, the only thing you're in danger of is traveling in the wrong direction."*

"As I said. Useless."

"I'm inclined to agree," he conceded. *"At least where you're concerned. You get into some odd scrapes."*

She kept her eyes closed while she waited for her head to stop pounding. There were plenty of spells she could manage without hand gestures, especially where healing was concerned, but cutting rope wasn't one she'd practiced much. She could do it, but only with steady concentration.

"I hate to interrupt your solitude, but the lead moron is headed your way."

Her eye popped open, but the only thing she could see was stone. She was on her back with her head turned to one side and a rock under her right shoulder blade. Her arm was numb.

The scuff of a boot drew her attention, and she turned her head just as a kick to her ribs landed.

She grunted but didn't curl into it like she wanted. Instead, she glared at her attacker. It took a couple blinks for the early morning sunlight to quit blinding her, but she immediately recognized her assailant. It was the soldier with the sliced ear.

It was tempting to ask him what in Racha'o's name he thought he was doing, but she fought the urge. It was a stupid question. What he thought he was doing was kicking her. Instead she asked, "What's your name, soldier?"

He sneered down at her. "I'll ask the questions around here." He aimed another kick her way.

She grabbed his boot with both hands, using it for leverage as her other foot shot out, slamming into his ankle.

With a startled yelp, he toppled.

Hettie released his ankle as he fell on his backside.

Deryl snickered. *"These jokers talk a lot. That flickerwit is Lagri."*

"Listen, Lagri," she said, getting to her feet in one smooth motion despite her tied hands. "Touch me again, and I'll roast your liver for breakfast." She scanned the area, spotting four more men, each a dozen or so paces from her, spaced out in a semicircle.

Two pulled their swords.

They were in a small stone clearing with sharp, spiny peaks rising all around except one side with a steep drop-off.

One of the unarmed men muttered to the guy next to him. "She knows his name."

Hettie's eyes narrowed. *"Is that the one who doused me last night?"*

"Yarp. Grimli."

"Grimli," she growled, looking at him. "Nice to see you again."

He had sallow skin covered in pimples. His eyes went so big they looked ready to fall out of their sockets. He ducked his head, slinking behind the guy with a sword next to him, who was a good three inches taller. Five if you counted his head full of brushed back curly locks.

"Did these guys say what they want with me?"

"Just that they're taking you to someone."

"Temple stuff, maybe? Is Tinto here somewhere?"

"No. These dimwits are the only ones around."

"Why'd you ask for names if you already knew them?" Curly asked. He'd have been a looker if he wasn't just a bit cross-eyed.

Hettie ran her hands over her face, which still had a layer of dust on it. "Because it's useful to know how belligerent you idiots are going to make things."

"We're not idiots," Curly said, pointing his sword at her despite being too far away to use it.

"Really?" she asked, squinting sideways at him. "Because it doesn't seem like you've thought this plan through."

Lagri rolled away from her and scrambled to his feet. "Shut your mouth, stupid witch," he said, rubbing his tailbone. "Nothing's wrong with our plan."

"Yeah," Grimli squeaked from his hiding place behind Curly.

Curly cast a scowl over his shoulder before turning back to Hettie. "We've been training years for this moment. We've thought of everything."

Hettie had no idea what they were planning, but she wasn't about to let them know that. "Years?" she asked incredulously. "You've had all that time, and this is the best you've come up with?" She shook her head in dismay. "At this rate, you boys might be worthy opponents in another decade or so."

"Which way have we been headed?" she asked Deryl.

"It was hard to tell at first because they took turns carrying you over their shoulder, so I couldn't see much, but since sunup, we've been headed mostly east."

"Thanks," she said, turning her attention back to the men. "You do know you're headed for the desert, right?" Lagri's eye twitched. Curly and Grimli both stiffened. The other two men hung back, avoiding the confrontation. Hettie gave them all a look of disgust. "Without food or water? Tell me how that's a good plan."

The four men glanced from her to Lagri, waiting for his rebuttal.

"Don't listen to her. She's using her witch magic on you," he said.

"Logic is witch magic now?" Deryl mused.

"Block out her voice. We'll be legends once we turn her in. We just got to get her to Rousland."

Lagri's speech was gaining momentum, and she used the distraction to focus on the knots at her hands. Strangely, she could heal a stab wound easier than she could cut rope, but with enough concentration, she'd be able to manage it.

Or so she thought. The powder they'd used to put her to sleep did something to her magic. She could almost form a spell to weaken the rope, but it would go fuzzy at the last second. Now that she was paying attention, she wasn't even sure how much magic she had at her disposal, assuming enough of the drug's effects wore off that she could use it.

Her magic reserves had slowly regenerated after her big spell on Ouri. It had been back to normal by the time she'd gone to sleep. Had it grown since then? She wasn't sure if her sisters' magic had stretched her capacity, allowing her to hold more or if she would simply level back out to her pre-family-fight magic.

"They dosed you with the same stuff as in Garpoint?" Deryl asked.

"Maybe. Just in a different form? I think breathing it in was less effective than drinking it."

He let out a thoughtful sound. *"The drugs in Garpoint made you lose your magic, then pass out later. With this stuff, you were out in seconds."*

"True. Plus it took most of a full day for my magic to fully regenerate in Garpoint. This feels more like my magic is there, just slippery. It's hard to hold, but it's there."

"That's better than the alternative."

"Not really. If this drug works differently, it means there's more than one drug floating around that can neutralize my magic. Where is everybody getting this stuff from? Is there a black market for anti-sorcery drugs?" It was a sobering thought.

"That's a stretch considering there aren't any sorcerers left."

"These drugs might be why."

Lagri kept on about his grand plan, saying plenty without saying much more than where he was taking her.

"Rousland is west, dummy," she interrupted.

"You shut up." He pointed a finger at her, though he made sure to stay back and kept one hand on his sword hilt. Despite the implied threat, it remained in the scabbard, making him doubly a fool. Magic had a far longer reach than anything he could manage.

She just needed to stall long enough for the drug to wear off.

"We follow the code. We was trained by a true knight of the Temple. And it don't matter that *Rousland is west*," he said in a surly imitation of Hettie. "We got us a boat that'll take us there just fine."

"Nice of them to wait until after the battle to kidnap you," Deryl said.

That was a good point. "Convenient that you waited until after the battle to drag me off to the Temple. They call me a demon, but I guess demons are fine so long as they help you out, right?"

Lagri sneered. "There's no point in dealing with a problem that's going to solve itself, now is there? Either you was gonna die in battle or we'd just take care of you after. Asides, don't act like you was any help." He gestured at her in disgust. "We never needed you anyway. We could've won this battle by our own selves."

His men were nodding along with him.

"Now that we done tied your hands up, you can't even fight *us* off, much less a whole army."

She smiled grimly and managed to grab hold of just enough magic to make her eyes swirl like whirlpools. She'd practiced that one plenty, so it didn't take much concentration or require hand gestures. It was one of the few spells she could pull off in her current state since it hardly required any magic at all. "You have no idea what I'm capable of." She made sure all five of them got a good look at her eyes.

Collectively, they scrambled back.

CHAPTER 50
SQUAWKERJACK

Hettie

I'm not sure the eye trick was the best approach," Deryl said. "Unless you're just going to slit their throats."

Hettie had considered doing something similar but decided against it. "Even if I could pull that off, I don't want to. At least not yet. I want to know how far this conspiracy goes. If this has been years in the making, it's bigger than me. Besides, the longer I keep them talking, the more magic I can use."

She could feel the effects of the powder wearing off, but she needed more time.

"Tricks," Lagri said, though his voice wavered. "You can't hurt anyone with them swirly eyes."

She stared him down, and he took another few steps back. "For the sake of argument, let's say I go to your boat willingly." She let her eyes return to normal. "What then? You still don't have food. The army had just enough for supper last night." She tipped her head in a thoughtful pose. "You remember the army, right? The ones you stranded behind a giant rockslide? The rockslide I was going to clear out for them this morning?"

Lagri's lips pursed, telling Hettie she'd hit a nerve. "They'll move it on their own."

Hettie nodded. "Sure they will. It shouldn't take them more than a few weeks once they get the right tools. I'm sure their families won't miss them. Much. I mean, it's not like they've gone off to fight their first foreign battle ever against an enemy madman and his army of crazed cannibals."

"They fought crazed madmen at Penelope," Deryl pointed out.

"Hush." She kept talking. "I'm sure they'll be fine getting hard tack tossed over the boulders in the meantime. It's a fitting reward for putting their lives on the line to keep Poll's Wander safe."

"We fought too," Curly objected. "It's not like we didn't do our part."

"Sure. But that only goes so far when you strand the entire army," Hettie pointed out. "And for what? Glory? Fame? Money? It's certainly not to help your neighbors out." She paused, but none of them responded. "Like I said, you have not thought this through. If you had, you at least would have waited until after I cleared the path."

Lagri ran his gaze over his men. All four scuffed their toes on the ground looking like kicked puppies. When he turned to Hettie, Lagri's lips were peeled back in a silent snarl.

She stared him down, refusing to look at her hands to inspect the knotted rope. "How many people are in on this grand plan of yours? How many more get the privilege of working under your superb leadership, Lagri?"

He let out a low growl but didn't answer.

Grimli spoke up. "There's nobody else."

"Shut up!" Lagri shouted. "Don't you tell her a thing."

Sullen, Grimli said, "It's not like it's a secret, brother. It's just the five of us."

"Are they all related?" Deryl asked. *"Because that would explain a lot."*

"Five's all we need to get you to Joeri," Lagri said.

That name rang a bell.

Deryl said, *"I'm wondering if Vincent's babbling had something to do with that kid dicing him like a tomato."*

Coincidence only went so far. Hettie needed more information. "Joeri?" she asked, playing dumb. "Where's that?"

Lagri smirked. "It's not a where; it's a who." He glanced at his friends as if to say "See, she ain't so smart" then motioned sharply with one hand. "Enough talk. Start walking, witch." It was clear he wouldn't say more on the subject for the time being.

She waited another few seconds just to piss him off. There would be time to get more out of him once her hands were free.

She inhaled deeply, breathing in slowly and let her head fall back on her shoulders. She spotted Ouri overhead. He would have made a racket if he'd seen the men carrying her off. He'd probably been hunting for dinner at the time. By daybreak, he would have found her. Even if they'd been carrying her all night, Ouri could cover a lot of ground.

Being a smart bird, he would know the men weren't friendly, but one bird against five men wasn't likely to end well. He also knew Hettie. He'd wait for a signal from her and be ready to attack when the time was right.

"All right, let's move," she told the men, as if heading onward was her idea. She stepped forward, picking at the cinched knot.

The men kept their distance until they reached the far side of the clearing where a path led upward. As they approached it, the men closed in behind her.

She hadn't made it more than a few steps up the path when she heard a distinct sound. She stopped to listen, cocking her head and holding up a finger.

Everyone stayed quiet as the sound of horse hooves echoed from a path to the right.

"Who has a horse out here?" Hettie hadn't seen a horse since Garpoint. Stonehaven had probably eaten those from the stables.

"Beats me. Traveler from the desert?"

"Maybe. A horse means they've obviously planned better than these dufuses. I doubt it's someone fleeing from the battle. They'd need to have hidden a horse from an entire starving city. Still, what are the odds of us coming across the only traveler out here?"

A figure cloaked in silver entered the clearing with a horse trailing behind. Bulging saddlebags hung from its sides. The traveler was watching his footing and hadn't spotted their group yet.

"If he just finished crossing the desert, shouldn't his saddle bags be more empty?" Deryl asked.

Lagri called out, "Hey there, friend!"

The cloaked man looked up, and Hettie made out a wide face with a square jaw and an angular nose. His features were strongly Pavinn with medium brown skin and black hair, but he was taller and leaner, and something about the curl in his hair told her he had some Darrish in his bloodline. Or maybe it was the haughty look he wore.

He brought his hand up in greeting, then casually reached to his neckline and pulled something from beneath his shirt. The motion moved his cloak, revealing a dark red underside.

"Red cloak," Deryl warned.

"Drink me a tankard. That's Cayon." The cloak had been the single most defining descriptor Adyr had given. Hettie hadn't thought it useful since a cloak is easily removed but, apparently, he'd thought turning it inside-out would be enough to hide him.

"How did we get here before him?"

"We started on the ocean side of the chasm. There's no way he crossed that ledge without our soldiers spotting him. He must have taken a back passage through the tunnels."

A shift in the breeze brought the smell of horse sweat mingled with the distinct odor of the tunnels. Before she could second-guess herself, Hettie lashed out on instinct, just barely managing to grab hold of her magic. She did her best to open his throat, but her magic slipped at the last moment, throwing off her aim.

She barely nicked him, getting the horse instead. Its hide was thicker than human skin, so the gash wasn't deep, but it flinched and let out a startled whinny.

Cayon snapped the reins, which may have settled the horse in calmer times, but injured and agitated, it laid back its ears and bit the hand holding the reins. Cayon jerked his hand away, hissing. The horse pulled its reins free, prancing away from Cayon. Blood trickled from the shallow cut along its neck.

Cayon focused on whatever he'd pulled from around his neck, bringing it up to his mouth.

The shrill screech of a whistle filled the air, very different from the inaudible whistle Hettie used to call Ouri.

Cayon blew again. The sound was ear-splitting and invasive, rattling Hettie's skull. She cringed away from the sound. When it stopped, her ears rang.

She shook her head to clear them and took another shot at Cayon. Her grip on her magic was still weak, but her aim would have been good if he hadn't dodged at the last second. Hettie was floored for a moment before she realized Lagri had picked up a rock and thrown it at Cayon. He'd been dodging the rock, not her blow.

"Quit that, you bastard." Lagri waved a fist at Cayon. "I'll throw you off the cliff if you blow that damn thing one more time."

"Apologies," Cayon said, his voice emotionless. "I will refrain from further assaults on your ears." He became aware of the nick from Hettie's magical slash and reached up to touch the few drops of blood trickling down his neck.

His fingers came away red. He frowned. When he looked up, his eyes were calculating. They landed on hers, then took in her tied wrists.

"Uh oh. I think he just figured out you've got magic."

Cayon's journal entries about finding a sorcerer to experiment on made her nervous. The last thing she wanted was to be one of his prisoners.

She focused on lashing out a third time, but was interrupted again, this time by Deryl.

"Danger!"

Hettie dropped to a crouch, ready for Cayon's attack, but he was tucking his whistle back into his shirt front.

Out of the blue, a body collided with her from the side. She went flying, landing on her back hard enough to knock the wind out of her.

When she got her bearings, she found the most adorably malicious creature she had ever seen standing over her.

It was a bird. Of sorts. At least, that's what the scaly legs indicated. Much like a hatchling, it was covered in downy gold-orange fluff, but it was larger than Ouri by double, at least. It had stunted, flipper-like wings incapable of flying and looked like something young children would happily befriend.

The cuteness ended there.

Its beak, also distinctly un-birdlike, was closer in shape to the crocodiles of Darkfen Marsh. The not-bird clacked its bill at her, making a dull, hollow sound. The bill opened wide, revealing a rim of sharp teeth. It brayed like a foghorn loud enough to rival Cayon's whistle for sheer obnoxiousness.

"What in Bizzith-non's aching bowels is this thing?"

"Squawkerjack!" Deryl crowed. *"I named it first!"*

"What the—"

Deryl's second warning came a second before the thing lunged at her face.

With her tied hands at her chest, she couldn't do much to defend herself. Frantically, she rolled to the side, knocking the angry squawkerjack off balance.

It clamped its jaws shut on her shoulder as it fell, and its teeth tore flesh. Hettie fought back a scream.

Three more of the squawkerjacks leaped off rocky outcroppings overhead to land amid Lagri's men. Chaos erupted.

"What in the Murks are these things?" Deryl sounded more intrigued than worried.

"Your immortality is showing." Hettie's squawkerjack lunged at her again. She threw her hands up to fend it off. It chomped down on her thumb. Blinding pain shot up her arm as teeth scraped bone.

From overhead, Ouri swooped in, screeching with rage. Outsized and outnumbered, the amber hawk didn't lack for courage.

Hettie could always count on him. They'd been through a lot together. After losing her family, she felt his loyalty keenly, like an ember that warmed her heart.

The squawkerjack released her to scan for the source of the sound and Ouri's claws took out two clumps of fluff from the thing's head.

The squawkerjack puffed up a bulge in its throat, then deflated it with an odd vibrating hiss. It stepped back, letting Hettie roll away and clamber to her feet, each movement bringing on a wave of agony. Her thumb was a mangled mess, and her shoulder was no better.

She stumbled away from the demon bird. The ropes binding her had been partly severed by its teeth and she yanked her hands apart. They held fast.

"Watch it," Deryl said in a tight voice. *"You're close to the ledge."*

Hettie stopped a foot from the edge of the cliff to survey the scene. Cayon tried cornering his horse, but it dodged past him and ran back up the trail they had come in on. Clearly frustrated, Cayon took a different path. Presumably one that didn't lead back to the citadel.

Hettie's squawkerjack followed Ouri's path as he banked overhead, giving her a moment to assess the battle.

Three squawkerjacks fought her kidnappers. One chewed on Lagri's leg while he screamed hysterically, trying to bash its head with a rock. A second occupied the two men Hettie hadn't interacted with, sitting on one while chewing on the arm of the other, who slapped at it in vain. The creature was too absorbed in its meal to notice his flailing.

The last squawkerjack stood between Curly and Grimli, who had been smart enough to position themselves on opposite sides of it. Curly stepped back. The bird snapped its beak in his direction, and he froze.

Grimli took advantage of the bird's distraction. He ran for the nearest path out of the clearing. The bird's thick, scaled legs moved quicker than Hettie expected. Grimli only made it three steps before the sharp beak snapped shut on his arm. The bones cracked audibly and Grimli screamed. His legs buckled, and he crumpled in a heap. Easy prey.

If Curly had crept away slowly, he might have had a chance. Instead, he ran for Hettie screaming, "Help us!"

Hettie's squawkerjack zeroed in on Curly with predatory focus.

"Danger!" Deryl barked. *"Danger!"*

The squawkerjack plowed into Curly just as he reached Hettie.

Its momentum flung all of them off the ledge and into open space.

CHAPTER 51
THIS IS GOING TO HURT

Hettie

D*aaannngggeeeerrrr!"* Deryl screamed.

Reality came crashing down on Hettie. They were falling to their death, and she didn't think a shield would do much to save them, even if she could cast one.

The shock of her predicament made it hard to breathe.

"That might be the wind!" Deryl shouted, though she could hear him fine. *"We are falling really fast!"*

Adrenaline-fueled, Hettie tried once more yanking her arms apart. The rope held.

She clenched her jaw in pain as her bloodied hand sent waves of pain radiating through her. The wind pressing on her thumb was excruciating, but she didn't have time to focus on that.

If she was going to die, she was going to do it with that gods-blasted rope off her wrists. She braced herself for the pain and yanked again, simultaneously lashing at it with her magic. The slice was weak, but it got the job done.

The rope broke just as Ouri slammed into her.

His talons raked at her, trying to find purchase. She reached out to grab hold of his ankles, her hands fumbling with his claws. A sharp talon dug into her mangled thumb, bringing a burst of pain that had her seeing spots.

By reflex, she pulled her injured hand back. Her other hand managed to find its mark. She dangled awkwardly from his one leg, but he wasn't near big enough to support her weight.

Ouri let out a frantic *grawp* and flapped for all he was worth, doing his best to slow her fall.

Woozy, she almost realized too late that her grip was slipping. Ouri stretched his free leg out so Hettie could grab it without flailing.

"Smart bird," she mumbled, though the wind whipped the words away so fast even she couldn't hear them. She managed to latch onto him, though her grip was weak without the use of her thumb.

"Danger!" Deryl yelled again, even louder. For once, he sounded properly concerned.

"I know! Shut up!" she replied. *"I'm trying to concentrate!"*

He whimpered but stayed quiet.

They were coming up fast on a jagged peak, but if they could steer around the tip of it, a secondary drop off would give them a few more seconds to figure something out.

"Go around," she called to Ouri.

His honed reflexes had him moving almost before the words left her mouth. He banked as best he could with her weight pulling him down. He almost avoided the peak.

At the last second, Hettie swung her feet forward to run along the surface, then launched herself farther out, dragging Ouri with her. The change in direction got them away from the peak but forced them into a spin.

Ouri let out a low warble as he struggled to straighten them out.

"Now would be a really good time for a giant-sized bird!" Deryl called.

"Stop yelling. You're in my head. I can hear you just fine," she snapped. Holding on to Ouri was killing her shoulder. The squawkerjack had

disappeared below her, along with Curly. Good riddance to both. *"I need two hands for that spell."*

"Then use two hands," he snapped back.

She had no idea if she had enough magic to cast it, especially with the drug's interference, but falling to her death gave her a certain degree of motivation.

Still spinning, Ouri managed to maneuver them to where the mountain floor dropped out below them.

"Great Racha'o, please don't let us die," Hettie whispered. With a steadying breath, she steeled her resolve and released Ouri's legs.

She'd been convinced Ouri hadn't slowed her much right up until she let him go.

The wind whipped past so fast she found it difficult to breathe again. She tumbled as she fell, making it impossible to tell which way was up save for the press of the air.

Ouri crowed in alarm, an already distant sound.

With concentration borne of panic, she focused on her magic, pushing through the last of the drug's effects. The words for Avid Preservation poured from her. Part of the difficulty was in the way she had to contort her pinky and ring fingers, but for once she was grateful not to have to use of her injured thumb.

The twist of her fingers wasn't the only difficult part of the spell. Trying to keep her hands stable in the shifting wind proved nearly impossible. With painfully tensed muscles, she completed the last gesture, praying it took.

The rush of magic left her body. She'd done at least something right.

Her eyes watered, and the world was a blur. She couldn't make out the ground, the sky, or the peaks around her. The view was probably spectacular. It was almost disappointing she couldn't enjoy it.

Deryl's *"Woo hoo!"* was her only warning.

Ouri plowed into her, his enormous talons gripping her by one leg. He flipped her upright as if she were a toy and held her by her upper arms. With a shriek of joy, he stiffened his wings, slowing their descent far more than he'd been able to at his usual size. Judging by the wind force, they were still falling too fast for comfort, but it was slow enough there was at least a chance they wouldn't die.

Hettie blinked her eyes clear just in time to see the ground racing up at her. Flat ground would have been scary enough, but nothing was flat in the Little Gods. "Do you see a tree anywhere?" she asked Ouri. His eyes were far better equipped to see in blinding wind.

He let out a chirrup of assent.

"Good. Drop me in it."

"Are you sure that's a good idea?"

"If I have to choose between a pokey tree and a boulder to the face, I'm going with the tree."

"Good point. You'd hate to end up stuck between a rock and a—"

"Deryl," she said in warning.

"Fine," he conceded without a shred of grace. *"If you get stabbed in the brain by a stick, though, I hope you die knowing you could have enjoyed one last rock joke before you went."*

"Your jokes make me envy every person that can't hear your voice."

"You're really hurtful, you know that?"

"And you're hard to get along with." She was kicking herself before she'd finished saying it.

"You know," Deryl said slowly.

"Yeah, I know," she said sourly.

She could practically feel his laughter.

Ouri banked, making her stomach lurch. After a quarter-turn, she spotted a tree situated on a small ledge. It was far bushier than the ones near Stonehaven.

"Let's hope this one's as cushy as it looks," Deryl said.

It wasn't as cushy as it looked.

By the time she'd come to a stop, Hettie had two broken ribs, a broken arm, and a stick through her calf.

"Not so much," Deryl remarked.

Hettie just groaned. It hurt too much to think. She tried to breathe slow and deep but the stabbing pain of her ribs made her vision grow dark.

She might have passed out. She wasn't sure.

"You okay?" Deryl asked. *"I mean, you can heal. Just a reminder."*

A single word struggled to break through her thoughts. *"Useless."*

Slowly, her awareness returned enough for her to focus on her biggest sources of pain. She tried healing her thumb first, which surprisingly hurt as much as her ribs. Granted, her ribs made breathing difficult, but taking shallow, panting breaths was preferable to forcing the ribs back in place. That was going to suck.

"You say I'm useless, but you just proved my advice was pretty solid," Deryl remarked when her thumb was once again functional.

After casting Avid Preservation twice in two days, her magic was so depleted she had to pull on it to get enough of it to do anything.

"Shall I continue to be useful and informative?" he asked sweetly. *"And before you answer, you should know your bird is injured. I think he crashed into the mountain trying to get close enough to drop you in the tree. He wasn't quiet about it, but you were too distracted with breaking your own bones to notice."*

Hettie's brain cleared at that news, though it brought the pain to the forefront of her mind. She longed for the cloud of fuzziness that had shielded it from her. *"Is he okay?"*

"Careful," he said as Hettie tried to reposition herself.

She was cradled nicely between two large lower branches of the tree.

"He's alive. I heard him scrabbling around while you were out."

"Ouri?" she croaked.

A pitiful chirrup came from somewhere below her.

"Hang in there," she said, panting.

There was no help for it. She needed to get her ribs back in place so she could get down and help him. Placing one hand gently on her side, she held back a whimper. *"This is going to hurt."*

"I could have told you that."

CHAPTER 52
TRY BEING MORE INTERESTING

Hettie

It took the better part of two hours to heal their many wounds. By the end, Hettie felt drained enough to have healed a small army.

Ouri had smacked into the nearby cliff face pretty solidly, breaking one wing in four places, as well as his foot.

Hettie had to wait for her magic to regenerate between healings. Each time, it left her more mentally and physically exhausted than before. She ended up dozing in between.

"Time for wakey," Deryl said. *"Nap time is over. You've still got that stick in your leg."*

The force of her fall had snapped the stick off, allowing her to climb down to heal Ouri. It was the last thing she had to deal with and it spoke to her exhaustion that she'd been able to sleep with it in place.

She opened her eyes to blinding light. The sun hovered almost directly overhead.

"I'm starving," she said.

"I'm starving too."

"You don't have a stomach."

"Which is why I'm not starving for food. I'm starving for attention. I'm bored and it's killing me," he said.

She heaved a sigh and pushed herself to a sitting position, the better to scowl down at her leg. Why was healing so much work?

"I try to be patient with you at night. Gak and I have come up with a game we like to play, but it takes hours to get a good one going. Your naps aren't long enough to do anything with, so I just sit here like a pet pig, waiting for you to shower me with your witty conversation."

"Gak talks," she reminded him.

"Yes, he does, but you can only listen to the same person yammer on for so long before it gets really old."

"Tell me about it," she groused, reaching down to take a firm hold on the stick. She gave it a yank. Her leg came off the ground and a bolt of pain shot through her. She took several slow breaths until the pain died down. "Ow." That was an understatement.

"I feel like that was justice for your snotty remark."

"Well, it's no snapped rib," she said sarcastically. Her second yank was more forceful. The stick came out with a mushy squelch. A distant buzzing started in her ears.

Blood poured from the wound. She frowned at the hole in her leg like she would a disobedient child, which wasn't far from the truth considering her body wasn't behaving like it should. "Blood goes inside the body," she reminded it.

It ignored her.

"Are you trying to convey that your leg is a more interesting conversationalist than I am?"

"Do you mind? This is a private conversation."

"Well, excuse me. I'll just sit here in silence."

He stayed quiet while Hettie closed her wounds. When she was done, she lay back on the cool stone. *"How is my conversation any better than Gak's? We're each just one person."*

"Yes, but he is always just one person. You travel around and meet people and

have conversations with them. Half of our conversations are about the people around us. You're only technically one person. You feel like an entire cast of characters from a bard's epic ballad compared to Gak."

Hettie closed her eyes. The world was silent. There were no birds or pigs or people. No crashing of distant waves or rustling of wind in trees. Not even the buzzing of insects. Just the steady thrum of her heart and an ambient vibration from the mountains that felt like the pulse of the world.

The weight of everything that had happened came down on her, heavy as the mountains themselves. Elkin. Her family. This mission. Even with the handful of kids they'd saved, it still felt like they'd failed. They'd wiped out an entire city.

The only thing that made Hettie useful was her magic and that kept getting stripped from her at the worst possible times. And that was when her magic wasn't actively trying to murder everyone around her.

She'd been lucky to manage Avid Preservation a second time. After healing Ouri, her thoughts drifted to her sisters. How were they faring without magic, without her healing them every time they were injured? With their magic sealed up, their lives seemed so much less fulfilling.

Hettie needed to be more careful, or she'd end up stripped of her own magic, along with her life. She'd had too many close calls.

"You're not talking," Deryl said.

"I'm thinking and listening."

"Even the mountain is more fascinating than me now?"

"Depends on what you say. Try being more interesting."

He thought for a minute. *"Okay, how about this? You get moving, and I'll tell you more about my time with Cerissa."*

Hettie had waited months to hear his story. Tired as she was, she wasn't about to miss the opportunity. She tried not to think about the hours of climbing she had ahead of her. She was exhausted. Resigned, she said, "Deal."

She stood and searched the rocky surface for a way up. The mountains were like needles towering overhead, far steeper than the area near Stonehaven. It would be hard to find handholds. Luckily, it didn't take much magic to make some of her own.

Before she started climbing, she checked on Ouri, who had returned to his regular size. "You're probably hungry," Hettie said, reaching down to scritch his neck. "Go find food. You got me down safe. I'll figure out how to get myself back up."

He let out a *grawp* and stretched his wings, flapping them experimentally.

Hettie turned back to the mountain. She found a vertical groove she could shimmy up and wedged herself into it.

"Cerissa had me for a couple decades," Deryl started.

"That's all?"

"Yes. She didn't like me much."

Hettie snorted but didn't say anything.

"She had a box that she stored me in," he said conversationally. *"She spelled it to block the sound of my voice. She was really quite talented when it came to magic, but she was meaner than a snake with a crushed tail."*

"So she put you in a box whenever you irritated her?" That didn't sound like a bad idea.

"And left me there."

"For how long."

"Days sometimes."

That seemed like overkill.

"Those were the shorter stints. Occasionally it was weeks, but mostly it was a few months at a time."

Months? Wedged into the rock face with the silent, sunlit mountain wilderness around her, Hettie imagined being stuck in a dark cave for months on end with nothing to see, nobody to talk to, unable to die. How long would it take for a person to go insane?

Deryl followed her thoughts. *"I don't think it's the same for me. I can feel like I'm going insane from the monotony of my circumstances, but I think actual insanity comes from some kind of malfunction in the brain. Being in that box wasn't that different from being in the Murks, and I've spent over a century in there. Sure, I'm a little needy because I absolutely loathe being bored, but I'm not insane. At least I don't think so."*

"Don't worry, I'll tell you if you start getting crazy."

"You do that. For now, keep up. Your pity is killing the story."

"Sorry."

"So I spent plenty of time in the box until the day she found a job for me. She passed me along to a lieutenant in a position to become general if the general at the time died."

"Let me guess. Cerissa had the general killed."

"Of course. It's an age-old practice, but we're getting ahead of ourselves. Lieutenant Yeup was madly in love with her, and she told him I was a good luck charm so he would keep me with him at all times."

"But you were bonded to Cerissa." The opening Hettie was wedged in widened as she climbed. She had to do some creative leaping to get up the last of it. When she lay panting at the top, she said, *"So Lieutenant What's-his-name couldn't hear you. I'm guessing that means she was using you to spy on him?"*

"Yes. I gave her false information just to mess with her, but she had other spies around Yeup that I hadn't noticed. I learned the hard way she could reach out and zing me."

"Zing you? What does that mean?"

He chuckled darkly. *"It's sort of like having a miniature lightning bolt run through your whole body. And by 'whole body' I mean the body I didn't have. I could feel it all the way through my sensitive bits. It hurt like you wouldn't believe."*

Hettie considered that. She knew Deryl well enough to know he would take pain over boredom in a heartbeat. It was like he couldn't stop himself from needing some kind of outside stimulation. *"You had her do that all the time, didn't you?"*

"Every day. Sometimes more than once. She's a patient woman, but being in her head meant I got really good at pissing her off. It's why she created the box in the first place."

"I get pissing her off, but that sounds like a painful way to get attention."

"Exquisitely painful. But it did let me feel my body." His tone turned wistful. *"Almost like it's still out there somewhere waiting for me."*

Hettie gave him some time to reminisce while she surveyed the ledge she was on. It was a long skinny strip that ran alongside the mountain for a couple dozen feet. Some exploration revealed a spot she could climb up if she created her own hand holds in strategic places. Her magic regenerated faster now that she was healed.

With another seven hours of daylight, she hoped to make it back to the squawkerjack clearing by dusk. Her stomach grumbled. She'd missed breakfast and both the magic and the climb would sap her of strength eventually.

"Best keep moving," Deryl suggested.

"If your body's out there, maybe we can find it. I wouldn't be surprised if Liselle has more than the one spell book. Maybe she'll have an instructional guide to sorcery."

"Maybe, but unless she's preserved it somehow, it'll be a pile of bones by now. I'm pretty sure reanimating corpses counts as advanced magic. There are some spells I could teach you, though. I remember a few off the top of my head since they were used fairly regularly."

He'd never mentioned that before. She frowned. *"Why would you memorize spells when you can't do magic?"* She pushed herself to her feet.

"Mainly because I couldn't sleep. Plus, I figured it was possible I'd get passed along to another sorcerer at some point. Memorized spells can be useful. Good leverage and all that."

"What kind of spells did you learn?"

"Basic stuff, for the most part. How to open locked chests, though it doesn't work for doors, strangely enough. How to track stolen possessions. How to clean river or ocean water for drinking, though I hear it makes the water taste tart. How to bathe when you don't have water."

His words turned her attention to her thirstiness, then to her state of uncleanliness. The last time she'd had a proper bath was before they left Garpoint. With the rock dust from the tunnels and the sweat of battle, she'd probably never been so dirty. She'd been looking forward to reaching the ocean that afternoon. While the soldiers would have been nervous about the fish-men, Hettie wouldn't have hesitated to rinse off in the salty sea.

"You have a bathing spell? Why didn't you say something sooner?"

"Eh," he said noncommittally. *"Honestly, I keep forgetting how pathetic your magic skills are. I mean, in ways, it's really impressive that you've learned*

to minimize the use of your hand movements so much by memorizing so many spells. The way you heal is crazy. It's intuitive on a level I've never seen. But then I discover you don't know how to do something as simple as cleaning yourself off. It's a kick in the teeth finding one of your blind spots."

Hettie let him ramble on while she struggled with carving out a spot for her next grip. She'd never had much reason to carve stone. A crack big enough for her to stick her thumb in made for an easy start, but when she carved out the rock, it opened to a bigger hole deeper in. A spider the size of her fist scurried out, its front legs raised in anger.

Hettie jerked her hand back at the sight of the black, hairy creature with pale gray spots speckling its body. It was almost as big as her fist.

A moment later, it scurried up the mountain face. *"Whenever you're done critiquing,"* she told Deryl. *"I'd love to hear the spell."*

CHAPTER 53

YEUP

Hettie

Deryl explained the spell. Hettie climbed. She was eager to reach the next stopping point to try it out.

"This is a great spell for you," Deryl insisted.

Hettie rolled her eyes. *"I don't usually smell all that bad. And you don't even have a nose, so you don't get to comment."*

"That's not what I meant, though it wouldn't surprise me if you smelled like moldy seaweed by now. I just meant that while it sounds complicated when I explain it, it uses a lot of common hand positions that will be good practice for you."

After the hand positions, he went over the words several times and explained the timing in relation to the hand gestures. By the time she'd reached the next ledge, she felt comfortable trying it. She was tired and wanted to rest first, but it would feel better to relax while clean, so she began the spell before she lay down.

"Wait! Are you crazy?" Deryl asked. *"You have to strip first."*

"I have to what?" If any other man had said that to her, she'd have

smacked him, but Deryl couldn't even see her naked body unless she looked at it or took him off her neck, so she knew he didn't mean it the way it sounded. Besides, with him living in her head, she'd gotten used to bathing with him around.

He sighed. *"I forget how inept you are."*

"Hey, I created a triple-sized hawk of vengeance. My magic skills are just fine."

"Fair point," he said consolingly. *"You're not inept, just uneducated."*

"So educate me, wise one."

"Wise one. I like that," he muttered. *"Okay, so the spell is designed to remove all things that are not your body from your body. Meaning it'll poof away excess sweat, dirt, grime, and what not, including your clothes."*

"Seriously?"

"Mm hmm. Plus weapons if you're wearing them. I know a guy who got rid of a barbed spear through his gut that way."

Hettie was tired enough from climbing that the thought of taking off all her leathers felt like a hassle. She did it anyway, folding Deryl's pouch up in her shirt. She managed to work the spell the first time through.

"Yeow!" The spell washed over her, scrubbing as it went. Every inch of flesh felt like it had been scraped with a rock. It left her skin tingling painfully. "You didn't say it hurt."

"Oh don't be a baby. You wanted to be clean and now you are."

"Super clean since it took a layer of skin off with it."

"You heal fast. You'll be fine. I'll just be over here waiting for a thank you."

She sprawled out on the ground, wincing at the sensations on her tender skin. After a few minutes, the sting faded to a dull ache. Soon, even that was gone.

"Wake up," Deryl said. *"You've only got so much daylight left."*

Hettie sat up and yawned. She hadn't realized she'd drifted off. *"How long did I sleep?"*

"Half hour. I'm still waiting for that thank you."

She ran her hands over her body and basked in the cleanliness of it. Her hair was cleaner than it had ever been in her life. *"Okay. I think you've earned this one. Thank you."*

"You're welcome. And just to be clear, you might be able to adjust the spell based on how vigorously you perform it. Try smoothing out the gestures a bit next time and see if you get different results."

"Good to know." She put her clothes on, cinching her vest snug. It was a shame her clothes weren't as clean as her body.

Her boots went on last, and she stomped her feet to seat them. *"Tell me more about this lieutenant guy. How long were you with him?"*

"Yeup? A long time. The rest of his life, actually. He was a smart guy. And nice too. He was sent across half of Andos to deliver a message to a guy that was going to kill the general and put Yeup in charge, but I changed his mind."

"The guy who was going to kill the general? Or Yeup?"

"Yeup, obviously. I never met the guy who was going to kill the general."

Hettie scanned for her next climb, watching for creepy crawlies. The next section was short and didn't look difficult. *"How did you manage to change his mind if you couldn't talk to him."*

"With a lot of blinking. He didn't set me out very often. It freaked him out whenever I watched him. Or when I looked around the room. Or anytime I moved at all, really. I'm pretty sure my mere existence gave him nightmares."

She understood the sentiment.

"He got drunk one night and set me on the side table and began talking to himself. I started blinking madly and it was the first time he realized I was alive, of sorts. He asked a lot of smart questions that led to a system of blinkable communications."

For the most part, Deryl was happy to stay in his pouch. Hettie was grateful for that. His eyeball was almost hypnotically beautiful–an iris of bright green fading to gold near the center. His pupil was a vibrant blue, which was odd, but the sack of skin that could open and close to blink was downright icky. The fact that he had no eyelashes made him all the more disturbing.

"We started out with yes or no questions and moved on to learning the alphabet. I was able to spell out words for him. He wasn't all that good at reading though, so communication was slow."

Deryl chuckled at the memory. *"Eventually, I got across to him that Cerissa was using him and if he delivered her letter, someone would die. Granted, I didn't tell him the death would promote him to general, but he wasn't all that power hungry anyway. He wouldn't have wanted to get the position that way. Probably."*

"What happened to him?"

"He decided I was good luck in another way. He'd chatter at me whenever people weren't around, and we had conversations when he was feeling patient. We spent a few years together before he found a girl to settle down with. It was hard to miss the similarities between her and Cerissa. Tall, slender, curvy in all the right places. Hair like midnight and skin like honeyed mead. There's a reason men fell in love with that evil sow."

Hettie pulled herself up on the next landing, which was wider than the last by a good margin. Ouri was waiting for her with two fat lizards, bigger than her palm, lying limp at his feet. He picked one up and offered it in his big talons.

She grinned. "You brought me lunch. I knew there was a reason I liked you." She took the lizard and sat next to the hawk. It took a bit of concentration to heat her hands, then send it into the lizard so the meat wasn't so raw. She preferred it lightly toasted. When it was done, she bit into it, tail first. As the crunchiest part, it was her favorite, followed by the feet.

"So what happened?" she asked. *"With Yeup and his girl?"*

"She didn't like me either," he said glumly.

Hettie laughed. *"You don't have much luck with women."*

"Tell me about it. She thought I was creepy—which I am, but it still hurts to hear it. She didn't even know I could communicate. Yeup would apologize for her comments when she wasn't around, but I still ended up in a drawer more often than not."

Hettie couldn't imagine how depressing it must have been to be discarded like that. How long had he been left to himself? Days? Months? Years again? It was no wonder he'd been so bitter when she'd bonded to him. And why he couldn't seem to shut himself up.

Deryl's tone grew distant. *"At one point, she started bringing home the baker. I told Yeup as soon as I could, but he didn't believe me. The wife had worked out a fairly steady schedule by then, so I told Yeup when to check in on her so he could see for himself."*

Hettie shook her head in disgust. *"How did you know what the schedule was if you were locked in a drawer? You had no way of knowing what day it was. Or even if it was daytime."*

"Even blind people know when it's morning. That's when everyone gets up and starts moving around. Then everything goes quiet at night. Meals are a good indicator too, and I could hear when the streets outside were busy or who was home. Footsteps can be pretty distinctive."

Hettie couldn't imagine being stuck in a box for so long, needing to study the sound of footsteps in order to know what was going on. *"So did he check in on his wife?"*

"Yes. It took him a month to get up the courage. She'd just found out the baker had put a bun in her oven when she got caught. Yeup was devastated. He kicked her out. Told her to go live with the baker."

"At least he did that part right."

Deryl was silent for a long while.

Ouri finished pecking at the shredded remains of his lizard. He wasn't a tidy eater. He let out a grawp and hopped a few feet away. It was his way of announcing he was taking off, likely to find more food.

Hettie's lizard was delicious, but it wasn't much of a replacement for two missed meals. Still, she was grateful for what she had. She took another bite, savoring the crackle of its scaly skin. She waved Ouri off. Maybe he'd come back with another for her. She certainly didn't have time to hunt them down herself. *"What happened after Yeup kicked her out?"*

"He cried a lot. More than a lot. Far more than one would expect a reasonably intelligent, respectable man to cry over a two-timing tramp." He clucked sympathetically and muttered, *"Worse than a teenage girl."*

"And what happened to you?"

"I stayed in the drawer. I would periodically communicate with Cerissa, leading her on a goose chase whenever she asked for information. Eventually, she found out I'd run off with Yeup and threatened to track us down and kill us. She didn't bother following through until about a year after Yeup kicked his wife out. Not that I was keeping close track of time by then."

His voice went quiet. *"I sort of shut down at some point."*

Hettie's chewing slowed. She'd been so wrapped up in her own drama lately. It had been easy to forget about what Deryl had lost.

He'd been a good friend to her. She almost felt bad about all the snotty comments she made, though he seemed to thrive on them. *"Did your next sorcerer treat you better?"*

He barked out a harsh, humorless laugh. *"Not even close. So far, you're the only one I wouldn't have drowned in a puddle of piss if I'd had the chance."*

"Umm. Thanks?"

"You're welcome. Just don't fall off the mountain again. I'd rather not lose you. For once, being bound is better than being in the Murks."

"Is that a compliment? You hate the Murks."

"I hate sorcerers more. Present company excluded."

Hettie polished off the last of her lizard. *"It's a wonder women didn't want you around. You give the best compliments."*

"They just couldn't see my charm."

"Right. When you figure out what charm looks like, describe it to me."

CHAPTER 54

VOICES IN THE MOUNTAIN

Hettie

An hour later, Hettie spotted a trail overhead. She healed her fingertips and shins for the last time and pressed on.

Ouri scouted from overhead, watching for the vicious squawkerjacks.

Deryl had spent a lot of the time cracking jokes or lost in his own thoughts. When Hettie reached the next ledge, his comment took her off guard. *"I'm pretty sure your marriage to Elkin would have gone better than Yeup's."*

For a moment, Hettie could picture Elkin in a black vest with gold thread embroidery depicting a scene from his life, his black hair shining in the sun, and that dimpled smile he always saved just for her.

The image made her throat close, and her heart pound painfully as if it, too, were struggling for air.

"I'm glad we weren't married. We were young and our relationship was complicated. I had responsibilities. A set future. I didn't want to tie him down only

to neglect him when I took over the island." Hettie hadn't fully recovered from her previous climb, but she pressed on, needing something to take her mind off the topic at hand because her explanation was only half true.

Part of her wished she'd married Elkin long ago and run off with him and never looked back. She knew she would never have run off though. She'd wanted to take care of her people. Losing him had been so painful. It would always be painful. If she'd married him, it would have been so much worse.

"Do you hear that?"

Hettie paused to listen. Faint voices drifted on the air. The path ahead wasn't far. At first, she thought someone was on it, but the voices were coming from the opposite direction. *"Where is that coming from?"*

"Inside the mountain?" Deryl sounded dubious.

Hettie cast out, searching for heartbeats. She found them easily. They were the only ones around besides her own. *"There's three of them. And they are inside the mountain."*

"Last I checked, people can't walk through stone. There's got to be a way in."

Hettie shifted the focus of her search, checking for openings in the stone. She didn't find it until she'd scanned the far side of the rounded mountain face she was on. It took some creative navigating, but she managed to reach it.

The main path she'd been aiming for had a skimpy, windy offshoot leading to the opening, which was mostly hidden from view.

A tunnel wound into the mountain. Hettie summoned her night vision and headed in. The tunnel opened into a cave where two men sat talking and a third figure lay curled in the corner, sleeping. Three holes in the rock let in small shafts of sunlight, which didn't provide much illumination.

"Sorry to intrude," Hettie said, startling the men, who jumped up, cursing.

The third figure, a woman, sat bolt upright. "Zel?" she asked, blinking in the darkness. "Is that you?"

The two men stared at Hettie, though she doubted they could see her well. "I was just passing through," she said. "I heard you talking and was surprised to find anyone out here."

Both men were on the slender side. One was tall and gangly. The other was muscular in a lean, wiry way. The woman was wrapped in a blanket. All three wore torn, ratty clothes.

"Passing through from where?" the lean one asked. Suspicion laced his tone.

Hettie wasn't sure how to answer that. The bottom of the cliff? In the end, she opted for vagueness. "Down the mountain."

The taller man let out a sigh of relief. "The desert. Good. You're going to want to head north. Crossing the mountains here is dangerous."

She cocked an eyebrow. "Because of the giant bird things?"

"Among other things," the lean one said, his voice a scratchy baritone. "There are bird things and spider things, giant worms and killer lizards, but the worst of all is the madmen of Stonehaven."

Hettie grunted in acknowledgement. "The worm thing is dead, as are the madmen. I haven't met any killer lizards, but I know at least one of the bird things died falling off a cliff."

The two men exchanged dubious looks.

"I thought you said you came from down the mountain," the tall one said.

Hettie shrugged. "Most recently, anyway." It was true.

The woman asked, "What of the spider?"

"It's not so bad once you get to know it."

The woman wrung her hands nervously. "And did you? Get to know it, I mean?"

"Aw, Ska, don't start that again," the lean man said.

"But this proves it," Ska said, remarkably urgent in her declaration. "She spoke to it."

"She didn't say anything about talking to it," the lean man insisted, glaring at Hettie.

"Well how else do you get to know someone, Bisher?" Ska practically shouted at him.

The tall man stepped in close to soothe her. "Calm down, Skalina. We've been over this a hundred times."

"*Oh boy,*" Deryl said.

"*Oh boy, indeed.*" Hettie agreed. Skalina, the chitton's wife, was human?

"*Does that mean the chitton was human?*"

"*If it was, it's not anymore.*" Hettie turned back to the trio. "You sound like you've got stories. Tell me yours and I'll tell you mine. How'd you get holed up in here?"

Bisher glared at his two companions, but neither spoke. "It's not much of a story, really. We went to Egren on a business trip. When we came back, we found our village turned into a nightmare."

"The village outside Stonehaven?"

He nodded. "It doesn't have a name. We just call it the village."

"How long ago did you three return from Egren?"

Bisher sniffed. "There were seven of us that came back. After we found our friends and family dead, we weren't sure what to think. There were a few survivors, but they'd gone mad. Gebratin used to tend the vineyard and a nicer guy you'd never find. He tried to kill us when he saw us." Bisher shook his head. "It didn't take much investigating to realize that's what happened to the rest of the village folk. They straight killed each other."

Hettie nodded. "So you hid in the mountains. How'd you survive out here?"

The tall one spoke up. "It was easier with all of us. Kuser was one of our group of seven. He was a stealthy bastard. He'd sneak out to the village at night and fill up our skins at the well. He'd drink his fill while he was there, so he drank more than the rest of us."

"He was the first to start acting strange," Skalina said quietly. "Said the wind was full of darkness. He was convinced it was trying to eat him."

The tall man put an arm around her shoulders. "That's how we realized the water must be causing the madness. We found another water source partway up the path, tucked back behind a recess. It trickles through the rocks, so it's hard to get much to drink. We stay here because it's cool. We don't need as much water that way."

"Kuser kept sneaking into the village," Bisher said. "He ended up killing the last few villagers and convinced the other three in our group it was safe to live in their homes. All four of them were dead within a week."

The tall man said, "They wouldn't listen to us about the tainted village water. They just wanted to go home."

Hettie said, "This other water source you have isn't contaminated?"

"It's clean," Bisher said. "All of us have our wits about us for the most part." He nodded at Skalina. "She's mostly sane except at night when she rambles about her husband calling to her. All we hear is that giant spider making weird screechy noises all night."

"He calls my name," Skalina insisted. When he rolled his eyes, she said, "You be glad my foot is still in my shoe instead of planted in your backside."

Bisher threw his hands up. "One minute you insist your husband's a spider and the next you try to convince us you haven't lost your damn mind." He shook his head in disgust.

Skalina gave Hettie a challenging stare. "It's my husband, Zeloxahad. He stayed behind to tend the chickens while I crossed the desert."

"Should we tell her the truth?" Deryl asked.

"Tell her that the Element transformed her husband into a giant rock spider? I suspect she already knows. The trick is to convince her group that she's not insane."

"We can argue about this all day," the tall man said.

"And have," Bisher cut in.

"Tell us your story. What do you mean the madmen are all dead? Last we checked, Stonehaven was crawling with them."

"I came here with an army from Poll's Wander. We wiped them out. They're all dead." Hettie told her story, emphasizing they were at least partly on a rescue mission that didn't go as planned, but none of them seemed to judge her for killing everyone they'd ever known.

She mentioned the few children they'd managed to rescue, though none of the group had kids and didn't ask more about them. That didn't surprise Hettie. It wasn't like the group was in any shape to take on extra mouths to feed.

She left the chitton out of the story until the end.

"Where does Zeloxahad come into all this?" Skalina asked.

Hettie filled her in on the chitton. She'd never seen such joy on a woman's face. Or such a case of sour grapes as Skalina crowed about it to Bisher. While they slung insults and threats at each other, Hettie made her way out of the tunnel.

Outside, she scanned the sky for Ouri only to find him perched near the opening. With some work, she managed to explain what she wanted.

Ouri flew off just as a call came down the tunnel.

"Woman?" It was Skalina. "Where'd you go?" She spotted Hettie a moment later and stopped beside her on the ledge where the late afternoon sunshine lingered. "Out here, it's hard to believe there's so much wrong with the world."

Hettie grunted. "You don't seem upset that your husband is a giant rock spider."

"I don't care what form he takes. He belongs with me, and I with him."

"It may be more than his body that's changed. He may not be the man you knew," she hedged. "He isn't very bright." Remembering her translation bracelet, she added, "You may not even be able to understand his speech. He can barely form a coherent thought."

Skalina snorted. "That's nothing new. For all that Zeloxahad is a grand name, he's always been a big, dumb brute. But he's *my* big, dumb brute. I've always found that the best couples have both brains and brawn. After all, brains won't get you across the desert when your wagon wheel breaks. Heavy lifting is just as important as any other task." Her voice grew soft. "Zel would lift the very mountains if I asked him to."

They stood listening to the voices drifting from the cave.

"I'm going to find him," Skalina said. There was no mistaking the steel in her voice. For a moment, she reminded Hettie of her mother.

Ouri's distant cry came from the west.

"It occurs to me," Deryl said, *"that your translation charm may not work on animals at all."*

Hettie sucked her teeth. She'd already considered that. *"Liselle did say it was created from the bones of men. It makes sense that it works on humans."* The chitton was really just a mutated human, same as the rocktoads.

Ouri's cry came a minute later, closer than before.

Hettie smiled when she spotted the bulky figure scrambling across the mountain face after him.

CHAPTER 55
WHO'S USELESS NOW?

Hettie

Hettie made the last of the journey to the squawkerjack clearing as the sun set. Reuniting Skalina with her husband had helped take her mind off her aching muscles and joints.

"You keep saying this mission was a failure, but you can add Skalina and Zeloxahad to the list of reasons to be happy we came. We saved Pillar's kid, along with Grumpy's, and chasing off Cayon has made it safer for all the other rocktoads. We've got a gaggle of human kids that'll have a future now, plus Skalina's group won't have to hide in a cave anymore."

"True." Hettie couldn't ignore the number of dead though. Would her sisters have done better if they were here and still had their magic?

"The dead aren't your fault," Deryl said, following her thoughts. *"There's nothing you could have done about them. War comes with a price. You didn't start this one. You helped stop it. The body count would have been higher if you hadn't."*

Their conversation cut off as the trail opened to show the clearing Hettie had fallen from that morning. It was bathed in so much blood that it was hard to believe only four people had died there.

"Curly may have been the lucky one," she thought.

"He would have hardly felt his death," Deryl agreed. *"Emphasis on the hard."*

She ignored his attempt at humor.

Lagri, Grimli, and the other two members of their cohort were marked by large blood splatters spreading from chunks of corpses that had been hard to get at through the clothing. Hands and throats were gone, faces were mutilated, and the squawkerjacks had raked clean through the thick leather clothing in places.

Lagri's vest had come undone. The squawkerjack had made short work of his undershirt and gorged on his guts. Ribs were missing and it looked like pieces of him had been dragged off to the side, widening the bloody circle that marked the feeding zone.

A sound came from the far side of the clearing. Hettie spun, putting up a shield, but it was only a man, and that man wasn't Cayon. The tension drained out of her. She dropped her shield when she recognized him.

Bannot skidded down a boulder and stumbled to a stop fifty paces from her.

What was he doing so far from the army? "Are you looking for me?" she asked.

Bannot stood frozen for a long moment, his gaze taking in the carnage around her. "No," he said. "The rest of the camp is though."

His voice was still guttural, but she'd made some minor changes the day before, so he was easier to understand.

Hettie grunted. "Is Adyr out here with you?"

Bannot shook his head. "I left him behind. It's for the best," he mumbled.

She nodded. It probably was. Adyr would fight to keep Bannot in a mold he no longer fit.

"You left last night," he said conversationally, making his way to her. "Half the camp thinks you used magic to disappear. The rest think you walked away on your own two feet. Adyr doesn't think anyone but Cayon could force you to leave if you didn't want to go. Jonathan says you would never leave without saying something, especially when you promised to clear the rockslide." He skirted a corpse. "It's the one thing he and Vammi agree on."

"They're right. I wouldn't have left them stranded."

Bannot surveyed the scene. The late afternoon shadows did strange things to the hollows of his face. "Looks like whatever happened, you've got it in hand. I'm familiar with torture," he said slowly. "This looks worse."

"This wasn't me. There are giant killer birds out here. They tore these guys apart."

He eyed her. "Looks like you held your own." He rubbed a finger along the top side of his nose hole. "Can't help but notice there are only human corpses here."

Hettie chuckled. "I didn't manage to kill any of the birds. I was a bit tied up at the time. The birds ran off, I assume."

He tipped his head. "You assume?"

"I was thrown off the cliff when one of the birds plowed into me. Stupid move for a bird that can't fly."

His eyebrows rose. "You survived the fall?"

She didn't bother going into detail. "Magic."

"Sweet mother's milk," he muttered.

"Ouri helped." Hettie pointed up at where the amber hawk circled overhead. That just seemed to confuse Bannot more, but he didn't ask questions. "What are you doing out here if you're not looking for me?"

Bannot squinted past the blood stains. "Cayon came this way."

"You're tracking him over rocky mountains?"

"I've been around him enough to know his stench."

Hettie raised an eyebrow. "You can smell him without a nose?"

He gave her a toothy grin. "Better than I ever could with one. I can tell night from day underground by the smell. Did you know sunlight had a smell?"

"Can't say that I did."

"That pickled rat's anus took my family from me. He took my life. But he's given me strength, endurance, and a nose that can out sniff a gold-tip bear. I'm going to use it to find him and kill him."

Hettie had never seen a gold-tip bear. Named for their golden fur, they were infamous in Mirrik and Norrik. She clapped Bannot on the back. "I can't think of a nobler purpose for such a nose, nor a more fateful ending for that evil swank-wagger. Be careful though. If you find him, make sure he doesn't blow the whistle around his neck. It'll call the killer birds to him."

Bannot scanned the area again. "This was him?"

"Yes. You're several hours behind him." She gestured at the carnage. "This happened an hour after sunrise. You've got some catching up to do."

He grunted. "The price of good-byes," he said.

Hettie would have given anything to say goodbye to Elkin. "It never pays to cut those short," she said softly. "Best to make them count."

He nodded.

She cleared her throat, pushing past the tightness there. "Cayon went that way." She pointed to where she'd last seen the horse disappear. "Down the mountain. He had a horse, but it took off during the fight and headed up toward Stonehaven."

Bannot nodded. "Even hours old, I can smell the moldy leaves. I'll find him."

"Cayon smells like moldy leaves? The tunnels smell similar."

"It's the Element," Bannot said. "It runs all through that mountain. Cayon spent a lot of time in those tunnels. His smell is similar, but more oily."

Hettie sucked her teeth. With the rockslide trapping the army, she couldn't justify going after Cayon. She'd leave it to Bannot to make sure he met a deserving fate. Her duty was to the Widows' Will.

"You're sure you can track him?"

He grinned. "Like a pot roast."

Hettie grinned back at the comparison. She couldn't think of anyone more motivated to bring Cayon to justice.

They surveyed the jagged mountain peaks, tall and thin like pointy teeth. The mountains of Storm Flower had been more navigable. She'd seen drawings of stalagmites in caves from sailors who frequented the Troll Coast. This portion of the Little Gods looked more like those.

"It's going to be tough traveling," Hettie said.

Bannot nodded.

Hettie thought back through the day's climb. Deryl had talked the whole way up. He was strangely silent now. *"What's your stance on this? Do we clear the rockslide or accompany Bannot? You wanted adventure."*

"I did," he said thoughtfully. *"But when we fell of that cliff, I was pretty sure you were going to die. I still want adventure, but maybe we could do it in spurts."*

"We fall off one little rock and suddenly you're scared I'll die?" she teased.

"For the record, that was more than a little rock. And you of all people should understand why I want to make sure this relationship lasts as long as possible."

He was right. She did understand. She might be the only person who had ever understood and cared about his predicament. Well, besides Gak.

Bannot turned away from the cliff and faced the path Cayon took. "Go back to the army. Enjoy the people who love you."

"You know you have people who love you too," Hettie reminded him.

His shoulders slumped in weariness. "I know. This has been a crazy year. Not even a year. Gods, how can everything change so much in a matter of months?"

Hettie thought of the day her sisters tried to steal her magic. She'd crippled half her siblings, found out who her father was, lost the love of her life, and abandoned her homeland in a matter of hours. "Change has no respect for time."

"Gods honest truth," Bannot said under his breath. Without so much as a farewell, he strode off, disappearing into the deepening twilight gloom.

"Eat the angels," Hettie said to his retreating back.

"I wonder what angels taste like."

"Better than people stew, I'd wager." She cast her night vision spell. *"Time to go home."*

"You're not going to rest first?"

"I can rest when I'm dead."

"Knowing you, that'll be tomorrow, but you can't always count on death. Sometimes you get stuck for all eternity as an eyeball."

"If that happens, I won't need sleep."

"What happens when we get back to Garpoint? The Temple sent a fleet after your mother and now they've tracked you down and kidnapped you. I'm willing to bet they're behind that incident in Garpoint too. Are you planning to take the fight to them?"

Hettie hauled herself over a boulder and clambered up to a path that cut between two monoliths. She thought long and hard before she spoke.

"If the Temple of the Sky wants me, they know where to find me. For now, I'll wait for them to come to me. Next time, I'll be prepared."

"How long are you planning to wait?"

"We'll see how things go." Her confidence had all but disappeared since her life fell apart. She'd clearly thought herself more capable than she was. If the Temple had drugs that could strip her magic, she didn't want to go after them until she knew what she was doing. *"I need to practice the spell book. Besides, we promised to help build Valicor. It'll be nice to see the kids break out of their shells."*

"That might take a while."

"It might. But sometimes big changes come in short timeframes." She slowed, running her hand along a boulder as she passed it. *"You know you're part of this decision, right? I'm committed to getting the kids set up. The rest of it is open for debate. If you get an itch in your feet, we can compromise. Maybe start off with shorter adventures and work our way up to longer ones."*

Deryl was silent for a long while. His voice was hoarse when he spoke. *"You would plan your life around me?"*

"I didn't ask to have you stuck in my head, but you didn't ask for it either. I'm steering this horse, but it's only right to give you a say in where it goes."

He sniffled. *"Okay. Let's build a home and go from there."*

"Are you crying?" she asked.

"I can't cry, you moron. I don't have tear ducts."

"You also don't have a nose, but I distinctly heard you sniffle." She was tempted to pull him out of his pouch. Instead, she reached up and wrapped her hand around him.

"Deryl?" she asked, thinking of how he'd called Valicor a home. *"How long has it been since you've had a family of your own?"*

"Are you asking me to marry you?" he said in a droll voice.

"What? No."

His tone grew teasing. *"Are the kids going to call me Daddy?"*

She sighed in exasperation. *"The kids won't even know you exist."*

"We're going to have to fix that. If I'm going to be a father, I'm laying down the law. No deadbeat dad for those kids. They only get the best. I'll spoil them rotten and tell them bedtime stories and jokes that will have them farting when they laugh."

Hettie groaned. *"What is wrong with you? The second I think I can take you anywhere, you turn into a twelve year old."*

"But a twelve-year-old with a sense of humor, which is more than I can say for you. Give me a few months. I'll refine your joke palette."

She smiled. *"A few months it is. I'll need at least that long to teach you how to actually be funny."*

He felt all glowy in her mind.

"If you're going to change my humor, it may take longer than a few months. We're talking years, a lot of them."

She pressed on into the darkness, overcoming one rocky obstacle after another. *"I can do years. We can learn more spells together, starting with the ones you memorized."*

Deryl didn't respond for a long moment. When he finally did, he sounded nervous. *"About that. Remember how I said I knew a spell for finding stolen objects?"*

"Yes," she said slowly.

"I'm going to need you to learn that one sooner rather than later."

Hettie hopped down from a boulder. *"Why? What's been stolen?"*

"Gak."

Hettie froze. *"What?"*

"Gak has been stolen." Before Hettie could ask for specifics, he filled

her in. *"Liselle is in Garpoint, and bandits have snuck into Penelope. Gak's being loaded into a cart as we speak."*

Hettie's mouth went dry.

"It gets worse."

"How can it possibly get worse?"

"Gak says they're not taking anything else. Only him."

Hettie put two and two together. *"They know what he is."*

Deryl let out a frustrated groan. *"I hate that guy."*

"Who?"

His tone was dark. *"They're taking him to a guy named Joeri."*

Hettie cursed. *"Figuring out who that guy is just jumped to the top of my list of things to do, right after tracking down Gak."*

She ran some mental calculations. How many days before they were back at Penelope? After clearing the rockslide, they had a day's march to shore, then longer by boat before they even started the trek north across the marshlands. *"Gak will be long gone by the time we get home."*

Deryl let out a low chuckle. *"It's a good thing I know a spell to track him, then, isn't it? Who's useless now?"*

END

Acknowledgments

For this book and every book I ever write, my heartfelt thanks goes out to Kelly Colby and Kevin Pettway for giving me the opportunity to be in the cool kids' club. Cursed Dragon Ship Publishing has set the bar phenomenally high and has probably ruined me for all other publishing houses.

A special thanks to my editor Tracy Leonard Nakatani, my continuity editor Shannon Winton of Eyetooth Editing, and to my beta readers, Jennifer Flanagan Schoenbein, H.Y. Gregor, and Shannon Fox. Your patience and insight has made this book stronger than ever. Hats off to Molly Phipps for making such amazing covers for this (and every other *Misplaced Adventures*) book.

Thank you to Kevin Pettway (again), Jessica Raney, William LJ Galaini, Ethan A. Cooper, and C.M. McGuire for putting out such phenomenal books in this universe. I love what you've done with the place.

Zaepho, Greg, Birdee, Ligia, Jesse-the-mean-one, Lena, Og, Northern, Jeremy, Mia, Jorep, and so many more who contribute regularly to the feelings of camaraderie on the CDS Discord channels, you are my writer-home. Anyone reading this who is not on our Discord channel, you should join us. We are a *lot* of fun.

I've saved the best for last: Bryant, dear husband, thank you always for your dedication and support (and for reading my messy first drafts). You are the best! Remind me I said that the next time I complain.

ABOUT THE AUTHOR

Jen Bair is an Air Force brat, Army veteran, and military wife. She loves traveling with her family to foreign places, real or imaginary, whenever she can. Her family is her life. Her writing is her passion. You can find her published works at http://jenbair.com.

Join her newsletter below:

facebook.com/AuthorJenBair

JOIN THE CURSED DRAGON SHIP NEWSLETTER

Love what you just read? Want more just like it? Sign up for our newsletter so you don't miss out on the adventure. You'll get:

- A free book for signing up
- Advanced notice of new releases
- First word of books on sale
- Opportunities for free books
- Most up-to-date information on author appearances.

We're busy and know you are too. We won't send more than one newsletter a month.

Register below.

DID YOU MISS THE FIRS
GET IT NOW!

What happens when you drag your magic
into a war they want nothing to do with?
feud of epic proportions.

CHECK OUT THE ANTHOLOGY FEATURING CHARACTERS FROM EACH MA SERIES

A card cursed with self-awareness seeks a hero to retrieve his creator from the afterlife. Nothing could possibly go wrong.

www.ingramcontent.com/pod-product-compliance
Lightning Source LLC
Chambersburg PA
CBHW031435200726
48289CB00001BA/191